☑ W9-DID-370

New Year's Eve, 1999

The last day before the millennium. The craziness of the century is coming to a close. In the White House, the President plays with her toys. On nationwide television, Doctor Love of Faith, Ltd. prepares a momentous announcement. In the Southwest, millions of True Seekers gather for a Great Revelation.

And Circe McPhee, a corporate sorceress who has seen disaster in a pack of tarot cards, races to prevent it before midnight strikes . . .

ARMCHAIR "FAMILY" BOOKSTORE
Paperback - Exchange - Comics
3205 S.E. Milwaukie
238-6680
Hours 10 a.m. - 7 p.m., Sat. 10 a.m. - 6 p.m.
PORTLAND, OREGON 97202

Bantam Science Fiction and Fantasy
Ask your bookseller for the books you have missed

ALAS, BABYLON by Pat Frank
A CANTICLE FOR LEIBOWITZ by Walter M. Miller, Jr.
THE CENTAURI DEVICE by M. John Harrison
CENTURY'S END by Russell M. Griffin
CRYSTAL PHOENIX by Michael Berlyn
FANTASTIC VOYAGE by Isaac Asimov
THE GATES OF HEAVEN by Paul Preuss
THE GOLDEN SWORD by Janet E. Morris
THE GREY MANE OF MORNING by Joy Chant
HIGH COUCH OF SILISTRA by Janet E. Morris
HOMEWORLD by Harry Harrison
THE HUMANOID TOUCH by Jack Williamson
THE INTEGRATED MAN by Michael Berlyn
THE JANUS SYNDROME by Steven E. McDonald
JEM by Frederik Pohl
THE MAN WHO FELL TO EARTH by Walter Tevis
MATHEW SWAIN: HOT TIME IN OLD TOWN by Mike McQuay
MATHEW SWAIN: WHEN TROUBLE BECKONS by Mike McQuay
MERLIN by Robert Nye
NEBULA WINNERS THIRTEEN Edited by Samuel R. Delany
THE PARADISE PLOT by Ed Naha
QUAS STARBRITE by James R. Berry
RE-ENTRY by Paul Preuss
THE REVOLT OF THE MICRONAUTS by Gordon Williams
SLOW FALL TO DAWN by Stephen Leigh
STARWORLD by Harry Harrison
THE STAINLESS STEEL RAT WANTS YOU! by Harry Harrison
THE STEEL OF RAITHSKAR by Randall Garret and Vicki Ann
   Heydron
A STORM UPON ULSTER by Kenneth C. Flint
SUNDIVER by David Brin
THE TIME MACHINE by H. G. Wells
TIME STORM by Gordon Dickson
20,000 LEAGUES UNDER THE SEA by Jules Verne
UNDER THE CITY OF THE ANGELS by Jerry Earl Brown
VALIS by Philip K. Dick
WHEELWORLD by Harry Harrison
WIND FROM THE ABYSS by Janet E. Morris

For my mother

Acknowledgements

I should like to express my gratitude to Sheila and Morgan, whose patience and forbearance made it possible for me to write at all; to George Beker, Peter Clark, Curt Suplee, and especially Fred Davis, whose initial suggestions, encouragement, and later willingness to read the finished manuscript were of inestimable value; and to Virginia Kidd, whose genuine interest was as important as her skill and judgement in bringing this all to fruition.

1

A Tale of Two Sigils

10 AM Friday, March 12

It was the best of times, it was the worst of times, an age of wisdom and foolishness, an epoch of belief and of incredulity, a season of light and of darkness, a winter of despair and a spring of hope. It was the threshold of Aries in the year of our Lord one thousand nine hundred ninety-nine, opening of the zodiacal short year that would bridge the close of the twentieth century before its end in Pisces: Ram to Fish, soup to nuts. It was the anniversary of the moment God made heaven, earth, and man, but not even the scrubbed and groomed corporate astrologers could agree whether in the ponderous backward reel of the zodiacal Great Year mankind would also see the close of the drawn-out Piscean Age and the beginning of the Aquarian when it woke to the dawn of the third millennium after Christ.

Even with computers, it is not easy to tell one epoch from another, Gregorian or astrological.

In the White House, a monumentally gregarious woman with a Mount Rushmore jaw sat in unaccustomed isolation, oblivious to the sun outside her window diminished to a pale yellow wafer by another dust-blizzard fifteen hundred miles away, oblivious even to the swelling green blush of the official lawn below or the Ellipse beyond. Perhaps ten years ago, as Republican junior senator from Tennessee, she'd at least noticed the first and even the second time the cherry trees along the Potomac had blossomed well before March twelfth, but these days she waited for the morning briefing display to find out what ought to be noticed. Noticing was a staff function.

Anyway, she was preoccupied with the round and square blips on the liquid crystal display of the Oval Office microcomputer.

1

The eleven red squares had been programmed to think and act precisely as she would—eleven electronic clones exercising her will, her intelligence, and the majesty of her office against the eleven green circles of the computer's microgamesman chip.

At the face-off, her center got control and telegraphed the old egg straight to her right wing, who came down the side breathing fire and sparkplugging a wild offensive sweep by the reds. Down past the twenty-five-meter line, a halfback outmaneuvered and another vaporized, both defensive fullbacks dazzled by the lightning thrust—it was going to be a piece of cake for the big red machine. Whammo! Her wing made his grab for the old brass ring and took his best shot. It blooped out of bounds three meters wide of the cage.

Helplessly she slumped back in her swivel chair as the circles and squares arranged themselves on the display screen for the defender's free hit five meters from the goal line. If she'd been born fifteen years later, she thought gloomily, she could have played football with the boys instead of this field hockey crap.

The blips froze. Now what? The computer was calling five of her electronic doppelgangers off sides.

What the hell kind of a game was it when the computer not only controlled the opposing team but refereed, too? She sighed. Maybe they could bring over an impartial second computer from Defense or State to officiate.

Meanwhile, up Pennsylvania Avenue, gaggles of senators and representatives moved up and down the aisles of their respective chambers, smiling frightfully or looking grave, maneuvering to pass again and again before the camera's unblinking eye, peripheral dancers in the gavotte of voices from elsewhere in the rooms. Did the United States have any moral obligation to keep accepting refugees from the radioactive wastes of Pakistan? What sanctions could be taken against the rapacious Canadian wheat barons? Was it really in the national interest to continue preaching population control as national policy when citizens of other countries were reproducing like lust-crazed fruit flies?

High policy, weighty decisions, and the dancers, ponderous and sedate as bank buildings, sweated in concentration over the intricacies of the steps without worrying much where the dance's end would find them, secure in the certainty that whatever they or the president did was of no consequence whatsoever.

For years, after all, government had been effected by the occasional "presidential" decree from one cabinet bureaucrat or another, and by the slag heap of directives trundled from the labyrinth of regulatory agencies where, bent like mining dwarves, whey-faced civil servants toiled at charting the average continental temperature (up five tenths of a degree Celsius in twenty years with what was said to be the greenhouse effect), recording the population's decline (better than half a percent annually), and plotting the spread of drought land and dust bowls across the Great Plains and the shrinkage of grain production (down from sixteen hundred million tons to little more than nine hundred).

And at day's end, when they laid aside their graphs and printouts, they picked up their rebellious children at day care, perhaps stopped for advice at their family astrologers, shamans, and witches, and then went home to adjust their headbands and televisions for the reassurances of Doctor Love's commercial minispots and megahypes brought to them by Faith Ltd.

Yet there were others less satisfied. In a Seattle street, Brother Moonbeam solicited handouts for the Seekers and urged contributors to repent, and in a New Bethel, Ohio motel, his spiritual leader the Monad instructed her latest roomful of teenage converts; in Valhalla, North Carolina, Chrissy Binks stared through the diamond mesh of a chainlink fence into the radioactive waste beyond, while just outside Amarillo, Texas, T-Boy Tucker stood in line at the DP camp waiting for the week's bag of groceries and dreaming about the freedom he'd have soaring through tomorrow's maneuvers with the Texas Air Guard; near Apple, Kansas, Andrew McCallum peered through the swirling dust at the polytents flapping in the wind, trying not to think about where his daughter might be, and in Woodbridge, Connecticut, Raymond Soames gave his wife another mescaline spansule to ease the pain; in Lowell, Massachusetts, Sister Catherine, last of her order, rubbed her chilled hands after a confession to Father Camillieri that hadn't begun to mine the rich lode of sin that ran through the core of her being, while nearby on Route 2, James Augustus Pilcher III sat in a thorazine stupor beside James Augustus Pilcher II in the family car, released from Shady Pines because he had finally agreed that he could no longer be absolutely certain he was Jesus Christ, Son of Man, and was prepared to pick up his academic career at Stoddard College in Tennessee where he'd left it during his senior comprehensives just prior to his Incarnation; in New York City, Jervis Santalucia thought it might help to remove the blank sheet of paper he'd been staring at in his typewriter and roll in a flatter one, while

3

twenty blocks away, Circe McPhee, following the directions in one of her old student texts as a kind of lark, ripped open a polypak and dropped three eyes of newt and a dash of spiderweb into the blender and set it on mulch/stun.

And in a Soho loft, Sinbad Schwartz, earliest exponent of the Crapart Movement and still its most daring voyager on the uncharted sea of how much the art world would stand for, lugged the last of his supplies and his infant son down to the street where his rented semi waited for him, ready to carry him into the windy center of the Great Plains—exactly where, he'd be at great pains not to discover until after the fact—until he'd found the perfect place for the erection of the greatest monument of Crapart the world had ever seen.

2

Hamlin's Children

Noon, Thursday, March 25

The girl's unwashed hair hung in lank clumps, face streaked, jacket and jeans powdered with the dust of Kansas, Missouri, Indiana, Ohio. She eased a shoulder and arm out of one strap and swung her backpack to the cracked pavement, peering westward along the road, half hopeful, half fearful. Over the horizon, the great brown clouds were piling up as though the storm were pursuing her.

Not exactly a main route, and hardly busy, but that was why there wouldn't be any smokes to pick her up for hitching or vagrancy—and maybe check their runaways printout at headquarters.

At last, far down the road, a cloud of dust boiled. Something coming toward her. She still hadn't gotten used to how fast people drove in the east; where she came from, people drove slower to keep the dust down.

Dust. That, more than anything else, was what she was running from. It could come in a solid tidal wall, or hug the ground like a morning mist, or roll over in great clouds, black at the bottom and reddish tan on top; it blew from morning to evening, usually, but sometimes straight through the night and into the next day. Last year, her father had said, there had been three hundred and eight dust storms; that had left only fifty-seven days of sun.

During the storms, she would listen to the roar and whistle of the wind and the sizzle of dust against the windows, wishing that, like Dorothy, she could feel her house ripped from its foundations and whisked off to the Technicolor land of Oz. And when the storms were over, she would see where the dust had collected like snow on the muntins and sills, and where it had drifted against the machinery in the compound. Whenever she walked in the fresh dustfall, she would always stop to look back at her footprints from the agristation living module, as crisp and clear as an astronaut's on virgin moon-soil.

Usually she'd find five or six motionless little mounds when the wind had stopped, birds overtaken by the storm and suffocated. The wind would sift ramps of the finest dust against them, always on the west side. Occasionally she'd find the bigger mounds of jackrabbits buried as they'd crouched choking in the thick air.

Even their module, sealed tight with ionizers at both doors, couldn't keep the dust out. It powdered and permeated everything: when you sat down, chairs coughed great clouds; when you pulled down your sheets or took clean clothes from the bureau drawer, billows rose into the light; when you came to dinner, your food was peppered with grit and your glass of milk gray. And for days after a storm, the dust could turn the sun munchkin blue.

The column of dust grew closer and began to slow. It was a pickup with a big blue Ford ellipse on the nose. It looked, she realized, older than it was, red paint weathered a chalky pink, and sides streaked with rust and dirt, like the trucks of the farmers she saw occasionally, passing by or stopping at the compound for the latest government stats and forecasts.

Buzzing like a monstrous June bug, the pickup drew even with her, tarp over the back flapping. The door sagged open and a round, olive face appeared.

"You hitching?"

The girl smiled.

"Soon as I saw you," said the young woman, "I told Moonbeam here you were good people. We're headed for New York. Can we drop you along the way?"

The girl couldn't believe her luck, but she showed no emotion. "New York would be fine," she said.

"Woody!" called the woman gaily and squeezed herself over to make room as the girl clambered in, wedging herself against the seat back between the woman and the door, her pack bundled onto her lap. With a shiver, the truck began to move again.

"I'm Sister Moonrose," the woman said, looking expectant. She was in her late twenties, earth-mother huge, draped in a muumuu, with tan skin and Indian-black hair.

6

The girl gave no answer.

"This is my man, Moonbeam," Moonrose went on, jerking her head toward the frail man at the wheel. His reddish beard was baby fine and wispy, as though it had grown in at adolescence without ever being shaved. "Course, we don't get it on any more, being purer vessels and all that, but I still call him my man."

The girl looked steadily out the front window, wondering what Moonrose was getting at. She'd learned fast that some drivers considered giving a lift to a hitchhiker the first half of an open transaction: the ride she'd gotten from eastern Kansas into Missouri had been with a dumb jimmy who'd opened his fly and made her say hello to his thing and told her his thing's name was Alfie. She'd seen worse on TV, but if it hadn't been for her being able to slip away when they stopped at a diner because the jimmy had to use the comfort station—or at least Alfie did—there was no telling what would have happened.

"You going to New York for any special reason?" Moonrose tried again.

The girl looked down at the floor of the compartment. Beside her left foot lay a red box of shotgun shells.

"No," she said. "No special reason."

"Oh," said the woman, a note of disappointment in her voice. She gave the man beside her a look too quick for the girl to decipher.

"We thought you were a T-True Seeker," the driver said at last.

The girl nodded doubtfully.

"A True Seeker's someone t-tuned in to Personal Human Evolution," Brother Moonbeam explained. "Someone looking for the road into the Next Evolutionary K-Kingdom."

For the first time, the girl noticed how tense and strangled Moonbeam's voice seemed, how nervously his eyes flicked from the road to her to the mirror and back to the road.

She looked away uncomfortably, saw the shells again, and looked up to the open glove compartment. Out of the rat's nest of misfolded maps peeked the brownish white handle of a pistol. It was a little like the one her father kept in his lab office for when jackrabbits got into the polytents and gnawed the experimental crops.

Should she stay with these people? Moonrose seemed lowcal enough, but there was something eerie about Brother Moonbeam and his limpid eyes, a pale, pale, unnatural blue.

She'd hit the road without any definite destination in mind—she'd been intent on leaving something and not on arriving someplace else. Still, New York had consistently popped up among the alternatives whenever she'd really tried to settle on a goal. The offer of a ride straight through to New York not only saved her getting further rides but spared her having to decide where to go. But these people . . . At first she'd taken them for farmers like those she'd grown up near, but Moonrose and Moonbeam were into something very different.

It wasn't the guns that bothered her; she was used to guns. What she wasn't used to were people that didn't share her mother's way of looking at things. No matter how long she'd yearned for the variety she knew existed in the world beyond their compound fence, actually confronting these two new mindsets in the confines of a truck cab was frightening.

Still, the thought of getting out on the highway again without knowing where the next ride would take her was worse. No, she'd stay with these two, for now, at least.

"How do you do Personal Human Evolution?" she asked to be sociable.

The man winked at Moonrose. "You t-tune in on the Monad, see, for this cosmic energy she's got. Then you see your human faults and you can shuck them. The more you can get away from things like sex and food and c-comfort, the farther you are on the Road to the Next Evolutionary K-kingdom."

"That sounds kind of tough," said the girl.

"Tough?" said Sister Moonrose. "You'd better believe it! But the Dinks make it even harder. They're always keeping up this spiritual bombardment to trick you into carnling down, like getting mad or horny."

"Or hungry," said the frail Moonbeam, eyes working ceaselessly. "Those Dinks are really bombing me right now, let me tell you. Just when you think you're not human anymore, your stomach g-growls, you know?"

"What are Dinks?" asked the girl.

"Disincarnate Beings," the woman said. "They're the Devil's agents and they're everywhere. Hell is out on Pluto, and Satan keeps sending his Dinks everywhere to trap you, so you got to watch out for them all the time. Parents, teachers, smokes—it could be anyone. The worst are the Doctor Love people. They're really dangerous."

"But if you beat the Dinks, then you're in the Kingdom?" asked the girl.

"Oh, no," laughed Moonrose. "Humans can't get into the Celestial Jerusalem—not by ourselves. All we can do is turn our bodies into indestructible vessels of purity, so we're *ready*. It's like always having your suitcase packed."

The girl nodded. "To go to Heaven?"

"Our heavenly home, right. See, being pure generates all this heat, so it turns your spirit into like a hard-boiled egg or something. Then when the Day comes, the Saucers can kind of beam your consciousness up out of your body shell and into the next dimension."

"That's the fourth dimension," Moonbeam added. "I th-think."

"The *saucers?*" said the girl. "You're Saucer People?"

"That's what the T-TV news always calls us," said Moonbeam. "We call ourselves True Seekers. The *real* Saucer People are actually up *there*." He rolled his eyes up into his head to indicate the sky.

"So you're going to New York and get evolved into the fourth dimension!" the girl said happily. She was interested now: these were flesh and blood incarnations of the shadows she'd seen on TV. "Your leader is the Pied Piper!"

"We call her the Monad," said Moonrose. "Right now she's missing again, cause the Saucer People have to keep beaming her up to the Mothership to tell her what to do. Meantime, we've got to tune into where she might be beamed back. We were all out in Washington State, see, when she disappeared, and then some of us flashed on big cities, and finally Skyflame thought New York, so we all packed up and headed east."

Sister Moonrose beamed with pleasure at the girl's interest.

"The Monad's just like the old prophets in the Bible, you know," she went on. "She's one of the Ones from the Next Level who's come down to show us the Road, like Ezekiel. That's why it's kind of woody, cause being from another dimension, you never know where she'll be for the next meeting, and we've got to hit on the right place using our spirit radar—that's what all the Beings of the Next Level have, and we're supposed to be evolving it."

"Usually w-we're wrong," said Moonbeam. "That's the d-discouraging part, but the Monad says it takes a while to grow radar. But what makes it woodier is that the Time's really close.

9

Some people are even saying New Year's is going to be the Day, so there's no time to waste."

"Anyway," Moonrose said, "she says first there'll be these Demonstrations to prove her prophecies. A big city's going to be destroyed—"

"Like the L.A. earthquake?"

"We thought that was it last year, but the Monad said it was going to be something even worse, with flame and lightning from the sky, like Sodom and Gomorrah. Then this Beast is going to rise and slay the Monad after she's preached forty-two months—that's what she says, and she's real brave about it—and she'll be left unburied for three and a half days."

"In Sodom or Egypt or someplace," Moonbeam said.

"And then," Moonrose continued triumphantly, "she'll rise into the sky in this cloud, which is the Bible's way of describing a UFO, because they weren't all that smart back in olden days when they wrote the Bible. They didn't know all the stuff we do about outer space and aliens and all. They thought the prophets were just a bunch of old Jews."

"And the next Demonstration is some big D-Dink leader is going to get killed," Moonbeam said. "I hope it's that bastard Doctor Love—I'd like to do it myself. And that's when we'll know we've got to be at the Place, because the Monad will be reborn there and everyone will be beamed up to the Mothership."

"What kind of place?" the girl asked.

"D-don't know. We haven't flashed on it yet, and the Monad isn't allowed to say where it is."

"Why Egypt? Did she mean in Illinois?"

"That's symbolical," Moonrose said. "It means someplace sinful, like Pittsburgh or L.A."

The girl was silent for a time, considering. "But if you know how long the Monad's supposed to prophesy, then you could figure out when it's going to happen, couldn't you?"

"Well, yes and no. It's soon, because twelve hundred and sixty days is what she said, which is forty-two months, or three and a half years. Trouble is, we know the Monad's been preaching *about* three years, but nobody knows *exactly*."

"Nobody was listening too much when she started out down in Texas," Moonbeam said. "So nobody knows what exact day to count from."

"The Monad must remember," said the girl.

"Oh, yeah, but she isn't allowed to say."

The inscrutability of the mystery prompted a unanimous silence.

"G-God, am I *hungry*," Brother Moonbeam said at last.

"You better put a lid on those carnal appetites, Brother."

"Maybe, but we're c-close to four hundred miles since the last charge, and we're going to have to stop somewhere for a battery."

He pointed to the bright phosphorous digits of the heads-up readout glowing on the bottom of the windshield: *HED 25 KM*. The high energy density batteries were down to a range of twenty-five kilometers at the present rate of energy consumption.

"We'll hit the next Zapstop," Moonrose said. She turned to the girl. "You know, a lot of kids your age are True Seekers."

"I know," the girl muttered. She didn't want to be pressured—she'd just gotten away from that kind of thing. "I don't really know kids my age."

"How come?"

"I grew up on a government compound in Kansas."

"A D.P. camp?" asked Moonrose.

"An agristation. I guess there might have been kids when I was really little, but I don't remember. They were all relocated—even Apple is empty. That's the nearest town. I mean, it used to be."

"Yeah," said the man. "Just before we found the Seekers, we were squatting on an empty farm in Missouri, right on the edge of the dust bowl. Guess it couldn't grow enough for the pig that owned it, b-but it was enough for us. At least till we heard the Monad the first time."

"We were looking for something even before we knew what it was, kind of," Moonrose said. "After we quit this community college, we hung out with this bunch of antique Moonies, and then Moonbeam here got into a little trouble, so we figured what the hell, we'd plow our educations under like potato fertilizer and try farming, you know? I mean, who cares about that crap anyway? But then we heard the Monad and we decided we wanted to get in on the Evolution."

"Anyway," Moonbeam added, "those days our Level of B-Being really b-bit the b-big one. God, am I hungry."

"They'll have food in New York," said the woman.

"Zapstop ahead," said Moonbeam.

The girl saw the white box of an old gas station. The sign had been taken down, but the pumps were still in place, painted over in Zapstop's red and white, as a display stand for dry lubes, upholstery cleaners, and car polishes. As they drew closer, the girl could discern the outline of the old "Gulf" logo, stenciled by rain and dirt where the letters had once been bolted. Over the roof on a single pole was the familiar Zapstop lightning bolt in red and white plastic. As they swung off the road and eased to a stop beside the pumps, she was able to make out the additional "Subsidiary of Gulf-Mobil" and "A Solarsystems International Company" worked into the lightning bolt's border. Below it on the pole was a large yellow oval with red lettering: "BATTERY RENTALS BY DAY WEEK OR MONTH—RETURN OR EX-CHANGE AT ANY ZAPSTOP IN OUR NATIONWIDE TRAV-EL NETWORK."

An old man shuffled out of the building, the heavy insulated cables of a battery tester dangling from one hand like the tentacles of a captured octopus. "Charge or change, son?"

"Change," said Moonbeam, getting down from the truck as Moonrose passed him the rental papers from her bag. "You got a coin machine for food in there?"

The old man nodded as he leaned under the hood. "Jesus, this HED of yours is dead as Congress."

"Remember we're short, Moonbeam," Moonrose called as the young man disappeared into the building.

Moonrose shifted her weight, and the girl sighed at the relief from the pressure. Idly she glanced at the advertisements taped inside the station's windows. "DUMP TIMED CHARGES," read one. "30 MIN 100% DTC, 5 MIN 70% MEDICHARGE, 2 MIN 40% SPEEDICHARGE."

Her shoulder was still hot where Moonrose's meaty arm had pressed against it. She thought again about splitting, but she couldn't help remembering how many times she'd sat at home while her parents were in the fields, alone except for the microcomputer that made her lunch, regulated the light and heat, and fed her set theory and rhetoric and narrative history and invertebrate biology because there weren't any schools within two hundred miles. Hadn't she yearned to have people this close? Hadn't she watched with envy the TV clips of normal kids crowded together in daycare centers?

"Lucky you stopped," the attendant was saying as he wrestled the exhausted battery module out from under the hood and onto the dolly-jack. "Stations are rare as robins around here."

12

"How many kilometers to New York?" Moonrose asked.

The man peered in the window, his face a mask of red starbursts of ruptured blood vessels. "Kilometers? Jesus, lady, I never could get that stuff. I could tell you in miles, if you want."

"That's all right," said Moonrose.

Suddenly from inside the station came the tinkle of breaking glass.

"Oh, no," Moonrose murmured as the man shuffled toward the building as quickly as he could.

The girl read on to pass the time: "GET AHEAD, GET A HED," "CONVERSIONS OF COMBUSTION AND FLYWHEEL SYSTEMS TO HED BATTERIES BY FACTORY-TRAINED TECHS—TRAVEL TROUBLE-FREE THE MODERN WAY."

A shout from inside the station was suddenly cut off. A few moments later, Brother Moonbeam emerged pushing a new battery on a dolly with one hand while in the other he balanced a stack of small packages. He stopped on the girl's side and handed the stack in through the window, a pile of Twinkie Nature-Cakes.

"Help yourself," he said, opening one and stuffing the whole cake into his mouth. "That guy was definitely a real D-Dink." He pushed the dolly to the front of the truck to install the battery.

"What can you expect?" Moonrose said to the girl. "The Dinks outnumber us. But we'll have the last laugh at the end when we're beamed up and they're left down here."

The girl nodded, too tired to wonder why the old man hadn't helped Moonbeam put in fresh batteries. A moment later, Moonbeam was back behind the wheel, opening another Nature-Cake as they eased out of the station.

In a way, the girl thought, what these people were saying made a lot more sense than the Bible did about heaven and angels and things. You couldn't relate to sitting on a cloud playing a harp—how could anything that dumb be true? But she was always hearing about the fourth dimension, and lots of people had seen UFO's and flying saucers. It was a lot easier and more scientific to believe in another dimension instead of heaven, or in super-brainy aliens instead of something vague like God.

And without quite realizing it, she drifted off into her old dream. Passing by the ionizer and the dustlock, finding their barren compound yard transformed into yellow brick, the leafless

13

skeletons of stunted bushes into lush greenery and the diminutive forms of welcoming munchkins. And slowly her head drooped forward until it rested on the bulky, dusty pack in her lap.

They reached New York well after dark, the compartment aflutter with empty Twinkie wrappers. The girl had no idea where in the city they were going, nor whether Moonbeam had a map or was following his spirit radar. She was too overwhelmed by the cliff-like black buildings towering over her on every side. Even Moonrose's closeness was no comfort. The instrument readouts made her round olive face glow with an unearthly green pallor.

Wherever they were, it seemed dark and deserted. Soon, however, the girl began to catch glimpses of people on the sidewalks, many children her own age, drifting along in twos and threes. Within another block, the sidewalk was crowded, and some had spilled over onto the street. Moonbeam steered the truck over to the curb and parked, waited for Moonrose and the girl to clamber out, stuffed something from the glove compartment into his coat, and followed.

They joined the stream of pedestrians, moving at first with an aimlessness that gradually gave way with each block to a growing sense of vague but powerful purpose. Already the girl felt uneasy at being hemmed in by so many people, and she glanced quickly from one side to the other. Most were young, some in rags, others in packs and camping gear, still others bundled into expensive coats and boots as though they'd just come in for the evening from Westchester and Port Washington. They carried floppie-players and portavees; the entire length of the street flickered with the rectangular elfin lights of video screens, and over the click of heels and murmurs of hurried conversations shrieked the competing hits of the top-forty UHF stations: —*you are the rainbow in my sky-yiy—in those good old fash-shoned pis-stone-driven day-yay-ya—why don't you f—got a fire in the Delta, whay down th—*

"You stick with Moonrose," Moonbeam said, eyes flicking faster than ever. "Got to find the Hundred and check in." He increased his pace, sidestepped two children playing tag, and was gone.

"What's the Hundred?" asked the girl.

"Kind of an honorary group," Moonrose said. "They watch out for the Monad in case she's attacked or something and forgets to shoot fire out of her mouth."

14

"Is someone going to attack her—before the time she's supposed to die?"

"We've had a lot of trouble," Moonrose said. "Even a few Seekers killed. Haven't you seen it on the news?"

"I guess so."

"The Hundred thinks it could be the Love people. The more people see the light and join us, the more money they lose."

"But I've seen Doctor Love on TV with my parents lots of times," the girl said. "Anyone that sincere—"

But she couldn't finish because the crowd had thickened, slowing their progress, packed with bodies as school yards at recess she'd seen on TV, more living people than the girl could have imagined in one place, no matter how many pictures she'd seen of old Pakistan or China. Timidly she dropped back to follow in Moonrose's ample wake as the woman angled away from the street and jostled her way up to a chain link fence that ran along the sidewalk and across what had once been a street before disappearing into the crowd.

Gratefully the girl pressed herself against the fence, reassured by its likeness to the one around her compound back home. In the darkness beyond was a wasteland of deserted buildings, and she yearned for the sweatless, humanless air on the other side, hooking a finger into one of the metal straps that bound a sign to the links above her. "NO TRESPASSING," it read. "CLOSED BY ORDER OF CENTRALIZATION SAFETY COMMISSION OF NEW YORK PER PUBLIC ORDINANCE 18903 SECTION 55.B.1. VIOLATORS SUBJECT TO NOT LESS THAN $25,000 FINE AND 1 YEAR IN JAIL."

"Oh, *rude!*" she heard someone saying. "It's Sister *Moonrose!* You flashed on it, too!"

"We brought someone with us," Moonrose answered.

"She eaten the Book?"

"Not yet, but she will, I know it. Picked her up this morning outside Erie."

"Let's see her. You give her a name?"

"Not yet," Moonrose said. "What kind of name would you like, honey?" she asked the girl.

The girl wasn't listening. She heard only the pounding of her own heart, saw only the beautiful emptiness where buildings had been bulldozed into a kind of no man's land between the fence and the derelict neighborhood beyond. She wondered if this kind of place frightened city people the same way the crowd behind

15

frightened her. If only she could slip through the fence and wander there, just long enough to fight down the panic.

"What about Starfire?" someone was saying. "That's a nice name."

"Yeah, but I just met a Starfire down the block," someone else answered. "And I knew two in Parma."

"She's special," Moonrose said. "She's got to have a special name."

"How about Starbud? Like a star being born."

"Yeah, a star being born," said Moonrose. "That's just what she is."

The girl felt Moonrose's hand on her shoulder and Moonrose's lips at her ear. "Starbud—that's your new name. Like it?"

The girl formed the words soundlessly with her lips: Starbud.

She was suddenly aware of movement behind her, of shuffles and sighs and murmurs of disappointment.

"You mean we flashed on the wrong place?" someone asked.

The girl turned to find Moonbeam back, chewing thoughtfully on a Granola bar. "No," he said. "The Monad isn't here. G-Glitter heard something about Ohio."

"Guess the Beings needed more Seekers from Ohio."

"Yeah, but that leaves us stuck in New York."

"What now?"

"They're p-passing out stuff for a service," Moonbeam said. "Then maybe we'll get the cosmic strength to flash on exactly where the M-Monad is."

Already a reverent silence was spreading through the crowd, TVs and players being flicked off, until at last the only sound was someone hidden in the crowd playing on a recorder, a thin, woody, alien strain that echoed plaintively back from the street and wisped into nothingness in the empty air beyond the fence.

Suddenly there was a distant stuttering sound. In the black sky over the deserted buildings appeared the three angry red points of a helicopter's landing lights. It swung over them, clacking loudly, traced a long, watchful parabola to the far end of the crowd, and then circled back.

"Children," blared a voice from across the street. "May I have your attention, please."

The girl had to strain to make out what was producing the sound: a human figure floating lazily at eye level, apparently someone on a hoverbike with a bullhorn.

"Please, children," the voice rang. "You're blocking a public—"

16

An inarticulate roar rose from the crowd and drowned the voice out, then subsided, intimidated by the chatter of the rotor blades slicing overhead again.

"—for your own good. And the Commissioner of Labor wants to assure you—"

More movement in the crowd, people passing piles of mimeographed sheets. Moonbeam handed one to Moonrose and another to the girl, and kept one for himself before handing the rest on. The girl glanced at the paper, but it was too dark to read.

"—several thousand jobs begging for qualified—"

Something else coming, boxes this time. She felt Moonbeam shove a waxy candle stub into her hand from one of the boxes, and she was suddenly aware of spots of warm, yellow light bobbing in the crowd, like thousands of stars, as though the Milky Way had settled onto the street and was stretching out to engulf her. A moment later Moonrose's face was lit by the starlight of a single match as she touched it to the girl's candle, and then the girl watched the starry glow spreading from her to flicker through the rest of the crowd beyond.

"—time of crisis," the bullhorn boomed, "it's the patriotic citizen's duty to take up the mop and pail—"

"Clean it up yourself, you old fart!" shouted a voice from the crowd, and a shower of cans and wrappers arced from the sidewalk onto the street.

"We'll show you what you can do with your broom!" shrilled an excited child's voice. "You've had your chance!"

On every side the girl now heard the rustling and tearing of paper. They were stuffing the sheets into their mouths.

"Go ahead," whispered Moonrose, her mouth full. "Eat the Book."

Reluctantly the girl tore a strip from the piece of paper and put it to her mouth, even as she realized that behind the suspended form of the speaker hung more grim shadows in the dimness on the far side of the street. Smokes.

"—have no permit for public assembly," rang the voice.

"Fuck your permit!"

Laughter eddied through the crowd, a momentary nervous relief from the electric tension. More cans and paper bags and one or two candles flew toward the speaker, and the shadows on the far side of the street began drifting forward, top-heavy with gleaming tanks and strange nozzles.

"Faggots!" bellowed an unamplified voice. "Loafers!" One

of the shadows emerged from anonymity to loom over them, a paunchy figure teetering on a hoverbike, face hidden behind the featureless plexiglass of his head shield. "How long before you get jobs?"

"Till your dork falls off, plate-face!" answered a boy from below, skimming something upward at the policeman.

"Everybody!" Moonrose pleaded. "You're carnling down! Don't let the Dinks get to you!" She turned desperately to the girl. "All we want is to flash on someplace to go and get out of here."

But already more hoverbikes were easing in at either end of the crowd, bunching the Seekers tighter and tighter toward the middle. The girl felt herself jostled and then squeezed as the crowd compressed about her. Moonbeam was already gone, and the girl felt herself being forced inexorably away from Moonrose and into the heart of the mass. She could no longer see what was happening. Again the helicopter clattered over, a menacing shadow. She spat out the curds of half-chewed paper, began to scream. Beyond her, the center of the crowd surged at the curb, tensed, burst onto the street like a ruptured boil.

Released, the girl staggered onto the pavement. There were balloon-like poppings from above, and suddenly a yellow fog rolled over her. Her nose and throat burned, her eyes streamed as though smoldering sticks had been plunged into them. She heard a hoverbike swoop over her, felt the rush of the motor-heated, oily air. For an instant she opened her streaming eyes to see, as though in a blue-gray fog, the hoverbike sweeping on.

Suddenly there was a wet splattering somewhere to the left, sudsy streamers, writhing festoons of crowd-control foam, then a terrifying crack.

She knew without seeing it that it had been a pistol. The hoverbike just beyond her jolted back, then careened on in a wide downward arc to slam horribly against the pavement.

"Screw, screenfaces! Just screw!"

More of the yellow gas. The girl couldn't breathe. Choking, burning, drowning, she clawed blindly at the bodies hemming her in. Where were Moonrose and Moonbeam?

A hand grabbed her arm from the darkness. She opened her tearing eyes just enough to see that the hand came out of a uniform cuff, bluer than the haze of her gas-blurred vision.

"Can't breathe!" she gasped, struggling. "Can't breathe!"

"Quit it!" said the muffled voice of the face behind the plexiglass mask.

"Let me go!" she screamed, pounding at the blue arm with her free fist. "Get air!"

And then something horribly hard struck the side of her head and she went limp as Dorothy on the bed of her airborne farmhouse.

3

The Monad

Like flash photographs clicked in succession.

An old jail had been reopened for them. Somebody called it the Tombs. She'd been herded into the back of a dank, long-vacant cage with ten others. Nowhere to turn, no escape from the press of bodies. She had crouched on a mesh cot, staring at the barred door, her back against more bars that looked into another cage filled with bodies. It smelled of sweat and damp concrete. The only relief was in the aisle between the rows of cells, but even there the air was hot and close, and the door kept her from it. She knew she would die. *Flash*.

The smokes came in every hour and searched them. Officer Christmas Williams had been killed—*killed, scumbags*—and they wanted the gun and its owner. Starbud was thrown against the bars, patted down by one set of hands, then another—*you creeps know he had a wife with a kid in the oven?*—while she wondered why they'd kept a kid in the oven, then her own hands examined, sprayed with something—*checking for gunpowder, but you could save us all a lot of trouble and tell us who the fucker was*—stubby fingers pinched her hard on the breast, she screamed, they pushed her away and she sprawled on the floor surrounded by feet, their feet, the others' feet, two were women—*it was a forty-four killed Christmas, we figure a Smith and Wesson. Anybody want to come forward, save your friends? You all want to spend the next twenty years here?*—but why were almost all of them black?

Flash.

Starting Monday morning, they began taking her blockmates out one at a time, and they never came back. "It's all right," somebody said. "They're being arraigned, and our brothers and sisters are making bail for them. We just have to endure, like the Monad says. Just smile at the Dinks and we'll be out."

Still, when the press of bodies had decreased so she could breathe, and her turn came Wednesday morning, Starbud was afraid. Maybe it was true somebody outside was putting up bail and getting them out. But maybe the smokes were just taking them off to some darker cage below and suffocating them, one by one.

The room they brought her to was spacious, reasonably bright, paneled in old wood. The light and cleanliness were impossible to comprehend; Friday night and everything since had melted into a single nightmare of animal screams and faceless monsters. Somehow even seeing the man that had arrested her without his helmet or body armor in the court couldn't convince her that the sane world she'd once known still existed.

A scruffy little man with bushy hair—*I'm your attorney, babes, unless you've got something better and want to wait for him to get here*—stood beside her listening to the charges: resisting arrest, assaulting an officer, aggravated assault, unlawful assembly, disturbing the peace, conspiracy. The dream got stronger, but she told herself any minute she'd wake up to the wind's low moan back in her bed in the agristation.

The judge, a bush of white hair, a glint of spectacles over the edge of a tall desk, said something about five thousand dollars and promising to appear at Superior Court on August eleventh.

"As in the other cases, Your Honor," the scruffy little man said, "the Seeker organization has arranged to post the five thousand dollars."

"Where is the money *coming* from?" the judge said to no one in particular.

"No idea, Your Honor," said the scruffy man. "I just got a phone call asking me to represent them Monday."

"Next case," the judge said.

Flash.

Someone led her to a side door and down a corridor. For an instant she panicked when she saw the bars, but it was only ornamental grillwork like a bank teller's cage. Someone who looked like Moonrose but who wasn't Moonrose greeted her. She had already paid the five thousand dollars.

"I've got no way to pay you back," Starbud said. The smoke behind the counter was looking for her pack.

21

"It's all right," the woman said. "You're one of us. We're your *people*."

The girl felt tears burning at the corners of her eyes. "I didn't think anybody cared," she said, voice trembling. "I thought I'd be there forever."

"Take it easy," the woman said. "Were you alone or with some brothers and sisters?"

"I was with this woman named Moonrose and—"

"Oh, shit, there are so *many* Moonroses," the woman sighed. "But most everybody is down at the park. Someone outside'll take you down and help you find whoever you're looking for."

She made her way outside, stunned by the realization there was still a sun, and a stranger took her to the park. They found Moonrose late that afternoon, when the last warmth was dissipating from the reddish light.

"I think we got it this time," Moonrose said cheerily, as though nothing had happened. "People have been flashing on Ohio all day, and then some sisters were down in front of this D-store watching the demo sets in the window and they saw it on the news, all about this place called New Bethel, where the Monad's been the last couple days. We were going to have to leave without you, because we figured if we pushed it'd take us ten, twelve hours. Lucky thing you came along."

The girl looked away. "I don't know if I want to go to Ohio," she said. "It's like going backwards."

"Not go hear the Monad after we bailed you out and everything? We're your family now. New York put you in jail, right? You want to stay in a place that put you in jail?"

"No," she said.

"There's Dinks everywhere," Moonrose said. "No wonder—this is where Doctor Love's headquarters is. Tell me you're not going over to the Dinks."

"All right," the girl said. "I'll stay with you."

Within the hour, Starbud found herself wedged inside the truck cab again with Moonrose and Moonbeam, this time with seven or eight others huddled in the back of the truck. And hours later—how many she never knew—she was back in another crowd. But this time, at least, there were no buildings towering over her on either side. Dark trees poked up from gaps in the crowd, and above she could see the black night speckled with real stars. Except for all the people, it was almost like home.

22

They stretched out on all sides of her, clustered around the squat cinderblock rectangle of the Dew Drop Inn Motor Hotel and surging out through the parking lot beneath the floodlamps and the Dew Drop Inn neon sign that fogged the stars with sudden buzzes of red and electric yellow. There were still the usual whispers, the squawks of instruments, the indistinguishable electronic gush of portavees and floppie-players, but it seemed quieter than New York. The noises were like the creaks and groans of an old house, the inevitable consequence of many people gathered together, but throughout ran the tense hum of anticipation.

Somehow Moonbeam managed to get them close enough to the motel to see the folding banquet table that had been lugged out from the Dew Drop Inn's conference suite and the semicircle of the Dew Drop's full complement of folding metal chairs. Most were already occupied by a variety of people, mostly older and looking stern, the deacons and subdeacons of the True Seekers.

At last, several of them rose and began to distribute sheets of paper like those she'd seen on Thursday night in New York. As the papers rustled back into the crowd, another of the elders rose and began to read from his own copy.

" 'And the voice which I heard from heaven spake unto me again, and said, Go and take the little book which is open in the hand of the angel which standeth upon the sea and upon the earth. And I went unto the angel, and said unto him, Give me the little book. And he said unto me, Take it, and eat it up; and it shall make thy belly bitter, but it shall be in thy mouth sweet as honey.' "

Another of the deacons rose. "Children, let us do even as the Monad has done." He paused meditatively. "Uh, *haveth* done."

Starbud was able to see by the parking lot lights that the paper she held was a mimeographed version of the text that had just been read. But she could do no more than glance at it—already the others around her were stuffing the sheets into their mouths. Her throat was dry, but she tore off a corner of the paper and slipped it between her lips.

" 'And I took the little book out of the angel's hand,' " the reader continued, " " 'and ate it up; and it was in my mouth sweet as honey; and as soon as I had eaten it, my belly was bitter. And he said unto me, Thou must prophesy again before many peoples, and nations, and tongues, and kings.' "

It tasted awful. As Starbud tried a second piece to the sounds of slow chewing around her, a short round woman with gray hair piled insanely atop her head shuffled out of the motel and up to the table. Gasps and whispers rippled through the masticating crowd. She was wearing a pair of old slippers and either a bathrobe or a cloth coat. A deacon handed her something, and she held it up to the inarticulate lowings of the adoring herd. It was dark on the top and bottom and white in the middle, like a pocket Bible or an ice cream sandwich. With a flourish, she bit into it, finished it with a second bite, and licked her fingers.

"I am the Two-in-One," she chanted.

"Two," they chorused. "Two-in-One."

"Hallelujah," she said, puffing a loose strand of hair from her eyes with pouted lips.

"Hallelujah," they answered. "Two-in-One."

"What are they talking about?" Starbud whispered.

"Just listen," Moonrose said, eyes fixed on the Monad.

The deacon who had read before cleared his throat. "'And God said, I will give power unto my two witnesses, and they shall prophesy a thousand two hundred and threescore days, clothed in sackcloth. These are the two olive trees, and the two candlesticks standing before the God of the earth. And if any man will hurt them, fire proceedeth out of their mouth, and devoureth their enemies.'"

"Hallelujah," cried the worshippers.

"See," Moonrose whispered, "we figure the Beings changed their minds after they wrote the Bible and just kind of economized the two candlesticks and two olive trees into the Monad. It's kind of like two for the price of one. That's why she's the Two-in-One."

"'And these have the power to shut heaven,'" the deacon read on, "'that it rain not in the days of their prophecy: and to have powers over waters to turn them to blood, and to smite the earth with all plagues, as often as they will.'"

Starbud thought about the plains parched by years of drought. Was that really something the Monad had done? And turning waters to blood—maybe it meant the blood rains. They weren't as frequent as the black blizzards, but that only made them scarier, dust storms of red silt. Her father—she winced even at the thought of him—had said they came from the Permian beds of Kansas and Texas.

"'And when they shall have finished their testimony,'" the

24

deacon continued, " 'the beast that ascendeth out of the bottomless pit shall make war against them and overcome them, and kill them.' "

The Monad looked off into the distance, vaguely preoccupied, not listening.

" 'And their dead bodies shall lie in the streets of the great city, which spiritually is called Sodom and Egypt, where also our Lord was crucified. And they of the people and kindreds and tongues and nations shall see their dead bodies three days and a half, and shall not suffer their dead bodies to be put into graves. And they that dwell upon the earth shall rejoice over them, and make merry, and shall send gifts to one another; because these two prophets tormented them that dwelt on the earth.' "

Starbud watched the Monad's face, thinking about her death, her unburied body festering beneath the hot Egyptian sun. Was this woman really willing to die for all these people?

" 'And after three days and a half the Spirit of life from God entered into them, and they stood upon their feet; and great fear fell upon them which saw them. And they heard a great voice from heaven saying unto them, Come up hither. And they ascended up to heaven in a cloud.' "

"The Beings' Mothership," Moonrose whispered.

" 'And their enemies beheld them. And the same hour there was a great earthquake, and the tenth part of the city fell, and in the earthquake were slain of men seven thousand: and the remnant were affrighted, and gave glory to the God of heaven.' "

And Starbud, swaying silently to the rhythm of the words, shuddered, contracted into herself as she imagined the earthquake toppling the cliff buildings she had seen in New York, the squat Dew Drop Inn, the solid prefab slabs of her parents' agristation, the walls collapsing again and again on her father and mother. And she looked around at the adoring faces, and she wanted more than anything to be among those that followed the Monad up into the cloudship of the Beings from another space and time.

The Monad listened to the drone of the words, trying to keep her eyes clear, because sometimes other things would interpose themselves between her retinas and the physical objects she focused on. Long white corridors and dim gray shapes that were the Beings from the Mothership talking in tongues—*on a maintenance dosage of fifty milligrams valium q.i.d., and then she just went off the wall*—who had kept her for an eternity before they let her out with the Word. The test that made her one of Them was never to mention the Word directly to Them, because whenever she had done that, They would decide to keep her longer, and it kept happening until she learned to keep the Word and the visions of fire and toppling buildings to herself. It was important to *know* that the space everyone called empty was actually alive with humming pods, but not to say it to the Pod-masters. Because then you had to stay, and she knew They wanted her to pass Their test so she could bring the Word to her own poor world, which was, of course, so small and minor as to be beneath the notice of the Beings except that nothing escaped Their notice.

She felt more than heard the soothing voice stop, and she breathed deeply to compose herself. Tonight she would talk about her latest Dream because it had obviously been sent by the Beings for her world's instruction.

The vacuum of space was lush. It teemed with pods. The earth grew dead and sterile.

"Now I want to talk to you about a couple things tonight," she heard herself saying. Her own voice startled her, but that was always the way—when she spoke, the Beings took over, and she could just sort of sit back and watch herself talking. "Now the first thing's the first Demonstration. It says in the Bible—"

Her preacher father stood behind her. What is thy mother? she recited. A lioness: she lay down among lions, she nourished her . . . um . . .

The terror of a word forgotten.

Slick! The flat of his belt uncoiled itself across her buttocks, the sting instantaneous through her thin polyester dress.

You forgit again?

Slick!

I can't remember, Pa. Please, Pa.

Whelp! The word's whelp, you slut! Think of the belt and remember whelp. How you expect to be saved you can't remember—slick!—whelp?

She closed her eyes against the pain, seeing red spotted with white. She nourished her whelps among young lions.

She opened her eyes, hoping she would not see the old kitchen, and with growing confidence found again the darkness spotted with the white ovals of upturned faces.

She remembered.

"Uh . . . in the Bible, that 'the angel took the censer, and filled it with fire of the altar, and cast it into the earth: and there were voices, and thunderings, and lightnings, and an earthquake.' Now that's the Demonstration. That's what's going to happen—a disaster, a big city somewhere blown up with thunder and lightning and earthquakes, because the Beings tell me They need to make some more believers, and that's what it takes to make believers out of most people. It's going to be Sodom and Gomorrah ten times over, and that lightning's going to fry the Dinks like so many sausages.

"Now I'm not allowed to tell you-all where it's going to be, so you've got to get that old spiritual radar *evolved*. But one thing I'm seeing out there is you've all got these portavees and floppie-players. Think about it, kids. Who's on TV all the time?"

There was an expectant silence.

"Who runs TV?"

Again silence, uncertainty.

"Doctor Love, that's who. And the more you watch them things, the harder it's going to be to evolve your radar. The more likely, in fact, you'll be tricked into going over to Doctor Love. And that'll leave you down here with the Dinks when the End comes. Do you want that?"

"NO!" they chorused.

"They can *use* that TV," she said. "The smokes can watch you through it, Doctor Love can make you crazy through it. I've seen it a million times. So let's get *rid* of them! Show Love and all the rest what we think of them!"

The crowd stirred uneasily. Destroy their TV's? Cut themselves off from the world? Live without the background of sound and movement flickering from the little screens?

"DO IT!" she screamed.

And suddenly there was a crash as someone swung a portavee against the trunk of a tree. And another, and another. Everywhere, the lights of glowing screens winked out.

"That's better," she said. "That's better. Cause it's going to be hard enough after I'm killed and I'm waiting for you with my brother and sister Beings in the Mothership." She leaned over the folding banquet table, her deacons on either side frozen in attitudes of concern like a fresco in some new Sistine Chapel. "Wherever the Place turns out to be, it won't be a piece of cake. The Dinks aren't going to loan you ladders to climb on board.

27

They're going to be after you with guns. Love and his thugs are going to want to stop you. You know what happened last night?''

Again the crowd waited, hushed. From somewhere the crunching of a foot on the shattered glass of a portavee.

"Two brothers and three sisters were ambushed outside a little town on their way here. Vigilantes did it, nailed them coming off the highway for a Zapstop. They say it was because someone killed a Zapstop man last week, but we know who did that. And we know who those vigilantes really were. We *know!* So let's have a moment of silence for those brothers and sisters, like the Lost Tribes of Israel.''

How doth the city sit solitary, her father recited. That was full of people! How is she become as a widow! She that was great among nations, and princess among provinces, how is she become tributary. She weepeth sore in the night, and her tears are on her cheeks. Supper ready?

"But we're like those Lost Tribes,'' she said. "We're outcasts. Has any jump to a new level of awareness for mankind ever come easy? What did they do to Socrates?''

There was an uneasy silence. "Cut his head off?'' asked a voice from the back of the crowd.

"Right,'' she beamed. "Cut his damned head straight off. And how about, um, Galileo, when he told them the sun was round and everything?''

"Cut his head off?'' asked the same voice, emboldened.

"Yeah, cut it off,'' muttered other voices. The pattern was emerging, and the first voice giggled with nervous pride at having seen it first.

"You bet they did,'' the Monad said. "People are always afraid of new truths, and you've got to be ready to fight, like all those antique Christians with the lions and all. Dollars to doughnuts, the minute the first caveman invented the wheel, someone whacked his head off with a club. So that's why you've got to wander like the Lost Tribes, looking for your true home.''

Just looking for a home, the old record player buzzed. Just looking for a home.

I guess that means a trip to the woodshed, her father said. If you don't punish sin, then it just grows like Topsy.

"Sure, it's like a punishment,'' she said, "but it's to save you from the worse punishment later on, when the Beings take the Dinks out to the woodshed. It's what's going to make you perfect, pure, blameless—''

We're all sinners, her father said. Lord, forgive me for what I got to do to this child.

"—and save you forever and ever. Nobody said it was easy. A lot of you already suffered in jail in New York, and a lot of others worked the streets to get the money to make bail. I wish there was some way I could just tell you They'll be at such and such a place to beam you up, but I can't. They want you to evolve that spiritual radar some more. But I *can* tell you two things."

A silence fell at the front of the crowd, moved back into the darkness of waiting bodies.

"It'll be before the end of the year!"

Gasps and cries.

Her throat was very dry, polished dry, gleaming like the long dry corridors of the Mothership. *We won't hurt you, they said. You'll be safe in this room. It was dry because there was no toilet and no sink.*

"It's not near the ocean! They hate water!"

Excited whispers scurried ratlike through the crowd.

"So be ready, that's all."

She turned and was gone.

Later, lying tucked under the comforting maternal arm of Moonrose, Starbud chewed thoughtfully on her thumb.

"What did you think of her?" Moonrose said.

"The Monad? I thought she was...I don't know, but she's got this look in her eyes, like she really *has* talked to the Beings."

"Of course she's talked to the Beings."

"Will she talk again tomorrow, do you think?"

"She'll probably be gone," Moonrose said. "That's her way. As soon as we're all here, she goes, and then we've got to try to follow."

"Where do you think it'll be next?"

Moonrose sighed. "Hard to say. Moonbeam told me a lot of people have been talking Denver over by the parking lot."

Starbud thought. "Denver's not near any ocean," she said. "You think Denver could be the Place?"

"Could be," Moonrose said. "All we can do is try to be ready."

Starbud closed her eyes. "Where's Moonbeam?" she asked.

"He's over with the people that brought the news about the

ambush in New York. It's funny—we were at that same Zapstop, you know. They're saying how it's time we stopped letting ourselves be kicked around and really did something about Doctor Love. Between you and me, I don't like their looks. I never saw them before, and they don't look like Seekers to me. I just hope Moonbeam doesn't let himself get talked into something stupid, because I'm getting very bad feelings over my radar. He's got a way of carnling down sometimes, forgetting our only real job is getting ready for the End.''

Starbud was silent for a long time. "Moonrose," she said dreamily. "What will the end of the world be like?"

4

Subdividing Space

10 PM Wednesday, April 7

Over the reassuring thrum of the dustcat's engine, Andrew McCallum listened to the sizzle of the gritty wind against his cab's metal exterior. The occasional pings were larger pebbles along with the usual miasma of fine soil flakes. Another killer wind, McCallum thought. Something better than a hundred kilometers an hour, because the average wind couldn't move aggregates bigger than eight tenths of a millimeter.

Even in a fifty-kilometer wind you lost three times as much topsoil as you did in a thirty-kilometer one—there'd be blowouts all over tonight.

Moisture, that was the key. Moisture made clods that even a two-hundred-kilometer wind couldn't move, but years ago the moisture-laden jet stream had looped far to the north, improving Canadian yields but leaving the Great Plains dry and open to the desert wind.

If only they could have done any of the things conventional wisdom dictated—planting alternate rows of small-grain crops and grasses, or tree windbreaks. But there was so much land and so little time. It was all he could do to keep after the covered experimental fields.

He eased the dustcat down the rows of tents, scanning the ghostly silhouettes of the guayule shrubs against the polytents' translucent sides, watching for flashes of inside light that might mean a tear in the tent fabric.

So far so good. At the end of polytent 043 he paused, then flicked on the searchlights in the housing over the cab to probe the alley between 043 and 044. A little dust devil swirled like a malevolent top, and then dispersed back into its parent wind.

A shadow at the groundline halfway down 044, possible tent bulge indicating a tear. He cut the spots, but there was no telltale streak of light. Maybe a rock or piece of trash; he could check in the morning once the wind had died down.

He gunned the engine to roll forward, and suddenly the shadow bounded away, moving in long frantic leaps through his headlights and disappearing into the darkness.

McCallum laughed at his sudden fear. Jackrabbit, that was all, trying to find shelter in the tent or maybe nibbling a prickly pear cactus. There'd been so much on the news about Saucer Kids murdering people and vigilantes taking revenge. And with Jessica missing . . .

Not that the prickly opuntia or the jackrabbits weren't a problem in their own rights, but at least they weren't a threat to his personal safety. The jackrabbits had moved out of their native Colorado fifteen years before, as the annual rainfall had dropped from seventy to thirty-five millimeters, five less than the worst years of the Dustbowl of the thirties. The dry weather allowed more of the opuntia young to survive, and the population mushroomed. They'd infested over one and a half million metric tons of western Kansas pastureland alone—or rather, former pastureland.

But at least they hadn't gotten the locusts, like Indiana and Ohio. Still, he'd have to keep the rabbits out of the tents. They'd be harvesting soon, and this was an important harvest for the project. Up till now they'd taken only the guayule tops because the growing cycle took three years, even with sunlamps and precious irrigation.

But for the first time, this year they had enough plants to afford harvesting a ninth of the total as whole plants. That meant getting not just the latex from the stems, but the resins leached out in the acetone bath to improve the latex's flexibility and longevity could be made into terpenes, shellac, cinnamic acid, and drying oils for the paint industry, while the wax from the leaves was as good as carnauba wax and, at sixty-two Celsius, had one of the highest boiling points of any natural wax. Even the pulpy bagasse left over in the flotation vat could be sold to the paper industry.

It was gratifying, no question about it. Who'd have thought fifteen years ago that the Kansas dustbowl would ever yield anything again? They'd said there was no way this time to reverse the damage done in those crazy, hectic days thirty years

32

ago when they'd used every chemical possible to increase wheat yield to meet domestic and foreign demands, depleting the humus in the soil and the land's ability to produce. And when the oil shortages had come, they'd switched from energy-intensive chisel plowing to old-fashioned moldboard plowing, and that had left the bare surface soil even more vulnerable to erosion.

So intensive farming had retreated eastward and westward, to California and Ohio and Pennsylvania. But McCallum and his colleagues in the Farm Security Administration had worked their butts off to find hybrids or natural crops suited to the impoverished soil or, like guayule, able to survive with minimal aids like heat lamps and polytents. Such semiarid crops might eventually tempt private farmers back, but in the meantime guayule would insure the country a growing supply of natural latex to take the strain off what was left of petroleum reserves.

The dustcat lumbered forward on its great balloon tires, past 044 and then 045, and finally to the end of the field. Dusk already. It was easy to forget in the growing spring warmth that the days were still winter-short.

He rolled down the slight incline to the old farm road and turned toward home, watching his headlights catch the dust whipped in streamers through the twisted mesh of the old wire fences along the roadside. Carol would already be back from the agristation by now, punching out supper and catching up on the national news and the directives and updates from FSA.

And thinking about Jessica.

He shook his head. You couldn't keep torturing yourself about something that was over and done. There was no way to undo it. If she were coming back, she'd come back. Worrying wouldn't make it happen.

He pulled the dustcat to a stop where Road 389 made a ninety-degree intersection with the remains of Route 4. Diagonally across from him was something that hadn't been there the hundreds of times he'd passed this way. He flicked the servo motor to swing the outside spot to bear on it.

A deserted farmhouse.

He grunted. The wind did things like that. It had covered a lot of houses like this in the last twenty years, but every now and then there'd be a blowout and it would start digging away at one of its own mounds until whatever lay beneath it was uncovered.

He eased across the intersection and up the incline. Better go and look now. The wind would undo things like this as quickly as it had done them; by tomorrow, the ocean of dust would already be rising around the house again.

He came to a stop in what had been the barnyard, pulled his respirator up from around his neck and adjusted it over his mouth and nose, tightening his hood and checking the seals around his face and between his sleeves and gloves. Then, grimacing against the wind force he'd feel, he pushed the cab door open and hopped to the ground. The beam of his flashlight writhed with phantasm snakes of dust.

He decided to check the barn first. The door was rolled part-way open, dust silted on either side of it to hold it as firmly as a cement footing. He was just able to squeeze his way inside.

He scanned the interior. Chalk marks on the wall of a stall: "Cow took bull 2/7."

Must have been one hell of a small farm, he thought, no more than recreational livestock. He'd check the computer records when he got home. A 1970 calendar on one wall with a picture of a wheatfield labeled "Manhattan, Kansas, The Union Pacific Railroad." A little older than he'd have guessed, maybe, but then you didn't keep current calendars in barns. No doubt the old codger had liked the picture. Next to it were car and tractor plates from the fifties, sixties, and seventies, but no priority-user plates from the eighties. Well, that might explain why the place had been abandoned. Farther back he found a bald tire and a shovel, and beyond these something covered by a tarp.

He walked to the tarp, ranging with his flashlight, and lifted it up. Wood. Jesus, a fortune in plywood. And it wasn't damaged at all. In fact, it looked brand new.

He pulled his respirator down and sniffed. Smelled brand new, too. Maybe being sealed off by the dust had played some kind of biological trick, like the way buried seeds and corn had been preserved in Egypt. With just enough moisture it would stay fresh indefinitely without rotting.

Behind the plywood he found rolls of foil-backed insulation, twenty cartons of aluminum foil, a box of gallon cans of paint. He pulled a can out—anti-fouling marine aluminum. Not exactly what you'd expect to find on a Kansas farm, for God's sake. Maybe the old farmer had been one of those nuts who spend their lives building themselves a boat without ever seeing the ocean and then put it on a trailer and head for the Pacific.

Beside the paint was a roll of zinc and a pair of cutting

34

shears—roof flashing, maybe?—a box of assorted nails and screws, some hand tools, a power saw, a compressor, and a spray gun.

All in perfect shape, that was the bizarre part. But it all fit—when the old farmer set off for the sea, he hadn't had any use for the equipment and supplies and he'd left them behind, and then somehow the dust had covered them over before looters or rangers had found them. A future archeologist's dream, except McCallum would come back in the daylight and take whatever had any value. The plywood alone would pay for his time.

He turned to go out and investigate the house. Maybe the old codger had left a fortune in bills in the stove or something. And then it hit him.

He'd looked right at it and it hadn't registered. The HED batterypak for the power saw and compressor. The things weren't just well-preserved—they were brand new HED tools.

So somebody had been squatting there. It was no surprise; there were squatters all over the wasteland. But after all the trouble with Saucer Kids and vigilantes . . . He hefted his flashlight, debating, then squeezed himself through the door and headed across the yard for the farmhouse. He wasn't exactly anxious to tangle with anyone, but the farm was government property, and that made it his business.

A broken length of clothesline snaked in the wind from its hook just beside the backstairs railing.

The kitchen door still worked. Usually these places were filled with dirt, and you had to hammer your way in.

The kitchen was pretty much what he'd expected. A vinyl blind flapped over a broken window. The piping to the missing stove was still intact. A shelf over the space the stove had occupied still had greasecloth thumbtacked to it. A yellow scrap of newspaper trembled against the pantry doorjamb, and a brittle page from a Bozo the Clown coloring book lay just beyond. He followed his flashlight beam into the living room.

The boards on the front windows had been blown in at some point, and the room was drifted with silt. But no footprints—that was what he was looking for.

There was a noise from above.

McCallum tensed. It had sounded like a cry, the kind a Siamese cat might make.

He found the hall stairs and started up. Some dust had drifted down, but it was probably recent. Whoever was using this place had probably started by coming in an upstairs window before the wind had uncovered the rest. At the head of the stairs he swung his beam toward the front bedroom and onto a ramp of dust leading to two missing boards over one window. That was how they'd gotten in, all right.

But there was something—a bit of cloth, a blanket corner just visible, curling up from the dirt. He swept his light across the miniature Sahara of the room, but there was nothing else. Swallowing back the sour taste, he went to the back bedrooms.

It was in the second bedroom that he found the battery cooker, surrounded by grease spots. Whoever it was had been here a while; their activity around the second-floor window had probably given the wind its fingerhold to tear away what it had piled up.

The cat noise again.

He swept his light across the four walls, lower and lower, probing the corners, then the closet. He peered in. A bundle of rags lay at his feet.

He knelt down, shining his light into the interior of the rags, and a baby's head emerged, squinting and turning away from the light, and beginning to cry in earnest.

Could whoever it was have left a baby unprotected in the dust desert? Had they abandoned it or were they coming back? Who but Saucer People could be that irresponsible?

He tucked his flashlight under one arm and scooped the baby up.

"There, there, little girl," he cooed, more from habit than any intuition of the child's sex. Had it really been thirteen years since he'd held Jessica like this?

"Take it easy," he said. "You'll be all right. We'll get you back to the station and fix you up. Who knows, maybe there was some purpose in me finding you."

He wrapped the blankets tighter to protect the child's face for the walk back to the dustcat, purring in the wind outside.

"Hey, jimmy, where you going with the kid?"

McCallum swung around. Something loomed in the doorway.

"Who the hell are you?" McCallum snapped, heart still pounding. "This is government property."

The figure came forward into the beam of the flashlight under McCallum's arm. He was less threatening than McCallum had thought—below average height, balding, rotund, squeezed into a pair of jeans three sizes too small that rippled at the zipper with stress. He squinted against the light and adjusted his glasses. The cheeks and chin of his round face were blue-black with the sheen of a five-o'clock shadow.

"I don't give a shit who owns the place," the man said. "But that's my kid you got there. Did my wife send you?"

In his hand, McCallum noticed, was a long crowbar.

11 PM Wednesday, April 7

Carol McCallum had promised that morning to check the vats in the autoprocessing factory. Once the harvest was in full swing, they had to be sure the machinery would shut down fast enough to avoid damage in the event of any sub-systemic failure. But the lingering odor of terpenes and shellac from the trial runs gave her a headache, and she had gone to spend the day at the lab. Andy was the farmer, after all; he liked tinkering with big, dirty machines, he liked blacksmithing.

Her dream—if the endless flatness and the dustwinds had left her anything like a dream—was to finish the research she'd begun in graduate school. Amaze the world with her discovery of the answers the dustbowl needed, amaze the world that she'd done it alone, with inadequate equipment and no university laboratory.

She understood that what was needed was an architect, an artist, who could step back and understand the whole. Instead, she found herself mired in day-to-day patching and niggling as a kind of agricultural janitor. Maybe that was enough for Andy, but to her it seemed that if you spent all your time sticking your fingers in leaky dikes, you'd never find out what the hell the dam looked like.

She'd been working with wheat and rice, the Calvin systems plants of the three-carbon-atom first product group, trying to increase the yield and stress tolerance of the C_3's to the level of C_4's like corn, sorghum, and millet, which were sensitive to chill but withstood heat and drought better. She wanted a staple crop that she could wield like a sword to reclaim the wasteland from the dragon, not a halfway desperation measure like guayule.

The problem was at night, when photorespiration formed glycolic acid which in turn broke down the carbohydrates and

37

released the carbon dioxide the plant had formed during the day through photosynthesis. At first she'd experimented with stopping photorespiration by lowering the oxygen and increasing the carbon dioxide in the atmosphere, but that would have meant growing wheat in polytents, and that would have been as pointless as guayule. The battle with the wind wouldn't be won until she had a crop she could force to grow under the open sky.

Now she was experimenting with hybridizing C_3's with Crassulcean Acid Metabolism plants. None were field crops, but they could survive in extremely arid regions because they fixed carbon dioxide at night and were incredibly water-efficient.

Coming up from the lab tunnel, she stopped at the house terminal to check for messages. How many times had she done this with the same mixture of hope that Jessica had at last decided to call and fear that a ranger had found . . . something awful.

Nothing. A videphone message from the Sears-Ward Catalogue Service wanting to know if she'd be ordering anything this month, a call from the regional school board asking how many children resided at this address—she sighed, swallowed, dug at something in the corner of her eye, piece of dust, probably— but the computer had answered that one for her: none.

She called for the federal weather, and the LC flashed 100 km. winds and a travelers' advisory. She skipped the news—the New York Saucer riot had made her inexplicably uneasy, so many *children*—and tapped for the FSA stats.

First came the pestographs, laid out as ovals on graphs of ascending moisture and temperature. Pale western cutworms in Alberta, ten percent crop loss. Pathogenic soil fungi, wheat pathogens like S. nodorum and S. tritici, wheat rust, P. graminis tritici. They had to watch for S. avenae triticea and S. tritici because they liked aridity better than S. nodorum.

Field bindweed up—to be expected because of the drought. But the one that bothered her was the warning flash at the end, spottings of swarms of Melanoplus sanguinipes, migratory grasshoppers, locusts.

The spottings were in Canada. In 1949, they'd destroyed a quarter of the Saskatchewan crop. When drought diminished the wheat supply, it diminished the grasshoppers' food but improved their breeding conditions. That was why they had already swarmed in places like Indiana. It was one thing to wish the cutworms and locusts on the Canadian wheat barons after all these years of profiting from American miseries, but the fact was that if the Canadian grain pirates had nothing to sell, even at inflated prices, the famines in the Middle East and the Orient were going to begin in the U.S.

She passed by the standard prognostications from Dragon Rouge—had things really gotten so crazy that FSA had hired a consulting firm of witches like everyone else? It was disgusting, the whole institutionalization of the occult in the face of uncertainty. It was the same mass insanity that made the Saucer Cult and the Lovites possible. It was like Medieval Europe trying to escape the Black Death by practicing self-flagellation. At least the Cult would be finished when none of their Pied Piper's predictions came true. But Doctor Love was something else. He was television.

She put a report on hybridizing cytoplasms within species and another on the improvement of nuclear and cytoplasmic genomes on hold for after supper and called for the sensor readings from the spot collectors on the acreage they were responsible for.

They had the makings of a blowout in 8942NW. The tolerable level for climatic stress periods was just over thirty kilograms loss per hectare per day, or eleven metric tons a year. At 8942 they were running twenty times that in today's wind.

She called for data on the parcel: silty clay loam. "Best countermeasures?" she asked.

Strip-cropping of erosion resistant and erosion-susceptible crops 130 meters apart—

"Jesus Christ, I want something for right now, not next spring! This is an emergency."

The screen was blank.

"Emergency measures," she droned in a monotone the machine could grasp.

Tillage tools set at 1.25 meter spacing.

1400 kg./ha. vegetable residue, stubble, mulch, + chemical stabilizers—

"Haven't got it on hand," she said. "Next?"

Cut level backslope benches seventy meters wide for 60% projected erosion reduction.

"No time. Next?"

Try 0.6 meter earthen banks or 1.2 meter snow fences.

"Thank you," she said. They had a roll of snow fencing in the shed, but even with the fence-laying machine it would take both of them. Another lab day lost.

Suddenly she heard the familiar high-voltage crackle of the dustlock. Jesus, Andy back from his polytent check. He had just stepped on the negative plate to ionize and remove the dust. She had to hustle before he got in—today was her turn to arrange supper.

"House status," she said. "Menus."

The screen showed temperature, electrical consumption, light levels, and a list of foods ready for preparation. She heard the hum of the vacuum removing the dust. "The hell with it," she said. "Pick something nutritious and cook it. Something unusual."

The door behind her opened. She turned, ready to flash a relieved smile at appearing to have taken care of those things she hated taking care of.

She froze.

It wasn't Andy in the doorway. It was a swarthy, round-faced man, hair wild from the wind outside.

"And just who do you think *you* are?" she demanded, trying to sound authoritative despite her fear.

"Sinbad Schwartz," he answered.

"My husband's due home any second," she said.

"I know," he said. "He's right behind me."

At that there was a second crackle from the dustplates and what sounded like a baby's frightened cry. Andrew McCallum pushed through the door, the vacuum suddenly loud and then muffled again as the door swished shut behind him.

"Carol, I want you to meet Sinbad Schwartz."

"We've met," she said. "Where in the world did you get a name like that?"

"Probate court," he said. "I got it changed. Who'd want a last name like Jones? This way, everyone remembers me."

"He was down by the south polytents," McCallum said. "Squatting in an abandoned farmhouse."

"Like hell I was squatting."

"Had his kid with him," McCallum said, holding up the still-bundled baby.

"Can I help it if I had this really sticky divorce? If I'd left the kid back in New York with my mother, my ex would have been through the courts like prunes and Ex-Lax and come out with a reversed custody decision. Face it, who wants visiting rights for off-peak hours at the Kit-Kat House of Pleasure and Discipline? I *had* to take him with me."

40

"Oh, he's so *cute,*" Carol said, peering into the folds of ragged blankets at the pink face. "And you had him out in the dusters?"

"I kept him in the house the whole time. He *loved* it. I think he's an Early Americana freak."

"Parents!" Carol snorted. "There isn't a responsible parent left." She took the bundle from McCallum and held it against her. "Which house was it?"

"One we never saw before. Dusted over till a day or so ago," McCallum said.

"Look, I had to set up *somewhere,*" Sinbad said. "I figured if the land belonged to the government, then it was as much mine as anybody else's. I didn't hurt anything, anyway. In fact, I was going to make it famous."

"Get this," McCallum said. "Tell her, Sinbad."

"I was going to create a sculpture."

Carol nodded and went to the terminal to order up another dinner. They had milk, but nothing else for the baby. Well, after all—how many years had it been? Parents nowadays. If they kept their kids under control, there wouldn't be these Saucer Cults and Jessica wouldn't have been lured away.

"You hear that?" McCallum said. "He wants to build a statue or something in the middle of the dustbowl."

"Why don't we talk about it over dinner?" Carol said.

Through the course of dinner—the computer had taken literally her injunction about having something unusual and had microwaved a pecan pie and a stack of pancakes to a turn—Carol decided that Mr. Schwartz would have to stay with them. They had a spare room, after all, and, she told herself, it might just serve Jessica right to come back and find out that they'd *given* her bedroom away.

"So what do you *do?*" Sinbad asked, smacking his lips.

"Agricultural research," Carol said.

"And a lot of practical stuff," McCallum added. "We're trying to reclaim this land for farming. Right now we're experimenting with guayule. It's a shrub you can extract latex from. The Aztecs used to make it into little rubber balls."

"And now we're going to make it into big rubber balls," Carol said. "The improvement is that we don't have to chew up the stems in our mouths to get the rubber the way they did. We've got a machine."

McCallum glared at her while Sinbad drained his glass with a

41

zooful of loud sucking noises. "And we're doing other things, too. We collect samples for the paleoclimatologists so we can fit this area in with their records for the south and southwest."

"That important?" Sinbad asked. "Anybody want that last pancake?"

"Very important," McCallum said. "There have been droughts before, you know. Now if we could find out what happened to the Anasazi at Pueblo Bonito in New Mexico, for instance—why it got too arid for trees to grow in the eleventh century and why it actually turned into a desert in the sixteenth century—"

"Sixteenth century?" Sinbad said, brightening. "Rubens."

"And Marlowe, Shakespeare, Queen Elizabeth," McCallum said. "And in this country, ecological disaster. And there was a two-hundred-year drought in Iowa that wiped out the Mill Creek Indian culture. If we could fit the big picture together, maybe we could predict what's going to happen this time around, or learn how to prevent it next time. Or even reverse it."

"Speaking of pictures, Mr. Schwartz," Carol said, wiping the baby's chin, "exactly what kind of art is it you do?"

"A lot of people have asked me that," Sinbad said. "I used to be into pure abstraction, but all these critics kept insisting my work *meant* something. Well, what was I back then? A kid, right? So I gave in to their representationalist fantasies, even got into Talkart. Had these videphones set up all around the gallery, and when you tapped zero, I'd come on and tell you to shit in your shoes or whatever. Critics loved it, but they're all a bunch of masochistic limp-wristed fruits anyway, and they love being humiliated. Biggest gallery hit in the last ten years was Rinaldo Fawcett's 'Blood Rain.' He set up this little booth, and when you stepped inside a machine dumped chicken guts all over you. The reviewer from *Art Today* came back *six times* just to get off on it. Course, Rinaldo recycled the guts, but you couldn't do that nowadays," Sinbad said wistfully. "Meat prices the way they are, the first critic would *eat* the goddamn thing."

"Baby got a little gas?" Carol said, patting the baby's back.

"Anyway, after a while I just said the hell with it. Fuck the conceptualists, I said, fuck the formalists, fuck the minimalists, fuck the figurativists, fuck the abstractionists, fuck the super-realists, fuck the colorists, fuck the constructionists, *and* fuck the objectivists."

"That's a lot of people," McCallum said.

42

"Yeah, but I wanted to get to the roots of the modern malaise. See, art isn't visual perception anymore."

"It isn't?"

"Oh, that was okay for Rembrandt or Caravaggio or that bunch, but for me it's not enough for art to be a vision of truth. It's got to be, well . . . it's hard to explain, but what I'm trying to do is a little like taking plaster casts of the footprints of our emotive sensibilities. Know what I mean?"

McCallum looked blank. "And that's what brings you out to the dustbowl?"

"Right. See, forty years ago Pop Art was on the right track, but it was a celebration of the everyday artifacts of the present. When I founded the Crapart movement, what I wanted wasn't the mediocrities of today, I wanted to get right down to the *roots* of the crap. I wanted to celebrate the *plumbing* of modern *angst*. So what I'm planning is this big silver column—"

"Is that what the insulation and tin foil are for?"

"Right."

"But what's it *mean*?"

Sinbad drew a shaky square in the congealing maple syrup on his plate. "You see? Everybody's into representationalism. A spindle."

"A spindle?"

"A great, silver spindle. And up on top I'll have this huge silver disc a hundred, two hundred feet across. It'll set up this spatial dichotomy, see, kind of crystallize all the space around it into the volume of air from the ground to the disc and the air from the disc to, say, Pluto. Above and below, see? More than a visual perception—people will move *through* the space underneath, like a progression through life or some everyday situation. It's a sculpture in space and time using a vocabulary of, well, basically plywood and a saber saw."

"What for?"

"I told you—to experience one defined space, and to *yearn* for the one you can't reach up on top of the disc." Sinbad paused. "Unless, of course, I put a ladder up. Then they could get a taste of *both* spaces."

"It sounds like it's supposed to look like a flying saucer."

"Flying saucer? Shit, no. A big silver disc on a spindle? It's an ode to the past—before floppie-discs and top-forty TV. It's an ode to the essence of yesterday. It's a two-hundred-foot ode to the forty-five-rpm record!"

43

5

Circe McPhee

1 PM Friday, June 4

Whoever Mr. Soames was, he was late, and Circe McPhee found herself glancing anxiously toward the entrance with every flurry of movement.

"Is the madam of interest for a—aha! Ms. McPhee! I never realize you!"

Circe removed her sunglasses and smiled at the waiter, a vision of starched red cloth and gold braid incongruously topped by a bald head laced with livid scars and deeper blue radiation blotches. "Afternoon, Chaudhuri."

"A cocktail of the usual?"

"Not yet, I'm waiting for a client. Just water for now."

He bobbed affirmatively.

"And maybe a plate of chapaties."

He turned and was gone. Zarda's had its bad points, but at least it was quiet and it had enough class not to remind you bread and water were extra. Most of the refugee Pakistani places were fast-food reenactments of the Five-Minute War, faceless people pushing and shoving through fumes of red pepper.

And God knew she needed a little quiet today. In fact, if this Soames jimmy hadn't been so insistent on the phone—desperate even—she'd never have agreed to meet with him at all, let alone have him intrude into her few moments of peace for the day. But there had been no other time she could see him—two appointments and then the League meeting for the rest of the morning, and back-to-back consultations all afternoon.

She was almost too distracted to cope with any of it. Adele had been perfectly bitchy the last three days and was probably getting her period; whatever the reason, life in the apartment had

44

been stretches of sullen silence interspersed with angry staccato exchanges. And if home life weren't disruptive enough, things were getting worse and worse at Ashtoreth, Incorporated, where Circe was halfway through her probation as a junior account executive.

For one thing, in every one of this week's consultation readings the Tower had appeared, the sixteenth card of the Major Arcana. Invariably it had shown up either as the unalterable future card in the Celtic method or, when she'd switched to Tree of Life to escape it, as the first of the Daath's seven cards, the client's immediate future.

The face of the card showed a tower being struck by a jagged arrow of lightning. From its top tumbled the papal tiara of worldly thought, while two flaming victims plunged from its fiery windows into the abyss.

Traditionally it indicated a change in the style or substance of a client's life. It could be the kind of change that brings new knowledge or eventual improvement, but normally it was a card of ill omen—bankruptcy, bereavement, loss of power, catastrophe.

It was statistically impossible—and any self-respecting witch knew the probability curves—for her to have had such a run of clients all headed for individual demotions and bankruptcies, even if as a probationer she didn't exactly get the best ones. It had to be some single external event that was going to touch them all, perhaps a national or world disaster, for Circe had learned to intuit at least a little beyond the mechanic's established meanings for the cards, and that clairvoyant sense told her the Tower presaged more than a few petty personal problems.

Maybe something like the New York Saucer Riot in March, a policeman killed and all those Saucer Kids arrested. They were still criss-crossing the country in caravans; another clash with authorities was inevitable.

What she needed was something to jog her limited clairvoyance. She knew her Gift was meager compared to those of the full partners and the better junior executives; but she'd never get to the corporate top at Ashtoreth if she couldn't figure this one out. Maybe there was some common thread among the clients—their occupations or places of residence. This morning there'd been a Connecticut woman from the Sikorsky Division of United Technologies, though hers had been a rare private consultation, and a man from Solarsystems International.

Both were big corporations. United Tech was more established, but Solarsystems was a new solar power conglomerate that had used its Denver satellite monopoly to gobble up most of the old oil and nuclear power companies. Could it be a business disaster, then, a stock market crash like '29 or the long slump of '93? Or another natural disaster that could affect a lot of different people like the California earthquake?

Chaudhuri appeared with Circe's plate of flat bread and a glass of water. As he bent to lay them before her, she saw again the purple radiation blotches that scarred his face and neck.

Could the Tower mean something like the Five-Minute War that had brought Chaudhuri and his fellow Paks here? She remembered that at the time news commentators had agreed it was too bad the war hadn't been mutually devastating; India's dazzling success was an open invitation not just to the fifty countries with the bomb, but to the shabbiest satrapy with an imported atomic power plant, to risk the same kind of preemptive first strike.

She ran through this morning's clients again. One worked with helicopters, the other with solar-power microwave satellites. Both had possible military applications, but she'd have to check her appointment book to see if the rest of the week's clients had related occupations. It would be a relief—a little war in Bulgaria or Yemen was a lot better than another earthquake or depression at home.

"Still wait?" asked Chaudhuri.

Circe nodded. Still wait.

She decided to calm herself with one of her exercises, and reached into her shoulder bag for her Tarot. Every probationer was encouraged to build a rapport with the cards by going through them again and again in her spare moments, picking a different one to study each time. Through intense concentration you could lose yourself in it, become one with it, and return with a deeper understanding of its significance and a sharpened Gift. Dagon had described it as a kind of auto-hypnosis; certainly it always helped her forget her other problems. Anyway, it couldn't hurt her image if this Soames jimmy found her reading the cards when he arrived.

Idly she considered each of the cards in turn. King of Coins—a dark, vicious man. Knight of Cups—a rascal. The Hanged Man, haloed head, one foot tied to a T cross—a suspended decision, self-sacrifice. Seven of Swords, a man carrying off five swords

46

and leaving two—uncertainty, partial failure. Caesar, King of Wands—a good man, though Mademoiselle le Normand had written he signified an evil personality. And then, in succession, the dark and sterile Queen of Swords, the motherly Queen of Cups, reversed—potentially dishonest but essentially good—and her own card, the black-eyed, black-haired Queen of Pentacles—a strong but hopelessly earthbound intelligence.

Circe was hardly casting a fortune, yet considering this morning's meeting, it seemed more than chance that the three queens should appear together like this. The belief in the mysterious link between animate and inanimate things, of course, was the basis of prophecy.

Circe sighed. No wonder Ashtoreth always sent a probationary account executive as Sisterly Emissary to the League. Who else could be expected to do so miserable and thankless a job?

Pre-eminent at the meeting had been Madame Melba from Dragon Rouge Associates, which held the lion's share—or dragon's share—of government prognostication contracts. She had sat stern and silent as the Queen of Swords on her throne amongst the storm clouds. Next to her had been the woman named Clyve, white-haired and hazel-eyed, as motherly as the Queen of Cups but old enough to be subtle and unpredictable in political matters.

Circe had presented the position of Ashtoreth's full partners. The point, as she told the meeting, was for the Amalgamated Covens of the League to stop excluding other occult artists and seek cooperation. "It's a matter of self-preservation," Circe had told them. "We've got to start discriminating on the basis of integrity rather than which system we think is 'right.' Because if we don't set up a pan-occult commission to police ourselves, the government's going to start licensing and regulating us. I don't think any of us want to see bureaucrats controlling the occult arts."

"But meeting with *herbalists*," sniffed Madame Melba. "Really, darling, a lot of Slavic old crones ruining the good name of witchcraft. They weren't included in the League for a *reason*—we simply *can't* deal with that sort of people."

"What worries me is getting involved with the Astrologers' Guild or the Sorcerers' Union. Our whole industry is based on the coven philosophy of sisterhood under the Great Mother," Clyve said. "At least the herbalists are women."

"But the Great Mother's consort has always been the Horned

God," Circe said. "We all know there have been accommodations and compromises already. The Sisters of Shibboleth have at least one male astrologer on retainer—"

"But he's gay," someone interjected from farther down the table.

"Most of New York is gay," Circe answered. "Whatever his preferences are, Shibboleth bent the rules because he did work they could rely on—and we all know Shibboleth isn't the only one. When it's a matter of survival, you don't draw the line at arbitrary things like gender."

"I suppose, my dear," Madame Melba said, "that next you'll have us taking in phrenologists and alectoromancers."

"Better than taking orders from a government flunky," Circe snapped. "But the government's not the only reason we need a industry-wide organization. I imagine you all watched the TV coverage of the riot last March?"

There was silence as everyone gazed down at the table.

"And that's just a taste of the Pied Piper and her Saucer Cult. Things are bound to get worse, I can feel it."

Murmurs of assent rippled down either side of the table.

"Think what this woman means. In effect she's selling a kind of undisciplined mysticism—every soul its own clairvoyant and divinator. Our industry *depends* on the fact that only a few people have the Gift for mystic science—but it'll take a well-funded organization to counteract the brand of occult populism she's pushing."

"I don't think she's got much of a following except the very young," said Clyve.

"That's not entirely true," Circe said. "But whether it is or not, we're also up against what's got to be the world's first TV religion."

"You mean Doctor Love?" asked Clyve.

"Do you really think we can compete as individuals with an organization that peddles faith through a bunch of gadgets you can plug into your TV at home?" Circe said. "Especially when his electronic mysticism is aimed at relieving precisely those anxieties that bring us our clients."

"But darling," said Madame Melba, "I know for a fact that Doctor Love has never condemned witchcraft."

"He never condemns anything," Circe said. "He's all things to all people—that's his secret."

"But his organization is also a prime customer for our services," Clyve said. "You should know that better than any of us."

Circe looked down. It was a fact that Ashtoreth was Faith Ltd.'s major supplier of prognosticatory software.

"Really, my dear," Madame Melba said, "I've got to agree with Clyve here. We can't put sisterhood aside for every fad that comes along. You're too young to know what the League has accomplished, but *I* can remember when we worked out of one-room apartments and trailers and even did palms and tea leaves just to eat. We didn't just lack respectability or corporate clients in those days; we had to deal with the dregs of humanity. Why, I used to go weeks on end hoping for a customer that didn't drool or tell me how the Devil appeared every night in her dishwasher wrestling with the Angel Gabriel. If it hadn't been for the sisterhood of the League, darling, none of us would be here now."

"Sisterhood and selectivity," said Clyve, taking Madame Melba's side to return the compliment. "We fought like dogs to get rid of the jimmies with crystal balls and tassled curtains and all the rest of it, and I'm not about to risk letting them back."

And so the motion to approach the astrologers, sorcerers, and non-League occultists had simply been tabled by a sniff from Madame Melba.

Circe spread the three queens out on the table before her, studying them.

"She over there," came Chaudhuri's voice.

"Ms. McPhee?"

Circe looked up to find an older man bending over her. He was dressed in a neatly pressed denim suit, typical for his age, hair silver, face drawn, eyes tired.

"Mr. Soames?" she asked, and motioned him to take a seat. She pushed the untouched plate of chapaties toward him, but he shook his head. Hurriedly she gathered up her cards and stacked them beside her plate. He brought some terrible pain with him. "I don't think you mentioned what company you're with, Mr. Soames."

He seemed surprised by the question. "I, uh, I'm vice president of sales with Fish and Rasmutin. We make industrial lasers, mainly for mine boring. We've got the new lunar contract."

She nodded. "And you want to arrange for some kind of corporate forecast of profits or a competitor's plans? Of course there are certain ethical restrictions on my divining a third party's—"

"I'm afraid you don't understand," he said. "I want a personal consultation."

Circe blinked with surprise. "We don't usually handle private accounts," she said. "Our fee schedule—"

"I know," he said, compulsively drawing the fingers of one hand through the other's grasp and then reversing the process. "But they tell me Ashtoreth is the best in the business."

Circe smiled. "I'm flattered, of course," she said. "That's the kind of reputation we try to maintain." She waited for Soames to tell her what he wanted.

"It's not for myself, either," he went on.

She nodded. "I can't cast as well when the principal's psychic presence is too far removed—"

"It's my wife," he blurted. "She's in a lot of pain. It's her gall bladder, but we couldn't get Board approval."

"Which board?"

"At the hospital. Gall bladders are one of the things they use those CLASS machines for now, and you've got to apply for a place on the list for mechanized surgery."

"And you want me to cast the Tarot to see if the Board will reverse itself," Circe asked, "or if her health—"

"I want something that will cure her."

Circe's head snapped back. "Mr. Soames, we're a reputable firm. We deal exclusively in corporate futures. You're asking me to brew a *potion*."

"You're witches, aren't you?"

"Mr. Soames," she said slowly, "the only witches I know that stir boiling cauldrons are in *Macbeth*. Maybe in *your* generation people—"

"What the hell am I supposed to do? The medical establishment turns me down so I try to punt four centuries and do what my peasant ancestors did, and now I find out witchcraft's as specialized as doctors were twenty years ago!" He leaned forward. "If you're the best in the business, then why the hell can't you cure gallstones?"

"*Please,* Mr. Soames," Circe said, looking down at her deck of cards to calm herself as Chaudhuri approached with his pad to take their orders. She'd heard an important element in such hospital board decisions was usually the ability to pay, and she glanced back to Soames as he studied the menu. He *looked* solid

50

enough, but people were always overextending themselves on plastic. . . .

"I'd stay away from the *goshts*," she said kindly. "Meat dishes are pretty dear these days. Try the *sabzi;* that's a vegetable curry. Or the *pulao,* peas and rice."

"I'm not really hungry," Soames sighed, handing Chaudhuri the menu.

Circe ordered chicken *farooq* and pushed her untasted water toward him. Gratefully, he took a sip.

"It's not that we're not sympathetic," Circe said after Chaudhuri had gone. "You have to understand the curative aspects of the occult sciences aren't as well researched as the divinatory arts. A respectable firm like Ashtoreth that's famous for guaranteeing its work can't afford to get involved with unproven techniques. But have you really exhausted the medical possibilities? Aren't there still small-town hospitals that haven't gotten the machines for laser surgery yet?"

"A small-town hospital? Where, for God's sake? They've all combined into regional hospitals specifically so they can *afford* the damned machines."

"Well, I've heard of people going to less advanced countries like the Maldives, that WHO and UNESCO haven't gotten to, where they still do manual surgery."

"My wife's already too sick to travel," Soames said. "She's in a lot of pain."

"Then if I were you I'd find a herbalist or a faith healer—the League doesn't approve of them, but I'm speaking as an individual, now, not a representative of Ashtoreth."

Soames was silent while Chaudhuri served Circe's order.

"Can you recommend any names, then?" he asked, his eyes following the forkful of *farooq* to her mouth.

"I don't know any of them personally," she said. "We have no dealings with them."

"Please," he said. "I'm desperate. I can't go chasing from one to another trying to find one that's legitimate. I don't have time. My wife's dying."

"Dying of *gallstones?*"

"People used to, you know—back in Neanderthal caves and the court of Louis the Fourteenth. The gall bladder gets stopped up with stones, it swells up and gets so painful it's all you can think about. Finally it ruptures."

Circe put down her fork.

"I had no idea," she said.

"Most people don't, not till they get sick and find out the things they grew up believing about medicine aren't true anymore. It's a technology nobody can afford unless you've got something so exotic the government subsidizes it, like dialysis or heart pumps. Or unless you can be treated with drugs. They never worked for my wife. All I can do is give her mescaline for the pain." He studied his hands for a moment. "But it's not so different from anything else these days, is it? The world is full of gadgets that don't quite work. Not even witchcraft."

Circe watched the haggard face working, the eyes sunken with worry and another's pain. "All right, Mr. Soames. Maybe there is something I can do for you—as a private person, not as an account executive with Ashtoreth. I still have my old lore books from school, and maybe I can find something that—"

"I'll pay anything," he said. "I still have the equity in my house, and—"

"I don't want anything, because I can't promise results. All I ask is you never tell anybody about this—*ever*. If anyone knew I'd concocted a potion for a client, I could lose my job and my League membership. I'd be ruined."

"I promise."

"It'll take at least a day. I'll give you my home phone and you can call about when to pick it up."

The lower rims of Soames's eyelids glittered with tears. "Thank you," he whispered.

"Just don't tell anyone. And remember, there's no guarantee."

Afterwards, watching him go, she shook her head sadly. Poor man. She had no reason to think any potion was going to work. It went against everything she'd been taught, though secretly she sometimes brewed things up at home from her old *Roots and History of Gramarye* college text for the fun of it. But faith was more important than any medicine, and maybe if Soames and his wife *believed* it would work...

Absent-mindedly she shuffled the pack, just for something to do with her hands, then laid it down and cut it three ways, always to the left. Then she took the new top card and laid it face up. The pleasant clatter of forks and knives and china dimmed around her, the burble of conversation diminished to the faintest buzz.

She shuddered.

It was the Tower.

6

Future Perfect

6 PM Monday, June 7

It had been an uneasy weekend and a terrible Monday. Circe had spent the day firming up the prognostications for Faith, Ltd., the corporate arm of the Doctor Love organization, and it had left her troubled.

For one thing, Doctor Love's significator card, the dark King of Pentacles, had been covered several times by the Hierophant. Not that finding Doctor Love's aura was the tiara-crowned Hierophant's bondage to external ritual and creed came as any surprise, but it was still disturbing. The Devil had shown up repeatedly, too—mindless sensualism, materialism, violence— and in conjunction with the fourth card of the Major Arcana, the Emperor—manipulation of the masses, kingship or political control—she had come to the conclusion that Doctor Love was either going to rise to a position in government or was actively planning to seek such a position. And her intuition told her it was no minor office. Given his popularity, anything was possible. Next year, the year 2000, would be a presidential election year.

More upsetting had been the Tower's appearance again. But this time it had not shown up as some simple event in Doctor Love's future. Her Gift seemed to tell her that the Tower and its destruction were somehow part of Doctor Love's *plans*, in the same way political office was.

That, combined with the Devil's violence, had made her go to one of the junior executives at Ashtoreth, Ruth Geist, as a check against herself. When Ruth's repeated castings of the Tarot had turned up none of the connections with the Tower and the Devil, Circe had been more convinced than ever that she had no Gift at all, that she would never be more than a poor mechanic with the cards.

Shaken, she had left Ashtoreth's headquarters early and walked along the new Hudson River Esplanade for several hours. When at last she arrived at her apartment, she found Adele stretched languidly on a mylar slingchair, her hands pulling her hair tight against the sides of her skull, a page of Jervis Santalucia's latest bestseller shimmering on the computer LC display while she watched a floppie she'd bought at Sounds-n-Shit on her way home from NBC. In addition, from another corner of the room murmured dialogue from *Bachelor Father,* another of those ancient syndicated reruns that Adele favored. Not content with their portable floppie-players or the fact they could watch TV on the homeputer's LC, Adele had just gone out and bought a Slim-Vu set. One source of programing wasn't sufficient, she had argued; even with three TV's running with floppies, bestsellers, and reruns, she ran the risk of being bored.

In those good old-fashioned
Piston-driven day-yay-yay—

"You do anything about dinner?" Circe shouted over the din.

Adele closed her eyes and shook her head, retreating into the pulse of the music.

"How can you read with all that racket?"

"I'm not," Adele said. "I'm skimming."

Circe wrinkled her nose. In fact, Adele was one of the slowest readers in the world. Her idea of skimming was not reading past the first page.

"They just announced this pig Santalucia's going to write the Doctor Love New Year's special, and I want him off, so I'm getting evidence from his book. He's a real chauvinist."

Circe scanned the LC page from *Hausfraus of Venus.*

"Yes," Alba smiled endearingly at the startled earthling, "here in the moist heat of Venus's womb we see no need to compete with our men. For us, children and the hearth are more than enough. After, of course, our primary duty, always to seek new ways to please and titillate the man who has chosen us at the annual auction. . . ."

"That's funny," Circe said. "I thought he was a racist. Wasn't his last book *Niggers in Space?"*

"All I know is what I read," Adele said, tossing her head to the music. "And he's not writing shows for NBC if *I* have anything to say about it."

54

Circe shrugged and went on into the kitchen to rummage through the freezer. *Why* hadn't they invested in a Computer-Automated Kitchen? How expensive could they be? After all, it was just a plug-in module and adapters for the appliances.

Somewhere, she thought vaguely, there'd been a polypak of Pierre Cardin string beans, but she couldn't find a single designer vegetable. Adele had probably eaten them.

Selfish bitch.

She settled for a supermarket pack of New Jersey-style vegetables and dialed time and temperature into the microwave.

Soames would be coming at eight tonight. They'd talked by phone earlier in the day, and she'd promised to have something ready for him. It was no problem, really. She'd gone through her texts over the weekend and she'd found a potion she could whip up after supper. It was just a matter of not forgetting to do it.

"God, the UN was a *zoo* today," Adele said, leaning against the door jamb. UN was Adele's coinage for the NBC hallway she shared with the other resident special interest groups in Program Practices, because of the constant yammer of incompatible dialects and languages.

"I thought it was always a zoo," Circe said.

"Yeah, but today was worse. I mean, every now and then I get a script with *smudges* on it—that Maria from Mex-Rights is such a *pig,* you know?" Adele made a face. "Anyway, today I got three scripts from that new show—"

"Which new show?"

"I've been talking about it for *weeks.* It's got Labelle J'Ackson from Afro-American Gay Forum all bent out of shape. You know, *Sexchange,* where they get these three transvestites to compete in sack races and stuff and the winner gets a free—"

"How in the world can they have *scripts* for a game show?"

"Circe, don't you know *anything* about television? Anyway, there was this dried *stuff* on the back of one of them. Now, I'm as charitable as the next person, and I thought first it was Jack Magawaki from Nippon Power spilling chop suey on it or something—"

"I don't think the Japanese eat chop suey, Adele," Circe said.

"All right, because later I figured it had to be that oversexed little bastard in Puerto Rican Affairs. I mean, those people only think about *one thing* all the time, you know?"

"I *don't* know," Circe said, gripping the counter. "I thought your whole career was dedicated to fighting prejudice."

"Easy for *you* to say," Adele sniffed. "You don't have to work with them."

"I've had a pretty rough day myself. Did anything *good* happen?"

"That biddy from Whites Against Special Privilege croaked over the weekend," Adele mused, bending over to see how the cauliflower and lima beans were doing. "But I'll miss her, in a way. When you got a review script from her, you could count on the fact it wouldn't have any coffee drips on it. That's more than you could say about the others."

"What happened to her?"

"Probably dropped dead reviewing a *Sexchange* script. Is this all we're having?"

"If you want anything else," Circe said, "you can goddamned find it yourself and put it on."

After supper, Circe retired to her bedroom study and opened her old rolltop desk. Stuffed into the little cubbies were the polypaks she picked up from time to time in occult arts stores. From the bottom drawer she hefted her Hexenhaus Press reprint of the *Clavicule de Salomon, roy des Hebreux,* and looked up gall bladders in the modern appendix Hexenhaus had thoughtfully provided. Someday, she thought, they'd get the lore books on tape and you could access whatever you wanted from a standard home terminal. There was already a Coven committee looking into it.

She found the recipe. Bat's blood, belladonna, and aconite. Aconite would cause palpitations of the heart and belladonna would cause delirium. It reminded her of the potions for magic flight she'd seen. They'd been designed to give the user the *illusion* of flying—which was exactly how potions had gotten such a bad name among reputable modern witches. She supposed the aconite and belladonna would create a kind of euphoria that would take the user's mind off her gallstones, though God knew what the bat's blood was supposed to do.

She pulled the blender forward from beneath the cubbies, found a pack of dehydrated bat's blood and some aconite, but no belladonna. Damn it—how stupid not to have checked yesterday and picked it up on the way home! Decongestant spansules—they usually had belladonna in them.

She went to the bathroom, got a glass of water as a mixing medium, and found some spansules. She had no idea which color grain might be the belladonna, so she dumped the contents of three capsules into the water and brought the glass back to the blender to mix with the aconite and bat's blood. Well, it didn't matter all that much, she told herself. Its effectiveness depended entirely on Mrs. Soames's faith. And if nothing else, it would dry out her sinuses for her.

When the blender shut off, she decanted it into a plastic vial with a cap in the shape of a grinning gargoyle and went into the living room. Adele, the same page of *Hausfraus of Venus* still on the LC, was watching an *I Love Lucy* rerun.

Circe settled herself at the coffee table and took out her cards to wait for Soames. Lucy had her head stuck in a champagne bucket. Without enough children to support more than a few top-forty UHF stations and with the continuing rise of production costs for a dwindling number of new TV shows, more and more stations relied almost entirely on old movies and reruns populated by the walking, talking, mummified remains of thousands of deceased actors. Clark Gable, Mr. Ed, Bing Crosby, Judy Garland, Joan Davis, Francis the Talking Mule, Spring Byington. At any given hour of the day, there were more dead faces than live ones on the screen. It was an Ancient Egyptian's dream.

Circe shook her head and decided she might try running Mrs. Soames's fortune. She'd never met the woman, but she guessed she might be graying like her husband; she pulled the Queen of Wands out as Mrs. Soames's significator and laid it face up on the table. Then she shuffled the deck and cut it three times, always to the left, then picked up the deck with her left hand.

—*brought to you by the Society of Greater Love*, gushed the television.

Circe glanced up. There was the interior of the House of Love, a pulpit apparently hovering atop the fine gilt mist of a bank of golden showers, as the camera zoomed in on Doctor Love himself, face soft as a Buddha but with the aquiline nose and deep, burning eyes of a Jesus or Mahomet. Circe smiled at the aptness of her choice of the King of Pentacles as Doctor Love's significator.

There had been a time not long ago that Adele had wanted to get one of the Love headbands and adapters. Love-watching had become popular among executives and would-be executives, in some cases for the sake of being in on a fad, in other, more devout cases, for the spiritual convenience of regular worship in manageable sixty-second commercial segments. But Circe had said no, and, in one of the few arguments she'd ever won with Adele, she'd remained adamant. The headbands went against all Circe's training; perhaps more important, though it hadn't been something she'd noticed on a conscious level, none of the people who got the headbands ever seemed to give them up afterward, no matter how frivolous their reasons had been for sending for them initially.

Scientists tell us, Doctor Love intoned, *that all energy and matter in the Universe seek a kind of ultimate inertness, which they call entropy.*

The voice was deep, confident, reassuring, hypnotic. The eyes bored into you.

Indeed, they are correct. Now, the Great Masters of the East have long preached selfless meditation to achieve the salvation from all material needs and dependencies, which they call Nirvanah. Yet what is Transcendental Meditation but entropy, and what is Nirvanah but entropy writ large?

Circe felt her eyelids growing heavy. She shook her head and tried to concentrate on her cards. She turned over the first from the deck and placed it over Mrs. Soames's significator. "This covers her," she said. The Ten of Swords, a prostrate body pierced by ten swords. The aura surrounding the question of Mrs. Soames's illness: pain and affliction.

"This crosses her," she whispered, placing the second card perpendicularly across the Ten of Swords: the Fool, Zero in the Major Arcana. So the force opposing the evil of Mrs. Soames's illness was the need to make a right choice. The choice had been to go to Circe. But had that been the right decision?

Flustered, uncertain, she glanced up again and found herself transfixed by Doctor Love's gaze.

And as you recognize your urgent need for peace and accept my loving offer, moving from our Stresscard to our Insight Loveband, you will become wholly liquefied in the Golden Stream of Life. You will realize, wherever you sit, that you, YOU, are the unmoved creator of all things . . . absolute passivity fused with absolute creative power . . . the perfection of being the Motionless Cause, afloat in the starry bowl of infinity and eternity. And there, in your entropic bliss, you will discover that you are God.

No wonder, Circe thought vaguely, that the junior partner at Ashtoreth had found none of the baleful cards in Doctor Love's casting that Circe had found. Because Circe had been entirely wrong. She had no Gift at all, that was it. The smart thing to do would be to leave it all, chuck it, maybe turn to something that could give her real fulfillment. Doctor Love . . .

There are those in this world who would have you put aside your Lovebands and leave your chairs and televisions, who would have you squander vital creative energy on fruitless quests. One in particular seeks to mislead our children with bogus miracles and ominous prophecies of the world's end.

Yes, Circe agreed. The Monad was a terrible woman. They were all terrible, these people who interfered.

She foretells disasters by quoting from one of the holy books of human history, the Book of Revelations of Saint John the Divine. But let them beware. Perhaps these disasters she foretells for others will overtake her own followers. Perhaps they are not God's elect, but the Children of the Beast. Perhaps she herself is the Beast, the Antichrist. Let them look to themselves that they do not bear the mark of the beast on their foreheads, as Saint John describes. Let them ask themselves if it is not their own end their leader prophesies in her visions of rains of fire and toppling towers.

Circe's head snapped back as though she'd been slapped. The Tower. Suddenly Doctor Love's words were filled with the leering menace of the Devil and the complacent power of the Hierophant that she'd seen in the cards that morning. Could it be that she'd been right? But when she searched the face of Doctor Love, she found only innocence, as though he were ignorant of the malevolence behind the words he had spoken.

She was fooling herself again, trying to preserve her belief in her Gift when she knew perfectly well she had none. With a sinking heart she went back to the cards.

"This is beneath her," she said, placing the fourth card below the first three to form the bottom of the Celtic cross. The Page of Swords, inverted, meaning that the basis of the question was illness. Circe smiled bitterly. Even she could have read that.

"This is behind her," she said, placing the fifth card to the left of the first three. The influence just past was the Two of Wands, physical suffering.

"This crowns her," she continued, placing a card at the top of the cross. The influence that might come was the Hermit, a possible journey, a search for a wise person that might somehow help. It could mean Circe—or, more likely, someone else. If only she could see beyond the mere arrangement of the cards,

59

use them as they were used by true artists, as a bridge to the very forces of fate and destiny.

"This is before her," Circe sighed. The influence that would operate in the immediate future was the Nine of Wands, again inverted—delay and adversity.

The doorbell rang. Circe glanced up at the clock. Eight PM—Soames. She sighed again and picked up the vial from the table. She'd wanted to finish the fortune, but how much truth would it really have contained when cast by her inept hands? She nodded to Adele that it was all right, then opened the door and slipped off the chain.

"I don't promise anything," she said, handing Soames the vial. His face looked even older and more careworn than it had on Friday.

"I understand," he said. "Thank you."

Circe hesitated a moment. "I—I've been running your wife's fortune. I haven't finished it or anything, and I don't think it would be fair to ask you for any consultation fee because you didn't request it."

Soames peered at her anxiously. "Did you find out something I should know? Please . . ."

"I . . . I can't be sure. It could be that the potion isn't the answer."

Soames looked troubled.

"Possibly you should try to find a doctor somewhere that could help. I think it will mean going on some kind of journey. . . ."

Soames hung his head. "Thank you for telling me. But I think it might kill her. I've got to try this first."

"Whatever you think best, then," Circe said. "If I find out anything else, I'll let you know, because I want her to get better, I really do."

"I know that," he said. "Thank you. And I promise whatever happens, your name won't ever be connected with this. No one will ever know about it."

Circe closed the door, feeling rotten that Soames should have devoted even a moment to worrying about her, and went back to her cards. There was nothing else to do.

"What the hell was that all about?" Adele asked. Doctor Love's spot was over and *I Love Lucy* was on again. "You going bi on me?"

"I always told you I was bi," Circe said. "But this was strictly business."

"So you made him some kind of potion?" Adele asked indifferently.

"Something like that." Circe glanced at the completed cross of cards, then prepared to lay the next four out in a vertical row, starting at the bottom.

"This is what she fears," she said to herself. Judgment, twentieth card of the Arcana—fear of death and suffering. The next card, the feelings of those around her, was the Nine of Swords, a woman weeping in her bed. Death of a loved one. The next card represented Mrs. Soames's hopes—

"I thought brewing potions was a definite no-no," Adele said. "Against the rules or something."

"It is," Circe answered distractedly. As she'd feared, into the space of Mrs. Soames's hopes went Circe's own card, the Queen of Pentacles. Almost certainly a false hope. But it was the last card that terrified her more than any of the others, not just for Mrs. Soames's sake, but because it might again be the Tower.

She reached down to the deck for the last card, held it back up as she heard Adele get up and snap the TV off. A moment later she felt Adele's hands on the back of her neck.

"What do you say?" Adele said. "It'll smooth us both out a little."

"I don't really feel like it right now," Circe said, trying to keep the trembling from her voice.

"Come on, babes," Adele said, kneading her shoulders with both hands. "Otherwise—who knows? I might just go to the Big Momma at Ashtoreth and tell her how you've been mixing up illicit drugs for customers."

Circe looked up sharply and then down again to hide her fright. Adele's face had been smiling, so it was probably a joke, but Circe couldn't be sure. Adele was a very unpredictable person. Violent, even.

"All right," she said. "Why don't you go ahead into the bedroom. I'll be right there."

"Rude," Adele beamed and went off.

Circe turned over the fourth and last card in the row and let out an involuntary gasp. It was the thirteenth card of the Major Arcana, an armored figure on a horse, carrying a banner, other

61

figures falling before him. His visor was up, and from within the helmet stared the eyeless sockets of a skull. Death.

Circe swept the cards together and shuffled them back into the pack as though to lose them forever. Then she rose to go to Adele, waiting impatiently in the bedroom.

7

The Demonstration

5 AM Tuesday, July 20

They rose and washed in the cold stream by starlight, some occasionally looking up as if they might see the Mothership already hovering in wait for the Time which only the Monad knew. But even the lights of Denver were hidden from their campsite on the plain by the plateau; all that was visible was the black, jagged line of the mountains behind the city against the graying sky.

Her fingers burning with cold, Starbud dried her hands and face on a crusted piece of shirt and passed it to the next person squatting by the stream. She shivered, pulling her flannel shirt tighter, and looked again at the empty sky. The hours in the truck, hot oil smells, cold, wet shoes, stiff, unwashed clothing had all blended together in a conglomerate of sensations that lay like a rockslide between her and the world she'd shared with her parents so long ago. But it was all worth it. This time the Monad had found them.

"G-guess I'll work downtown," Moonbeam said back at their army-blanket tent, his breath smoking. "Get us some money or f-food or something."

Moonrose nodded, blowing at the fire, round-faced and puffy-cheeked as a wind-face in the corner of an eighteenth century map. "I'd head back about four, though," she said. "Wouldn't want to miss the Monad's first talk."

"N-no. I saw her for a minute when she got in last night. Quark and I brought in her luggage. She was talking to herself, so I g-guess something b-big's up."

"I think Starbud and I'll spend the day here," Moonrose said. "Just in case. You think this could be it?"

Moonbeam shook his head. "Haven't had the D-Demonstration. Some city's got to get it. And after that . . ."

He left the Monad's death unspoken, and Starbud shivered again. Then he turned and was gone.

"He's a good soul," Moonrose said at last.

Starbud nodded yes, though in fact something about Moonbeam still frightened her. She and Moonrose had both been glad when the Hundred had decided against taking the revenge that their self-proclaimed brothers had urged in New Bethel.

"We been together eight years, him and me," Moonrose went on. "A lot of people don't like him, I guess, but I always thought he was special. And he was always good to me. Don't know what he saw in me, matter of fact. Course, being purer vessels now, I don't suppose it matters, but back when we were all carnled down, he *still* loved me. And look at me. I'm a fat woman. And he's all thin and nice. He could have had anyone he wanted, just about."

"I don't think of you as fat," Starbud said. "I think you're beautiful and warm."

"Well, I think any Seeker that follows the Road gets a kind of lowcal spiritual beauty, but there's no two ways about it. I'm a fat Seeker."

Starbud said nothing, staring into the frail, smoky fire of green twigs that Moonrose had started.

"You just got to love someone like that, someone that sees past what you look like on the outside. That's what I liked about the Seekers—they don't care about your looks, they care about what you *are*. And you know, Moonbeam was really a Seeker even before there was such a thing. He could always look inside."

Thoughtfully Moonrose broke a frozen block of mixed vegetables and wedged them into an old coffee can. She pushed the can toward the edge of the fire.

"I guess you know he spent some time in jail," Moonrose said. "Even a mental hospital once. But he's basically *good*. See, he grew up without having anyone around telling him what to do, and he has trouble with people trying to tell him now. He just sort of grew and opened on his own, like a flower. Nobody pries a flower open, right? You just wait for the sun and rain, and when the flower's ready, it opens all by itself. And nobody had to tell it how to *be* a flower. That's probably why they're so beautiful."

"Yes," Starbud said with another shiver. A cold wind was picking up from the east. She wished she knew what the weather was going to be. Ever since the Monad had made them destroy their portavees, no one had known anything about the world beyond. And the loss of the flickering pictures and muffled television voices had made her feel very lonely.

"The thing that worries me," Moonrose mused, trying to separate the melting vegetables with a stick, "is how he's going to take it when we get to the Fourth Dimension and one of those Beings tries to tell him what to do."

2 PM Tuesday, July 20

Along a hundred-mile line from Wiggins to Calhan, black cumulus clouds were rolling westward along the gently rising apron of plain before Denver. Across West Bijou Creek and Comanche Creek they came; jagged threads of lightning licked between the shadowed ground and the dark undersides of the clouds and were gone. Ahead swept great gusts of wind, shaking highway signs and buffeting cars and trucks rolling their way up Interstate 25 from the south and 70 from the east toward the city.

It was rain at last. Again the winter had left no snow cover, and the rocky bones of the mountains lay parched and white, baking in the sun, while below, Denver waited for the rain that would at least lay the dust in the shimmering streets and wet the empty creek beds.

The winds roared into Denver, whistling around the Capitol and the Civic Center, past the Brown Palace and the Hampshire House. On top of the roof of the Conyers Building at the corner of 19th and Wazee overlooking the just-refurbished Union Station, two men in white coveralls with "Miles Refrigeration" stitched across their backs turned their collars up against the wind and increased the tempo of their work. Carefully, using lead-faced pliers and coated screwdrivers, they worked at the nails that held the strips of metal roofing. At last, one of them stepped back and glancing across the way to the microwave horns clustered like a rooftop garden of exotic metal flowers atop the Solarsystems International Tower next door, lifted up a corner of one of the roofing sheets with his foot. In a moment, fingers of wind began to dig at it, pry it, curl back one corner and then another as the two men hurried to the penthouse door. In another few minutes, the roofing sheet had been tugged nearly upright, flapping in the wind opposite the microwave horns, while the first drops of rain puckered the dust collected in cracks and crevices below.

Meanwhile, in the Solarsystems Tower, below the horns, below the corporate offices of Solarsystems International and its demiurge, Colorado Solarsystems Incorporated, below the acres of floor space leased to architectural firms, investment brokers, market researchers, computer consultants, credit analysts, corporate astrologers, tax lawyers, and sibyls, two stories below the street, Charles Wayne sat at his console in the Solarsystems monitoring station, eyes flicking from the banks of gauges to the liquid crystal display screen and back again. Beside him, a portavee hung from its wrist strap, laboring mightily through its tiny, ringing speaker.

> *Got a real Delta heat wave,* sang the cricket voice.
> *Way down there,* answered a cicada chorus.
> *Just steamy as the jungle,*
> *Way down there!*

On Wayne's display screen flickered a schematic of Solarsystems' eight-hundred-meter dish antenna atop a mountain miles away, overlooking Boulder, a great blue circle on which was projected in red the exact position on the dish of their satellite's hundred-megawatt microwave beam.

On the other side of the cavernous room, Helen Wokowski clicked "steamy as a jungle" with her long nails on a Coke bottle as she watched the telemetry readout from the SCAT satellite itself, arcing in synchronous orbit two hundred forty kilometers above her—precise attitude of the three-kilometer parabolic solar collector; temperature of the molten lithium in the heat-transfer system; status of the thermal-electric device. On a small screen flashed a recurring sequence of maps and charts to verify SCAT's position in relation to Boulder and Denver; beneath, a bank of lights reported SCAT safely locked into the microwave homing beacon relayed from her console to the control transmitter beside the mountain collector dish.

Way down there, squeaked the TV.

"I like it," she said.

"*What?*" he called over the noise.

"I *like* it!"

"Like what?"

"That song."

"Oh."

And now for all you Saucer Kids out there in the boonies, said the TV, *we had to go way back into the vaults for this baby. Give an ear and shed a tear, hams and hamsters, because here's an oldie called "One-Eyed, One-Horned, Flying Purple People-Eater."*

Helen Wokowski screwed her eyes shut. "God, what a lot of *noise.*"

Wayne ignored the tinny roar and scanned his dials and schematic. He'd reached the point where he could literally read the display as accurately as the gauges—the most intense red at the center where the horn collected the beam meant 2.4 watts per square centimeter on the surface of the dish. Gradually the intensity of the red decreased outwards, dropping to a purplish 1.3 watts where it met the blue safety margin at the dish's rim. Still, he always checked himself against the dials, the same way the computer constantly checked his responses against its own, as it checked Helen Wokowski's and the performance of the satellite and the receiving station.

Say, out there, that storm we promised earlier is here, and I mean HERE! We got six inches of rain expected with gusts up to ninety kilometers PEE AITCH! And don't go standing under any TREES, cause they say there's going to be enough lightning out there to straighten your hair. So stay inside and gear an ear to something a little new out this way, but they tell me already number seven on the charts back east. Okay, here we go, just nixon in on Sandra Cassandra, pokes, for some lowcal sights 'n sounds. And don't forget, this half hour's being brought to you by the Society of Greater Love, and later on we're going to hear a few words from the good Doctor himself.

Already the speaker crackled and the image jumped with the static of the lightning on the slopes. Idly, Helen swiveled around to watch the postage-stamp picture.

> *You are the lightbulb in the socket of my day-ay,*
> *You are the rainbow in my sky-iy.*
> *(Yes you, little boy,*
> *You know I'm talkin' to ya!)*
> *You are the pow-wer in my lifetime battery-ee—*

A great and insistent electronic bleep filled the room, rattling the metal cabinets and ringing from the walls. Instinctively, Wayne swung to his gauges, saw the needle on the line output from the receiver into Denver drop below 500,000 volts. At the same time, the blue rim on the left of the schematic waxed to a crescent as the intense red of the beam's center swept toward the opposite side.

"What the hell's going on?" he yelped. "I'm losing the beam!"

"It's all right, it's all right," she said, her voice still tight and high from the first fright of the alarm. "Something's happened to the homing beacon. The backup'll be on in a second."

Wayne knew the satellite's transmitter would shut down within a second of losing its directional signal, but it was still eerie to watch helplessly while the beam moved steadily off target. A beam that intense could turn whatever it focused on into a gigantic microwave oven. It had been the one aspect Solarsystems' lobbyists had had to fight hardest for in getting Congress to approve the actual implementation of this pilot project, but in the end there had been no arguing their point that the energy losses from a broader, weaker beam would have doomed the solar power project from the start.

Helen was already on the phone to the dish receiving station. "Lightning," she said with a shrill, nervous laugh of relief, her hand over her mouthpiece. "Boulder says lightning must have hit the station and knocked the beacon out. They're looking for the trouble now."

As she spoke, the lights beneath her screen ticked on.

"There," she said, hanging up. "The backup generator's kicked in."

The disappearing circle of red wavered and slowly moved back into position on the schematic.

Wayne sighed and slumped back in his chair. "God," he said, "that gave me a start."

"Yeah," she shouted over the continuing alarm, "but you got to trust the engineering, you know? SCAT's got her own laser gyroscope, her own computer."

The bleep stopped suddenly, and the music of the puny TV sounded strangled in the ringing absence of the great horn. They sat with their arms down and legs extended like spent swimmers, drained and exhausted.

And then the impossible. The bleep swelling again. The

beam's center began to drift off the schematic; the dish center gauges trembled and dropped to two watts per square centimeter, then one, while the right rim gauges surged up. The line voltage from the station began to fall.

Helen was hunched forward, her earphone pressed against the side of her head. "Generator's failed," she yelled. "Wish someone would shut off that damned horn."

The second stretched into an eternity as the beam's red circle swept from the screen and was gone.

"There," Helen said from her console, "the satellite's shut down. Now it'll go into a search mode while they get the homing beacon started again. Nothing worse than a blackout."

Again the horn's shriek was cut off, replaced by flashing lights on Helen's console. With a trembling hand, Wayne reached back and flicked the portavee off. Nothing they could do but wait for the Boulder technicians to get the homing signal working again, but at least nothing could happen in the meantime. And at least that damned alarm would stay off.

Helen got up and stretched. "All the inboard systems are operational," she said. "We're copacetic. Can we have the TV back? It's lonely down here."

Wayne was just reaching for it when he heard Helen's joyful call. "*There* we go—it's back!" she said. "It's on again, see?"

Wayne glanced up at his schematic. It was still blue and empty. "Couldn't be," he said. "I'm not getting anything."

Helen lunged for her own console in disbelief. "Jesus, you're *right*," she said, reaching forward and actually touching one of the darkened beacon feedback lights as though to confirm what she saw. "We're sending, but the homing signal relay at Boulder's still out. But *look*—SCAT's on! It's beaming power *somewhere!*"

"Where, damn it?"

She peered frantically into her screen for the coordinates from SCAT's telemetry. Wayne clapped his earphone on and punched the button for the supervisor.

Helen leaned back and turned toward him, her face white. "Denver," she whispered.

"What? Turn it off!"

"I can't," she breathed. "It's locked on a microwave homing beam. Except it's locked on the *wrong one!*"

"Override it!"

"I don't have the access code to the navigational computer.

69

Only Mr. Allen has that, and this is his golf day,'' she wailed. "It's a foolproof system."

"But how could it get the wrong beam?"

"How do *I* know? Sabotage, maybe? If someone aimed a beam from Denver with the right frequency and the satellite found it in search mode . . ."

"It's going to fry everything in an eight-hundred-meter circle," Wayne said. "And if it drifts— Where is it?"

"Next door," she said.

Andy Rogers was standing at the corner of Walnut and 18th, head tipped against the gusting rain, waiting to cross, his hand still in his pocket clutching his change after his run-in with the looney down the street.

Jesus, flying saucers coming from Jupiter or somewhere to evolve people into another dimension—what a crock. And a big, strapping kid, too. Not the kind of anemic you'd expect. It was one thing for some grasshoppery noodle to be gaga, but when it was somebody that could just as well be holding a job and doing something in an economy that was desperate for workers. . . . It was downright obscene for a kid like that to go running around unemployed. It was unpatriotic.

What was it he'd called himself? Brother Moonbeam, that was it.

Of course, he wasn't completely all right; Rogers was willing to admit that. He'd stuttered, and he'd had these kind of crazy eyes. Still, that wasn't any excuse for being a no-good. A couple of sessions with a good shrink or an astrologer, maybe a few evenings of Doctor Love, and he'd be just fine.

Rogers turned and saw Brother Moonbeam, collar up, working his way down the street, stopping passersby for handouts. Did the kid really think Denver people were going to support him and his shiftless friends? Did the kid think Rogers's hard-earned money was burning a hole in his pocket?

He turned back with a shiver of disgust, still jingling his coins and looking idly into the sky in response to the steady whap-whap of a passing helicopter. It was a big blue air taxi on its way to Stapleton Airport, belly full of business travelers.

Suddenly the helicopter veered off to the right, arcing crazily around and downward as though its pilot had lost control. A moment later, still several hundred feet above the rooftop of the Solarsystems Tower, it burst into a ball of orange flame.

Rogers stared with disbelief as the fragments spiraled away.

There was something weird about the sky, too, almost like a huge column of mist or steam, lighter and brighter than the driving rain on either side of it.

But even as he tried to digest what he'd seen, an antiquated fuel truck half a block down 18th disintegrated in a blinding flash, and a mushroom of flame leaped up, followed by a pillar of dense black smoke. Just a few feet beyond, a fat man in a Stetson and cowboy boots staggered and fell screaming to the sidewalk. A policeman sprinted toward him and crumpled halfway across the street.

Smoke was everywhere now, rising from inexplicable fires, and steam seemed to billow up from the river beyond Union Station.

Now directly across the street from Rogers, the tires of an old flywheel Rambler began to smoke, and great blue sparks arced from its metal body to a manhole cover beneath it and a lamppost near its fender. A puddle by the curb just in front of Rogers's toes disappeared in a cloud of steam.

And in the second that followed, Andy Rogers felt his own face redden and begin to burn while unbearable heat and pressure boiled in the very center of his skull. And yet for some unfathomable reason the sensation he felt most strongly was the terrible pain of his old DKE signet ring burning around his little finger and the daggers of heat from the coins he still clutched in his pocket.

"It's here!" shouted Brother Moonbeam, loping up. "Sodom and G-Gomorrah, just like she said! I told you, t-turkey, I told you! And I'm seeing it, goddamn it, I'm *seeing* it! And it's b-beautiful!"

Andy Rogers caught a glimpse of the young man suddenly stumbling, raising his hands to his eyes, and then the moisture in Andy's bone and muscle and blood vaporized, and he toppled to the sidewalk, his clothes smoking at his belt buckle, his zipper, and his pants where, in fact, his money had just burned a hole in his pocket.

The Monad was still on the plains outside the city. She had been hearing the voices again and trying to decipher what their message was when she saw the pure light slicing through the sky toward her like a great column of white fire.

"The Mothership!" someone shouted. "The Mothership's started the beaming!"

She saw people running towards the steaming shaft as it approached, and then a camper parked nearby burst into flame.

71

And then she was inside the beam. She felt hot, confused, her head pounding, and then she knew, even as the metal of the truck bed seared her palms and buttocks, that the Beings were at that moment probing deep within her skull for her soul.

And she tipped forward, her earthly body an emptied husk, into the everlasting, purifying fire.

The ambulances and fire trucks and police cruisers reached the downtown areas first, sirens whooping. They found the pavement cooked dry and cars parked at crazy angles in the street wherever they'd rolled to a stop. At first they were still too hot to touch, but when they broke them open they gagged at the sickly sweet stench of drivers roasted behind their steering wheels. They found a fat man in cowboy boots lying on the sidewalk, screaming for help, but when they tried to move him onto a stretcher, the flesh fell away from the bones even as the man continued to babble his gratitude, and steam rose from the opened sockets. In the basement of the Solarsystems Tower, they found Charles Wayne and Helen Wokowski badly burned but still alive. Further down the street they found Andy Rogers, dead, and Brother Moonbeam kneeling beside him at the curb, blind, sobbing with joy. It was hours before the National Guard reached the devastated campsite to the southeast of the city.

5 PM Tuesday, July 20

Circe didn't hear about it until she was on her way out of the building, a sheaf of accounts tucked under her arm. She'd spent the last hour with Marian Horning, the senior partner who took responsibility for the probationers. Ms. Horning had seen Circe's confidential memo concerning her suspicions about Doctor Love and her confusion over the recurrence of the Tower in her forecasts. Ms. Horning had not been in the least pleased, and she had assured Circe that it was not Ashtoreth's business to analyze the moral characters of its clients, especially second hand. Circe had been placed on warning for her indiscretion, and in an addendum Ms. Horning had pointed out that the quality of Circe's prognostications, especially in connection with her interpretations of the sixteenth card of the Major Arcana, was really not up to the standards people expected of Ashtoreth. A second complaint would mean her dismissal.

"Circe!" a voice called just as she passed through Ashtoreth's outer glass doors. It was Carol Arendt, another of the probationers. "You hear about Denver?"

"What about it?"

"Half the city's in flames. I just heard it on TV."

"Oh, my God," Circe said. "What happened?"

"Nobody knows. None of the officials will talk, but they had some spokesman for Solarsystems on, and he said it was natural gas trapped in all the old gas lines they'd shut down after they switched to solar power. Claimed it was proof the country's got to go to solar satellites and dismantle all the antiquated storage facilities for fossil fuels before there's another disaster like this one. Course, I guess he's all pissed because apparently the Solarsystems Tower was one of the places that got damaged. They're clients of ours, aren't they?"

"Tower?" Circe said.

"Yeah, their corporate headquarters are out there. Why?"

For an instant Circe thought of going back inside to confront Ms. Horning with this vindication of her forecasts. But it still wouldn't clear up the mess she'd made by questioning the motives of a major client like Love.

"Nothing," she said. "Nothing."

8 PM Wednesday, July 28

It took Moonrose and Starbud days to find Moonbeam. He'd been put on a cot in a basement corridor of the hospital where the authorities had hastily set up a clinic to handle the burn cases.

"Well, we knew it was coming," Moonrose said, easing herself onto the foot of the rickety bed.

Moonbeam, eyes bandaged, tipped his head to listen. "You mean the Monad?"

"She was sitting on the back of a truck between these two trees," Moonrose said. "Brother Quark and a couple others were there, talking or something—I was a good distance off. And then there was this light—"

"I saw it," Moonbeam said.

"Yeah, well, I don't know, but it just came over her all steamy and everything, and the two trees on either side of her . . . well, they *exploded,* is all I can call it, and then there was more steam—"

73

"Her body," Moonbeam said. "What happened to it?"

"Oh," Moonrose said.

"Damn it, what happened to her body?"

"The National Guard took it," Starbud said at last. "They took everyone that was hurt."

"That was the thing," Moonrose said. "We didn't know if she was dead or what, and we thought if there was any chance someone could save her. . . ."

"But her body was supposed to lie in the sun unburied for three and a half *days*. How could you forget that?"

"They had guns," Starbud said. "They sealed off the area."

"She's not buried anyway," Moonrose said. "They've got this high school they're using for a temporary morgue because I guess they want to do autopsies. The soldiers won't let anybody in yet."

"Doesn't matter," Moonbeam said, sinking back.

"Why not?"

"The body was supposed to lie out in the sun for three and a half days—not in a goddamned high school gym!"

"You're carnling down," Moonrose said.

"Don't you see? They're trying to screw up her p-prophecies. Now none of it's going to work out."

Moonrose's eyes widened.

"The whole thing's a goddamn p-plot. I heard all the crap about oil tanks rupturing or whatever, but I was there, I saw it. It was fire from the sky, just like she said. B-but they're covering up so no one will know she was right, and they're doing everything they can to keep her prophecies from being fulfilled. In f-fact, I think this whole thing was just to k-kill the Monad."

Starbud leaned against the plaster wall. It was a dirty green, cool against her shoulder. She tipped her head to lean her cheek against it. She didn't understand. If the Monad really *had* been a prophet, then how could anything anyone planned outsmart her? Shouldn't she have foreseen something like this? She was a fake, that was all. There were no Beings.

"Maybe it's some kind of test," Moonrose offered. "Maybe she deliberately didn't give us the exact information, just to see if we'd be able to—"

"She warned us, didn't she?" Moonbeam said. "She told us we could expect trouble, especially when the Time started getting close. Those guys were right back in Ohio. Their n-number's in the glove compartment in the truck. I'm going to get out of here, get the Hundred together—''

''You're talking crazy,'' Moonrose said.

Starbud tried to remember her parents' faces, but she couldn't. Her nose was filled with the smell of disinfectants and the damp plaster of the wall. She wanted to go home.

''I'm not talking crazy. Those guys said they knew where we could get weapons—really sophisticated stuff.''

''But you've got to let your eyes heal—'' Moonrose pleaded.

''They'll never heal,'' Moonbeam said. ''But that's not going to stop me, you hear? If we don't get these Dinks like Doctor Love, then they're going to get us. It's like those guys said— we're a real threat to the Love people. They were the biggest-growing thing in the country—till *we* came along. It's a fight to the d-death,'' he said, swinging his legs over the side of the bed and clasping his trembling hands together. ''It's a holy war.''

He was silent for several minutes. ''Look, tomorrow night you come b-back with some clothes. Then—''

''No, Moonbeam. Your eyes—''

''The hell with it. I was going to skip out tomorrow anyway,'' Moonbeam said. ''Shit, how else was I supposed to c-cope with the goddamned b-bill?''

8

The Boys from RR&D

8:15 AM Monday, August 2

Disheveled and bleary eyed, Jervis Santalucia pressed the ANSWER rocker on the videphone. There was a microsecond's delay before the screen glowed with his caller's image.

Santalucia knew what the pause meant. He was getting a call from one of those damned computers that, in dogged, sequential fashion, dialed every possible numerical combination in a telephone exchange: households with unlisted numbers, executives with secured lines, police dispatchers, CIA cryptologists, SAC bomber pilots, even rival computers couldn't escape the programmed sales pitches for freezer plans, cryonic funerals, computer-automated kitchens, and aluminum siding.

The micro-pause meant the computer was evaluating Santalucia's face and selecting a suitable match-image to generate for him. And then one of the most attractive black women Santalucia had ever seen flickered to life in the caller's screen before him.

Simply amazing. Of course, his wife, Martha, had been telling him it was coming for years, since her job made her part of the developing technology, and at supper the night before she'd mentioned there was a rumor that somebody had actually perfected the technique for commercial applications.

Actually, they'd been discussing the detailed news coverage of the Denver disaster two weeks earlier, and Martha had been pointing out that all the footage was Synthanuz processed, meaning it was neither a film nor a videotape, but a digital encoding of first-generation visual sources—a computer program. Ultimately, she'd said, the digital approach would lead the way to 3-D holographic television, but what had troubled Santalucia, as much as anything troubled him, had been her admission that

76

since the news footage was actually a computerized recreation or simulation, a talented operator could not only augment the images, he or she could reprogram them to look like anything he or she wanted. Unlike a doctored tape, an altered computer program would be just as "real" as the original.

The Russians could have bombed Denver, and the government, with network collusion, could have made it look like a church picnic.

But he was forgetting about his ersatz caller.

"Good morning, Mr. *hmmm* Santalucia," she murmured.

His name, too. An expensive operation; their computer had been fed the Manhattan telephone directory so that it could match the number it generated against the directory listings and come up with a name.

"I'm calling from Stress-Mate," she went on. "Because I want *very* much to know if you're really *comfortable* and *happy,* Mr. *hmmm* Santalucia, and if you're really at emotional and spiritual *ease.* Or are you, Mr. *hmmm* Santalucia, worried like so many of us nowadays? Do you feel a burning sense of urgency? Do you seek the genuine relief of eliminating all anxiety?"

"Jesus Christ," he muttered. "I haven't even brushed my teeth yet."

"Well, we all understand that the stresses of modern life become greater every day. That's why I'm calling to ask if you'd let me send you, without obligation, one of our free, self-scoring Stresscals."

She held up a flat blue pocket calculator like a golf scorecard.

"These Stresscals contain all the possible stress situations that can put us out of touch with our bodily needs, conveniently divided into attenuated long-term stress situations and intense short-term stress situations. Each is rated appropriately in Extended Stress Units or Intensive Stress Units, allowing you to evaluate precisely the total stress in your life. For instance, if your HED were to fail during rush hour traffic, you could check your handy Stresscal—"

She demonstrated, running her finger down the buttons and pressed one.

"—and find that your predicament was a total of six ISU's or Intensive Stress Units. On the other hand, if you had a terminal illness, you could find out that was worth a big nine ESU's or Extended Stress Units, whereas if you were undergoing a long and difficult divorce, you'd be faced with a full ten ESU's *and* an average of three ISU's per court appearance or accidental meeting with your estranged spouse. Don't you think that could be a big relief for *you*, Mr. *hmmm* Santalucia? Now if I may, I'd also like to send you free of charge a series of video-player floppies—''

Santalucia smiled. No mention of Doctor Love, but it was obviously the computerized convert crusade he'd heard mentioned at Faith Ltd. They hooked you with the stress analysis, and then as you watched the floppies you'd be bombarded with subliminal messages to tune in a Love show or one of his megahype spots. Eventually you'd sign up and buy one of his patented headbands and tune out for the duration.

''Sorry,'' he said, wondering why he was bothering to be polite to a computer, unless it was because the image, bogus or not, was so striking. ''As you can see, I'm painted blue from head to toe, which makes me an Orthodox Druid.''

''Many of those who've found relief through our Stresscal system have been *hmmm* Jewish, Mr. *hmmm* Santalucia.''

Santalucia snorted and tapped out the ANSWER Rocker.

''But Mr. Santaluch—'' the voice protested as the image faded.

''Who was it, Jerv?'' called Santalucia's wife from the kitchen.

''Faith Limited.''

''About the meeting today?''

''Nope, nothing to do with it.'' He wandered into the kitchen for a cup of coffee before his shower. ''Pure coincidence—their computer called us up to convert us to the faith.''

Martha was in her tattered terrycloth robe, peering into the toaster oven. Erin, their five-year-old, sat at the table shoveling Granola Sugar Flakes into her mouth.

''The Ferrises are doing it now,'' she said. ''They swear by it.''

''They also believe in astrology, witchcraft, and the ultimate perfectibility of man,'' Santalucia said.

''Are you picking me up at day care tonight, Jerv, or is Mommy?'' Erin piped.

''So does everyone else,'' Martha said. ''Honestly, I don't see how you could agree to write a TV special for those people and not even consider trying the thing you're writing about.''

''Honesty's got nothing to do with it,'' he said, pouring himself half a cup of coffee from the brewer.

78

"I suppose not," Martha said. "Honesty's never been your strong suit."

Without answering, Santalucia set his untasted cup down and stomped off to the bathroom to plunge into a shower. The steam, he thought, would clear his head.

Santalucia had been born in 1969, the product, his Child Welfare file had informed him when he'd demanded it on turning eighteen, of the rape of a black junior-high student by a white construction worker; the file included neither her name nor his putative father's, nor any indication of whether there had ever been an arrest or trial. He suspected not.

He had been adopted at six months by a pair of gentle, college-educated, infertile liberals who had decided to settle for a mixed baby instead of languishing on the waiting list for a white one. And so he had grown up listening to Paul Simon and Beatles records and being reminded he should be proud of his noble African heritage—with which, of course, he had no contact beyond Viewmaster reel #B618 "Wild Animals of Africa" and a copy of *Roots* given him by an adoptive relative. But of his real brothers and sisters in Queens and Hillsboro and Watts, he had known nothing.

After college he'd gone to work for the Abrams and Streicher Agency, writing copy for the new Dust-Buster vacuum cleaner campaign aimed at the growing househusband market—Dust-Buster was the first vacuum to have a gunmetal finish with crinkle-leather insert trim, external gearing for the drive transmission, and a rifle sight on the cleaning wand. From there he'd drifted into the editorial department of *True Housekeeping,* where the Dust-Buster ads had first appeared, and had eventually tried his hand at crafting the high adventure house-cleaning stories that were *True Housekeeping*'s staple—stalking the wild dust-kitty, fighting back the sour taste of fear in the reeking lair of the washer-dryer. From there it had been a junior editorship at *In the Groove,* a magazine devoted to reassuring the baby-boom college graduates of the 60's that they hadn't really betrayed the slogans of their protest marches by winding up as dermatologists or owning McDonald's franchises or living in Westport, Shaker Heights, and Atherton. Regular features included updates on the latest bourgeois turns in the lives of Eldridge Cleaver, Rennie Davis, and Bernardine Dohrn; consumer columns had insisted that buying Cadillacs, Marantz amplifiers, and Sony Trinitrons not only improved the Human Condition by keeping workers

79

employed, but preserved the Environment—the higher the price the better the quality, the better the quality the longer it lasted, the longer it lasted the more precious natural resources were conserved for future generations.

In the Groove's editor, a Mr. Sterling Burton—cherubic face and mop of curly gray hair—had one day taken Santalucia aside and explained his secret: go find an unexploited market and sell the ass off it.

"Catalogue their neuroses and find out what they want to hear, and tell it to them—again and again and again. They never get tired of hearing it."

Santalucia had never forgotten. After leaving *In the Groove,* he had discovered the disenfranchised white male who had fled to the Sunbelt to escape integrated schools, integrated housing, equal opportunity, and liberated wives, and he went for their jugulars. His first big book was *Niggers in Orbit.* It was sensational. People who'd never read so much as the inside of a matchbook clawed their way into bookstores to read about the darkies in zero-G with their watermelon squeeze-tubes.

If Santalucia had felt any guilt about any of it, he managed to conceal it. *Kikes on the Moon* proved less successful, largely, as he told himself, because he had misjudged his market, but *Hausfraus of Venus* earned him the censure of every women's movement from New York to Sri Lanka, the collected curses of the Amalgamated Covens of the Occult Arts League, and the highest praise from *Playboy, Penthouse,* and *Orifice.*

Since *Hausfraus,* however, things hadn't gone well. He seemed to have run out of exploitable prejudices; every time he sat down to write, the paper curled around his typewriter roller remained virgin white until he took it out again to flatten it under a dictionary. The money was still coming in, but he'd felt uneasy, even useless, and to make matters worse he'd been suffering from chronic prostatitis. Not even the tetracycline four times a day, that gave him horrendous diarrhea, had had any effect. "Just take it easy," his third urologist had assured him. "Give yourself a hot sitz bath every night, and try not to worry about your performance." He began to think he was falling apart faster than the country.

And so it had been with a certain amount of relief that he'd accepted the offer from Faith Ltd. to ghost a TV special for Doctor Love.

Suddenly the water lock snapped on and his glorious shower stopped. He fumbled his way out of the stall, blinded by soap and cursing the water shortage, found a towel, and did his best to clean himself off.

Thirty years old, impotent in bed, and still whoring at the typewriter the way he'd done at Abrams and Streicher. It was a wonderful life.

By the time he was back in his robe, Martha was clipping Erin's mittens to her coat sleeves.

"Say goodbye to Daddy," she said.

"Bye, Jerv."

"Have a nice time at school," Santalucia said.

"Why do you always say that?" she squeaked. "You *know* I hate school."

"Give Mommy a kiss," said Martha, bending down.

She kissed her, picked up her Sandra Cassandra battery-cooled lunchbox, and goose-stepped out the apartment door.

"I just can't get over how she walks to school all by herself now," she said, closing the door after her. "They grow up so fast nowadays, don't they?"

"Next thing she'll be voting," muttered Santalucia. "Aren't you going to be late for work?" He hated her terrycloth robe.

"I can go in late because I've got to stick around this evening to take a client to dinner," she said. "That reminds me, you've got to pick Erin up from day care at five, cause I'll be tied up."

"I've got a meeting, too."

"That's at ten," she answered, going off to the bedroom. "Plenty of time to get her afterwards."

Santalucia slumped down in a chair.

"Oh, by the way," she called back, "I took a look at that tape you brought home from the urologist. I got you something to help follow the instructions."

Santalucia's face brightened, his mind racing past the dietary prohibitions and vitamin and mineral supplements to the part about regular sexual activity. Did she have something that would finally turn him on? A filmy nightgown? Eensy little panties with a snap-open crotch and a peek-a-boo black bra? Already his throat was getting dry.

Martha swung around the door—still wrapped in her robe with a shower cap now clapped on her head. She looked like a vinyl mushroom. "Here," she said triumphantly.

"Provocative," he grunted.

She looked puzzled and held something toward him: a large brown bottle with a child-proof cap.

"Zinc pills," she beamed.

Santalucia took the bottle and put it on his bureau. "Zinc marital aids. Actually, I hear mercury's the last word in heavy metals erotica."

"What's the matter with you? Isn't that what the tape recommended? You've just got to stop being discouraged—that's all that's standing in your way."

"That's about the only thing that *is* standing around here," he said gloomily, looking down his open robe as he stepped into a pair of underpants.

"That's what's wrong with your body, that's what's wrong with your writing, that's what's wrong with our marriage. You're too damned cynical."

He smiled benignly at her. "I don't like to think of this as a marriage. It's a growing experience, like getting up on your tenth birthday and skipping outside just in time to see your dog run over by a garbage truck. Being married is like watching your dog get run over every morning."

They said nothing further before Martha left for her job as a systems designer for a computer music company that she claimed was going to make the audio disc, the cassette tape, and the video floppie obsolete in ten years. She was like that, Santalucia thought. In business she went after victories like a Hun. He poured himself a fresh cup of coffee and brooded over it until it was time to leave.

He arrived by subway, several minutes late. The House of Love was a vast web of abstract spires and arches spanned by great plexiglass planes, a jumble of mismatched grandiosities that excited the awe of passersby by conjuring up at once the monomaniacal spirituality of the Gothic cathedral and the limitless resources of a foundation that could not only afford to build such a thing in these Lilliputian times, but heat it, as well: the otherworldliness of Saint Francis and the wealth of Croesus.

He crossed the vast plaza and trudged up the great sweep of stairs feeling like a flyspeck trapped among the illustrations in a geometry text. At the top, he made his way between the columns and went in through the huge main doors.

Most of the interior space above ground had been devoted to

the temple itself, a monstrous cave of concrete and plastic vaults. On gray days like these, yellow plastic filter sheets were lowered from their recesses to cover the plexiglass windows and hype the dim light to the maximal efficiency of a wavelength something over five hundred millimicrons in the yellow-green region of the spectrum. Thus the faithful, seeing by dark-adapted scotopic vision as they entered from the grayness outside, would be dazzled by the brilliance of the temple. It was like putting on yellow ski goggles, or, as Santalucia once observed, like having the Guardian of the Gates lock green spectacles on visitors' heads to ensure that they would find everything as emerald green in Oz as rumor had made it out to be.

Beneath the windows was an amphitheater of row upon row of plush upholstered seats, referred to by the ushers as "pews," commanding an unobstructed view of a bottomless pool of water dyed yellow and laced with anodized aluminum flakes. It was supposed to suggest liquid gold, but, like everything else for the past year, it reminded Santalucia of urine. The water was circulated constantly through a bouquet of fountains before a column in the center of the pool, atop which perched a pulpit connected by a narrow bridge to the stage and choir behind. The earthly cinderblock foundations of pulpit and stage were thus perpetually obscured by a hedge of spraying water, over which colored spotlights played constantly to change the cascading water's hue every ten seconds.

Nearly blinded by the light, Santalucia at last found the bank of elevators on the far side of the foyer, and down he went into the labyrinth of staff offices. He rather liked C level, three stories below the street; it was never bright.

Hurrying along C corridor, Santalucia couldn't help pausing before a large fire door with the legend "Project Stress-Mate" stenciled neatly on it, followed by the warning "Authorized Personnel Only." He was tempted to step in just to ask if they'd used a real human as the basis for the beautiful phantasm that had awakened him on the videophone that morning, but he was already late, and on he went to the last door but one on the right: "Ritual Research and Development—Authorized Personnel Only." He checked to make sure his RR&D badge was clipped to his pocket and let himself in.

Inside was a long conference table at which were seated the scrubbed, bright-eyed historians, theologians, psychologists, anthropologists, and sociologists who made up RR&D, and who were known officially as ritual engineers, a term coined during the early growth of the Love movement fifteen years earlier, before "engineer" had fallen into disfavor and been replaced in job-descriptive compounds by "artist."

Santalucia found his arm being pumped violently by Leonard Percy, Director of Ritual Research and Development, immaculately tailored, fortyish, with short blond hair just beginning to gray, and a ferociously optimistic smile. He was known to his subordinates, Santalucia had learned, as Mr. Bubbles. He led Santalucia, still clasping his tingling hand, to the chair next to his own and introduced him around the table. Most were section heads, but Santalucia found himself introduced as well to another visitor, a dark-haired woman named Circe McPhee, from Faith Ltd.'s occult consulting firm, Ashtoreth. He gave her an extra smile and sat down as Percy explained that today's interface was to get Jerv in on the ritual ground floor so his New Year's script would dovetail with the main thrust of the ritual arm.

"That makes me a kind of group facilitator, Jerv, and I'm hoping to induce a kind of gang-bang mentality, if you follow."

Santalucia looked up from Circe McPhee. "Pardon?"

"You know, each one facilitates the others' thinking, loosens them up. Kind of a soft encounter session. You see, what we do here is emulate the true greats of the behavior modification field—you know who I'm talking."

"You're talking B. F. Skinner?" Santalucia ventured.

"I'm talking Werner Erhard of est, and the late, great Ray Kroc of McDonald's."

There were hushed murmurs of agreement around the table.

"Well, I guess if what I hear is any indication, you're pretty good at it," Santalucia said. "I was told you've got a Pentagon contract to revitalize patriotic ritual and military—"

"Well, well, we can't discuss any of that, Jerv. All right, before we get to your area of concern, we were doing a little values clarification and needs assessment mini-brainstorming, and Frank from Demographics was sharing some of his concerns with us."

Frank was a tall, whey-faced man who had never elected corrective surgery for his bald head. He pushed his glasses back up the bridge of his nose. "Well," he said, opening an oversized folder thick with computer printouts, "getting back to our target congregation, till now we've been shooting for the middle-aged members of the non-lower classes. Even with our Singles Outreach and Swapper's Hotline programs''—he nodded to a thin, blonde woman who reddened with pride at the acknowledgement—''our group's basically on the down side of the life-expectancy curve. And unless the trend in health care delivery costs is reversed, the death rate's going to double its present lead over births. Already we're way below our three hundred thirty million population high in the eighties. In fact, we're down to the lowest total population in over thirty years.''

"It's the times," someone said. "People don't spawn in troubled waters."

"Can you share your concern in a nutshell, Frank?"

"In a nutshell," said the demographer, "we've got to increase our *percentage* share of the total population or face a drastic decrease in revenues over the next two decades."

"Grim, Frank," Percy smiled. "What I hear you saying is very grim."

"Now we've done distribution studies of religion node clusters—"

"What?" Santalucia whispered loudly to Percy.

"Existing organizations, physical plants, congregations," Frank said tiredly. "Churches that could be absorbed intact on a franchise basis with minimal financial outlay on our part, like Unitarians and Episcopalians. We've optimized our procedures by running some multiplier studies and deterministic linear regression models to get some *very* useful equations—"

"Is this another of those damned projections, Frank?" someone asked.

"Now, now," Percy cautioned, "let's stay open and non-judgmental."

"Actually," Frank said, hurt, "most of it's from an Ashtoreth workup Circe McPhee sent over yesterday morning." Circe nodded assent. "And I hope we're still in agreement that a witch's no-bull forecast beats a ton of computer curve graphs?" Frank looked defensively around the table.

"What I hear you saying, Frank, to get back on target a minute, what I hear you saying is that our new Stress-Mate campaign isn't enough."

"I'm saying specifically we ought to be trying to get some converts from the Saucer Cult," Frank said.

"We've already made some progress with the Denver thing," someone said. "As far as giving their beliefs some purposive correction, Project Snuff should—"

Percy held up his hand. "We've got *visitors* today, Joan. That's a confidential matter."

Joan reddened and Circe McPhee, who had suddenly leaned forward, eased back in her chair.

Santalucia frowned. Did these people know something about Denver? Santalucia wondered again about Martha's passing comment that the video news coverage could easily have been doctored through computer augmentation.

"I grant you, it *was* a fortuitous accident," Percy was saying. "Not for us, but for the country. But how will this Monad woman's death impact on her followers? Are we going to be able to go in and scoop up the pieces?"

"Hard to say," observed Stanfield, a historian. "She'd already prophesied her death, so this could have a cuing or binding effect on a lot of them, make them more fanatic than ever. We're dealing with a typical millennial movement here—an obscure prophet predicting the apocalyptic destruction of the old order, rains of fire, her own martyrdom. Then there's a basic ritual for cohesiveness—"

Somebody snickered. "You mean when they eat those mimeographed sheets? I wonder if they're impregnated with some kind of drug."

"Well, I admit their notions about ritual are pretty uninformed by our standards—"

"Primitive, you mean," someone else sniffed.

"Even primitive, but they've got the advantage of being opposed to the established order, and that makes them very dangerous. Whenever the distribution of wealth is disrupted and a part of the population figures it isn't getting its share—say, when some people have a new technology that's not available to others—there's trouble. That's what started the flagellants in the Middle Ages—all of a sudden expanded trade made the middle class fabulously rich while the peasants were still living the way they did in the year six hundred. The Navaho Ghost Dancers are another example."

"Both groups were exterminated."

"But Naziism wasn't. Marxist-Leninism wasn't. Early Christianity wasn't. They thrived on adversity, and in the end they overthrew the existing order."

"I don't see how any of that pertains to the present," Percy said. "We're a brand new religion."

"But we're a television religion, and that makes us part of the establishment, that and the majority of our members."

"I don't see the rest of it," Percy said. "There's no one group nowadays that's well off—we're all short of food—"

"Water, even," Santalucia said.

"It's not one class envying another this time," Stanfield said. "It's a matter of envying the last generation. People today feel their ancestors ripped them off. They can't even have what they had ten years ago, let alone what their parents grew up with. They feel cheated, the young most of all. Look what the dust storms have done to eating habits—food takes up more of a family's budget than ever in our history, and world competition for Canadian grain makes costs higher all the time. Have you ever asked yourself why the revival of *Life with Father* is the biggest thing on Broadway for the last three years?"

"The good old days," someone said.

"The *eating* scenes. Imagine sausage and eggs instead of seaweed flakes. Imagine not having to save up your pennies and ration coupons just to get a beef heart for Sunday dinner. Imagine a cut of meat you didn't have to slice with a chain saw."

"Well, I certainly appreciate the food problem," Percy said. "Nobody hates lentil loaves worse than I do. But getting back to this millennial stuff, I wondered if I could piggyback on your idea a minute. What if *we* got into the millennial business?"

"I think you're missing out on the meat aspect," Stanfield said. "Americans used to get sixty-five grams of animal protein every day back in the sixties, and when you consider the Aztecs turned to human sacrifice and cannibalism because of the absence of large game animals in the—"

"We could develop a campaign about how there's a great religious leader every thousand years," Percy went on, ignoring him in the elation of having had an idea. "We could call him a . . . a charismaster, how about that? You know, charisma? First, let's see . . . Zoroaster, then Christ, then . . . um, well, we'll have to dig someone up for the year one thousand AD. And then in two thousand AD—Doctor Love!"

"I don't know," Stanfield said, miffed. "Buddha was *five hundred* years before Christ, and Muhammad was a little over five hundred years after."

"Then we just say there's a millennial charismaster every five hundred years," Percy sulked.

"What happened to the millennial thrust?" Santalucia asked. "I thought that usually took a thousand years."

A gloomy silence settled over the table.

It was at least another thirty minutes before Santalucia, feeling guilt-ridden about Erin in day care all those years, finally insisted they get to his topic. "Now what my agent told me was you wanted some patter for your Doctor Love and his celebrity guests on your New Year special, maybe some comedy sketches or—"

"Right," Percy said. "The major message texts and the Announcement itself will be handled on an in-house basis by the boys in Public Utterance, and what *we* want is the light transitions to blend the Announcement with the ritual centerpiece of the evening."

"And what would that be?" Santalucia asked.

"Well, that's a problem. We want something lowcal so it doesn't interfere with Personal Enrichment Day on December twenty-fifth, and something that's not too far off from the elements which our target worshiper will find familiar and comfortable, the way we incorporated Santa Claus into Personal Enrichment Day. That's Faith Limited's greatest strength—the ability to innovate without violating important traditions. The purpose of ritual, you see, is to reassure people, make them comfortable, so it has to grow out of what's gone before. Otherwise people get anxious."

"Well, I'd say the best bet for you is have everyone get drunk," Santalucia said. "That's what New Year is all about."

"Really, Mr. Santalucia, you're such a card," Percy said. "Actually, we've been thinking about interspersing cuts of old Guy Lombardo shows from low-anxiety years like the fifties to encourage transference of positive associations to Doctor Love, and maybe recreate the old lighted ball in Times Square with some kind of electrical gizmo right here on top of Love Central—"

"We've come up with a few things in comparative anthropology," said a dark, squat woman halfway down the table, as round and rough-skinned as a Neolithic fertility goddess of terra cotta. "We've ruled out the old Celtic New Year called Samhain, since it was basically a feast of the dead—"

"That's certainly not what we're looking for," Percy said.

"But in the Himalayas at New Years they used to get a dog drunk . . ."

Santalucia nodded his approval.

"... and then behead it to rid the village of bad luck for the coming year."

"What I hear you saying," Percy said, for the first time without his smile, "is you want us to climax a nationally televised three-hour special with the ritual murder of a beagle?"

"Well, we *were* thinking of a fairly *small* dog," said the woman, giving him a sour look. "Sort of get the essence of it without all the blood."

"Actually, ritual murder is a very attractive possibility," said another specialist. "Of course, we'd need to displace it somehow, not show anything on screen. But if we had some ritual act that suggested killing the bad old year..."

"Now I hear you," Percy said. "I'm comfortable with that."

"I hope this doesn't sound too dumb," Santalucia said, "but what's this Announcement you were referring to?"

Percy looked surprised. "Oh—I keep forgetting you're not one of us. Well, it's still hush-hush outside this office and Public Utterance, but I guess I can share it with you. I imagine Ms. McPhee has already seen it in the cards?"

Circe McPhee gave no indication one way or the other.

"You'll have to promise not to breathe a word of this," Percy said.

"Only my typewriter will know."

"On New Year's Eve, Doctor Love is going to kick off his campaign!"

"A fund-raiser?"

"No, his political campaign. For president."

"Of the *United States?*" Santalucia said.

"He'll announce he'll be in the New Hampshire primary. Imagine, a truly religious *and* media-conscious chief executive in the White House!"

"Instead of that fat old bitch we've got now," someone muttered.

An evangelist for president, Santalucia thought. A TV evangelist that had probably perfected—though no one had proved it—some form of subliminal communication with his viewers. Santalucia was almost worried. Almost, because the fee he was getting for the script was very fat indeed.

It was nearly four o'clock before the meeting broke up, and Santalucia, yawning ostentatiously, followed Percy down the corridor as he accompanied Circe McPhee to the elevator.

"Sorry we never nailed down the actual rituals, but you can see ritual design is a very tricky business. And I think we made some very, very solid progress today."

"Solid," said Santalucia.

A secretary stepped into the hall behind him. "Oh, Mr. Percy," he said, "there were some messages for you during the meeting. That special events producer called from NBC wanting to know what you thought about purple."

"Purple?"

"They're doing a mock-up of the set to check camera angles and colors, and he wanted to know if you could relate to purple."

Percy paused a moment. "Purple's very good live, but it looks black on screen sometimes. Tell him blue—blue's almost as inspirational."

"Check," said the secretary. "Also, he wanted to know if you'd like a gasp track."

"You mean those canned ooh's and ah's they dub into adventure shows? God *no*, tell him."

"Well, he said he didn't have anything hokey in mind. He said the Oral Roberts people used one with a bunch of devout murmurs and someone saying 'yes, yes' every now and then. He says they can cue the 'yes, yes' to the text."

"Hmm," Percy muttered. "Could be very helpful. Tell him I'll check with my RR&D people and get back to him tomorrow. Anything else?"

"Well, there was this," the secretary said. He handed Percy a small envelope. Santalucia just caught the word "Snuff" written in one corner as Percy hurriedly stuffed it inside his coat.

"And there was a call from the garage, too. There was a loose wire in your car or something."

"And?" Percy said.

"I guess it kind of blew up."

For the second time that day, Percy did not smile.

"But they said there's an Inner Circle car going out now and you could get a ride in that."

Percy brightened. "Well, well, I guess every cloud's got a silver lining. Can I offer either of you a lift?"

"No," Circe said. "My office is just down the street."

"I'd just as soon walk," Santalucia said. "It's almost time to pick my kid up at day care anyway."

They emerged at the rear of the House of Love. At the foot of the steps below waited a dark green sedan with the Love tetrahedron emblazoned on the doors. Percy was in the middle of offering them both a ride again, promising them a once-in-a-lifetime shot at automotive luxury, when a tall man in a dark overcoat slipped out of another set of doors further along the terrace and went down the steps toward the car.

"Oh, my God," Percy said in hushed tones. "Sorry, but I'll have to cancel that offer." And he hurried down the steps in pursuit.

"What's with him?" Santalucia mused, as much to himself as to the woman beside him, looking closely at the man in the overcoat. There was something vaguely familiar about him—the straight back, the glimpse of dark and deep-set eyes.

"It's Doctor Love," Circe said. She seemed to be staring at him with unusual intensity.

Santalucia wavered. Here was a chance to meet Love in person and maybe find out how much of his appeal was in his make-up, but even as he hesitated, the two men reached the car and the driver punched the rear door open from the dash. Then the door slammed shut behind them and the electric motor's whine rose as the car pulled away.

Suddenly Circe started down the steps. "No!" she shouted. "Don't—!"

There was a blinding flash. The car's rounded roof lifted up and flapped backwards like a lid torn from a tin can to release a stream of flame that carried three indistinct, fragmenting, dark shapes lazily upward. At the same moment the sedan's wheels rolled away in different directions as the car body bucked up and then rocked to the pavement.

Santalucia saw Circe dive for a pillar even as he spun around to protect his face. He felt the blast of hot air against his skin and heard the prickling tattoo of raining glass shards. A moment later he looked back to find the car a shapeless hulk from which a column of flame rose to top the nearby lamppost.

"Jesus," he whispered. "What was it?"

"An incendiary bomb," Circe said, rising slowly.

"How do you know it was a bomb?"

"I *sensed* it the minute I saw the car." Her eyes filled with tears. "But I *waited*. I didn't trust my Gift. I was afraid to say anything."

"Take it easy," he said, his knees suddenly shaking in a

91

delayed reaction. He grabbed a pillar to steady himself. "And look, if you happen to smell any more bombs, don't be afraid to speak up. I want you to know I really, *really* respect your opinion."

9

Tapestries Unraveling

10:30 PM Monday, August 2

Like storm-tossed Odysseus, Jervis Santalucia returned home looking like a bum. But there was no faithful, aged hound to greet him and expire (dogs not being allowed in the co-op), and, unlike the wily Odysseus, Santalucia arrived drunk as a skunk.

After the police had finished with their questions, Santalucia and Circe had slipped into a state store and gotten a ten-pack of weed, and then, still shaken, proceeded to the nearest bar. Somehow they'd gotten separated shortly thereafter, and Santalucia had gone on in search of her to the Roman Villa, the Hungarian Rhapsody, the Bengladesh, and, in a fit of nomenclatorial inconsistency, the Lickety-Split, by that time too numb to realize it was a lesbian bar, or feel its patrons' icy stares, though he had at least spotted the overwhelming preponderance of what in his step-grandparents' day would have been the distaff sex. "Lotta nookie here," he'd observed gravely to a towering woman in chains and leatherette next to him.

It was after she had carried him to the door and dropped him on the pavement outside that he had decided it was time to go home. Enough chasing after nubile Nausicaas.

"And stay out, nigger," the naugahyde woman had trumpeted.

Yes, undoubtedly time to get back and see how Penelope's weaving was coming along.

When he arrived, however, Penelope had left her loom: Martha had shucked her terrycloth robe and was on the sofa in her coat, apparently watching a top-forty station. The mass migration of top-forty stations from radio to television's unused UHF channels in consequence of the triumph of the video floppie's music-cum-visuals over the venerable forty-five disc's

93

straight audio was a phenomenon to which Santalucia had not yet adjusted.

"I'm home!" he announced.

"Shh, Jerv," said Erin, huddled in a shadowy nook of the sofa. "It's number *five* this week."

You are the lightbulb in the socket of my day-ay, sang Sandra Cassandra from the television. *You are the rainbow in my sky-iy.*

"What's *she* doing up?" Santalucia demanded thickly.

"Waiting for the taxi with me," Martha said. "I called my astrologer and my witch, and they both agreed it was the only way."

"It's too damned late for a five-year-old," Santalucia muttered, dropping onto the other end of the sofa. "Anyway, what's a five-year-old following the top forty for? That's for teenagers— least, it used to be. Kids grow up too fast these days. If we didn't make them grow up so fast, we wouldn't have this Saucer Cult now, and that's a fact."

"I'm glad you're such a concerned parent," Martha said through tight lips. "Is that why you never showed up to get her at day care tonight? Is that why the head day care artist had to call me in the *middle of a client dinner* and humiliate me with the news that my little girl was traumatized, abandoned, sobbing uncontrollably in an empty room *two hours after closing time?*"

"I had a really rough day," Santalucia said. He waited for Martha to ask him how rough, but she wasn't going to bite.

"And that was on top of the fact that the poor thing was in shock all day because she saw *two dead squirrels* in the park on the way to school this morning."

"What was it, a suicide pact?" Santalucia said.

"She *loves* squirrels, you know that. She adores them."

"Look," Santalucia said, "three *people* were killed *right in front of me* this afternoon. How does your astrologer feel about *that?*"

You are the pow-wer in my lifetime battery-ee, Sandra sang on, her plump, prepubescent face wreathed with fantastic green computer-generated wisps.

"Anyway," Martha demanded, "who do you think pop music is for if it isn't for kids?"

Why won't you fuck me, tell me why-iy? pleaded Sandra, vomiting a stream of crackling roman candles courtesy of the computer.

Santalucia was silent for several minutes. "Didn't you hear

what I said? I guess if you've been watching this crap all evening you didn't see it.''

"See what?''

"The news.''

"I watched the news at seven. So what?''

"So *what?* Somebody blew Doctor Love away not ten feet from where I was standing!''

Martha didn't look away from the close-up of Sandra Cassandra's pumping hips. "Honestly, Jervis, if it isn't one thing, it's another. There was no such thing on the news. But two men from Love Central were here earlier this evening looking for you.''

"You see? They want to talk to me about the assassination. Percy even asked me if I wanted a lift, and it was just pure luck I hated his guts so much I didn't want to be in a closed space with him.''

"My witch says you hate everybody. That's your problem. She said the only solution was to get out and phone in a divorce.''

"Don't give me that again,'' Santalucia said groggily. "Anyway, you're missing the point. I was *inches* from getting into the *death* car, and then a couple seconds later—*blam!* Percy, Love, the chauffeur, and a Cadillac Supreme were raining all over the sidewalk. *Now* do you see why those guys from Love Central want to talk to me? It proves what I'm saying.''

"They said they just had a few things from today's meeting they wanted to go over with you. I told them your regular hangouts and they went out to try to find you. They should be back any minute.''

"I don't see what for. There won't even *be* a church with Love gone.''

"Shh, Jerv,'' said Erin.

"Your mother's the one doing all the talking!''

"*Please.* I want to hear the part where she goes 'yay-yay yeah-yeah unhunh.'''

Ponderously, Santalucia rose, reached forward, and punched the VHF button. "Now we can watch the news and see how Daddy was almost killed.''

Erin began to weep.

"All right,'' Martha said. "Come on, Erin, we'll just go downstairs and wait for the cab outside. Jervis is just too stoned to care about anyone else's feelings.''

"What about *my* feelings?" Santalucia said.

"Just start taking your zinc pills and your tetracycline. Maybe you'll learn how to *have* feelings."

"Gives me diarrhea," Santalucia said. Glumly he watched the last minutes of *Airport '99* and waited for the news while Martha buttoned Erin's coat.

Brought to you by Tips Condoms and the Society of Greater Love!

"There's an irony," Santalucia said. "Doctor Love's obit is going to be sponsored by rubbers and the late Doctor's very own church."

But Martha and Erin were gone.

Fuck it, he thought. It wouldn't be the first time. Eventually he'd get lonely and talk her into coming back, and in the meantime they could both let off steam. Maybe he'd call that girl from this afternoon. What was it? Circe something. Circe McPhee. They could talk about old times. Bombings, murders.

Take a Tip from Charlie! sang an unseen chorus. In slow motion against a deep blue background—inspirational, Santalucia thought, that's what Percy had called blue—an enormous, screen-filling, artificial erection rose up and came sproi-yoi-yoing to a throbbing halt along the top left to bottom right diagonal, its turgid glans sheathed in semi-transparent blue plastic.

Tips is the brief one, but it gets the job done! smiled a happy fornicator from her pillow.

And, added her partner, looking back over his shoulder and up at the camera with a sheepish grin of pleasure and understandable pride, *Tips's patented bikini length keeps you safe without getting in the way of those oh-so-satisfying sensations.*

So for the peace of mind that comes from fool-proof family prevention or planning, protection from disease, immunity from prosecution, and just plain fun, gushed the voice-over, *take a Tip from Charlie. A product of the Charles Plastics Technology Corporation, a subsidiary of Leisuretime Industries, a General Foods Company.*

Santalucia watched with gloomy envy as the ersatz penis in the blue pith helmet repeated its diving-board imitation. Sproi-yoi-yoingggg. It reminded him of Martha's shower cap.

The news itself was uneventful, and inexplicably the assassination of Doctor Love wasn't even among the four lead stories. Another drop in the GNP, the latest bankruptcy threat to the overburdened Social Security System, another thirty-year-old school's collapse owing to shoddy construction, along with the usual rundown of local ranch house failures from rot and short nails. The Lapp Freedom Fighters had taken over the town hall in Biloxi, Mississippi and demanded the U.S. intervene to free Lappland in return for the lives of Deputy Thurmond and an unidentified occupant of the drunk tank.

Weather: a new dust storm in its third day covering 1.3 million square miles from Canada to Texas; Mount Washington observatory already reporting yellow snow, as fine New Mexican dust sifted down from the stratosphere to seed storm clouds over the White Mountains; eastern states could expect darkened skies for at least two days as effluvia of the storm rolled over, with residual dustfall anticipated as far as three hundred miles out into the Atlantic.

When the hell were they going to get to the Doctor Love murder? After all, Santalucia thought, he headed what was the fastest-growing and maybe even the biggest religious institution in the United States.

Personality roundup: President and her cabinet gone to Camp David to escape the humidity for the week. Monad buried by her bereaved followers in Denver, shouting threats of revenge.

Santalucia started. Could that be it—Saucer Kids had assassinated Doctor Love to avenge their insane leader's accidental death in an oil fire? He studied the plump face in the file photo on the screen. How perfectly ordinary and even dowdy she looked. And yet if her followers had really—

—*brought to you by the Society of Greater Love*, said the announcer's voice.

Santalucia rubbed his eyes as the camera zoomed in on the familiar figure perched in the pulpit above the golden spray. He knew it was only a tape prepared weeks, even months ago, but it was still eerie to watch a dead man speak. He was used to watching reruns and movies whose entire casts had been dead for years, like the *Wizard of Oz* or *The Honeymooners*—after all, Hollywood was as hard-pressed to find workers as the rest of the economy—but to see someone whose death you'd actually witnessed . . . And it was plain bad taste for WCBS to run the thing without so much as a mention of the man's death. Was it some station manager's idea of a late April Fool's joke?

Scientists tell us, Doctor Love said solemnly, *that all energy and matter in the Universe seek a kind of ultimate inertness, which they call entropy.*

97

For the first time since the explosion, Santalucia felt relaxed. His eyelids grew heavy. He could barely distinguish one word from another; they merged together in a soothing buzz like lazy bees idling from flower to flower.

political action ... false prophets ... gave you a warning only yesterday ... and an incident this afternoon in which an attempt was made on my life. ...

Suddenly Santalucia was very wide awake. An attempt on his life this afternoon? But he'd seen Love killed, and how could—?

—have decided, despite my natural reluctance, humility, and desire for peace of mind, to sacrifice my personal comfort and offer myself as the only viable candidate for the presidency of the United States of America.

The announcement of his presidential campaign? *That* could have been taped in advance, of course, but was it possible the bureaucracy at Faith Ltd. was so impenetrable that Public Utterance didn't know about the assassination? But the mention of the *attempt* on his life—it had to be a tape made since yesterday afternoon.

The time of democracy has passed; the time of theocracy is at hand. For who is better qualified to lead us through these apocalyptic times than a man of God?

Santalucia stumbled to the homeputer and told it to find Circe McPhee in the directory. After all, he *was* a little drunk. Maybe he hadn't seen what he thought he'd seen. But there'd been fifty cops on the scene, ambulances, fire trucks ... Yet it hadn't been on the news.

An unfamiliar face appeared on the videphone screen and Santalucia demanded to speak to Circe.

"This is her roommate, Adele," the face said. "She was called back on a job this evening and she's really zonked."

"I've really got to talk to her," Santalucia insisted. "It's important."

"Who is it?" he heard Circe's voice call.

"Some black guy that wants to talk to you. Sound familiar?"

"No," Circe said tiredly, "but I'll take it."

Adele's face disappeared and Circe's replaced it from an extension phone.

"Yes?" she smiled.

"Circe, it's me," Santalucia said. "From this afternoon, remember?"

Circe looked puzzled. "I'm sorry, did we have a consultation or something? I see so many clients...."

"No, no—this *afternoon,* when they blew up Doctor Love and we went to a bar afterwards and—"

"That's not possible," she said. "I've been at Faith Limited all evening revising some charts for them."

Santalucia stared at the face in the screen. It was possible she was lying, but her expression seemed so utterly devoid of any trace of knowledge, a perfect blank. Was it possible the Love people had taken her back to the temple and somehow washed out any memory of what had happened? It certainly fitted in with the fact that they'd somehow managed to keep the news away from the reporters.

"Hello, Mr. uh ... whatever your name is, are you all right?"

Jesus, he needed time to think. Actually, what he needed was a good stiff drink. It was a shame what grain prices had done to the price of whiskey. If only he'd remembered to ask Martha if they had any bourbon left before she'd taken off with Erin.

"Look, mister, I'm really tired. If you don't have anything else you want to say—"

"Uh, no, no. Guess I had the wrong person. Sorry to have troubled you."

Santalucia pushed the rocker to OFF and leaned back. Damn Martha, just when he needed her for a little clear thinking—or at least a hint about where the bourbon was—she was never there.

Suddenly he started forward. Men from Faith Ltd.! She'd said something about men waiting to see him, going out looking for him at his favorite hangouts. And she'd said they were due back any minute! That was it—they were planning to flush out his memory the way they'd flushed Circe's. Whatever their reasons, that was what they were going to do.

He cradled his head in his hands for a moment, trying to sort things out. Well, what the hell, why would he *want* to remember this afternoon? What good was a memory?

But he didn't want anybody diddling with his head. Not when he didn't even know why they wanted to cover this thing up.

The doorbell rang.

10

Parting of the Ways

11:45 AM Friday, August 13

They had stayed too long, and they were restless. In the mornings their campsite seemed naked and vulnerable to the rising sun's fire, and in the evenings the shadows of the Rockies crept out and covered them in comfortless darkness.

A few had trekked back to wonder at the scorched path the beam had traced through their old campsite, and they had mounded up a cairn of small stones on the spot where, as well as anyone could tell, the Monad had died. The truck in which she'd been sitting, and all other traces of the rain of fire, had been towed off and impounded by the National Guard for study, and their very footprints and tent-stake holes obliterated by the Guard's tire tracks. The shattered trees, the blackened swath, and the little pile of rocks were the only reminders.

And the grave, of course. One of hundreds in a plot set aside to the south of the city near an abandoned tract of houses. Like the others, it was still unmarked. The authorities said they knew which was which, said markers would be provided in due course, said they were too pressed for time to go through the records right now and find it. Come back after Christmas.

So they came in twos and threes and stood at the edge of the plot, wondering which was the sainted ground and waiting reverently as though one of the grassless rectangles of fresh dirt would suddenly tremble, and through an unfolding blossom of earth the Monad would rise up to greet them.

But she didn't, and already some of the faint-hearted had begun packing up and drifting off in disillusionment and despair, while at the camp the Monad's original lieutenants argued with each other and with outspoken newcomers like Levitt over what to do next. It was, even to Starbud's unpracticed eye, a struggle for power and dominance; each clearly lusted to assume the Monad's scorched mantle of leadership. Even Moonrose was getting involved.

Meanwhile, there were still the living to be fed and clothed, and contingents of the faithful would move daily through Denver, begging for coins, scraps of food, old clothes. It was never enough.

Today the air was hot and dry. Even the shadows under the browning leaves broiled. The girl squatted in the blue light against the trunk of a tree, her forearms hanging like counterweights. She was unhappy, miserable, even as Moonrose had been elated.

This was the day for Moonbeam's prearranged call to a phone booth at one end of the park, and Moonrose and the girl had been begging along its paths all morning. For a while, Starbud had snuck away to escape the heat by going into a D-store and watching the display televisions, remembering the days when she'd watched television every day. But she'd known Moonrose would miss her before long, and she'd left the coolness and gone back to the stifling park.

She saw a man approaching her. She'd noticed him several times that morning, watching her.

She looked away. Sometimes she wondered if the whole thing had been a mistake. There had been a time that the Beings and their arrival from another dimension had possessed a vivid reality; but since the deaths of the Monad and so many others, the vision had paled and dimmed.

And yet the Monad had foreseen her death. Didn't the fact that she'd been killed prove the truth of her prophecy? But it was a comfortless, unconvincing vindication.

Shit, the man was definitely coming toward her.

She felt him stop beside her, slide his back down the trunk, and squat next to her. She turned and saw the usual flaccid white face, red nose, slack neck, skin like sandpaper. Another boozer.

She'd seen enough of them since she'd started begging. She wasn't exactly afraid of them anymore, but she hated being too close to them.

He cleared his throat and spit. Out of the corner of her eye she caught the flash of the sputum's arc through the sunlight onto a patch of grassless dirt beyond.

"Been watching you," he rasped, patting the pockets of his

workshirt and pants until he'd found and extracted a crusted handkerchief. "Just wanted you to know I'm with you one hundred percent. 'Cause *I've* known they was all over the place for years."

"Who?" she said.

"Martians. See this?" He tipped his head forward, pointing to the furred opening of his ear. Inside something shiny like tinfoil seemed wadded. "They got a ray gun up in the mountains there, zapping everybody. Even got me a couple times, too, before I caught on. Fried these old brains. Used to be a genius, you know."

She said nothing.

"But I still got some smarts, and I figured it out. I'm the only one knows that their ray can't go through tinfoil. Bounces it right back at them. But I got cotton in my other ear. Know why?"

She shook her head.

"Ray goes *through* cotton. If I had tinfoil in *both* ears and a ray got in through my nose or something, it would just keep bouncing around in my head till my brain was oatmeal. I mean, *really* gone. This way, the ray can get out through the cotton. Don't do half the damage in there."

She nodded.

"My landlady's one of them," he went on.

"One of who?"

"The Martians. Sneaks around and changes the clocks so the end of the week comes a day earlier each time. In seven weeks, you know what that means? She's collected an extra week's rent out of me. That's how they're going to take over, you know. Screw up all our clocks and wreck our economy. Get everybody paying extra till we're out of money and then they'll just walk in. It started with the Arabs and their oil, when I was young. They're Martians, all of them."

Moonrose's huge form loomed over them. "It's just about time for Moonbeam's call," she said.

Relieved, Starbud rose and followed her toward the end of the park.

"You check them clocks and see if I'm not right," the man called after them. "And get some tinfoil and cotton for your ears. It's the only way to beat them."

Starbud sighed. He was no crazier than Moonrose or Levitt or the rest of them. She'd heard that just this morning on television, that people were getting crazier and crazier because it was the end of the century and the end of the second millennium. She'd noticed because they'd mentioned the Seekers as a cult, and a whole bunch of other groups she'd never heard of—some leader named Otto in Germany, someone else in France, some tribe in Africa or someplace that had started cannibalism again. And they'd said there were more people in mental institutions than ever.

It was like dogs. It seemed to her that dogs were supposed to sleep curled up with their noses tucked in their tails. (Had she seen that on TV?) But the only ones she ever remembered seeing always slept on their sides, with their tongues out.

The booth had been vandalized, the videphone screen smashed, and someone had written "REPENT" in lipstick across the shattered glass. When at last the phone rang, Moonbeam's voice seemed very far away through the tiny speaker.

"You p-probably heard the news last week, right?" his small voice cried jubilantly.

"The screen's broken at this end," Moonrose said. "We can't see you. Where are you?"

"N-new York. So did you hear anything?"

"About what? The Beaming?"

"About that D-dink Doctor Love being d-dead."

"No," Moonrose said. "Why do you think he's dead? You mean the Monad's prophecy?"

"I *know,* that's all," Moonbeam said. Starbud could imagine his sightless eyes still flicking ceaselessly, the way they always had.

"Well, we don't have TV's anymore, remember?" Moonrose said. "Maybe he *is* dead, but we haven't heard anything."

"No," the girl interrupted. "I saw him on TV today, talking about being president."

"Shit," said Moonbeam's strangled voice. "It's not p-possible."

"I *saw* him," the girl shouted at the speaker. "He said something about people trying to kill him and everybody going crazy and only religion could cleanse America's violence or something."

"I d-don't get it."

"Moonbeam, will you talk sense? Why do you think he's dead? Did you actually *do* something?"

There was a pause. "N-no. The scars aren't even healed, all right? But that's what's holding everything up, d-don't you see?

103

The Monad said some Dink leader had to be k-killed, and till that happens, there won't be any B-beings.''

"Moonbeam, just come back, will you? If the Monad promised it would happen, it'll happen. But I want you *with* me. I want us together."

"I'll be back in time. But I have these feelings. . . . It's like a voice in my head, you know? I'm not r-reading it yet, but it wants me to d-do something. And I know that's going to be the answer, just as soon as I figure out what it's saying."

"But what are we supposed to do in the meantime?" Moonrose said. "There's people wanting to go back to the West Coast, and some others want to head north. And those guys from New York—they've just got to be Dinks, Moonbeam. They want to go to *Texas*. I mean, our people have had real trouble in Texas. It's not safe."

The girl felt a chill. She didn't want to go anywhere near the Dustbowl. Even Denver was too close.

"You m-mean Levitt and those guys? They're all right, I tell you. They put us in touch with some real good people here, found a bunch of the Hundred places to stay, got me a doctor for the surgery, even offered to help us. You ask the Hundred when they get back. They'll tell you Levitt's completely lowcal."

"I don't like them, Moonbeam. I don't trust them."

The girl stood aside when Moonrose came out of the booth, her face a mask of anguish. "He's never coming back," she said. "I just know it. I've got to go find him, no matter what."

3 PM, Eastern Daylight Time

Moonbeam found the OFF rocker with his thumb. It wasn't possible. Everyone had agreed the damned thing had blown at the right moment, that Love was inside when it had gone.

He thought about smashing the phone box in case anyone had used coins instead of a charge card, but without his eyes he had no way of knowing if any smokes were watching.

He felt along the glass for the door. If only he could *see*, damn it, he'd do something about it himself. Because otherwise the Monad's promises were going to go right down the tubes. He knew that, through some strange conjunction of cosmic forces, everything now depended on him.

He smiled ruefully, thinking of the sightless reflection that was staring back at him, unseen. He'd heard somewhere that blind people developed funny expressions because they could never see themselves in mirrors, like deaf people talking funny because they couldn't hear themselves or—

Mirrors! A mirror image—that was it! Love had some kind of double.

But most of the Hundred had already left, thinking the job was done. Only Levitt's friends were still around, and he had no idea whether they could be trusted to handle heavy-duty stuff. Oh, they'd gotten him the doctor and all, but this was different. Proof again that everything pivoted on him. If only the surgery would heal. His head felt so heavy.

But it would, they'd told him. Soon. Then he could take care of things himself. Once he'd sorted out the voices.

10 PM, Rocky Mountain Time

They had parked several of the vehicles in a semicircle and turned on their headlights to illuminate the meeting. John Levitt was standing in the center, his frizzy hair a halo of light from the headlights.

"I keep flashing on Texas," he was insisting. "I just got this feeling that's where we should head for."

"It doesn't make any sense," Moonrose said. She stood mountainlike just inside the ring of the circle, shadowed from the headlights. "The Monad said the Beaming wouldn't be anywhere near the sea, and Texas is right on the Gulf. I ought to know. I was a kid there."

"Yeah, but the northern part is dry as anything," Levitt said. "I mean, are *you* flashing on something or what? Let the rest of us in on it." His face was twisted in a sneer.

"If it's all the same to you," Moonrose said, "I say we go back east to New York."

The girl, hidden amongst the others in the crowd, thought of the jail in New York. She didn't want to go there, either. But she was afraid to lose Moonrose.

"Well, I don't see how that makes any better sense, Sister," Levitt said. "New York's an island. It's got water all around it. I say we stick together."

105

"We never did before," Moonrose said. "When we couldn't get anything on our radar, we just followed our own *instincts*, right?"

There were murmurs of agreement in the crowd.

"You're acting like the Dinks don't exist," Moonrose went on. "What better way for them to get us than if we're all in one place? Look what happened when we were all together here."

"No," Levitt said. "If we split up, they can pick us off one by one. We're safest when we're all in a group."

"The hell with it," Moonrose said. "I'm following what my radar tells me."

"Then I say you're a threat to the Seekers—no better than any other Dink. You're breaking us up." His face was hard and he balanced forward on the balls of his feet. "How many are for Texas with me?"

There was a flurry of hands, but others stood unmoving. It was clear the disagreement had legitimized the old way of individual people following their personal intuitions. Levitt took a quick count, then faced Moonrose.

"I hope you're satisfied," he said. "Good luck when the Mothership comes for us in Amarillo."

6:11 AM Saturday, August 14

In the morning, the trucks, campers, and cars began to pull out, each following its own route, disappearing in as many different directions as points on the compass.

Starbud sat beside Moonrose in the truck that Moonbeam had left them. "Promise you won't go through Kansas," she pleaded.

"Why?"

"Be*cause*," she said bleakly.

"All right," Moonrose said. "I guess we could head south with Levitt's bunch, then swing east through Louisiana or something. Why don't you get the map out and check it? I can't say I like traveling in Levitt's direction, though. And I don't have any good memories about Texas. But I guess there's likely to be dust storms in Kansas, and if you're so set against it—"

"Thank you," Starbud said.

A car pulled even with their cab on Starbud's side. It was Levitt.

"You change your mind?" he called out his window.

106

"No," Moonrose shouted across Starbud. "We're just going south a ways before we head east. Dust storms."

"Fuck it, then," Levitt said and roared ahead, cutting dangerously close in front of them and blinding them with his cloud of dust.

5 PM

Starbud was asleep when the caravan reached Texas. Moonrose glanced down at her occasionally and smiled. She was a purer vessel, all right, no doubt about it. Face like an angel. Maybe that was what the Beings would look like.

Just as well she was asleep, Moonrose thought. She gazed out at the moonscape of empty bowls and craters on either side of the road, strewn with the rusting wreckage of abandoned rigs and earthmovers and pumps.

She knew its history well enough. First the domes had been emptied of oil, and then in the eighties a polymer had been pumped in with water to loosen the oil trapped in the sand. And when the ground had become unstable—nothing like LA, but unsettling for Texans—they had pumped in additional seawater to stop the quakes. But the water had proven to be a lubricant along the cracks and fissures, and the quakes had started again, and finally the domes had collapsed, leaving the ground pocked with sinkholes.

That had been before her parents had moved to the Kirkland Relocation Camp. Her memories of the days before the move were uncertain. Idaho, somewhere. First there had been bright skies and hot suns and endless stretches of golden wheat, but then the skies had darkened and the winds had begun. And the brown dust that was everywhere, pouring out of your shoes when you took them off, in a little pile in the center of your palm when you took a handful of change out of your pocket. It crackled against the enamel of your teeth whenever you bit into something.

That was why, she supposed, she'd felt such kinship with Starbud, though Starbud would never talk about her home or family.

Still, Moonrose thought, at least in Idaho they'd had the family home, despite the dusters. There had been something reassuring about seeing her father in the seat of his great tractor, a sense that everything was all right in spite of the wind, because

107

he was still in control. He could turn the wheel and make the huge machine change direction after his will. He could work the pedal to make it go fast or slow.

But the storms had gotten worse and worse, and finally her parents had given up, carried what they could into the cloth-roofed army trucks like motorized covered wagons, and let themselves be taken to the relocation camp. Backward pioneers.

Oh, they'd gotten an apartment in the Texas camp, after a while, a gray little place in which she'd watched her gray-faced parents rattle around as aimlessly as paper bags in the wind. Every two days they lined up with all the other gray-faced people for groceries to cook on their electric hotplate, and every night they went to the social room with the same gray-faced people to watch whatever was showing on the television whose channel selector and tuning controls were, like their apartment thermostats, locked away from them. When they went to the nearest town for an outing, they went with the other people on a gray Navy surplus bus, and somebody else drove.

The people running the camp hadn't been any better. They'd given orders, told you to clean your bathroom and clip the tufts of grass beside your gravel walkway, but they quaked in their turn before higher-ups, and so on all the way to that grinning baboon of a president who smiled, waved, and, whenever she was asked a specific question, pressed the hearing aid further into her ear to hear her chief of staff tell her what answer to give.

Moonrose had kept hoping her parents would stop taking it and get out. Maybe they had been right about turning down some of the opportunities that came their way, like when Solarsystems wanted miners to work on the moon, where they were going to mine the raw materials for their satellite. But there had been other things—she'd heard of people staking out farms along the margin of the Dust bowl. They wouldn't have made money, but they could have raised as much as they needed for a family farm. It would have been better than having a television you couldn't control or standing in line for a bag of groceries some nutritionist had picked out for them.

But they hadn't, and Moonrose had gone from the gray high school in the camp to the gray community college two towns away. And there she had met Moonbeam. His name had been John then, but he'd seen that there had to be something more to life than what was around them.

And so they'd gone off—to the Moonies, to a Dust bowl farm of their own, and finally to a new life and new identities with the Monad one day in a motel room. She hadn't seen her parents since. She supposed they had simply sifted down into two little piles of dust.

But that was why she wasn't giving up on the Monad now, or on Moonbeam. She'd seen what losing everything you'd believed in could do to people.

The sun had nearly set. To her right, Moonrose could just make out the crumbling concrete of a culvert. Along the top ran a guard rail, and far below ran the dry bed of a long-dead stream. When they'd first come to the camp, she remembered people talking about the kinds of rains that had made culverts like these necessary. Toad-stranglers, they'd called them. They could wash out the side of a mountain in minutes, fill a culvert like that in under an hour. That had been before her time, of course. She couldn't remember a Texas rain.

She glanced down at the folded map beside her. Route 180 should be coming up pretty soon. It would take her eastward through Anson, Albany, Fort Worth, Dallas, and eventually Shreveport, Louisiana. She began to slow down, letting the convoy pass her as she watched for signs for the turnoff.

It was then she noticed the car coming up behind her at high speed. As it closed on her tailgate, then swung out to pull beside her, she was sure she saw Levitt at the wheel, frizzy hair aglow in the red sunset. An instant later they were even, Levitt driving insanely in the wrong lane, and then he swerved toward her. The impact rocked the truck, snapped Moonrose's head back. She hung onto the wheel, trying to keep herself upright, barely aware that she was still steering the truck.

Again the jolt of Levitt's car, and this time she felt her truck lurch away from him and bounce against the culvert guardrail with a burning screech of metal and thocking of rivets on the fenceposts.

She caught a glimpse of Levitt's face, intense, murderous, and then his car closed again. She swerved to lessen the impact, caught her fender on the guardrail, lost her right headlight, fought the wheel to turn back into the lane, and suddenly felt the car spin wildly. Her head smashed against the side window, she felt Starbud's body slam against her, arms flailing, still half asleep, both caught on a carousel gone mad, and just as suddenly they swung squealing to a stop.

109

Moonrose shook her head to clear it. Broadside. They'd ended up broadside across the highway.

Levitt's car had disappeared.

From the arroyo came the dry, metallic twitter of some thirsty insect calling for a mate.

11

Triage

It was like so many other towns in Indiana. A main street bordered by one- and two-story stores on either side, some frame with false fronts, a few of brick toward the center of town, the rest single-story cinder-block boxes, built four and five together, relative newcomers. An Aubuchon hardware store, Medi-Mart, a clothing store that had been run by the same family for four generations, a police station in the basement under the town hall and courthouse. And down the street a hospital built by money raised at hospital fairs and book and cake sales to replace the old frame house where Dr. Haddon had set bones and administered elixirs.

And after Dr. Haddon had come Dr. Lyndon, a woman trained at Yale-New Haven, a woman who knew medicine.

Dr. Lyndon pushed her chair back but did not look up, concentrating on her hands grasping the edge of the desk.

"I'm sorry, Mr. Soames," she said, looking down to pick some lint from her Superman jumpsuit. "I'd like to help your wife, I really would, but my hands are tied. Literally tied."

"I can't believe it," Soames said, leaning forward across from her in his rumpled denim suit. "You're not that much younger than I am. You must have done manual surgery in the old days."

"Of course I did."

"Then why not now?"

"Because that's the way it is, Mr. Soames. Times have changed. A doctor can't just pick up a knife and go cutting someone apart. Not when we have Computerized Laser Assisted Surgical Systems—"

111

"I'm asking you to do it yourself, not one of your damned machines."

"Not use CLASS?" She was genuinely astonished. "How could you do excisions without biolasers? What would you do about cauterizing severed vessels in surgery unless you used an argon light knife?"

"Doctors used to manage."

"*Manage?* What about photocoagulators? The computer focuses the laser through the lens of the eye and *spot welds* the retina. Doing it by hand used to mean impossibly painful surgery—the patient had to spend weeks flat on her back so she didn't undo the work. Now, the patient gets up off the table and goes home."

"Okay, I'm not arguing with progress, just with things that aren't progress at all. If you make even an appendectomy prohibitively expensive, where's the progress? If no one can afford surgery, what difference does your recovery rate make?"

Dr. Lyndon checked her watch, running her fingers along the keys of the prescription computer terminal. "You simply can't have someone aiming a laser by eye. CLASS has made surgical error obsolete."

"But why not a knife? I'm not asking for exotic brain surgery, Doctor. Gall bladders used to be a simple operation—"

"No surgical procedure is simple, Mr. Soames, and neither is my duty in this case. I'd be violating hospital regulations, I'd be forfeiting any right to reimbursement from Fedmed. And my malpractice insurance would be cancelled. Surely you can appreciate my position."

Soames leaned back wearily. "Well, at least we've gotten to the heart of the matter. I appreciate your honesty about it. It's the money, then. And I don't suppose it matters that I've sold everything I have, that I was so desperate I even went to a witch—"

"You and everybody else."

"But are you going to let a woman die—?"

Dr. Lyndon fixed him with her most serious look. "I don't want to, Mr. Soames. But you can't expect me to sacrifice a *career* of helping the sick just for the sake of one life." She paused, allowing what she'd said to sink in. "You might as well face the fact that there's no place in this country to get what you're looking for. You could try taking a plane down to Panama, maybe, or—"

"Plane? Jesus, you people amaze me. Can you for one second try to understand what it is to be broke? I CAN'T AFFORD A PLANE TICKET!"

"I don't need to be shouted at, Mr. Soames," Dr. Lyndon said, rising. "I don't need people raising their voices at me. And there are ill people all up and down this corridor. I think you ought to leave."

"SHE'S DYING!"

"We're all dying, Mr. Soames. It's not for any of us to say when the process should be completed in any one case. It's for the Regional Board. All I can do is submit her name to the Board and when they have the facts—"

"They'll turn her down. I've been through this before."

"Well, naturally, the Board's screening has a limited triage function. There's a waiting list for the CLASS machines, and you don't expect a hospital to let a salvageable patient die in order to treat a hopeless case, now do you?"

"Hopeless case? It comes down to the fact you restrict yourself entirely to welfares and wealthy people with a hundred percent recovery probabilities. That way, your ass is covered—you rarely fail, you're always paid, and your patients are either socially acceptable or guilt-reducers. So they'll turn my wife down because it'll take months to qualify us for Fedmed. It's that simple."

She waited with her hand on the door to be sure there would be no more outbursts. "Mr. Soames, I have patients waiting."

"A pain-killer, then—?"

"If you won't let me handle her as a regular patient, I certainly can't play Doctor Feelgood and make out prescriptions for every hard-luck story that comes through the door. Now, if you'll excuse me..."

It took Soames several moments to collect himself in the stuffy cubicle after the doctor had closed the door behind her. Then he rose and let himself out, moving slowly down the hall, occasionally passing another open door that revealed a room decorated with precisely the same two chairs, desk, diplomas, and plastic tulips he'd seen in his own cubicle.

He paused at the receptionist's window long enough for her to note his health insurance number—no need to tell her it had long ago expired—and then made his way back out onto the hot street. The sky was still darkened from the Kansas storm.

He stopped at a state store, limiting himself to a ten-pack of

113

weed and a card of five mescaline spansules, knowing that his Omnicharge was still in the grace period and no red lights would blink on as long as he kept individual purchases under the hundred-dollar limit.

From there he headed back to the car, pausing only once, just behind it, to see the silhouette of his wife sitting rigidly in the front seat.

He wished he could keep it that way. Wished he didn't have to slide in beside her and see her face drawn by pain. But he forced himself onward to the driver's side and opened the door.

12

Circe's Cave

9:30 AM Tuesday, September 7

Circe sat straight-backed in the cushioned chair, wiping her sweaty palms on its puffy vinyl arms and squinting at the brightness of the bare, alabaster-white office. Across from her, Marian Horning folded the gnarled roots of her arthritic fingers on the gleaming plane of her ebony plexiglass desk.

"I'm sorry it had to come to this," she said. Her eyes glittered like diamonds from inside the tired folds of her skin.

Circe felt her shoulders sag. It was the sense she'd had as a child when, close to the finish line, she knew there was no way to close the gap to the front runner, no longer any point to forcing herself on. But she was an adult now. She couldn't let down.

"If it's about the Tower, I think what happened in Denver explains it. I checked through all the clients that had the Tower in my forecasts. The air taxi that went down was a Sikorsky product. The Solarsystems man was from their Denver office, and in fact it was the Solarsystems Tower that was the worst hit. And—"

"You're saying, in other words, that you can do things with the cards that Ruth Geist—not only a junior partner but one of the most talented clairvoyants I've ever trained—*can't?*"

"I don't mean it that way exactly. But it's possible in this particular instance that maybe I was somehow . . . I don't know . . . I had some lucky *insight* that was denied to more talented readers."

"Well, perhaps so," said Marian Horning. "But the discrepancies in your forecasts have nothing to do with our decision."

"Then it's about the things I thought I saw in the Faith

Limited forecasts? I can't tell you how sorry I am. And he *did* announce he was running for the presidency—"

"No. As a matter of fact, Mr. Percy called just last week to say how highly they all thought of you."

"Mr. Percy?" Circe looked blank.

"The head of Ritual Research and Development. The man you were working with. . . ."

"Oh, of course," Circe said, trying to remember who he was or what she'd done for him.

"No doubt it has something to do with your significator being the Queen of Pentacles, the mate of Doctor Love's King. You're highly compatible spiritually."

Circe nodded.

"But I'm afraid this has nothing to do with any of that. Frankly, if it were up to me, I'd prefer to keep you on, despite some indiscretions and inaccuracies in your work."

Circe looked up hopefully.

"But this is a League matter. It's out of my hands."

"A *League* matter?"

"Oh, come now," Marian Horning said. "You know perfectly well you brewed a potion for some man named . . ." She glanced down at the LC display screen built into her desk. "Soames."

"How in the world—?"

"It's not for us to wonder how the League gets its information, but on the basis of past experience I'd imagine they've known about it for some time and only recently got it through committee to the vote."

"I only did it because he seemed so desperate," Circe said.

"And I suppose I understand. Again, it's something I might have overlooked if it had been up to me, though I confess I'd have the severest reservations about any probationer that flouted League rules, however good her intentions. But the fact is, we've been informed that the full Council will be convened for a final vote this afternoon. And I'm afraid there can no longer be a place for you here at Ashtoreth. The scandal of having someone still on our staff being censured—"

"But it's not *fair*," Circe said. "Only *one* mistake and—"

She stopped herself, full of hatred for Soames. The potion hadn't worked, probably, and he'd wanted revenge—that had to be it. If only she hadn't told him how important it was to keep the matter quiet, he'd never have known it was something he could use against her.

116

"In the occult arts," Marian Horning said, "one mistake can be fatal." And she looked briefly toward the door; the interview was over.

"Oh," she added just as Circe was letting herself out, "you'll want to turn in your washroom key, of course."

Circe cleaned out her desk quietly, and none of the other probationers dared say anything to her, though at one point her eye caught Carol Arendt's and Carol flashed her a brief, covert smile of sympathy.

There wasn't much, really. A presentation Tarot pack, some lore books, and her untested necromantic Bell of Girardius which she'd had cast for herself while she was still in school, before she'd fully realized that the big firms like Ashtoreth disapproved of flirtations with astral projection. She slipped the bell over her head and let it hang from her neck by its ribbon, and packed the rest in a cardboard carton. She left the paper clips, rubber bands, stationery in the desk. Office issue.

Her shoulders didn't sag until she was outside. Today the sky was gray-black with the blow-over from the dust storm in the middle west. The streetlamps were lighted, and cars hummed cautiously with headlights on. It was like a December dusk.

End of a dream.

The only question was whether Soamès had really been the one that turned her in to the League. Barring electronic eavesdropping, he was the only one who could have known.

Except Adele. Adele had overheard what Circe had said to Soames. Had even joked about informing on her. Joked? Now Circe wondered. Adele was perfectly capable of it—Circe had seen her harbor enough resentments against her coworkers at NBC. And Adele and Circe certainly hadn't been getting along lately—that argument about the Lovebands, for instance.

She hefted the cardboard box under her arm and started slowly down the street. She could deal with Adele later. The immediate problem was what to do with herself now. The rent and all her other bills would still have to be paid. There was always the possibility of setting up shop as an independent, but without League approval she'd never get the kind of corporate clients she was used to at Ashtoreth. And League membership had been her goal for so many years.

Her mother had been a witch of sorts. She'd worked the night shift as a carder in a specialty woolen mill near Nashua, New Hampshire, but she'd kept a hand-lettered sign posted outside the door to their mobile home in the trailer park, and she'd always managed to get a few regular clients—phrenology, palm reading, forecasts with the cards. That was back when most people still had some faith in rational approaches to problems, and interest in witchcraft and astrology was still confined to trendy people in the arts in Boston and New York and LA; but her mother had believed, and Circe could remember her reading with great interest the occasional news items about the early days of the League.

Her clients had been mainly first and second generation immigrants—Poles, Italians, French Canadians. Her mother herself was Finnish, though her father—if indeed her parents had ever been married—had apparently been of Irish extraction. Her mother had never said.

Circe had grown up in the tall grass behind the trailer park. There were other children, of course, but she'd preferred to wander by herself through the sweet smells and warm buzzings of the field. Sometimes she would come back to watch her mother practice her arts, perhaps hiding in the rear of the trailer or even standing on the tire and peering in through the back window, except when it was one of the gentlemen callers. Then Circe would go off into the field to play at what she'd seen.

It had been a sprawling, messy world of gas stations, many already shut down as gasoline supplies dwindled and HED-battery cars gained popularity, fast-food restaurants, abandoned Dairy Queens, and a drive-in that showed X-rated movies which she watched sometimes high up in an old maple when her mother wanted the trailer empty for entertaining. Even families better off than hers lived in sagging frame houses whose front yards were littered with bathtubs, car bodies, old Coke machines. As she'd grown older, the car bodies had begun showing up along the roadsides, as well.

She had loved and hated her mother. Determined not to lead her mother's life, Circe had studied social engineering on government loans at UNH, but witchcraft was all she really knew; she had come home to work the graveyard shift at the mill with her mother for the money for the apprenticeship year at New York's Institute of Occult Arts. It was directly from there, through the standard year-end competitive interviews, that Circe had gone to Ashtoreth as a probationer.

But that was over.

She paused at the walk light, glancing behind her as she

waited. A man several meters back stopped at precisely the same instant, and drifted toward a store window as though suddenly consumed with interest in its display of discount jewelry.

The light changed, and she started across. At the curb on the opposite side, she turned again, saw the man, hat down and face obscured in the noontime twilight, scurrying to make it across after the light had changed and cars were starting to move.

Almost as if he were following her.

She quickened her pace, past a Pak-Shack fast-food outlet, Soulfood Heaven, camera store.

He was still behind her.

But Circe knew the neighborhood. Her heart beating faster, she swung around the next corner, carton of personal effects suddenly millstone-heavy, and doubled back down two alleys to emerge back at the Pak-Shack. Cautiously she peered out to the sidewalk, then waited for footsteps behind her. The seconds crawled by, but no one appeared at the far end of the alley.

Probably just her own paranoia. But what could you expect after being fired? Actually, she'd been nervous ever since that day she couldn't remember at Faith Ltd. Maybe she *had* said or done something so horrible or embarrassing that she'd completely repressed the whole day, and Marian Horning hadn't let on in order to protect the League's sources.

But at least she'd made certain no one was following her. She walked another few blocks to calm herself, felt her carton growing ever heavier, and finally decided she needed someplace to sit down—preferably in a large crowd where she could find a wall to keep her back to, like Wild Bill Hickock.

The Dying Tiger Bar wasn't far away. She'd been there once or twice with Adele. It had a reasonably catholic clientele at lunchtime, tending toward intellectuals and people in the arts—but most important, it was far enough from Ashtoreth so she wasn't likely to run into any of her former colleagues.

Inside was dim and cool, the air feathered by an overhead fan. A woman with sensuous Monroe lips painted around her eyes was dancing alone in the middle of the floor, naked above the waist except for the loose bib of her overalls, behind which her breasts bobbled like magicians' assistants working furiously behind a curtain. She watched Circe come in with stony eyes, never losing the beat.

You are the rainbow in my sky-iy, sang the juke box.

119

Circe moved along the bar. A man and his dwarf lover were melded at the lips in a passionate kiss; two stools down a willowy young man had slipped his hand inside the pants of a plump young man with fashionably greased hair, his fingers visible through the tight fabric clutching one buttock the way her mother had tested grapefruit.

"End of the world?" he was saying. "Hell, New York's been living at the end of the world for twenty-five years. I mean, we're right out there at the cutting edge of Armageddon. I mean, *nothing* works—power's out half the time, every snowcat's in the garage whenever it snows, the garbage men can never remember which street they supposed to collect on Tuesdays. It's the raunch, darling, the pitteroos."

Past a man with a face painted clown white, finally reaching the curve of the bar from where she could watch the door. She placed her box of mementoes on the floor by her stool and sat down next to someone in a floppy western hat. To her other side was a vacant stool with a half-empty glass. She told the bartender she wanted a Blackbeard.

"Er is ein recht guter Narr," shouted someone in a mask.

"Ja, ein Esel bleibt ein Esel," another agreed.

"God, I'd *love* to get it on with one of those witch wenches, hons, but they're so *butch*—"

"—another twenty years, there won't *be* any families *anyway*."

"That's what they said twenty years ago. Maybe not here, but in Wisconsin—"

"Sweetikins, in twenty years Wisconsin will be anus-deep in *dust*—"

You are the pow-wer in my lifetime battery-ee—

The stone-faced woman danced on, in a fog of drugs and alcohol.

The bartender brought her Blackbeard and she sipped. The Kahlua was rich and sweet; the bourbon gave it bite. It felt good just to sit. The faces of Marian Horning, Adele, the shape of the man who'd followed her flashed through her mind, sent a chill across her shoulders. She sipped again.

The man in the hat turned suddenly and awkwardly, catching the rim of her glass with his cuff and spilling some of her Blackbeard.

"Would you *watch* it?" Circe snapped, happy to have a handy target for her anxieties.

The man tipped his head toward her, apparently sighting off to one side. Blind, she realized.

"I'm sorry. I didn't know you couldn't s—"

"F-forget it," the man said.

Blind or not, he was damned rude. He didn't so much as apologize, let alone offer to replace her drink. In fact, he seemed preoccupied, as though he were listening for something. A moment later someone sat down on the other side of her, returning to the half-finished glass, and the man in the hat seemed to relax.

Circe turned to the newcomer. She realized at once there was something terribly familiar about his dark, deepset eyes, soft face, aquiline nose.

She couldn't resist the impulse. "Don't I know you?" she asked.

He shook his head. "Doubtful."

"But I've seen you somewhere, I know I have."

"Well, maybe," he said. "I'm an actor."

"I knew it!" she said. "On television?"

He looked into his glass.

"Come on, that's it, isn't it?"

"I really can't say."

"You mean you do porn?" she asked. She found herself suddenly interested. For one thing, she'd never bought Adele's line that bisexuals were just straights trying to avoid admitting it to themselves; she'd always maintained that whoever interested her interested her. Right now, in fact, a little companionship wouldn't be such a bad idea—especially since she owed Adele one. And it wouldn't hurt to have someone handy in case the man who'd followed her showed up again and she needed help.

"I guess you could say I do a kind of porn," he laughed. "But that's all I'm allowed to say, so why don't we just leave it at that, okay?"

She studied his face. Why couldn't she place it? After that missing day at Faith Ltd., she'd wondered if her memory was going. "So do you do free performances or do you always get scale?"

He laughed again.

"—in one of those sun-death cults, you know," a distant voice was saying. "Wagging your bare ass and tiptoeing around the altar with a knife at your throat hoping to God you didn't trip—"

"Well, what do you say?" Circe asked. "You busy right now?"

"Nothing till late this afternoon," he said.

"Your place or mine, then?" She felt guilt, shame, saw the men carrying six-packs trudging up the dusty path past her mother's palm-reading sign to the trailer door. Fuck you, Adele.

He glanced around nervously, as though he were afraid someone was watching him. Circe tried to follow his eyes—an old woman with a facelift looking like the mummy of Rameses III, the man and the dwarf woman, the people with painted faces, the solitary dancer, the gay now arranging a fruit dish by putting cherry nipples on two grapefruits to the giggles of his companion.

"*Ig* of unattractivenesses," said the plumper one, brushing back his oiled hair and taking a spoonful of grapefruit. "So the creature just *perched* there and *shrieked*—"

"Your place," he said.

The blind man tipped his head and Circe realized he'd been listening the whole time. Well, what the hell—why did she have to be so paranoid about *everybody?*

They walked to her apartment in the night-black afternoon, all the darker for the limitations on commercial lighting displays. Halfway there, Circe felt loosened enough by the drink to talk a little about herself, always glancing over her shoulder for any sign of the man who'd followed her. So far, so good.

"So you're a witch," the actor said, surveying her living room and taking a seat on the couch after she'd let him in. "Where are the cauldrons?"

"I said an *ex*-witch," Circe said. She still had the mesc spansules she'd gotten to intensify her clairvoyant trances; at least they'd be useful for intensifying the sex. She offered him one, took one herself.

"And do you cast spells?" he asked, leaning back as they waited for the mesc to work.

"Spells? What do you take us for?" Circe found it always an annoying question. "I did corporate prognostications."

"I know, I know," he said. "I was only joking. I go to a witch *and* an astrologer. I'm still not sure I believe in it, though."

She shrugged. "Then you've got nothing to risk if I run the cards for you. If you won't tell me what you do, maybe the cards will. Let's at least see how you'll be in bed."

He laughed, already feeling a little silly from the mesc, as she picked the Knight of Pentacles for him and began to shuffle the cards.

"I've never understood what good a random bunch of face cards is supposed to do," he said.

"There's nothing random in the universe," Circe said. "That's the foundation of witchcraft—every event in creation is the result of preestablished law. There's a magic relationship between us and these cards created by our presences here, and the random order created by shuffling them will in fact make their final order significant."

"And then you just read them off, like my witch?"

"It's not that simple," she said. "A true Tarot reader goes into a clairvoyant trance, and that concentrated psychic energy allows her to divine the meaning of the cards as they're modified by their proximity to each other in any individual reading. If you want mechanical divination, you go to that astrologer of yours—they're basically mathematicians who think they can find the future with abstract calculations. But it's *intuition*—that's the *only* way to understand cosmic law. It's incomprehensible to logic."

"My witch says it's a kind of autohypnosis," he said.

"For good readers. I usually need the mesc first."

"But you don't do trips outside your body into the spirit world or anything?" he asked.

"None of the reputable firms approve of it," Circe said, motioning him to cut the cards three times. "It's perfectly possible, according to everything I've read, but anyone that doesn't have a real Gift would be crazy to try it. I've never tried it. Okay, do you have a question for the cards to answer?"

He nodded, and she turned the first card over on his Knight of Pentacles. King of Pentacles, Doctor Love's significator. Funny coincidence. The second card was number one of the Major Arcana, but not the Magician. It was the Juggler. Damn, she must have picked up the souvenir presentation deck she'd brought home from the office, a set of historical reproductions of a pack designed in the nineteenth century by Oswald Wirth, de Guaita's pupil.

She was about to sweep them up and start with a new deck when the growing lassitude of the mesc told her not to. Maybe her choice of packs was somehow ordained. Better to stick with this, try to figure out the significance. The modern Magician was will, mastery, occult power, his head surmounted by the symbol of infinity. In this older version, the Juggler's hat brim formed the infinity symbol, and the pips of the four suits were all represented—coins, swords, cups, with the Juggler himself holding the wand.

She tried to remember. Papus had written that the wands were the intellectuals, the cups the professors and writers who preserved the verities of the thinkers, the swords the warriors, while infinity was the masses from whom the other three castes came—eternity uniting the three other principles, each cabalistically linked with the Hebrew letters YHVH, Yahweh. The Aleph in the right-hand corner was the Cabala symbol for the spirit of the Living God who manipulates the things of the universe as a juggler manipulates earthly objects. Yet here, the Juggler was reversed; that meant a charlatan who used dexterity to exploit human credulity.

A god that practiced deceit and trickery? She wanted to glance up at the man opposite her, but she was too far in now, and she feared to break her frail trance. She had to pursue the truth through the cards.

"This is beneath him," she whispered. Five, the Hierophant, the Pope. Traditional teaching of the masses, purveyor of external religion as opposed to the intuitive witchery of the High Priestess. Creed and ritual, the outer husks of religion, conventionalism.

Suddenly it was clear to her. She leaned back, looked him directly in the eyes. "Doctor Love," she said.

His head snapped back. "No," he protested. "I told you, I'm just an actor."

Circe bit her lip. She should have known better than to trust her intuition. She opened her lips to apologize, but time seemed slowly to grind to a halt, mesc-stretched into an endless, unmoving plane before her. "You're Doctor Love," she heard herself saying, ". . . and yet you're not."

"All right," he sighed. "You win. I'm one of his TV stand-ins. I was reading for a part in some little summer theater in upstate New York—I wanted to play the young intellectual in Gorky's *Summerfolk*, you know? Then after the reading these people came up to me. They didn't say what they wanted. They just gave me an air-taxi ticket and told me to be at Love Central next day."

Circe closed her eyes. His words seemed to take forever.

"They've got this really elaborate production facility tucked into some rooms under the Temple," he was saying. "They dressed me up and shot me against a blue wall so they could mat in backdrops later. I didn't even recognize myself the first few times—they used a computer to rearrange what I said, the sound of my voice, even my face. I didn't look like me—I looked like Buddha, Jesus Christ, you name it. I *was* Doctor Love—or rather, they'd taken what I'd done and turned it into Doctor Love.

"I guess I didn't like it much. What actor would? But they paid me enough so I agreed to keep quiet and not take any other acting jobs. I've just gone along ever since, getting frustrated and bored, but I've never told anyone till tonight. I guess you can't hide the truth from a witch."

Circe smiled in triumph and vindication. If only Marian Horning could see *this*. "So you're the Doctor Love I see on TV?"

"Actually, I gather there are several of us that are used as models to freshen up the image the computer generates."

"I wonder why the real Doctor Love doesn't just do his own minispots?" Circe mused, struggling with her heavy tongue.

"Who knows? Maybe he's too old. Maybe he's too busy planning his presidential campaign. God knows it would take twenty Doctor Loves to keep track of all the projects they've got over there. Frankly, I never wondered about any of it till the other night. That's what made me suspect we were used for something else. For decoys."

"Decoys?"

"Awhile back somebody was killed right in front of Love Central—blew the fucker up in a car."

Something tugged at Circe's memory, but she couldn't quite make it out.

"Nobody'd talk about it," the ersatz Love went on, "but I was in the building and I heard the explosion. When I got out I could see it was one of those Inner Circle jobs they use to ferry us around while we're in makeup, and I just got this feeling that the guy in the car had been another one of the doubles. I mean, it's possible there were other explanations, but I'm sure it was somebody gunning for Love that didn't know about us stand-ins."

"How do you know it wasn't actually Love himself?"

"Because nothing changed over there afterwards."

Circe pondered. "I wonder who'd want to kill him. Half the country treats him like a god." Suddenly Circe began to giggle despite herself. It was the Blackbeard and the mesc, the release from the tension. "I've never been to bed with a god before," she managed through her laughter.

"Neither have I."

"What?"

"I said neither have I."

"Now *that's* flattery," Circe said. "I was just reporting what I read in the cards."

"No, I meant your name. Circe was a goddess, you know. You look like a pretty worthy namesake." He reached over and took her hand, began to knead her forearm.

"Maybe I'll turn you into a pig," she laughed.

He rested his head on her shoulder. "Maybe that would be better than what I live with now. Every now and then I think about how they're using my face, and I'm scared, really scared. It's like it's somehow my responsibility because it's my face, but I've got no control over what they do with it. It's like slavery or something."

The old sympathy routine, Circe thought dreamily. It was such a drag. She'd already made it clear to him it was just going to be a simple fuck. Why did people have to make such a game out of it? Such an elaborate ritual . . .

Suddenly the room was plunged into blackness.

"What the hell was that?" he said, sitting up.

"Power failure, what else?" Circe said. "I thought you'd been in the City a while. We get them all the time. Probably too many people turning on their lights because it's so dark out."

Gradually her eyes grew accustomed to the dim light, and she felt his head settling on her shoulder again, his hand on her upper arm, knuckles just brushing her breast. She was beginning to make out the silhouette of the top of his head when against the wall just above it she saw a circle of intense light, smaller than a penny, begin to glow and then burst into flame.

For some reason she glanced over at the window, saw the ring of a burn hole still glowing in the curtain, smelled the smoke, and knew without ever having seen one in action that it was some kind of laser.

"Down!" she shrieked. "Get down!"

And she dove for the floor under the coffee table even as the actor, suddenly without her shoulder to support his head, sprawled sideways on the couch like a marionette whose strings had been cut.

13

The Denver Connection

2:53 PM Tuesday, September 2

Circe watched in horror as the glowing dot, pulsing on and off like punctuation in a neon sign, swept down the wall. The actor rolled off the couch and scuttled around the doorway into the kitchenette. The penny of light followed, stopped, began to bore through the wall, sputtering as it burned away the vaporized plasma of plasterboard in the hole.

"Keep moving!" she shouted. "Get behind something else!"

There was a spark and a puff as the beam burned through to the other side. A scream echoed off the kitchen tile and the light was gone.

Oh my God, no, Circe thought. It couldn't be. It couldn't. Things like this didn't happen.

All at once the light was back, searching, crossed the wall and sliced mindlessly through one leg of Adele's cherished 60's Mediterranean cabinet in its pursuit. The cabinet pitched forward, spilling odds and ends from its opening doors—coasters, matches, booklets, headphones, floppies—as the beam pulsed on, seeking her.

She had to find out where the assassin was. She tensed in the darkness, trying to focus her mesc-fogged mind. If she moved, she was likely to draw fire; whoever it was had somehow known every move the actor made.

There was only one solution. Frightened, she took a deep breath and closed her eyes, trying to remember the descriptions of the technique she'd read in her student days. Calm, concentration, that was what she needed. She drew inward, pooled herself at her very core until she could feel the concentrated energy

128

roiling within, then exhaled, forced herself outward, drifting, misting through her forehead (so easy, it suddenly seemed), reaching out until she had materialized the sofa out of the blackness (out there or behind her own eyelids? She no longer had any sense of her physical orientation), then the lamp and the end table. Farther. (A disembodied eye with three hundred sixty degrees of vision.) The door.

Was she really doing it, a voice inside her wondered, or was she just hallucinating, fooled by the mesc into imagining she saw the familiar things?

She felt her vision leach through the wall into the hall outside her apartment. There, in the window beyond, something crouched on—yes, on the fire escape. Somewhere she felt elation, excitement; she coiled herself, sprang toward it.

There was an impact like crashing through a wall of brick, and for an instant she was looking through something (the sights of a gun?) into her own living room. She could see herself as a reddish silhouette fading sometimes into black in regular horizontal lines like a weak television image, flickering, curling like smoke. She could see the actor sprawled dead in the kitchen beyond.

What had she done? Had she somehow broken into her attacker's consciousness and was seeing through his eyes, or had she entered some unknown plane separated from her body, another dimension or universe?

And then she heard—or heard through him (angry mind)—footsteps in the hall. She felt the squeeze of panic, her own and another's, and involuntarily jerked back. Her eyes flicked open and she found herself back in the darkened living room with the acrid smell of burned plaster and paint.

Someone was knocking at the door.

She froze, trying to collect herself for another psychic probe. But she was too exhausted; the calming and intensifying power of the mesc had dissipated.

There was a knock again, then a rustling and scraping as whoever it was tried the doorknob.

Stealthily Circe crawled out from behind the couch to the wall beside the door and rose into a crouch. The doorknob rattled, the door swung open, and a dark figure eased itself inside. Locking her fingers together in a double fist, Circe swung as hard as she could at where she thought his crotch might be. She caught him in the lower abdomen.

"Holy shit!" the figure gasped, dropping to the floor. "My goddamn prostate!"

At that moment the lights flickered on, and Circe found herself staring down at the collapsed form of an oddly familiar black man.

"Don't move," she said. "Don't move or I'll do it again."

"I'm not going anywhere till the ambulance gets here," Santalucia grunted.

"Just give me the laser gun or whatever it is," she said. "Slide it across the floor to me."

"Gun? Don't have any gun," Santalucia said. He pushed his back up against the wall until he was in a sitting position, all the while rubbing his lower abdomen. "You think I could take a hot sitz bath while we're talking? Maybe have a tetracycline cocktail?"

"You're the guy that followed me this morning!" Circe said. "I recognize the way you hunch your shoulders."

"My wife finds me very furtive and ratlike," Santalucia said.

"But what did you do with the gun just now?"

"Honestly, I just got here. After I lost you in the alley this morning, I looked up your address, and tonight I came up the back stairs, knocked on your door, and let myself in. All I wanted to do was *talk* to you, for Chrissake."

"It *could* have been somebody else," she said thoughtfully, "and you scared him off. But why did you want to talk to me?"

"Same reason I called on the phone a few weeks back," Santalucia said.

"I *knew* you looked familiar. But I already told you, nothing happened at Faith Limited that day." She said it even as she remembered what the actor (What was his *name*? She hadn't even asked his name.) had told her about the double killed in front of Love Central.

"You mean you don't *remember* anything unusual," Santalucia said, now apparently somewhat recovered and sitting up straighter. "But in point of fact, I don't imagine you remember anything about the day at all."

Circe winced. She didn't want to think about it because it brought her back to the dead man in the next room, and she hung, paralyzed with shock, between breaking into tears of sorrow for him and tears of elation at her first venture into the spiritual plane. "What's your name?" she asked dully.

"Jervis Santalucia, and the reason you don't remember anything before my phone call is that after they blew Doctor Love away, his little pixies sponged your memory clean with some kind of electronic Windex. In fact, they came over to my place to do the same thing, but I beat it out the back way. I like my memories intact, thanks—they're not much, but they're my own."

"It's not possible I could forget seeing a murder," she insisted, knowing she would never forget what had happened tonight. If she had finished the actor's Tarot, would she have found the card of Death?

"Actually, it was a triple murder," Santalucia said, "if you count the driver and Mr. Percy from Ritual Research and Development. I don't know whether he counts as a whole person or not."

"Marian Horning told me just this morning . . . Never mind. There's a man in the next room that saw what you're talking about."

"You know somebody that saw it?" Santalucia said. "I've been wondering if all these days without sleeping in a decent bed had affected my mind—though frankly, in a way it'd be easier if I could just chalk it up to good old fashioned dementia praecox and turn myself in for the cure, because the alternative is accepting the idea of an organization that can blank out your memory, and that scares me a whole lot more than a vacation on the funny farm. Well, why don't you trot him in here?"

"Because he's dead."

"What?"

"He's dead, Mr. Santalucia. Somebody killed him just like they killed the other double."

"Double?"

"That's what he said," Circe sighed. "The Love organization apparently hired a bunch of doubles for Doctor Love."

Santalucia whistled softly. "So that's why Faith Limited hasn't fallen apart—the real Doctor Love's still alive and well. My, my, I hope no one from the Saucer Cult finds out. You mind if I sit down?" With some difficulty Santalucia got up from the floor and made it to the couch, pausing to admire the burn hole in the wall.

"The Saucer Cult? What have they got to do with it?"

"Since I couldn't go home, I've had plenty of time in the public library. One of the Monad's key prophecies was that a major leader would be killed. Doctor Love would be the prime candidate, considering how paranoid the Monad was about the Love movement. Thought they were the major concentration of 'Dinks' this side of Pluto—that's Disincarnate Beings to the uninitiated. So when the Monad fulfilled another of her prophecies by getting fried out in Denver, it would be logical for a hit squad from the Cult to try to nail their biggest enemy and validate their leader's prediction at the same time. Since they were here tonight, it looks like they caught on to the fact they didn't get the right Love last time.''

"My God,'' Circe said, "they're even worse than Love has been saying on TV.''

"Well, you're a little biased from being shot at. They're still just a handful of zanies. It's the Love organization that's got the hardware.''

"Whoever it was tonight had a laser,'' she said.

"Yeah, they're better armed than I thought, but they've got a good reason. I don't suppose you remember Percy getting all upset when someone mentioned something called 'Project Snuff' at the Temple that day, but I've been wondering ever since why he didn't want outsiders like us to know about it.''

Circe studied Santalucia's face, trying to read her intuitions. "You mean like snuffing someone out? You think Project Snuff was Doctor Love's plan to murder the Monad?''

"In part,'' Santalucia said. "But think about the fact that the Cult is Love's biggest competition.''

"You mean mass murder?''

Santalucia shrugged. "If it were purely a matter of hygiene, I can't say I'd miss the Cult all that much, but it strikes me as tacky for a major religious leader and presidential candidate to have people eliminated in boxcar lots.''

Circe eased herself into a chair. There was no way to grasp the enormity of something like that. "So . . . you came hoping we could figure out something to do about it?''

Santalucia looked surprised. "Do I look like the Lone Ranger? I told you—I just had to know whether what I thought I saw really happened. Now that I know I'm sane, I'll just fold up my tent and steal away—''

He stopped himself and stared at the pile of debris beside the fallen cabinet.

"Well, well,'' he said. "I came here to compare notes, and it looks like I'm going to get my head washed, curled, and blow-dried. But that's what I get for talking to someone that hangs around with Doctor Love's double. I suppose you've already signaled them?''

''Who?''

''Doctor Love's mind-bending squad.''

''I don't know what you're talking about,'' Circe said.

''I'm talking about these.'' Santalucia rose and snaked something like a bicyclist's cap from amongst the cabinet's spilled contents. ''A geniune, patented Doctor Love headband, the latest model.''

''I don't have the faintest idea where it came from,'' Circe said indignantly. ''I hate those things. Adele must have gotten it despite our argument.''

Santalucia looked at her sourly. ''Okay, let's pretend you're telling the truth. It'll give us something to do while we're waiting for the goons to arrive. Have you got any idea what's inside these things?''

''They're alpha-wave stimulators,'' she said. ''It's a nice high—supposed to be healthier than mesc or weed.''

Santalucia flipped the adjustable velcro headband inside out to reveal two metal discs. ''You mean these electrodes that fit over your temples? You're right, they do mellow you out. It's even psychically addictive. But have you ever asked yourself what these earphones are here for?''

''So you can hear the megahype.''

''But why not just an alpha-wave stimulator over your temples and listen to the regular audio from your TV?''

Circe shrugged. ''Doesn't it have something to do with the fact the stimulator's keyed to Doctor Love's message, brings you up and down depending on what he says? You've got to have one of those little adapter boxes on your TV—''

''To coordinate the headband to the audio, right, along with providing a handy slot for your credit card when he calls for the offering. But I was curious, so I borrowed one of these from some friends—they've got a trunkful—and brought it over to a guy named Fred that does the prototype designs for my wife's company—a real tech freak, wild eyes, long hair, dreams about resistors. What he found out was very interesting.'' He pointed to the slim oblong of plastic that fit over the user's head. ''On one side's the stimulus level, and on the other's the volume control. The plastic bubble on top is the infrared receiver to modulate the alpha levels to match the megahype.''

''So?'' Circe asked.

133

Santalucia took a penknife out of his pocket and pried at the electronics package for several minutes before the cover finally popped open. "They really seal these things up to discourage people looking inside," he said. He pointed to several round silicon-covered substrates plugged into a circuit board. "Now I don't know an integrated circuit from Brown versus Board of Ed, but Fred tells me this is the low-frequency generator for the alpha waves. Here's the constant-current amplifier, and this drives the electrodes. What's interesting is this extra audio circuit here. It's for a high-frequency carrier channel."

He put the open package on the table.

"Normal TV audio doesn't go much above seventeen, maybe twenty kilohertz, but the soundtrack of a Love megahype also carries an inaudible high-frequency signal up around seventy-five or eighty kilohertz. It's not to convert dogs—it's fed directly through the adapter and sent via infrared to the headband's receiving bubble. Then this circuit demodulates it into an audible signal."

"I don't see the point," Circe said, troubled by Santalucia's agitation.

"Well, there's a circuit here for a bio feedback loop that tells the demodulator when the user's pulse is down to trance level—in other words, when the user's hypnotized by the alpha waves. Then it cuts in the carrier channel. Fred and I tried it out; it delivers what amount to post-hypnotic suggestions. In fact, they probably used one of these to wipe out your memory of that day at Faith Limited."

"But what kind of suggestions do they send? Is it on every megahype?"

"More or less. All we heard were bits about which products to buy and a couple of vote for Doctor Love's—relatively harmless stuff if you don't object to the basic concept of unconscious manipulation. But it does give Love the potential to control millions of people, a virtual army, if he wants to. And by modifying the carrier channel regionally, the same way ads are tailored to specific areas, he can even give local commands. In fact, using this he could tell other listeners to ignore something and give direct orders to specific people, and when the rest of them woke up, they wouldn't know a thing about it."

"Then if the Love people wanted to get me out of Ashtoreth for some reason," Circe mused, "say in case they were afraid I might get my memory back and realize I'd seen more than an attempt on Doctor Love's life, they could just order Adele to find some way to get me fired, and she might not even know she'd done it.''

Santalucia nodded. ''I guess you can see why Love's going to win the election hands down.''

''There's only one trouble—there's no adapter in the house.'' Somehow it made Circe feel better; it was simpler to live with the idea of a vindictive Adele than it was to live with the kind of evil Santalucia was suggesting.

''No need to anymore,'' Santalucia said. ''That's a Slim-Vu over there, isn't it?''

''Adele just bought it,'' Circe said. ''She wanted to be able to watch TV and read a book on the homeputer screen at the same time.''

''Well, another of Fred's discoveries is that the new Slim-Vues come with a built-in adapter. If you look at the Slim-Vu logo, you'll find a little plastic bubble in the center.''

Circe ran her hand down the flat screen to the thin base that held the electronics and the trademark. She found the bubble.

''Inside are little optical reflectors for LED's, an infrared transmitter.''

''But they sell these things everywhere. It's not a special Love model.''

''Exactly. Somebody's mass-producing TV sets with built-in Loveband adapters whether you need one or not. And for a company to absorb that extra expense out of the goodness of its heart sounds like . . . well, part of a very ambitious long-range plan.'' Santalucia levered himself to the edge of his seat and heaved himself up. ''So I think it's time to go rent an apartment under an assumed name somewhere in Australia and pull the covers over my head.''

''Wait a minute,'' Circe said. ''You can't just walk away from this thing—fold up your tents, like you said.''

''I most certainly can.''

''But we've got to tell somebody, warn people.''

''The really good practical joker never tells,'' Santalucia said.

''How about calling the FBI? Or even the president?''

''Because they're probably all Love-freaks already,'' Santalucia said. ''Doctor Love's too big to fight. All we can do is stay clear of him and avoid being manipulated.''

135

"No," Circe said. "With these TV's in D-stores all over the country, things are going to get worse instead of better. Think how many people you know already use Lovebands. In a few years there won't be anyone left you can trust. He'll use TV to turn the whole population into zombies." She was enthusiastic, even frantic. As long as she could keep herself safely occupied with plans and theories, she wouldn't have to face what had happened tonight. Wouldn't have to think about what lay in the next room.

"TV did that years ago," Santalucia laughed. "Doctor Love's just doing away with the untidiness of having several networks fighting to see who does the manipulating. Becoming president will just make it neater. Anyway, what would you do, go busting into Love's office and dress him down?"

"I don't know, maybe get this Fred of yours to set up a way to monitor the carrier channel and keep track of what Love's telling people to do. And in the meantime find out all we can about Love himself."

"You won't find a thing," Santalucia said. "I've been through every newspaper and magazine and book, and about all there is about the guy is he started out as a urologist in Cleveland before he got charisma and hit the evangelical trail. He's a very shadowy character."

"All right, then, we start somewhere else. How about finding who actually makes these TV's?"

"That's a nice, lowcal approach," Santalucia said. "What possible good could it do you?"

"Everything's a subsidiary of something else these days," Circe said. "If you tracked the ownership of Slim-Vu down . . ."

"You'd find out Doctor Love is actually the puppet of some South American dictator?" Santalucia watched with amusement as Circe examined the television.

"There's nothing here except 'Denver, Colorado' on the back."

"That's a hell of a note," Santalucia said. "Denver hasn't exactly been a healthy place recently."

"All right, there's a lot of poking around we could do right here. Maybe we can find out what we need from Standard and Poor's *Register* or by talking to a broker. And if that doesn't work, then we could go to Denver."

"Never in a million years," Santalucia said.

"Yes, we will," Circe smiled. "Because I just lost my job today, I don't have money for breakfast, and I couldn't possibly afford a ticket to Denver by myself."

14

Sister Catherine

2:30 PM Saturday, October 30

"It's like the world has gone mad," Sister Catherine said, pacing back and forth in front of the picture window in Father Camillieri's study. "Absolutely mad."

Father Camillieri nodded, seated at his writing table, and tipped a teaspoon of sugar into his coffee. Experience had taught him that in cases like this you let the person talk it out, the way a psychiatrist would. That, after all, had been the essence of the priest's role as confessor and adviser for almost two thousand years.

Father Camillieri watched her continue to pace. She appeared of indeterminate age, though he knew in fact that she was in her late sixties, because she'd announced her retirement from the Mill Street School at the end of the year.

She probably did a good job teaching first grade and overseeing the school's afternoon daycare operation for students of working parents, but with reluctance he admitted to himself that something about her had always made him uneasy. Partly it was her looks. Obviously, she'd never been attractive. Even as a young woman she must have been lumpy and mismatched, like a bad idea. Her eyes bulged, her eyebrows grew together, and with each year the gray hairs had become more discernible across her upper lip and in the cleft of her chin.

But more than that it was her desperate intensity. Not surprising, he supposed, for a nun who had seen her vocation as the cloister but who had lived on into these dark times when covents were a thing of the past and what few nuns remained lived singly and worked in the community. For Sister Catherine, it had come to a job as a teacher in a federally funded ghetto school.

"And not just in this country, you know," she was saying. "I was

138

reading in the *Transcript* that church attendance is down all over the world, in all faiths. I guess over the years I'd gotten used to churches being almost empty for daily mass. But last Sunday I happened to come to the eleven o'clock—*eleven o'clock*. There was virtually no one there. When I was a girl, Father, you couldn't turn around at an eleven o'clock mass without rubbing shoulders with a dozen people."

"I know," he sighed. "These are very troubled times."

"And false prophets and heresiarchs springing up everywhere like weeds. In Germany there's that dreadful ex-priest named Otto, or whatever, convincing people with that hare-brained story of his about some ancient king returning from under a mountain to restore their military glory."

"King Frederick," Father Camillieri said.

"But didn't they learn anything from World War Two? When I was a girl, everyone said . . . Well, never mind. And then some pagan candlelight parade, and Druids in England. And here we've got some television evangelist running for president!"

"We've had religious men in Congress before," Father Camillieri soothed. "It's not without precedent."

"But a man that tells people every man and woman is his or her own *god?* Blasphemous. And then the Saucer Cult! The newspapers were right when they called that awful woman the Pied Piper. The way she's lured our children away . . ."

"I imagine you find that particularly disturbing," Father Camillieri said. "Considering your work at the school, I mean."

"Wouldn't anyone?" she demanded. "Every time the Cult gets news coverage, another one of my children runs away to join them. Ten in the last year—*ten!*"

"These are things that worry all of us, Sister Catherine," he said. "The other day I went to see a rabbi I've known from some committees we've been on together. I just needed to talk to someone—a wise man, a scholar, but not another priest. That would've been too much like talking to myself in the mirror. I needed a different perspective."

"And what did he say?" she asked.

"He reminded me there have been worse times, especially for his people. And he reminded me that the Jews have had their millenarians and false messiahs for a lot longer than we have—in fact, they're where we got it from. The Apocalypse in *Baruch*, the Lion of Judah in *Ezra*, Daniel's Dream. Some Jews thought Simon bar-Cochba was the Messiah when he fought the Romans.

And he said it's still a passive obsession with them, believing they'll someday return to a new Holy Land and a communal millennium."

She sat down on the opposite side of the table. "I know," she said. "And sometimes I wonder if there isn't some grain of truth in all this."

"All what?"

"All this talk of a millennium. The year two thousand. Think about this latest rash of flying saucer sightings out west."

"Don't tell me *you're* planning to join the Saucer Cult, Sister Catherine."

"No, of course not. But you can't help wondering. I know there's no such thing as flying saucers, but weren't there strange events in the heavens the First Time, before Christ's birth?"

Father Camillieri scowled. "I imagine it's some kind of atmospheric disturbance."

"But the Bible is filled with talk of the certainty of a Second Coming. What if the end of the second millennium *is* the beginning of the New Age?"

"And you think there's a John the Baptist somewhere out in California getting ready to prepare the way?"

"Not necessarily. But it *is* a thrilling possibility. It's something you *have* to consider, Father."

"I suppose anything's possible," he said, finishing his coffee. "But we can't exactly reorder our lives around that kind of speculation. We wouldn't be much better than the Saucer Cultists if we did."

"I know," she said. "But if ever there was a time when Mother Church needed Him again, it's now."

"That's not really for us to say," he said. "The difficulties of the present always seem worse than the past. Would you like more coffee, Sister?"

She shook her head. "No," she said. "I think I'll go back to my room. It's Saturday, so I have the afternoon off, and I was thinking I might just take a nap."

"I think that would be a splendid idea, Sister Catherine."

On her way back to the school, Sister Catherine did not feel better, despite her talk. Father Camillieri didn't seem to understand the seriousness of the situation. He wasn't like the priests in the old days.

Nothing was like the old days.

When Sister Catherine had ended her juniorate and taken her perpetual vows, the Order had already begun its great modernizing reforms, and, in tune with the times, she had chosen the newer and less severe options: her habit had been a dark blue dress cut just below the knee, and she had kept her own name in preference to the other sisters' identity-submerging assumption of the names of Mary and a favorite saint; though, in point of fact, her favorite saint had always been her martyred virgin namesake, Catherine of Alexandria.

Well, what did it matter? The others were all gone, now. They had left the Order or died. Small wonder. Without tradition, without morality, what modern girl would be willing to submit to the life of sacrifice and self-denial that was required? So the Order's convents and schools had been closed, and the Order's few remaining faithful had been sent out into the world to teach beside the laity, observing what they wished of the old discipline they had known as novices and postulants, each one her own Mother Superior. And now, as far as she knew, she was the last of her Order.

It had all started with the new habits. She was as much to blame as any of them.

She was approaching the end of the commercial district, the last few stores before the wasteland of thirty-year-old housing projects. She glanced up at one of the signs.

ABIGAIL'S BOUTIQUE, read the lucite letters over the door. YES, WE HAVE EDIBLE PANTIES! said the hand-lettered sign in the store window.

It made her sick. A world of debauchery and depravity that thought only of one thing. Just like the doomed world that Saint John had seen in his revelations. Things had been different when she was growing up. It was terrible that today's children were exposed to such things. Even worse that adolescents were.

Because, she thought, puberty was such a horrible time. The glands drove you to the most humiliating exhibitions to find channels for those new, unwanted energies. She remembered as a girl, after all the mixers and hops spent in gymnasium shadows on folding chairs, sweating and talking to Angela Plotnik and tearing little strips from the rim of her paper cup, how one day Jerry Klimezewski had said hello passing her on the stairs at school. Said hello even though he was always with that awful Ada who'd been so fat in grade school they'd chanted "Ada potatah the big fat tomatah." And Catherine had stayed at the

141

railing of the landing to smile down and talk to him, knowing he would be able to glance up her dress, ready to stand there yielding and let him do it, without letting on she knew. And he'd kept going down the stairs without looking up at all, saying "I gotta go, Candy." *Candy.* He hadn't even known her name and she'd offered herself to him. He'd married Margaret Champeaux, who was two years behind her, and she'd told her parents never to tell her anything about the new Mr. and Mrs. Klimezewski. Later she'd cried about her brazenness, thinking how only a year before she'd imagined she might someday see a vision like the children at Fatima, and knowing now that the innocence and purity in which she'd had such dreams had been forfeited forever.

Well, that was what puberty did to you, but it was that kind of consciousness of it, that kind of sensitivity to it, she told herself, that made her a better teacher than the rest of them. Genuine concern for the children—it had been her distinguishing feature since her arrival at Mill Street School.

But she understood them, that was why. She was the only one native to the area. She gloried in being, like the children, a product of the dark cotton mills along Pawtucket Boulevard. She sympathized, identified, and gradually she even transformed her parents' garageless five-room ranch and treeless lawn in a lower-class suburb into one of the tenements on Massasoyit Street. It gave her a unique insight into the feelings of the poor, the disadvantaged, the rejected. Just as the unbearable suffering of her lonely adolescence allowed her, she knew, to understand the pain of the crippled and afflicted.

She loved the children passionately. Desperately. Like a second family.

They did not, she suspected, love her. She knew she was easier to manipulate than even Susan Meiers, but the children meant no harm in doing it. It was a matter of survival instincts for them, not personalities. When she'd first come, she'd tried to make them call her Sister Kitty the way they had in her convent classroom, or at least Sister Cathy. They had tried, but behind her back they had experimented with "Brow" and "Beard" and had finally settled on "Froggie."

She knew about it. She considered it a playfully affectionate reference to the lovable gremlin on *Smilin' Ed and His Gang.*

She had never considered that Smilin' Ed was from the Saturday mornings of her own childhood, not theirs.

She realized suddenly that she had reached the schoolyard. There was no daycare on Saturdays, but a few boys had apparently scaled the chain-link fence to play basketball. The asphalt playground echoed with the portavee they had set out of the way on a bench to keep them company.

> *You are the lightbulb in the socket of my day-ay,*
> *You are the rainbow in my sky-iy. . . .*

Children today couldn't be without electronic sights and sounds, not even for a minute. She waved hello. When they didn't respond, she called to them.

They stopped playing, let the ball roll away, and came reluctantly toward her. She knew them all; they were older boys who had long ago ceased to need daycare, but she still remembered each one's name.

"Asshole," she heard one whisper to another, "I *told* you if you peed against the wall she'd see you. Her apartment's right up there."

She glanced behind them at the brick wall, saw the irregular wet stain. She wished they wouldn't use that word. She wished they'd say "urinate."

"Playing ball?" she called cheerily.

One of them shrugged, looking over his shoulder at the basketball hoop and ball, still rolling. "Kind of."

"That's good," she said. "I've always thought it was a shame the way they locked up the playground on weekends. Where's Ronnie? Doesn't he usually play ball with you? He got a girlfriend now?" She tried to sound playful, to catch the spirit of boys at the age where girls were anathema, remembering too late that feelings like that had been common in her day but that times had changed.

"Ain't you heard?" one of them said. "Ronnie's gone."

"Gone where?"

"Where else? Saucers."

"That's terrible," she said. It was like being crushed by some huge weight loaded onto her ounce by ounce; she grabbed hold of the chain-link fence to keep from falling. On the portavee beyond she could see another of Doctor Love's commercials flash, hear the reassuring drone of his voice.

"No, it ain't. Makes as much sense as hanging around."

"You give me your word, now. You promise you won't go off

143

like that. That's faith misplaced. No flying saucers are going to come and take anybody away.''

They nodded, but she could feel the psychic tugging; they wanted to get back to their game, were afraid to because if they offended her she could always call the police and report them for trespassing. She tried for a few more minutes to engage them, but they would not meet her eyes, and at last she said goodbye and went to the apartment building next to the schoolyard, the one on whose brick side one of them had urinated.

Imagine, right out in broad daylight. No one would have dreamed of such a thing when she was a girl. But then, no one would have dreamed of seeing private parts flaunted on television, either.

Finding an efficiency apartment right next door had been a real stroke of luck. Almost like the old days, she thought, fumbling for her key to the outer door. Like the sisters' dormitory overlooking the classroom building.

She let herself in, checked her empty mailbox (well, wasn't that silly of her when there were no mail deliveries on Saturdays, hadn't been for years?), and went up the stairs to her room. It was like all the other furnished efficiencies: a bed, table, straight chair, built-in range and refrigerator, bathroom behind an accordion vinyl curtain. The only individualizing touches she had allowed herself were a crucifix over the bed and the threadbare coverlet her mother had sent her during her novitiate so long ago and the Mother Superior had consented to her keeping. It had seemed such a luxury then.

The room's solitary joy was its window overlooking the playground. Even when she had fallen ill this past year, she'd been cheered because she could still hear the sounds of the children playing below. She paused at the window, watching the boys scuffle beneath the basket until one of them wrestled the ball away and shot, and then she crossed the room to her bed.

It was time for her devotions, self-imposed since the dissolution of the Order, and today's were especially significant because she wanted to add a prayer for Ronnie, the latest of the lost lambs. The prayer would give today's devotions a special virtue.

Her devotional formula was like an author's creating a character. She tried to put herself in some saint's place and imagine the sensations and emotions he or she would have felt.

As devotional objects she avoided the too elevated and remote—Mary and Christ. It would have been too great a

144

presumption. Her first favorite was still her namesake, Saint Catherine. Again she tasted the triumph of refuting the elders and scholars in debate, the delicious agony of torture, the renewed triumph of feeling the wheel on which she was to be broken break beneath her, the brief and shimmering moment of pain as the ax severed her head from her body, the ground rushing up to meet her dimming eyes. Would her face feel the impact? And then the glory of her apotheosis, the ecstasy and perfection of her mystic marriage and union with Christ while at the same time, down below, she was a strangely sentient corpse rocked gently by angels as they carried her to Mount Sinai, where Moses had received the Commandments.

Now she turned to her second favorite, the Holy Innocents. She felt herself flung to the floor, felt her body's crevice begin to close and then well out tender and exposed and hairless (had he really done that, peed against her wall?). And she lay naked and abandoned on a straw mat in the cool shadow of the mud brick wall, a Jewish boy waiting, hearing Herod's cruel soldiers outside in the street, knowing that death was coming, but ignorant of the Christ for whom he/she was to die and who even now journeyed with his parents into Egypt, forewarned of Herod's plan to slaughter all male infants, abandoning him/her. The doomed boy that was Sister Catherine waited for the door to slam open and for the rough, armored men to enter, all unyielding planes and angles, to snatch him up and hold him by the legs, slashing and cutting, arms, legs, sex. An exquisite agony of innocent suffering, Christ's first martyr.

Now she was whole again, growing larger, hairier, clad in clothes of hairy skins. *He's coming,* she heard herself cry in a deep male voice. *I am not the Christ,* she protested. Again her head on the block, again the swift, electric slice of the sword. *I am the voice of one crying in the wilderness,* her disembodied head sang from the silver platter. *Make straight the way of the Lord as said the prophet Isaiah.*

Behind her she heard the whirring and rumbling as He rode His cross, lying spread upon it, supine, the cross floating horizontal, bottom first down from its hill. Faster and faster he slid toward her.

Behold the Lamb of God, which taketh away the sin of the world, cried her head, but already it was slicing toward her like some primitive, alien flying machine. The air crackled with its approach.

145

Later, trembling, Sister Catherine slid from the bed and sank to her knees to pray. For Ronnie. For charity toward boys that did things against walls, for charity even toward those poor deluded misleaders of children. And then she sought with all her concentration to empty herself, the sweat forming on her forehead and along her upper lip, listening for some sign that she had been heard.

"Don't do that." A voice from far away. Outside. "You want her to catch you again?"

"Who?"

"Froggie."

Sister Catherine's eyes filled with tears.

15

Library Work

Santalucia straightened up, wiped off the surgical jelly, and pulled up his pants.

"Prostate's distended and boggy," the urologist said, stripping the rubber glove from his machine.

"Boggy? What should I do?"

"Take a hot sitz bath every night." The doctor wheeled his machine back from the table, pneumatic arm bouncing, and parked it by the waste basket.

"What about coffee? My last urologist back east—"

"What difference does coffee make?" the doctor demanded impatiently. His consultation hall's cubicles were overflowing with other patients. "It's a diuretic, maybe, but it's got nothing to do with the prostate."

Santalucia thought gloomily of all the mornings he'd felt guilty about a half-cup of coffee. "And liquor?"

"Same thing. You've got a bacteriological infection there, my friend. Drink anything you want to. I'll punch you out a prescription for Minocin."

Santalucia watched sourly as the doctor went to his office terminal. After sitting out the flight from New York to Denver in agony, oppressed by all the woolly sweaters and heavy boots of the vacation skiers, he had called the first urologist in the phone book as soon as he and Circe had landed, while Circe had rented a little electric car and gone off to see what she could find out at the Slim-Vu plant.

It was not clear to Santalucia whether his prostate attack had been the result of too much bourbon or the fact that, when he'd last checked his abandoned apartment, still torn apart by his

147

uninvited guests from Faith Ltd., he'd found a message from Martha that she'd phoned in a divorce and gotten a final decree.

What the hell, it had been a stormy marriage anyway, and it had lasted five times longer than the average. Five years with anyone was a goddamned lifetime.

On his way out with his printed prescription, Santalucia paused for the nurse to imprint the bill with his credit card, then pushed through the double doors into the December cold. His face tingled in the frigid Denver air.

Hot baths—was that the best medical science could offer? He couldn't even get two doctors to agree on the rest of the treatment—no coffee, all the coffee he wanted; no bourbon, drown in bourbon. He was no longer sure whether he hated Doctor Love for wanting to be a religious dictator or because he had once been a urologist.

The doctor's office was in a neat little house on what had once been a residential street bordering the University of Denver, and Santalucia had arranged to meet Circe at the university's library. He climbed the slight rise onto the campus, his lower abdomen heavy as lead, mulling over the fact that he hadn't bought a single Christmas present for Erin.

His mistake—Personal Enrichment Day, she and her mother were calling it now.

The frozen grassy knoll doubled as a kind of park for local residents, and by a boulder next to the pathway a small black boy, apparently playing hookey from school, was winging gravel at some pigeons.

"Hey," the child called. "You got a dollar for a brother?"

He shook his head; he hated that kind of assumed bond. "I'm not your brother," he muttered. "Anyway, I only carry plastic."

Further on, he paused to watch more of the mangy pigeons, feathers ruffled by the wind, troop tiredly across the dirt, staying safely out of range. They eyed him carefully to see if he might throw them something edible, as though they had some genetic memory of how prodigal past generations had extravagantly thrown bread and popcorn to their ancestors.

"Sorry, brothers," he said. "Catch you next incarnation."

Vaguely he became aware of something behind him. He turned quickly, found only a tall young man in a large, floppy hat coming toward him, reaching from tree to tree, his breathing congealing into little clouds behind him. At first Santalucia thought the man was drunk or drugged out, but then he realized

148

he was simply groping: he couldn't see. A beggar of some kind? Welfare kept most of them off the streets, and this fellow didn't really look like a bum, anyway. His clothes were worn, but relatively clean, and his fine hair and beard seemed freshly washed.

"Somebody here?" said the young man, reaching out. He had run out of trees.

When Santalucia stepped forward to help him, he saw the young man's head move in response, as though he'd seen him. No, Santalucia thought, the angle of the head was wrong, but maybe he could see light or moving shadows. "I'm here," he said. "You looking for someplace to sit down?" The young man nodded, and Santalucia took his hand to lead him to a bench just off the path.

"You a student here?" Santalucia asked.

"N-no," the man said. "Who n-needs that shit?"

"Professors, I guess," Santalucia said. He watched the pigeons for a moment. "You around here during the explosion?" he asked, partly to make conversation and partly on the off chance he might pick up something useful. One of the reasons he'd come to Denver, after all, was to see if somehow the explosions and fires across half a city could have been engineered as a cover for the Monad's assassination, and if so, whether any connection to Doctor Love might exist.

"Explosions?" the man said. "You mean the *rays* when the Dinks killed the Monad?"

So, a member of the Saucer Cult, Santalucia thought. He caught a glimpse of the eyes as the man spoke. The pupils were cloudy, gray. "They said on TV it was exploding gas or something. I never heard anything about any rays."

"L-look," said the man, suddenly agitated. "I *saw* it. That's how I lost my eyes, in fact. I was right on the edge, and the ray just brushed me."

People didn't lose their sight in gas and oil fires, Santalucia thought. Not unless they were badly burned, and this kid didn't have any scar tissue on his face. "There *were* explosions, though, right?"

"Sure, l-lots of them, and fires. Saw a helicopter fly through the beam and get fried and blow up."

"When it flew through the flames?"

"N-no, man, it was an air taxi, way up. Nowhere n-near the flames. It flew through the ray."

Santalucia thought for a moment. "Could you actually *see* this ray? Was it red or green or what?"

"No, it was like invisible. Or more like it was *brighter* than the sky. It's hard to s-say. I just wish I knew whether it was the D-dinks down here that did it, or they sent ships from Pluto or somewhere. Cause there was all this cosmic energy everywhere. It was like lightning jumping from c-cars to streetlamps and sewer covers, and puddles turning to steam and metal getting red hot—"

Santalucia scowled. Well, Martha had been right about one thing: the video coverage of the Denver disaster had been doctored. Assuming, of course, that the kid wasn't crazy and was telling the truth.

"I gather you're still a member of the Cult," Santalucia said. "Losing your eyesight and your leader hasn't discouraged you, just made you more certain?"

"Look, she *said* she'd get killed. The fact they murdered her just *proves* everything. You'll see when the Mothership comes and b-beams me up and I g-get a new body and everything."

"What kind of bullshit is that?" Santalucia demanded, surprised by his own sudden anger. "Why don't you just face the fact no superbeings are going to come down and rescue you or me from this mess? We're stuck with things the way they are. We either live with it or we make it better. It's that simple."

"Then why've people been seeing UFO's in C-California?" the man said. "If that doesn't *p-prove* the Beings from the other Dimension aren't here already and waiting, I d-don't know what does."

"Look," Santalucia said, trying to be more reasonable. "If there *were* beings from the fourth dimension or whatever it is, we couldn't begin to comprehend them."

"The Monad comprehended them fine."

"But you know that old saw about how the inhabitants of a two-dimensional world could imprison a criminal by drawing a square around him, but three-dimensional creatures like us could just step over the line. Now think about how those two-dimensional people would see us. They'd be living on a plane, and if you stuck your finger into their world, all they'd see would be a line that was a cross-section of your finger where it intersected their plane. If you stuck your other fingers in, they'd see the other fingers as separate lines; they have no way of

150

knowing those lines were related unless you went in further, and suddenly those five lines would merge into one huge line. They'd be frantic.''

Santalucia glanced over to see how the young man was taking what he said, but he was sitting hunched forward, the hat obscuring his face.

"It's possible, I guess, that when our radar picks up blips taking ninety-degree turns at two thousand kilometers an hour, we might be seeing parts of one fourth-dimensional craft moving at conventional speeds, but there's still no way for us to comprehend that, let alone communicate—''

"I don't need to listen to this *shit!*'' the man said, standing up and angrily pushing Santalucia aside. "I g-got enough troubles. I'm c-cut off from the other Seekers, and the B-beaming's close—hear that, nigger? The Mothership's coming any day!''

He stalked away along the path.

"All right!'' Santalucia shouted after him. "You just go on living in that fairyland of yours! Suit yourself!''

It took him a moment to realize that in the man's anger he was negotiating the path without groping or faltering. And it wasn't until he'd disappeared that Santalucia thought to wonder how a blind man had known to call him "nigger.''

He shrugged and headed for the library. Wouldn't it be a joke if after all these years it turned out that the KKK had been right and black people *did* smell different? Jesus Christ, it sounded like something he might have written in one of his books.

Well, the hell with it. They'd have recall terminals for periodicals at the library, reference works. What the blind man had said about cars being energized enough to discharge into grounded metal, about puddles vaporizing, about his own blindness—there was a pattern there, some thread that tied the whole thing together.

It sounded, in fact, like microwave radiation. Except that the only thing capable of delivering that kind of radiation over so large an area was Denver's pride and joy—the world's first commercial solar satellite, traveling in synchronous orbit to keep the homes and offices of Denver warm and bright.

He was turned away at the door for not having a student ID. He finally managed to bribe a student to bring him in as a guest, paid her off just out of sight of the circulation desk, and took the elevator to the periodicals floor. Luckily, one of the terminals was

151

open. He slipped into the cushioned chair, got the bibliographical request code from the instructions on the wall, and punched in for anything on solar-power satellite systems.

Article titles ticked onto the liquid crystal display. *New York Times, Washington Post, Scientific American, Ecology Today, Aviation Week, Space Research, Aerospace Monthly.* He called for those that looked promising, skimming the words as they rolled up across the screen. Most of what he read he knew already, background stories about experiments in the late eighties with dish antennae seven kilometers across to pick up beams of ten or twenty-five milliwatts per square centimeter from photoelectric satellites with collector panels also seven kilometers across. These early jobs had been prefabbed and assembled in orbit, and then pushed out to 320 kilometers with permanent crews to monitor wobble, minimize error, and do repairs.

But despite protests from conservationists, they had turned to more powerful beams from ever closer orbits; power loss being the reciprocal of the square of the distance meant that only twenty-five percent of the power from the satellite could reach a dish antenna 320 kilometers away.

Eventually they'd come up with the heavier but smaller Denver prototype, an unmanned parabolic mirror that focused the sun's heat into molten lithium that was pumped through ceramic ducts to a thermo-electric device which sent a beam of 2.4 watts per square centimeter back to an 800-meter dish on earth.

Again the conservationists had protested—that the microwave radiation was dangerous and might damage the delicate flora and fauna of the Rockies near Boulder, that the tremendous booster rockets to put it in orbit could cause the damage of an atomic bomb if they strayed before expending their millions of gallons of oxygen and hydrogen, that the satellite itself, designed to withstand intense heat, would be invulnerable to reentry damage and when its orbit decayed would come in like a single meteor of thousands of tons, enough to flatten a huge area.

To the last question, Solarsystems International offered no answer. To the problem of booster rockets, they responded by mining and processing the raw materials and actually fabricating the satellite on the moon, where the one-sixth gravity demanded far less power to boost the satellite into an appropriate orbit. And to the problem of acquiring enough land in the Rockies, it turned out that Solarsystems International had in fact held large contiguous tracts around Boulder for many years.

But nowhere was there anything on the *effects* of microwave radiation, Santalucia found, except the unsubstantiated claims of environmentalists. He punched in a request for hard data on biological effects of microwave radiation in any scientific study done during the last ten years.

"NONE," the screen flashed.

He slumped back in his chair. Nothing on a subject so crucial? It was as though all research in the area had been banned. Or at least classified. He asked the computer for the same information over a twenty-five year span.

This time more titles ticked onto the screen. *New York State Journal of Medicine, Journal of Occupational Medicine, Aerospace Medicine,* assorted government publications.

He scanned one after another. Many dealt with the question of what constituted safe and lethal doses. The U.S. military claimed ten milliwatts per square centimeter was a safe maximum, the Consumer Protection Agency settled on five milliwatts as safe leakage from a microwave oven, and the Russians declared no more than one milliwatt per square centimeter was safe, and proceeded to zap the U.S. Embassy building in Moscow.

Next came articles dealing with microwave radiation symptoms: diseases of the blood vessels, disturbances in the body's heat conduction systems, nerve disturbances, something they called "mental inertia," even insanity. And cataracts.

No doubt about it. Whether the beam came from a flying saucer or the satellite, it was microwave radiation. Those gray pupils had to mean cataracts. That would explain why he'd sometimes seemed to have some vision—he could distinguish light and shadow through the cataracts. Poor kid. If he'd gone to a doctor, he could probably have had surgery and gotten his eyes fixed as soon as there was an opening on one of the CLASS eye machines.

Here was something—some scientist roasting rats in styrofoam containers. Not only did it look like a fascinating and rewarding hobby, but it provided Santalucia with an equally fascinating conclusion: rats heavier than 195 grams died faster than rats that weighed less. And at .165 watts, it took 40 minutes to kill a rat, but only 35 minutes to kill a rabbit. At a third of a watt you could kill a guinea pig in 17.5 minutes and a dog in only 15.

Santalucia paused. At two watts per square centimeter . . . well, he'd have to figure out the volume of an average human being to compare it to the charts in the article and he hadn't the vaguest notion how to begin, but it looked like if the same curve applied, it would only take a minute or two for a beam that powerful to kill a human being.

Of course, this still didn't prove any connection with Doctor Love or even that the disaster had been planned. What it did prove was that everyone in authority had lied about what had happened, and even suppressed any of the telltale details from the news coverage. But Santalucia never expected anything more than venality in his fellow humans, so he assured himself that none of this bothered him any more than any other academic exercise in logic. The key element, however, was whether he could trust what the young man had told him in the park. That would mean going down to the Solarsystems Tower and seeing if there were any physical evidence of microwave radiation. It was a long shot: whether it had been the satellite beam or something else, the fires and explosions that had been touched off had been real enough, and they might well have obscured any traces of what had caused them.

He felt a hand on his shoulder.

"I figured you'd still be here," Circe said.

"You bribe a student, too?"

"What for?" she asked. "They let me right in."

Well, that was the price he paid for looking furtive and ratlike, he thought.

"So did the doctor say you were okay?" she asked.

"Yeah, I'm great. What did you turn up at the Slim-Vu plant?"

"Very heavy security," Circe said. "But the sign outside the plant is a little more explicit than we'd expected, considering the stone wall we ran into in New York. It says they're a subsidiary of Sylvania-GE. Since corporate forecasting's my former special-ty, I can tell you Sylvania-GE is owned by Leisuretime Industries—"

"The people that make Tips Condoms?" he asked.

"I wouldn't know."

"Neither would I anymore."

"Pardon? Anyway, Leisuretime is a General Foods company."

"And General Foods is owned by Professor Moriarty, Sherlock Holmes's arch-enemy?"

"General Foods," Circe said slowly, "is owned by Solarsystems

154

International. So in addition to HED batteries, Zapstops, and the rest, they own—"

"The world's first city-sized death ray."

"I don't follow you," Circe said. "I was talking about Slim-Vu."

"I thought you were supposed to read minds or something," Santalucia said. "Never mind, I can lay it out for you in a minute. But first, I'd like you to help me go over the newspaper accounts and try to make up some kind of map of the areas that were destroyed—see if there's any kind of pattern. Then I'd like to swing down to the Solarsystems Tower and see what there is to see. Their connection with Doctor Love's Slim-Vu makes it all very interesting."

16

Taking Flack

"You seem a lot more interested in this than you were in New York," Circe observed, negotiating the Denver traffic. An old fly-wheel job had gotten in front of her and she was watching for a chance to get around it.

"It's just the hunter in me," Santalucia said. "In fact, I still don't give a shit what happens to the Cultists or anyone else."

"I can't believe that."

"Believe it," Santalucia said. How did you explain what it was like to have been a black man raised by white parents, cut off from both races by background on one hand and pigmentation on the other? It took a long time to learn to live with that kind of isolation; it took even longer to learn to love the protection it afforded. "I just happened to run into one of them this morning, and if it was up to me, I'd dump them all in the Gulf Stream."

If Erin were older, he thought, she might have been one of them.

The Solarsystems Tower was not terribly distinguished as corporate headquarters went. It was the standard monolith of prefab forms, solar panels, and windows. It showed little or no signs of damage, though burned-out buildings and boarded-up shells clustered around it on every side.

After a quick glance in at the Solarsystems lobby, carpeted with brown-uniformed security officers, Santalucia led the way to the Conyers Building next door.

"Why don't we start with a look from the top of this one?" he said. "See what there is to see—scout out the enemy before we confront him."

They took the elevator to the top floor of vacated offices and found the stairs to the roof. At one time access had been barred by a locked fire door, but the metal door had fallen from its hinges in the heat of a flash fire and hung askew, a broom still leaning against it, handle charred black where it had rested against the metal.

"It really is a lovely city, still," Circe said when they had gained the roof, peering across the vista of Denver against the dust-gray sky.

"And it was mighty hot here," Santalucia said, pointing to where the roofing tar had melted and sagged around the metal weather stripping, and to where the bricks by the metal roofing sheets had been scorched.

With their rough map of the areas of destruction gleaned from newspaper accounts, they studied the panorama below. At first the devastation seemed random and general, but as they began adding to their map the damage that was still visible but which the newspaper accounts had omitted, a rough pattern seemed to emerge, something like the arms of a fourteen-pointed star radiating outward from the area of the Solarsystems Tower. One of the arms, however, had not stopped in the city; it had continued outward and ended somewhere in the distance at the campground to the south where the Monad and hundreds of her followers had died.

Santalucia moved toward the edge of the roof to get a better look at the Solarsystems Tower itself. If there had been much damage over there, Solarsystems had spared no expense to get it repaired; if there hadn't, it would raise an interesting question. No, he remembered accounts of the injured being taken from the building. He could see nothing across the way but the usual roof ducts, solar panels, and a cluster of communications microwave horns atop masts.

Suddenly he found himself sprawled flat on the roof.

"You all right?" Circe laughed.

"Loose piece of roofing," Santalucia muttered. "Caught my foot. That's another thing my ex-wife hated about me. Clumsy."

All at once Circe stopped laughing. "It was deliberately loosened," she said. "I can feel it."

Grudgingly, Santalucia examined the flap of metal. She was a good kid, but he was sick and tired of all this witchcraft crap. "No sign of it. There aren't any scrapes or tears like a crowbar would make. Looks to me like the metal just worked loose in a storm, say, and—"

"No, it *was* done on purpose," she insisted. "Look how many nails would have to work loose—there's a good two meters of it that's free. That's just *too* much coincidence."

"I thought you were a great believer in coincidence," Santalucia said. "Anyway, it would be a pretty dumb joke thirty stories up. I'm afraid the point eludes me." But as he spoke the Solarsystems microwave horns happened to catch his eye again. "Wait a minute. The satellite's homing device uses a microwave loop that originates here and runs to the satellite via a relay at the Boulder dish. If somebody held this piece of roofing up somehow, it could block the beam. Which way is Boulder?"

The direction in which Circe pointed formed a line that ran straight across the loose piece of roof to the microwave horns. "I see it . . . rising and falling," she said, eyes closed.

Santalucia frowned. "There was a storm that day, a bad one. If the wind pulled this strip of roofing up enough to deflect the beam, then when the satellite went into a search mode, somebody could set up a decoy beam somewhere else and get the satellite to lock onto it. If they had just the right frequency, and the transmitter were in a van parked at the Monad's camp, say . . . Except that wouldn't explain why Denver itself was hit."

"What if it were an accident?" Circe suggested. "What if that was their plan but there was some kind of foul-up?"

Santalucia thought for a moment. "You know, it's just possible that if this piece of roofing were held at the right angle, it could deflect the beam directly to the satellite. Let's say they pried this piece of roofing up and trusted the wind to make it flap enough to interrupt the beam, figuring that if anybody checked it out, the more things that could be passed off as accidents and coincidences, the more easily they could cover their tracks."

"Except the decoy beam wasn't turned on when it was supposed to be," Circe said.

"Right. So this beam was deflected up to the satellite, the satellite locked onto it, and Denver started to cook. But as the roof kept flapping and changing angles in the wind, the satellite would drift off, but still sending its beam for sixty seconds. Then the angle would be right again, and the satellite would focus back here."

"Fourteen times," Circe said. "It kept coming back and drifting off."

"Thirteen," Santalucia corrected. "The fourteenth time it was finally locked on the decoy beam. If I remember what I read this

158

morning, at the SCAT satellite's altitude of a hundred-fifty kilometers, it would take only a slight shift to move the beam. If it traveled at, say, fifty kilometers an hour, the eight-hundred-meter diameter of the beam would take a full minute to pass over—more than enough time to fry a human being."

"Well, that settles it," Circe said. "Let's go see the brass at Solarsystems International and tell them what's happened."

"Are you kidding? They *know* what's happened—they did it themselves. Or they ordered a crew to do it."

"Impossible," Circe said. "They're a major corporation. They've been *used*, that's all. Obviously Faith Limited planted stooges in Solarsystems—*you're* the one that told me how those Lovebands can control people. The stooges are the ones that sabotaged the satellite, just the way they've been making unauthorized modifications to the TV sets manufactured at Slim-Vu. We'll help management launch an investigation and bring the whole plot out into the open."

"I wish I had your faith," Santalucia said.

"Look, I've been dealing with American business for five years. Do you really think the chairman of the board at Solarsystems gets up every morning trying to think of ways he can hurt people?"

Santalucia shrugged. "It's not inconceivable," he said.

Their reception in the lobby of the Solarsystems Tower was something less than Circe had hoped for.

"Look, lady, you don't just walk in here and see somebody," the guard at the desk said. "You call ahead, you make an appointment, you get security clearance. . . ."

"But we know what caused the explosions," Circe protested. "We have *evidence* that the SCAT satellite was sabotaged and redirected—"

Santalucia noticed another of the guards tapping in a number on his phone. Calling upstairs, no doubt. "Hey, no problem," Santalucia smiled. "We'll just be on our way and call for an appointment later, okay?"

Down the corridor from the security desk, Santalucia saw four more brown-shirted security men step off the elevator.

"Anyway, we had a long night flight out from New York," Santalucia babbled, "and we really need to freshen up."

The second guard whispered something to the one at the desk.

159

"All right," the first one said. "As it happens someone *will* see you. Those officers down there will escort you up. May I see your briefcases?"

"I *knew* I forgot something," Santalucia said. "Let me go back and get it."

The four guards were approaching the desk.

"Actually, I think this could be handled adequately with just a short note. Let me stop by a printer's and order some letterhead stationery—"

Circe kicked him in the shins.

"You can come with us," the first of the four guards said.

It seemed to Santalucia that the man was not sincere about the degree of choice usually associated with the word can. But then, the average person's command of language was down the shit-can along with everything else these days.

Circe smiled reassuringly and stepped around the desk to follow the guards.

Crowded into the elevator with the guards, there was no way for Santalucia to convey his rage to Circe, but if he survived this walk into the lion's mouth, he intended to have a lot to say to her about avoiding obvious traps, looking before one leaped. . . .

They got off at the twenty-ninth floor, but Santalucia was too nervous even to notice the title on the door through which they were ushered. A broad-faced, gangly woman rose to greet them. She looked like a retired army colonel and obviously dressed by the book—in this case, *Dress for Success—2000*—in a smart business sweat suit.

"First of all," the woman said in a rich contralto, "I wanted to thank you for coming forward to share your concerns with us."

Santalucia groaned inwardly; the woman sounded exactly like everyone at RR&D. Obviously she'd had a lot of Communications Arts training.

"Solarsystems International wants to do everything in its power to encourage an open-ended dialogue with responsible sectors of the consuming public at large. Won't you have a seat?"

Santalucia sat next to Circe on the edge of a straight, functional, comfortless chair. To one side of him was a picture-window view of the Denver skyline, to the other a coffee table strewn with colorful brochures—*Power from Old Sol, New Horizons in Home Heating, HED Batteries: Traveling Trouble-Free the Modern Way, Zapstop Story, Tips on Tips: Carefree, Child-free, and Disease-Free*, and *Slim-Vu: New Slant on an Old Medium*, and the Shape of Things to Come.

So, he thought, they'd been brought to the PR flack. That explained it—they were invariably retired colonels dressing for a shot at the company presidency and unaware that PR was a managerial dead end. But at least he and Circe hadn't been taken to the VP for Rubbish Disposal; that meant they were being treated as no worse than average meddlers. "I take it you're not the chairman of the board," Santalucia said to make sure Circe could see how much Solarsystems cared about what they had to say.

"I'm here to make things happen in the public relations area," the woman beamed. "Now, our security persons downstairs told me that you had a totally new and unique line on the gas fires and explosions this past summer."

Circe nodded and summarized their conclusions, ignoring Santalucia's frantic eyebrow-waggling signals to say as little as possible.

"What I hear you saying," the woman said, "is that it's your feeling that someone *or ones* actually *misdirected* our SCAT satellite?"

"That's the long of it," Santalucia said.

"I'm so *glad* you brought these feelings to my attention," gushed the woman "So *many* people have similar mis-information about the mechanics of synchronous-orbit collector satellites that I feel genuinely *lucky* to have this chance to share with you how these things actually operate. You see, our SCAT satellite is a marvel of modern mechanical and electronic artistry. Its onboard laser gyroscope and computer make an error such as you've imagined *impossible*."

She smiled and made appropriate eye contact with each before she continued. "Moreover, access to the ground-control override and backup navigational computer is strictly limited to appropriate senior officers of the corporation. So you'll agree that there's no way the SCAT satellite could have been linked in any way with the rupturing and explosion of Denver's antiquated gas lines and oil storage systems. You *do* see that, don't you?"

"What I saw," Circe said, "was evidence of someone blocking the homing beam, and what I *felt*—"

"Was that you're absolutely right," Santalucia interrupted. "I think the best thing is for us just to forget about this whole thing."

"I'm so glad you shared that particular insight with me, Mr., ah . . ."

"Milton," Santalucia smiled. "John Milton."

"Mr. Milton. And I'd like to piggyback on your thought just far enough to suggest that perhaps this kind of misconception oughtn't go beyond these four walls, if you follow my train of thought here."

"I couldn't agree with you more," Santalucia said.

"Woody!" the woman grinned. "As the kids say nowadays. But let me give you some brochures, our annual report. . . ." The woman ducked behind her desk and emerged with a handful of booklets from a hidden supply by her feet.

"Jesus," Santalucia breathed, once more safely in their rented car beside Circe. He was reading one of the brochures as she drove. "Did you know their Tips subsidiary makes a whole line of HED marital aids and inflatable Fetish-Mates? They also own—"

"I don't see why you wouldn't let me press the point," Circe said.

"Because her job was to make us drop the subject, forget about it. If we didn't—"

"I read her face," Circe said. "She wasn't hiding anything—she believed she was telling us the truth. If we'd taken the trouble to convince her—"

"Jesus Christ," Santalucia snorted. "Mind-reading again. All right, maybe she was honest. But if we hadn't agreed with her, we'd have had trouble leaving the building. We'd have been passed from one VP to the next until we ran into somebody that knew what had to be done with us."

"Typical anti-corporate bias," Circe said.

Santalucia snorted again and went back to the brochure. "Get this—they make a line of designer cake mixes, they own hotels in the Bahamas, they've got drilling rights in Arkansas, they—"

"What do you say we get a hotel room?" Circe yawned. "I haven't slept since New York."

"That's your first good idea since you led me into the snake pit at Solarsystems."

They took a room at the Brown Palace, and Santalucia called room service for two oat-burgers, drinking water, and some ounce bottles of bourbon. Then he called Fred the tech freak in

New York. Not that Fred had any real interest in anything that didn't carry a current, but, with Martha gone, Santalucia felt better having at least one person he trusted know exactly where he was. Fred was out, so he left a message with his room number on Fred's scratchbuilt homeputer, then flicked on the Fednews cable channel and lay back on the bed.

The TV was carrying something about a famine somewhere in Africa. Santalucia watched the pans across dark faces with bulging eyes, and swollen stomachs, sparse curly hair, thin arms, bony fingers. He thought of the kid on the knoll this morning. His brothers and sisters, some might say.

Still underdeveloped, still doubling their populations in less than thirty years. They'd flung themselves into industrialization by fiat and edict from straw-hut capitals, but then oil prices had soared, and eventually oil itself had disappeared. The industrialized nations, preoccupied with converting to flywheel engines and nuclear power, and then HED batteries and solar power, had refused to help them. Meanwhile, the land taken out of production for industrial sites and the farmers turned into factory workers had meant food shortages, compounded by over-intensive farming of the remaining land with chemical fertilizers and miracle crop strains. When the fertilizers had been cut off, the miracle crops hadn't been able to grow. Famine.

He felt that he ought to feel sorrier for those children than he did. But were they really better off than their American peers, whose fuller bellies had given them emptier heads? Which was worse, a physical death or a mental one? Whether it was a matter of food or thought, the modern world had become a place defined mainly by its deficiencies, its shortages, and its vacuums.

He tapped the remote control to change to one of the commercial channels. He ran the risk of a Doctor Love megahype, but at least he wouldn't have to look at things that, despite his every effort, troubled him.

When he got up the energy, he'd take a sitz bath. Shit, he'd forgotten to get the Minocin prescription filled.

"What do you know," Circe was saying, chewing on her oat-burger. "That woman gave us the annual report and their Ten-K supplement."

"What's a Ten-K supplement, some kind of vitamin?" He wondered if you could get antibiotics from room service.

"A form they file with IRS and distribute to stockholders.

163

Complete financial report—major products, plant locations, that kind of thing."

Take a Tip form Charlie! said the TV. *Tips is the brief one, but it gets the job done!*

"Oh, my aching infection," Santalucia groaned.

"Let's see," Circe said. "Common stock, debentures, outstanding debts, locations, five-year summary of product lines, assets and liabilities. . . ."

"Is that the Ten-K?"

"No," she said. "This is the annual report. Did you know they own acreage in forty-six states?"

"Probably land acquisitions for receiving dishes," Santalucia said. "You too can have a death ray in your back yard. That's why they're so anxious not to admit any connection between their satellite and those fires. According to one of the articles I saw this morning, they have five years to prove this thing's safe before they get monopoly rights to set up in the rest of the states."

"Now you can understand why they wouldn't dream of sabotaging their own satellite," Circe said. "Now let's see . . . Research and Development . . . Parent Company and Subsidiaries. . . ."

"Aha! Who actually owns it?"

"Nobody. But *this* is interesting."

"What's that?" Santalucia was having trouble focusing on the TV screen. The TV penis had just gone sproi-yoi-yoing again.

"The board of directors. Did you know that Leonard Percy is on the board?"

"If you're talking about the head of Ritual Research and Development at Faith Limited, the operative verb is 'was.' "

"I keep forgetting that," Circe said. "Anyway, his name's right here. And so is that expert in history, Stanfield."

Santalucia sat up. "You recognize any other names?"

"As a matter of fact, I do. There's someone here I met in their Marketing Department and—do you realize what this means?"

"It means exactly what I thought," Santalucia said. "Faith Limited is a tool of Solarsystems International. Corporate interests in the religion biz."

"That's not how these interlocking directorates operate," Circe said. "Percy's the only one actually listed as an employee of Faith Limited. The others have listings like 'Demographics Consultant' and so on. But for a bunch of middle-level management people from one firm to be on the board of directors of another means that *Solarsystems* is the satellite. Of the Love church.''

"Jesus, is Doctor Love on the board, too?"

"Not by name. I wish I had access to tape two of Standard and Poor's,'' she said. "Maybe there's a general access terminal in the lobby. It would be interesting to know what other boards these guys sit on.''

—Cult is on the move again, the TV was saying. *Instead of dwindling, as many analysts had expected after the death of its Pied Piper, this Children's Crusade has swollen to amazing proportions, and Texas Rangers have virtually given up on periodic ID checks to track runaways, much to the despair of parents nationwide—*

"You know what happened to the last Children's Crusade?'' Santalucia said. "They went out to show what innocence and purity could do, and a bunch of religious grownups slaughtered them. Which just shows you the relative positions of innocence and swords in the Great Chain of Being.''

The TV screen flickered with shots of the caravan, ancient trucks and cars overflowing with children and young adults while others trudged on foot.

—estimates running into the tens of thousands, the TV droned on, *as after a series of increasingly bloody clashes with local residents and personnel from Amarillo Air Force base they have apparently decided to head northward, for some as yet unspecified and perhaps undetermined destination. Meanwhile, reported UFO sightings continue to deluge authorities in several—*

"It's so sad,'' Circe said, laying her hand on Santalucia's shoulder. "And I'll bet anything those so-called clashes weren't accidental.''

Santalucia lay back and turned toward the wall. A moment later he felt Circe lie down behind him, the TV still on, and snuggle up against his back. He could feel the hard rim of that stupid bell she wore around her neck pressing between his shoulder blades. Then he felt her hand moving along his thigh, upwards, then slipping under the elastic waistband of his underpants.

"Look, no offense,'' he said, rubbing his eyes, "but I really can't.'' He rolled onto his back to look at her.

She extracted her hand from under his weight. "I thought we'd been getting really close,'' she said.

"It's not that," he said, "though in point of fact we barely know each other."

"It's just the stuff about those kids makes me feel so sad," Circe said. Her dark hair had fallen forward, almost obscuring her face. "Being close to someone makes me feel better. . . ."

"Well, I'd like to oblige you, I really would," Santalucia said. "But maybe you don't understand precisely what the symptoms of a prostate infection are."

"Of course I do," Circe said. "But that kind of thing is usually more a matter of self-esteem. . . ."

She was just beginning to squeeze Santalucia's tensed thigh when the phone rang. He leaped over her and hit the ANSWER button.

"Hello?" he shrieked in desperate gratitude for the interruption.

The balding head and shoulder-length hair of Fred the tech freak appeared, eyes blanked out by the eyeglasses which for thirty years he'd steadfastly refused to exchange for contact lenses. "Got your message," he said.

"Thank God," Santalucia breathed.

"Beg pardon?"

"Nothing. How's everything in New York? How's your work? How's—"

"Look, this call is costing me a fortune," Fred said. "I just wanted you to know I've been monitoring that high-frequency carrier channel like I promised. I thought maybe that was why you called."

"That's great, Fred, really great."

"Yeah, well, anyway, I just sample the tapes every now and then. Constant regional directives these days—the Bronx, Queens, stuff like that."

"Right. Good thinking."

"But you were mainly interested in illegal hypnotic suggestions, weren't you?" Fred asked.

"Among other things," Santalucia said. Circe had climbed out of bed and was watching over his shoulder.

"Who's your beautiful friend?" Fred asked.

"A witch. What was it you were saying about illegal suggestions, Fred?"

"Oh, yeah, well, I'm no expert on the statutes or anything, but I just happened to stumble across something that, well, strikes me as definitely on the gray side of the law. I'd guess it

166

was being aimed at housewives and househusbands and people on the night shift, cause of the time, but—''

"Fred, what are the suggestions they're sending?"

"Basically, people are supposed to do anything they can around here to turn any stray Saucer Kids back and make them head west. They want to make them join up with the rest of the Cult out in Texas."

"And what was that gray area of the law you mentioned?" Santalucia asked.

"Oh, well, when they talked about 'doing anything,' the word that kept popping up was 'kill.' 'Kill as many as you have to' was the way it went, I think. I figured you'd want to know."

Santalucia felt Circe's fingers dig into his arm, and he thought about their foolhardiness this afternoon in going in and laying out what they knew for Solarsystems. *If* that PR flack had reported their meeting to any of her superiors, then . . . It would be interesting to know what the Denver area carrier channel was telling people to do. Whether it had anything to do with a certain white woman and black man . . .

"Those poor kids," Circe murmured.

17

The Welcome Wagon

12:33 PM Thursday, December 16

Ed Binks shook his head and took off his girlfriend's Loveband. He got after his daughter Chrissy for watching TV all the time, and here he was doing the same fucking thing. But she was still a kid, and she ought to get out in the sun more—if the fucking dust storms in the midwest ever stopped and North Carolina ever got any sun again. Anyway, the Love stuff always mellowed him out nice and easy, made everything lowcal, and he did need it. It wasn't his fault the trucking industry was down the fucking tubes and he'd been out of work for—

Well, what the fuck did it matter? It wasn't his fault. He didn't have to count up the days or anything. He didn't have to answer to anyone for it.

He felt suddenly bored and ill at ease. He went to the closet where he kept his Remington Woodmaster .30-06-caliber semi-automatic. What he'd do, he thought, was give it a good cleaning. It needed a good cleaning. And it would relax him.

He took a box of .30-06 150-grain soft-point bullets off the top shelf and put them in his pocket.

Then he got out his cleaning rags and the rest and went to the dining room table. When he was finished, he washed his hands.

Chrissy was still at school or something, probably. Or diddling with that Benjie kid. Some daughter. And Mary was still at work.

Well, maybe he'd take the gun and go for a walk. No reason. Maybe go for a walk down to someplace and shoot at tin cans or something. Get ready for deer season.

Maybe go down . . . what the fuck. Maybe go down to the

thruway exit ramp. Maybe some of the other guys would be there.

They could trade stories or something.

Behind the exit sign.

4:35 PM

Starbud had not been paying attention to the road map or the route signs, and she had lost track of the days. Their progress had been incredibly slow. Time and again they had stopped to spend days on end in one small city or another. Moonrose had said it was to beg the money to make phone call upon phone call to various New York numbers she'd flashed on, but Starbud wasn't sure. It seemed Moonrose no longer believed she was going to find Moonbeam in New York, and she was dragging her feet to put off the inevitable. She had lost faith.

Now they were headed north through one of the Carolinas. Starbud didn't know which.

Along their leisurely way they had picked up others. A slightly older girl named Gwen was crowded into the cab between Starbud and Moonrose, though Moonrose had told her Gwen was no good as a name and had christened her Cosma. Two more women and three men were huddled in the back of the pickup under the tarp.

"How much longer to New York?" Gwen-Cosma asked, trying to make room for her right leg by kneeing Starbud's leg out of the way.

"Two days, maybe," Moonrose said. "Wouldn't you say, Starbud? You got the map."

Starbud shrugged. She hated reading maps.

"Let me see that," Gwen-Cosma said. "I still don't see why you want to go to New York. I tell you, we're supposed to be heading toward Oklahoma or somewhere. I saw it on TV."

"That's Levitt and his crowd," Moonrose said.

"But that's most of them," Gwen-Cosma said. "Us, I mean. I keep forgetting."

"But Moonbeam's in New York," Moonrose said. "And it's just a matter of days before the Beaming. You can just feel it in the air—it's like electricity. Can't you feel it?"

Gwen-Cosma nodded. "That's what they were saying on TV before I left, too. They did these interviews—"

169

"Well, Levitt's in for a big surprise if he thinks the Beings are going to take him," Moonrose said. "You can't fool the Beings."

"But aren't you afraid you won't get to the others in time? Aren't you afraid you'll miss the Beaming?"

"Yes, I'm afraid. But I can't leave without Moonbeam."

It was the first time Starbud had ever heard Moonrose actually express doubt. Starbud had felt the growing tension, the sense of urgency. Even separated from the other Seekers, she had sensed their united yearning and their conviction that it would be soon, very soon. A few weeks. Maybe, as Gwen-Cosma had said, days. It was a dizzying, exhilarating feeling, but at the pit of her stomach was the leaden fear that this mad pursuit of Moonbeam would cost them their chance at immortality.

"But I thought you said you hadn't heard from him for weeks," Gwen-Cosma persisted. "What makes you so sure he hasn't already headed west to join the others?"

"One thing you've got to learn about the Seekers," Moonrose said. "We stick together. We don't leave any brothers or sisters behind—ever. So we have to go to New York and make sure he's not there before we head west."

"How are you going to be sure, anyway? New York is a huge place."

"I'll know," Moonrose said. "Spirit radar."

At that moment something appeared on the highway ahead. At first Starbud thought it might have been an overhead sign that had fallen across the road, but as they drew closer she realized it was the broad side of a truck.

"Some kind of accident?" Gwen-Cosma wondered as Moonrose began to brake.

There were men on top of the truck and beside it. They were carrying long things that glinted in the weak sunlight. Rifles.

Moonrose slowed to a stop. "They're blocking the road," she said.

"Get out of here!" one of the men on the truck hood was shouting. "Go back where you came from!"

One of them came forward, gun in the crook of his arm. He leaned down to look in the window. "You're going to have to turn around," he said.

"Why?" Moonrose asked.

He looked blank for a moment. "Because. Because of the trouble. We don't want any trouble in town."

"But we're on a thruway," Moonrose said. "We weren't

170

going in *any* towns. We don't want any trouble either. We just want to get to New York.''

"If you don't want any trouble," the man said, "you'll head back that way and pick up I-Eighty-five west. That's my advice." He indicated some fresh tire tracks across the median leading to the south-bound lane.

"But that's illegal, crossing the median," Gwen-Cosma said.

The man guffawed. "I think Charlie there'll let it pass this one time, just as long as you're heading that-a-way to the Eighty-five turnoff." He jerked his thumb back toward one of the men on the truck, a tall figure in the broad-brimmed hat and gray uniform of a state trooper.

"Please," Moonrose said.

The man suddenly stepped back, whipped his rifle into his right hand, and fired into the sky. The air inside the cab slammed with the report.

"You *get*," he said.

Hands trembling, Moonrose backed up a few feet, swung the truck around, and lurched forward across the median, touching down onto the cracked pavement of the south lane so hard that two of those in the back were nearly thrown from the pickup.

Another concussion of a gunshot from the other side of the divider, and she pressed the accelerator to the floor. The rear passengers huddled against the back of the cab for protection from the bitter wind.

"I guess that settles it," Gwen-Cosma said. "We pick up the thruway west as soon as we hit the intersection."

"No we don't," Moonrose said. "Starbud, you find the next northbound highway on the map."

"Where are we?" Starbud said, trying to unfold the map.

"Here, give me that," Gwen-Cosma snapped. She studied it briefly. "Exit after this next one," she said. "It's a state highway."

But as they approached the ramp they saw a great column of black smoke rising in the air. Moonrose took a deep breath and swung off onto the exit.

The arc of the exit brought them around toward the smoke again, but before they had even reached the stop sign, they could see what had happened. A small pickup was parked across the north lane of the highway, and in the south lane the skeleton of a van tipped on its side still billowed smoke. They did not need to see its occupants to know that they had been Seekers.

Moonrose hunched down as she ran the stop sign and accelerated, squealing between the pickup and the smouldering van like a slalom skier and making it onto the ramp back to the thruway across the road even as a scattering of shots rang out behind them.

There was a ferocious pounding on the rear window as they careened back onto the thruway. A face appeared, one side covered with blood whipped into streamers and droplets by the wind.

"Stop," cried the muffled voice. "Stop!"

"He's been shot," Starbud said.

"We can't stop here," Moonrose said. "How far's the next exit?"

The pounding fist made bloody smears on the window glass.

"Just a few kilometers," said Gwen-Cosma's strangled voice.

The man's face was pressed obscenely against the glass like a child making faces against a window, blood oozing down one side, the others struggling to get him to lie down in the truck bed. Even inside the cab they could hear his screaming.

"How do you know we can get off here?" Gwen-Cosma asked.

"I don't," Moonrose said evenly. "But they can't be *everywhere.*"

The ramp seemed empty as they approached. Moonrose eased downward, glancing up and down the road as they neared the intersection.

"I think we've made it," she breathed. "Which way's the nearest town?"

The windshield turned opaque with the intersecting cracks of the first spray of bullets from behind the exit sign.

18

Elfin Lights

6:05 PM Thursday, December 16

Even flattened by the television screen, the dead girl's face was unnervingly gray and real.

Chrissy Binks pressed her own face close to the set, not because the Saucer girl mattered to her, but because she didn't want to hear the shouting in the next room. Her reflection hovered ghostlike over the dead girl's electronic image, veiled by the old glass's criss-cross mesh of scratches, her staring eyes superimposed on the motionless whites of eyes rolled upward into the skull when the shotgun had ripped her open.

That was the key, Chrissy thought. You couldn't let anything get inside. You had to stay closed up.

"What the hell *is* this?" her father bellowed, his breath smoking in the frigid kitchen. He'd been drinking and doing weed since he'd gotten home and put his gun away. "I can't even open the damned thing." He waved the salami-like plastic tube of food.

She pulled her coat tighter and held her breath to squeeze their yelling from her ears. *At least fifteen killed statewide in the last twenty-four hours,* the announcer droned as the camera moved lovingly from the dead girl's face to the black, blood-soaked back of another of them. *And at this particular location five known dead when the pickup you see here, carrying a truckload of the Cultists, came off the highway to recharge its HED batteries for the long haul to Greeley, and vigilantes apparently hiding behind that very thruway exit sign opened fire, presumably in an effort to prevent the kind of trouble here that Cultists have caused in various other—*

173

"I made a mistake, all right?" her father's latest friend said. "I bought the wrong one."

"How could you buy the wrong one? It says 'CAKWRAPT' all over it—that means, stupid, that it's packaged for Computer-Automated Kitchens . . . which we have not got. And look here—these sensing bands. What the hell did you think *they* were for?"

"I thought they were the price code," she said. "All right?"

—including the only known vigilante fatality in these shootouts, an unemployed civics teacher from—

"The price?" her father sneered. "That's *these* lines down here. Don't you know anything? These others are so when you drop it in the slot, the computer knows what it is and how much of it you bought and where to store it. Then it puts it on the menu someday and microwaves it for diner."

"How the hell do you know so much about it? You buying us one for Enrichment Day?"

Before she'd died, Marie had talked a lot about the Saucer kids, Chrissy remembered. Even about joining them, till she got too sick to even think about traveling. What she liked was the thing about the next evolutionary stage being another dimension, and how the Beings would just reach into your old diseased body and yank out your soul or whatever, maybe your brain, and then put it in a perfect new body in the new dimension.

Marie had been hung up on that because she'd known her insides were being eaten away; even after she'd given up, she used to say she was glad she had what she did because at least the doctors wouldn't cut any parts of her away like Annie Flemming's mother's cheek and jaw. She'd die whole.

At the end, when she'd been all drugged up, she'd get confused about whether she was dying or the Beings were going to take her.

"Oh, so that's it, is it?" her father shouted. "I guess it's my fault Empire Trucking folded?"

"Forget it, will you? I'll just slit it open and cook it like anything else. It's perfectly good food."

"Perfectly good food—and you only paid twice as much to buy it in a package only a computer can open!"

"Look, I thought it was a fast food like soypork or something," the woman said. "I'm *tired* after work. But you wouldn't know about being tired after work, would you?"

Chrissy glanced at the clock over the TV: *6:07.10*. She'd promised to meet Benjie by the fence at seven, but if her father and his friend didn't finish their fight soon, she was going to have to figure some excuse for leaving before supper, and her father was sure to object. Not that she cared one way or the other about meeting Benjie, but at least it was something to do.

"So Empire Trucking *is* my fault," her father said. "I guess that makes the whole fucking world my fault, too."

"Did I say that? But what about the goddamned garden you were going to plant to help out with food costs?"

"What happened? Take a look around, friend. The dirt glows in the dark, for Chrissakes. I can't even grow ragweed out there. It's probably why I feel rotten all the time."

"You've got enough energy to go out and shoot at tin cans every day. If you feel rotten it's probably because you spend all day waiting to get zapped out with your Loveband and drinking beer."

"I suppose Dave Garowski at the corner died of a bad attitude? I suppose Dotty Flemming and the Matthews kids are figments of my imagination? And Chrissy's girlfriend there, what's-her-name..."

Involuntarily Chrissy folded her arms across her chest, closing herself in. She had to go to a doctor, but she was afraid to find out for sure. Anyway, there was no money, every credit card had been revoked. She tried again to concentrate on the TV.

"Then why don't we move, damn it?" the woman shouted. "If not for yourself, then for her in there. She's only fifteen—and she's *your* kid. What about *her* future?"

"Don't you think I tried to move ten years ago?" he said. "Nobody in his right mind would buy this place after what happened. I'd take a complete loss. I'm stuck, fenced in, like a prisoner."

"The fence is around the old Valhalla plant, not around this house," the woman said evenly. "Our driveway goes right down the street, and the street goes right to the Interstate."

"I can't afford to lose my investment here. It's all I got left."

—isolated clashes nationwide, reporters covering the main body of Cultists have found a growing sense of frenzy and a general consensus that New Year's Eve will be the time of the so-called Beaming prophesied by their late leader, the Pied Piper, whose death last—

He was cut off by an ad. Chrissy saw within her own reflection a couple embracing tenderly by the glow of an old-fashioned fireplace. It was just a Tips ad, but it made her feel warm to

175

watch their tender fondling, even though she knew it was manufactured with cold deliberation for the camera. Over their amorous murmurs, the camera panned down for a tight product shot. Why wasn't her life like that?

There was a sickening *splack* as the plastic tube struck the side of the woman's face. Chrissy looked up impassively as the woman spun sideways, lost her balance, and sprawled through the doorway onto the living room floor.

"You bastard!" she shouted. "Get away from me!"

As he loomed over the woman, food tube dangling from one hand, Chrissy rose, glancing at the clock. He looked over at her stupidly, still trying to grasp what had happened. "You sit down, young lady."

"So you can beat me up, too?" Chrissy taunted, backing toward the door. He was too slowed by drink and weed to frighten her, and she didn't care one way or the other what happened to the woman—she was an adult; if she didn't like it, she could always take her own advice and leave. But it was the excuse Chrissy had needed, and after she got back from Benjie, her father would be too sheepish to ask where she'd been. She could even stay late—not that spending extra time with a dumb jimmy like Benjie was a whole lot better than coming home.

"You're like the rest of the kids nowadays," he muttered, slumping against the wall. "No respect."

The woman's groan distracted him, and Chrissy made it out the front door.

"CHRISSY!" she heard him screaming behind her. "YOU COME BACK HERE IF YOU KNOW WHAT'S GOOD FOR YOU!"

There were no sidewalks, and she scuffed a path for herself through the brown carpet of leaves along the edges of the withered lawns. Hadn't fall come earlier when she was little? She checked to make sure she had her flashlight in her pocket; she couldn't remember ever having seen the streetlamps lighted.

It occurred to her she *ought* to have been more upset about what her father had done. Violence and all that. Marie would have wanted her to pity the woman, or hate her father, or at least forgive him, the way she ought to love Benjie like the people in the Tips ad.

But she didn't. Life wasn't like that. She'd learned to be closed and self-contained as an oyster. No one had ever taught

176

her in so many words, but you could always tell what grownups wanted. It had been that way since the melt.

Maybe Marie had changed her for a while. Marie used to say that people had to open up, the way a flower would die if it never opened its petals to the sun. Marie picked up things like that from the fairy tales and garbage she read because she believed she was a poet. But Chrissy hadn't minded. She'd loved Marie *because* she was different.

And now she was dead. Sometimes, like tonight, Chrissy let herself feel how much she missed her. It was like she'd lost part of herself, the important part.

Up at the corner ahead she saw Colin Matthews watching his father pack leaves around the yellow shrubs beside their house, and she crossed the street to avoid him. He had no arms.

She'd babysat him once or twice when she was desperate, but he made her uneasy, like the other gruesies. They were under ten, because they'd been born after the melt, but a lot of them were already in her school. It was easy to exaggerate, but it seemed like every time she turned around they were putting in more handbars or ramps or extra-wide handicapper toilets. She was looking forward to high school because she'd be safe there for three years, until the first of them began turning thirteen. They'd follow her all her life.

There were others no one saw, people said, gruesies so awful they'd been sent away or kept hidden. She'd heard the Campos had a five-year-old with no arms or legs. It just lay in a crib like a pillow with a head, and they stayed home all the time, feeding it, wiping it, watching it grow bigger and bigger. She clutched her coat tighter across her breasts against the wind.

And there weren't just the gruesies that had been born that way. There were people who lost parts and turned into gruesies, like Annie Flemming's mother. Chrissy had gotten a good look only once since they'd cut her cheek and jaw out. Mr. Flemming was helping his wife get out of the car. She hadn't had her ski mask on, and the wind had blown her scarf aside. Her face had been all caved in, like a Halloween mask somebody had stepped on. Annie had cried because Chrissy had seen.

She found that by crossing the street she'd put herself in front of the Gorowski place, and she hurried on. It was only a month ago, but already she'd forgotten. Leukemia or something.

She was early for Benjie, so when she reached the path by the

177

fence she took her time, clattering a stick along the chain links that closed off the hundred square miles of forbidden forest. The Valhalla plant had been in the middle of it somewhere. They said that in the clouds of radioactive steam the silicon in the dirt had turned into molten globs, and the debris and paint flecks from the explosions had been fused inside. They said they were still there, millions of little sealed glass balls like dark pearls all over the place, filled with radioactive crap.

Of course, like her father always said when he was really stoned, it was the stuff that wasn't sealed away you had to worry about. The stuff that came down the hill in rivulets with every rain and ran right under the fence to pool along the edges of their streets and seep into their cellars and reservoirs. He said it was just dumb luck it hardly ever rained anymore.

But all you could see from her side of the fence was the dark tangle of sumac and second-growth trees no bigger than her wrist. For an instant she had the strange sensation that eyes were watching her from the shadows.

She laughed to herself. When she was little, they'd told stories about bogeymen with extra arms and mouths that grabbed you and carried you deep into the poison forest and ate you one part at a time for days and days till you died.

She wondered if the gruesies and the regular kids nowadays believed the same stories. Still, as she began to climb to the top of the bluff, she couldn't shake the feeling that something was watching her. It made her colder than the wind.

There probably were still vigilantes looking for Saucer Kids. And she was the right age. They were the kind to shoot first and ask questions later.

She wondered where her father had been when she'd gotten home from school today.

Benjie wasn't at the bluff, and she leaned against the fence to wait, staring in. From up here you could get a good look inside. In summer you could see the dead trees like white spikes, and the farther in you looked, the more of them you saw among the green leaves. This time of year, all the trees were spikes, dead and white.

Marie's idea had been that parents or the government had made up the bogeymen stories because it wasn't really a waste-land at all, but a secret place so beautiful they'd fenced it off just to keep the kids from getting in and enjoying it. Instead of bogeymen, Marie had said one afternoon on the bluff, elves danced in the forest; once, she said, she'd even seen their elfin lights twinkling under the trees. If you could find the sacred tree, the elves would take you off to their magical land for a minute or a thousand years or whatever. And she'd claimed the spikes of dead trees were just the beginnings of the thorn forest that guarded Sleeping Beauty's castle.

Chrissy tried to imagine Sleeping Beauty, eyes closed in magical slumber on her royal bed, but instead she saw the dead girl by the thruway sign. In a way, she'd looked a little like Marie, maybe younger. If Marie had lived, she'd have gone off and joined them, and then it would have been Marie lying dead by the highway. It just showed how once something was fated, nothing you did could really keep it from happening. One way or the other you'd die.

She threw the stick at the fence and it rattled furiously. Fences—they kept you out of melt areas, they closed off empty parts of cities, they ringed military bases, power plants, cemeteries. If there was anything that summed up this last year of the old century, it was the chain link fence. Marie would have written a poem about it. It would have had a lot of short lines that didn't rhyme, and probably the words "love" and "dew" and maybe "mist." Chrissy couldn't be sure, because she wasn't a poet herself.

And then, the fence still ringing, she shivered. There *had* to be something down there, watching.

The crackling of Benjie's feet on the fallen branches distracted her. He emerged from the twilight, a vacant smile on his face, a cord running from the earphone in his ear to the floppie-player he was carrying. She glimpsed the closeup on its screen of gyrating buttocks and wisps and knew he had the Sandra Cassandra floppy on.

"Turn on the sound," she mouthed.

Dreamily he unplugged the earphone.

> —in those good old-fashowned
> Piss-tone-driven day-yay-yay-yay-yay
> Yay-yay yays—

"Where the hell were you?" she said. "It's late."

"December trash pickup's tomorrow," he said. "Had to help my old man get the bags out front. Lotta shit this month." The screen flickered out with the auto cutoff. "Really woody," he said. "Ripped it at a D-store."

179

"So you're a hero," she shrugged, watching him unbutton his coat. "Look, I don't want to do it here tonight."

"What do you mean?" His eyes narrowed.

"I didn't say I didn't want to *do* it. I just don't want to do it *here*." She glanced over at the undergrowth creeping up toward the far side of the fence. "This place makes me nervous tonight. Besides, anybody could see us up here. Let's go down to the hollow. It's more private."

"Well, Jesus, this is new," he said, but he followed her down the far side of the bluff and in amongst the trees away from the fence. At last she stopped, opened her coat, pulled her jersey above her breasts, unzipped her pants to give his hand room without taking them off, and lay down.

He knelt beside her, squeezing her breasts while she lay stiff and cold on her back, holding her coat shut over his hands and staring at the darkening sky.

"You feel okay?"

"Sure," she said. He was a year older, and he always told her how he really cared how his partner felt, like it was a sense of responsibility that came with maturity. He'd learned it in grade-school Sex Ed. She felt only the slit of cold on her belly where his wrists made it impossible to reseal the coat. She thought of the caresses of the Tips Condoms couple, the dead girl—

"You got a zit, babes," he said. "A pimple right on your left boob here. Or something. Lemme see."

She held her coat shut. "I know," she said emptily. "I found it Saturday. Big deal."

Maybe it *was* just a pimple.

"Do the other part now," she said. "I'm freezing."

"But you're not on yet."

"Do the other part." She had to fight to forget the pimple. She had to think about the sky, pink-blue-black, the faint stars beginning to appear the way pictures slowly emerged in those special coloring books where she just wet the blank pages with clear water when she was little.

He reached into her pants, began to probe. She felt nothing, staring now past his left shoulder toward the darkness of the fence and brush. Could someone be in there, someone crazy enough to ignore the signs and climb right in?

He wet his finger with saliva and began again, more vigorously, more roughly. "How the hell long you planning to take?"

"Forget it," she said. "I'm upset, is all. Everything went wrong tonight."

"Again? You been upset for months. Ever since Marie died. It's like you were queer for her, you know that?"

"I said forget it. It was nothing like that, but you wouldn't understand. Let's do your part."

He withdrew his hand and straddled her hips, still kneeling, and undid his fly. She reached in without taking her eyes from the woods and began to pull at him.

"Careful," he said. "You could hurt—"

"Don't I *know* by now?" she snapped.

"Look, why does it have to be this way?" he asked, closing his eyes in preparation. "It's so . . . I don't know, mechanical or something. Why don't we just do it the way all the kids do. I could go on the pill—"

"No," she muttered. "Nothing in, nothing out."

"What?"

"I said maybe if you got some Tips. They keep everything all sealed up, clean."

"Those stupid things? You believe those dumbass—"

"Hold still," she said. "If we did it and had a baby, it would have all these sores or two heads or something."

A moment later he shuddered above her. Angrily she realized she hadn't been paying attention, and his stuff was all over her right hip. She twisted so he would get off her and stood up herself, her thumb wet and freezing in the cold, trying to scrape her jeans clean with a stick.

"You mad?" he asked when she had thrown the stick away. "I'm sorry I said anything about the zit. I know girls are uptight about—"

"Forget it," she said. "I'm just tired."

"Okay, I'll walk you home."

"I don't *want* to go home." She pulled her jersey down and zipped her pants.

"Look, is it because I said something about Marie? I didn't mean anything. I know it's tough to lose a friend like that. It's scary—like you're afraid you're going to die next, it's so easy. And you were like sisters."

She looked at him in the dim light, fly still open, and she laughed.

"What the hell is it now?" he said.

181

"You," she said. "Sitting on a toilet."

"What?"

"Don't you remember? Toilet training at day care. They used to march us in and there were like hundreds of these teeny little toilets and we used to sit there pissing and shitting away with our feet just kind of dangling down."

"I don't remember," he said. "Must have hated it."

"I don't remember feeling anything about it one way or the other. I just did it because they said to. In fact, that's all I remember from when I was little. I don't remember my mother. Just sitting on a toilet."

"Look," he said. "I got to go. You coming?"

"No," she said. "Not till my father sobers up."

He shrugged and she watched him go back up the slope into the darkness. At the top of the hill she saw the flicker of light as he flipped on his floppie-player to watch Sandra Cassandra again, and then he was gone.

She did remember something else. Story hour. The books they had read to them by the daycare artists, about children whose parents got divorced or turned out to be gay or whose grandfathers died. Stuff to get you ready for life. Never once had anyone read her about elves or magic, until she'd met Marie. Marie had been in the other toilet group.

Back at the path she paused. She was getting hungry; if she went home now, at least she could get in bed after she ate and warm up under the covers. Except the truth was her father's friend was right: if she was smart, she'd head for the Interstate and just go. There had to be places that weren't gray with radioactive crud, places where you didn't have to stay closed up. Maybe she'd find a doctor who could help her.

But what was the point? She'd have an operation and they'd cut something out and whatever it was would just keep on growing away inside.

There was a rustling on the far side of the fence and a glint of something. For an instant Chrissy thought of elfin lights and bogeymen, and then a vague figure congealed out of the darkness. It struck another match. In the flare of light, a girl's face appeared behind the grid of chain links, and then the match went out. Chrissy pulled her flashlight out of her coat and shined it at the girl.

"Please—don't yell," the girl said. "It's all right, really."

"How did you get in *there?*" Chrissy said.

"Oh, I just climbed up a big tree on your side a mile down and shinnied out on a branch and dropped in."

"How long have you been ... watching?"

"Long enough," the girl said. She paused. "Did it feel ... good?"

"Maybe."

"I wondered," the girl said. "I'd never seen it except on TV."

"Nobody's supposed to go in there, you know." Chrissy shivered. "It's *poison*."

"It's better than letting those crazy guys with rifles catch me."

Chrissy came closer to the fence for a better look, and the girl approached from the other side until her face was only inches away, staring back through the links like a mirror image. Her ragged clothes made her look a little like the dead girl on the TV. "Are you one of *them?*" Chrissy said. "From that truckload of Saucer kids?"

"You won't tell, will you? I'm just trying to get back to the highway. My name's Starbud."

"No, I won't tell, but you've got a long way to go. The next nearest interstate ramp is over by Sterling, the other side of the forest. You'll have to circle all the way around."

"Can't I just cut through the woods?" the girl said.

"Through the middle of the *melt?* You can't do that—you'd get sick. You'd die eventually."

"Oh, I'm not worried about that," Starbud said. "I'll get a new body when They come for me."

"I knew someone that used to talk about that," Chrissy said. "About yanking your soul out of your body and all."

"I *sensed* that," the girl said. "That's why I waited for you. I *knew* there was something about you. You know, this is the first time in I don't know how long I've been alone, really alone. Open up your soul to the megalove in the universe, the Beings. Come with me."

"Where?"

"We were going to New York," Starbud said.

"New York? I thought you were all headed somewhere out west, Oklahoma or something."

"Yeah. But we were looking for someone there. Now that there's just me, and my radar isn't all that good ... I guess I'll head west, too."

"To the Dustbowl?"

Starbud was silent for what seemed like a long time. "If that's where the rest of the Seekers are, yes," she said. "They're my real family."

Chrissy thought of the empty vastness she'd seen so often on the news, the distant horizon boiling with dust, and she pulled her coat tighter, shivering so her flashlight trembled. But she liked the bright, dancing sound of the girl's voice; it was almost irresistible, despite the sadness in it.

"The world's going to end any day now," the girl said. "If you stay here, you're going to die like the rest of them. The earth'll be blasted, and you'll wind up like the animals I used to find after the dust blizzards, that'd choked to death on the air. Just little lumps, drifted over with dust. But if you come with me you'll get a new body, live forever—"

For an instant Chrissy felt an overwhelming urge to clamber over the fence and follow. Maybe she could escape the lump of the thing eating away inside her. At least she'd find out what was really at the heart of the forest. But then she imagined some vague, gigantic power forcing her open, reaching into her, pulling out her essence.

She shook her head. "No," she said.

Nothing in, nothing out. Sealed up like a sausage food-tube or a Tips condom.

"You won't take a chance?" Starbud asked. "Even if it saved your life?"

"There's no way you can really change things," she said dully.

She'd go home, patch things up with her father. Tomorrow night she'd meet Benjie, not that he was any Prince Charming about to waken Sleeping Beauty. But he was solid. He was real. And things would go on the way they were intended.

"You're sure?"

"I'm sure."

The girl studied Chrissy's face hopefully, but at last she sighed with resignation. "All right. I'm sorry."

"Here," Chrissy said, pushing the handle of her flashlight through the fence and pressing her face against the links. "You'll need this."

"Don't you need it?"

"I know the way home by heart," Chrissy said. "But be careful—there's going to be vigilantes everywhere. If any of

184

them stop you, tell them you're a college student on a hike or a field trip or something.''

"Thank you." Starbud leaned forward and kissed her through the fence. "If you change your mind in time, I'll be with the rest of them. At the end of the road.''

Starbud turned and Chrissy watched the beam of light swing away and move off, flickering among the trees until at last it disappeared.

Suddenly Chrissy spread her arms and reached as high up on the fence as she could to give it a gigantic shake. It clanged, and she sagged forward, arms out, hanging, forehead pressed against the links. She felt the empty cold on her front through her open coat, as though something more had been taken from her, and where the kiss had wet her dry lips.

But there was no going after the girl, no changing what was bound to be. No elves, no magic cures. Only a jerk would believe in them. And she gave the fence a second, ringing, final shake.

19

Calvary Charge

1:15 PM Tuesday, December 21

James Augustus Pilcher III picked his way carefully along the deserted and overgrown dirt road.

He knew perfectly well that the reason the brothers at AO had let him design and build the racer all by himself for the annual exams'-end soapbox derby was that they thought he was crazy.

Some of them were afraid of him; the others figured the racer project was good therapy because the last time he'd flipped out had been during exams. He didn't really care. The important thing was getting his way.

There had been a time where the Alphas had called him crazy as a kind of accolade, like when he climbed North Tower and crawled around on the cornice five stories up, bare-assed, or when he'd gone up and down Fraternity Row sideways, draped in Christmas lights, absolutely gone on three hundred milligrams of Pale Riders and hooting that he was the Crab Nebula.

But a lot of those people had graduated in the year he'd been sent away to Shady Pines Home, and the newer pledges and brothers hadn't seen him climbing North Tower bare-assed or being the Crab Nebula. They just thought of him as a former mental patient, an unfortunate like some ghetto kid they'd taken in as a community service or something.

But that was all right. That was how much they knew. A bunch of dumb jimmies. They'd find out.

It was still not altogether clear to him why he had wound up being arrested. He knew he had been sent to Shady Pines because it was near his parents back in Massachusetts, but why the court had let anyone send him anywhere was a real mystery. Nothing he could remember having done struck him as particularly bizarre or illegal, though he was the first to admit that the thorazine at Shady Pines had really wiped out his memory.

It had had something to do with going to Chicago and living with Mary after he'd left school. He'd met her by accident down by the edge of the lake and they'd found a rundown apartment together. But later Mary had smeared blood all over the apartment and gone off, and he'd run outside without his shoes to find her. It might have been winter, and they might have arrested him for being barefoot. He wasn't sure.

Warmth. That's what the psychiatrist had said he didn't want to leave, and yet he'd gone out in the cold, barefoot, looking for Mary.

Had the landlord ever forwarded his shoes to his parents?

Warmth, the psychiatrist had said. The real reason he'd gotten up and walked out in the middle of his Senior Comprehensives that May morning and left Tennessee and college and hitched to Chicago and found Mary, the real reason, the psychiatrist had said, aside from too many caps of Pale Riders and God knew what else, was that he was afraid to graduate. Afraid of leaving the womb and going out into the world. And no wonder, the psychiatrist had sympathized, because today's world was not an easy place to live in. But he had to understand that most people *did* manage to live in it, and he had to try, too, no matter how cold and cruel it was. That was part of growing up.

Well, that was bullshit because he'd gone out after her without his shoes. And it was also bullshit because here he was, back at college and finished with his Comprehensives and the Tennessee Minimal Literacy exam, and he couldn't wait to graduate in January.

Of course, it was still better than being in Shady Pines with all the sicks. He'd really hated them.

They're like this ashtray, he'd told the psychiatrist.

How are they like that ashtray?

What a stupid jimmy. *Because it has six sides.*

Oh?

Stupid stupid stupid. No right to live. *Six—sicks. Get it?*

And you're not sick?

Of course not.

Then why did you tell me again the other day that you alone held the power of life and death?

Beause I'm Jesus Christ, Son of Man.

You see? We're not making any progress.

187

Let him think whatever he wanted to. If you just said good morning and thank you and kept the rest of it to yourself, they always let you out. They were *dying* to let you out. They needed the room. And one of these days, Mary would turn up again and wash his feet with her hair and put on his shoes.

Unless the landlord had stolen them.

By this point, Pilcher had reached the abandoned chicken coop which he'd appropriated for his project. A mile from campus, overgrown with brambles and creepers, it was the perfect place for the secrecy he needed.

A lot of the soapbox racers were jokes. Bathtubs on wheels, barstools, that kind of thing. Because the derby had always been an end-of-fall and end-of-exams Saturnalia, and no one had seen the seriousness of it.

But he was going to change that. When the crowd saw his racer, they were going to shit in their pants. It would show that psychiatrist. Just in time for the year 2000. The dawn of the New Age.

Someone had been inside his hideaway.

The night before, he had wetted a single strand of his own hair with saliva and very carefully stuck it across the crack between the door and the frame. Too inconspicuous for the average intruder to notice, but an infallible way of knowing if anyone had been tampering with the door. He'd read it in a yellowed old James Bond paperback he'd found in the AO garret. Or had Bond used it on a briefcase?

He flattened himself against the side of the chicken coop, pressing his ear against the weathered wood to listen for breathing inside.

Nothing.

The spies from the other fraternities were desperate to know his secret design. The soapbox derby was a cutthroat business. He picked up a rock from beside the coop, flung open the door, and leaped inside.

"DEATH!" he roared.

A small voice screamed for help.

He balanced on the balls of his feet, uncertain, blinded by the outdoor sunlight as he tried to scan the dim room for the source of the voice.

She was lying right on top of the goddamned racer!

"GET OFF THAT!" he bellowed.

"Look, I'm sorry," Starbud said, scrambling to the dirt floor.

"You could have damaged the bearings in the roller skates," he said. He threw the rock down angrily.

"I said I was sorry," Starbud said. "I just thought it was an old piece of plywood with a sheet over it."

"It *is*," he smiled. "The racer's *under* it. To hide it from snoops like you." He grabbed her wrist. "Who sent you?"

"Nobody," she cried. "I've been hitching rides through Tennessee. I was just so *tired*." She began to sob. "I thought nobody was using this place."

"That's why I picked it." Tenderly he put his arm around her heaving shoulders. "Okay, I believe you. The derby's only an hour away. Even if the other frats did get my design now, it'd be too late to do them any good. Where you headed?" He let go of her wrist.

"West."

"You one of those Saucer Kids? You hitching?"

"I *said* I was hitching." She sniffled, wiping a tear away at the corner of her eye with the tips of her fingers.

"Hungry?"

"Yes."

"I brought something to eat," he said. "I'll share it with you if you'll help me."

"How?"

"Well," he said, taking his arm from around her and beginning to rummage in the pockets of his army fatigue jacket, "for one thing, I need someone to give me a push down the hill at the derby. Your name isn't Mary, is it?"

"It's Starbud," she said. "But I guess I could give you a push."

He grunted his thanks and extracted a thermos of water and two peanut butter sandwiches from his pockets. They sat cross-legged on the dirt floor, white with ancient chicken droppings, using the sheet-covered plywood as a table.

"Good water," she said.

"Tennessee always had the best water," he nodded. "Lots of rivers and shit around here."

"But I don't see how you have a racing car under here," Starbud said, picking a bit of pocket lint off the dry bread of her sandwich. "It's so low."

"That's the *secret*," he confided. "Aerodynamics. The lower to the ground, the less wind resistance. That plus a time-tested aeronautical configuration."

189

"You probably shouldn't be bothering with this," Starbud said. "The world's going to end any day." She spoke with the same emotionless certainty with which Moonrose had always repeated the phrase, but it had lost much of its meaning for her over these last days.

That first night, when she had met the girl at the fence, she had been still fresh from the comfort of Moonrose and the terror of the windshield shattered by the gunshots and splattered with blood. But since then, deprived of Moonrose's reassuring litany, she had become less sure.

And there was something else. She had violated the code; she had abandoned her brothers and sisters. She had fled without even pausing to see if any of them were still alive. Even Moonrose.

So there was no reason to go on to the Beaming. Because the Beings would never forgive her.

"I *know* the world's going to end," he said.

"Then you're a Seeker, too? How come you're hanging around here?"

"I'm a Finder," he said. "I'm like a warning. Did you want to see it?"

"See what?"

"The racer?"

She shrugged. He stood up and, fingers trembling, reached under one edge of the plywood and lifted it up just enough for her to see under it. "There," he said triumphantly.

"That's a soapbox racer?" she asked, peering in at what looked vaguely like the crude skeleton of an airplane. "It's just a couple of boards."

"The conjunction of simplicity for its own sake coupled with its symbolic value," he said. "It'll go like lightning." Carefully he laid the plywood back in place. "We'll have to drag it to the hill with this on it. I don't want anybody to get a look until the right moment. Here, you can sit on it with me."

She sat down beside him tensely. "I thought you said it would break the bearings."

"Not if we lie back. It'll distribute the weight better."

She lay back and stared at the striations of skylight filtering between the boards of the roof. The peanut butter had made the back of her throat dry.

"Anyway, it's all right if you're with me," he went on. "It needs a christening. A christening of blood."

190

"What?"

She felt his hand close over her arm again.

She almost pulled away, but she forced herself instead to wait. She had been so alone without the motherly weight of Moonrose's arm next to her, the sense of purpose in Moonrose's voice. She wanted someone to tell her what to do.

His face loomed over hers, silhouetted against the skylight lines above. "You won't fight me," he said. "You can't." He stared at her for a long time, as though uncertain what he was going to do. Then he lowered his head and closed his mouth over hers.

She thought of how she'd watched the girl that first night alone. This was what people did to bring themselves together. Shielded themselves from the loneliness with another human body.

She put her arms around his neck and drew his face against her throat. She felt his hand brush across her breasts, then tug at the waistband of her pants.

"The velcro's gone," she murmured. "It's tied with string." She reached down and undid the string and he pulled the pants away with one hand as she twined her arms around his neck, felt the muscles in his back ripple and tense with a fluid, mad, inhuman strength. He pressed his mouth against hers harder, hurting her lips, and she held him tightly, surrendering, waiting to be overpowered and consumed.

When he was done, he sat on the edge of the plywood with his pants still down, and somehow she had not been consumed. Still, it had been adequate, even pleasant. She could see why people did it sometimes. It just hadn't been the overwhelming submersion she had wanted in return for no longer being a purer vessel.

"We've got to get going," he said suddenly, standing and pulling up his pants. "We'll be late for the race."

After she was dressed, they had to tip it on its side, plywood, sheet, and all, to get it through the door. Then Pilcher looped a rope behind the front roller skate and they each took an end, dragging the assembly behind them like a low, cloth-covered, Japanese table on casters. It bumped and lurched over the rutted path, catching them on the backs of their ankles as they staggered forward, straining against its weight.

She ought to get back on the highway, at least try. She wanted to see it through; whatever fate the Beings decided for her, she

191

wanted to be there with the others for the end, even if she were one of those left behind.

But she couldn't. The faces of the dead at Denver, of Moonrose and the others in the truck hovered between her and the scene she'd always imagined of the great, shimmering Saucer with its bright beam, like a glowing tube, that reached from its underside to the ground, sucking up the faithful.

And now she felt bound to the boy beside her. Maybe it would be better to be with him when the end came. At least she would not be alone, and she wouldn't have to face the avenging Beings.

"For a minute, inside back there, I thought I saw you dead," he said. "But I like you."

It took them a good twenty minutes to make their way through the scrub of the abandoned road, then past some empty gas stations and a boarded-up McDonald's. She'd heard from one of the older Seekers how they'd sold nothing but meat hamburgers. But at last she saw a cluster of old brick buildings, and soon they found themselves moving in the same general direction as little clusters of students. They were dressed in outrageous Mardi Gras costumes of ribbons and tatters of old clothes.

Starbud couldn't help remembering that first night with Moonrose in New York. The excitement of so many bodies crowded together, the exhilaration of realizing the singleness of their faith.

These students were nothing like the Seekers. They walked in twos and threes, engrossed with themselves.

Together they dragged their burden up a slight incline, and then Starbud found herself overlooking a long, narrow street with large, old-fashioned houses on either side. There were people everywhere, glints of bottles, the smell of weed. Things she had never seen among the Seekers.

"What the fuck is that, Jim?" somebody was saying. "You Alphas racing a coffee table or something?"

"You just wait," Pilcher snapped. "You'll see."

"Take it easy," the other person said. "Everything's lowcal, Jim-boy."

"They will, you know," Pilcher whispered to Starbud. "They'll all see."

At the top of the rise was a kind of junk yard of mobile trash. Behind a chalked line was an old brass bedstead on which lay a boy and girl in football helmets beneath a cardboard sign that read Phi Psi. Next to them was the low, sleek Chi Rho entry, apparently a professionally-made fiberglass soapbox racer. Next to it stood a garbage can mounted on three roller skates from DKE, then something from PKA made out of parts of a fiberboard packing crate and mounted on bicycle wheels, then a toilet bowl on casters, complete with water closet, lettered Delta Phi.

Silently Pilcher pointed to their spot beside the toilet bowl.

"When do we get to see it?" someone else said, coming up the hill toward them. "The whole House is dying to know what we're running."

"When the moment's *right*," Pilcher smiled. "The Alphas have to wait, just like the rest of the world."

"DRIVERS, PLEASE REPORT TO YOUR VEHICLES," echoed a voice from a loudspeaker somewhere. Down below, banners covered with Greek letters fluttered from poles, signs written on sheets flapped from windows, and the crowd began pulling back toward the sidewalks like the Red Sea to leave the street clear.

Now in the clear view of the expectant crowd, James Augustus Pilcher III stood serene and calm in the midst of the other drivers' last-minute bustle. Slowly, he unbuttoned his shirt and removed it. Then, gracefully, he kicked off his shoes. Finally, with all eyes riveted on him, he unzipped his trousers and let them drop. Save for his underpants, he stood naked beside his covered racer.

There were cheers and guffaws from the other drivers and hoots and whistles from the crowd below. "Take it *all* off!" shouted a voice, but Pilcher only smiled.

At last he nodded toward the sheeted board, and Starbud took one end while he bent down and took the other. At his signal they lifted the cover back and let it flop over onto its top.

The fraternity brother gasped and stepped back as though he'd gotten too close to something hot. The drivers and crews at the top of the hill stared silently at the stark cross of two-by-sixes mounted on rollerskates.

"Get behind me," he said to Starbud. "You have to give me a push."

He lay down feet first, testing the brake treadle that served as the crucifix's footrest, then reaching out with his hands to the opposite ends of the transverse piece where the steering wires came up through the holes he had carefully bored in the wood.

"GET READY!" barked the loudspeaker. "GET SET!"

Starbud crouched behind his head, her palms against the end of the two-by-six.

"GO!"

They were all launched at the same instant, in a confusion of clanks, clatters, and rumbles.

Down Pilcher thundered on the roller skates mounted beneath his head, hands, and feet. Down he came, head raised slightly to see over his toes, face transfigured by a smile of absolute, seraphic joy.

Down the hill and down. Past the brass bedstead, which had collided with a tree because it had no steering mechanism (*he* hadn't forgotten a steering mechanism, thus confirming the Alphas' wisdom in leaving this great work to his solitary discretion). Past the toilet bowl, as it fell and split into four porcelain pieces rocking lazily on the pavement beside the sprawled form of their driver. Past the garbage can, as it slowly swiveled around, then caught on something and tipped backward, dumping its pilot.

Somewhere deep inside, a small part of him knew that even in the midst of this great act of sacrifice and transcendent fulfillment, one of his brothers at the Alpha House was probably already on the phone to Massachusetts trying to reach his parents. And then they would be calling Shady Pines, and the whole hateful cycle would start over again.

But he forced it out of his mind, watching the faces of the crowd flash past as he roared ever downward, rocking, rumbling on his grinding rollerskates. Why hadn't he caught up with the Chi Rho entry? How was it they could still outrun the terrible bright glory of his immense, absolutely undeniable majesty?

At the top of the hill, in the center of the mocking crowd, Starbud watched his swift descent, eyes burning.

20

I'm Dreaming of a White Personal Enrichment Day, Just Like the Ones I Used to Know

6:30 PM Friday, December 24

Circe and Santalucia had wasted two precious weeks in Denver, but Circe had insisted they try every possible avenue for help, even as Santalucia had warned that if they kept at it, eventually they were going to step on a tentacle of the Love organization; and once Faith Ltd. was aware of all they knew, they would be marked for fates too dire for Santalucia to speculate on.

They had started with the police, of course. Chief Inspector Trample of the Bunco Division, to whom they had been referred, turned out to be a visionary who saw the law and human behavior in terms of Stop, Go, and Proceed with Caution. The scope of the plot Circe tried to outline was utterly beyond him. He did not deny it; indeed, he seemed to accept it, much as he accepted the fact that some people apparently believed in atoms and molecules and some judges thought the criminal code required interpretation. But he didn't see how he could do anything about it, any more than he could do anything about Saturn, which he had also never seen and did not understand.

He tried to be obliging, but as far as he was concerned it was not Go, and it was not even Proceed with Caution. It was Stop. He suggested they try the FBI, where the law and human behavior were understood in terms of more subtle classifications, such as Feint, Lie, and Cover Up, but when they finally got clearances for entering the Federal Building, they found that all the field agents had been assigned to a remnant of the Saucer Cult still south of the city.

A week later, when they finally got their appointment to see the deputy bureau chief, they were assured that if any such plot existed, the FBI would have known about it. The deputy bureau chief wanted very much to call a doctor for them, but they excused themselves and left.

"The old flywheel storage drives were actually a lot more efficient," Santalucia mused as Circe drove toward Stapleton Airport. They were on their way to catch a flight back to New York. There didn't seem much choice: they had exhausted the possibilities in Denver. What they thought they still might accomplish in New York was a question which Circe, at least, had not addressed.

It was dusk, and an easterly blowback from the Dustbowl had kept the sky dark all day, though now, the storm in the east apparently over, the sun hung at the horizon like a great red ball.

"HED batteries are pretty cheap to run," Circe said absently. She still burned with anger and humiliation at Santalucia's rebuff on their first night in Denver, and at the same time she felt guilty for worrying over her own petty problems when all her thoughts ought to have been on the children of the Saucer Cult. Between Fred's monitoring of the New York carrier channel and the pattern that emerged from the news accounts of clashes between Cultists and vigilante groups nationwide, it was obvious that stray Cultists all across the country were being systematically herded toward the Dustbowl.

"You're forgetting who really owns Solarsystems International," Santalucia said. "What keeps the price down when the last flywheel car's gone and there's no more competition?"

"Regulatory commissions, government," she said. Really, she thought, Santalucia was forever going off on tangents about everything except what really mattered. The more remote and abstract, the more he seemed to like it.

"When Doctor Love is president?" Santalucia asked. "Already, in one community after another, home windmills are being legislated out of existence. The taxes on individual solar collector panels in private homes go up every year. The reasons are always different, but the pattern's the same. No matter how you look at it, once the transition technology that developed independently is gone, then they've got us by the balls. It's the story of the oil companies all over again—who are, after all, reincarnated in Solarsystems. Except for their empty oil wells that Congress nationalized too late to do any fucking good."

"It's typical of you to worry about Solarsystems where it might affect your wallet," Circe said tightly. "I hate them too, but I think we ought to be worrying about what Solarsystems and Love are trying to do to the Saucer Kids."

"In point of fact, I agree with you," Santalucia said.

Circe shot him a quick look of surprise.

"These cults thrive on persecution, you know. The more of them get killed, the stronger they'll grow," Santalucia said. "For one thing, everything that happens to them fulfills some prophecy of the Monad's. It doesn't seem to bother them that she cribbed everything from the Apocalypse or that Doctor Love still falls short of Saint John's Antichrist by two gospels and a megahype."

"Why do you hate them so?" Circe asked.

"Common sense. Most chiliastic movements are embryonic totalitarian governments run by inner circles of fanatics around a central figure that foams at the mouth. Once the messiah's gone, the leadership's taken over by more practical and dangerous people. Look at German National Socialism, Marxist-Leninism, the Islamic Revolution in Iran. If people just left the Cult alone, it would peter out."

"Maybe not," Circe said. "These kids are the future. Now that the old baby-boom bulge from World War Two is on its last legs, these kids are beginning to flex their muscles and realize how much power they have. They've got a chance that we never had, because we were squeezed out in the middle. The baby-boom generation had clout in the sixties because they were the majority; these kids have clout because there are so few of them. Their parents want them, the economy needs them. They don't have to march and demonstrate to prove anything; all they need to do is withhold their labor and America is through."

"America's through anyway. What the kids like is the security of knowing when the end of the world is coming. It's like belonging to a club."

"More and more of them seem to think it'll be New Year's Eve," Circe said.

"That's their leadership's mistake," Santalucia said. "Once that day comes and nothing happens, it's going to be all over."

"Maybe. It's possible that they're right, of course."

Santalucia looked at her sourly.

"I said it was *possible*," Circe said. "But I've been thinking about it a lot, and it seems to me that what they're doing is looking for fathers and mothers They've found out their parents and grandparents aren't omnipotent—that in fact the last generations have blown it in energy planning, agriculture, everything. So they want cosmic fathers and mothers for the whole race. That's what these Beings are all about—the Monad just created a common focus for a general need. What they're doing is perfectly understandable and natural and human. It's the same reason older people are drawn to Doctor Love.''

"Taking a shit is human, too," Santalucia said. "But the thought that at this minute millions of people are doing it all over the world somehow doesn't make me all misty-eyed.''

"I'm just trying to make you *understand* them a little, that's all." Circe gripped the steering wheel tighter. "For a writer, you don't seem very interested in people.''

"I hate everyone regardless of race, creed, or national origin," Santalucia said.

"What's with you? Have you got a ticket to get off the boat the rest of us are in? Does being half black and half white give you a license not to care about anyone?" She was sorry the instant she said it, but it was too late.

Santalucia looked coldly out the windshield.

"I didn't mean that," she said. "I was just trying to say that all these kids are doing is looking to the stars for the superbeings they used to think their parents were. It's something we've all been through.''

"Yeah, well, we'd all like to have parents," Santalucia muttered. "Whether it's the Saucer Cult or Doctor Love in the White House with his religion of the very latest in media technology, I give democracy in this country another five years. It gives me worse constipation than Granola bars." He watched an airport sign flash by. "Anyway, Merry Christmas.''

"Merry Personal Enrichment Day, you mean," Circe said.

The woman at the Rent-A-Car desk was on the videphone and ignored them, no matter how many times Santalucia jingled the keys at her, once right by her ear and a second time between her eyes and the videphone screen. Finally he slapped them down on the counter in disgust and stalked off with Circe.

"Now *there's* an example of the decline of the west," he grumbled. "First the extinction of the carrier pigeon, then nuclear superiority, and now common courtesy.''

"Maybe it was an important call," Circe said, but she was troubled by the fact that nothing she'd been able to read in the woman's face had indicated that the woman was even aware of their presence.

To save time they avoided the ramps and cut across the access road toward the United-American terminal.

"Look out!" Circe shrieked, yanking Santalucia ahead just as a taxicab barreled through.

Santalucia stumbled up onto the curb, panting, "Is someone out to get us, or is it just me?" he said. "I told you if any of our visits to Solarsystems International or the authorities got back to the Love organization, no matter how cumbersome their bureaucracy is, it was only a matter of time before we were fingered."

"He was just careless," Circe said. She had caught only a glimpse of the driver's face, but she'd found not even a flicker of deliberate intention there. "Let's just get on a flight and get out of here."

"Assuming the pilot isn't a convert who's ready to fly us into a mountain for the Faith."

It seemed unusually difficult to get to the ticket desk. People kept stepping on their toes, walking in front of them. A woman with a slotted can collecting for Save the Californians, Inc. walked directly into Santalucia.

"At least you could say you're sorry!" he snapped, rubbing where her can had rammed his stomach.

The woman turned, seemed to look through him with a puzzled expression on her face, and continued on her way.

"BITCH!" Santalucia screamed. "I WON'T CONTRIBUTE A *CENT* TO THE FUCKING BASTARDS *EVER!* THEY CAN GO ON LIVING IN TENTS TILL THE *NEXT* GODDAMNED EARTHQUAKE!"

Only one or two heads turned to see who was shouting.

"And I thought I was ignored at Rent-A-Car," he said as they approached the flight desk.

Not even the aging Hari Krishna solicitor approached them.

"Two tickets for New York on whatever the next flight is," Santalucia told the man.

"Next," said the clerk.

The woman behind Circe handed her return ticket forward for validation.

"What the hell is this?" Santalucia fumed. "Am I invisible or something? You want to give me two tickets to New York or do you want to die a slow and agonizing death suspended over a boiling pot of decaffeinated coffee?"

The clerk turned to his idle colleague at the next station. "You see the game last night? Rude, wasn't it?"

"I guess you'd know rude if you saw it," Santalucia said.

"And that woody play Hakim made in the third, you know, when the—"

Santalucia hit the man in the face.

"—utility man burned it—"

Santalucia hit him again.

"—right between Jordan's legs—"

"He doesn't know we're here," Circe said at last.

A businessman walked smack into Santalucia's back, seemed confused, and stepped to the side to reach the desk.

"He honestly doesn't see us. It's like hypnotism demonstrations I've seen. The only possibility is that the Love people sent post-hypnotic suggestions about us over the high-frequency carrier channel. Maybe they even used subliminal flashes of our faces from the ID photo file at Faith Limited."

"You mean we *are* invisible?" Santalucia asked, letting go of the clerk's tie.

"For all practical purposes," Circe said. "Unless you can think of some other explanation."

"Hey, who can see me?" Santalucia shouted, clambering up onto the flight desk and waving his arms. "Look at me—I'm a duck. Quack, quack, quack!"

Perhaps a dozen faces glanced up, mainly children; the few adults hurriedly looked away to hide their embarrassment, hoping someone would come and take the lunatic away.

"Jesus, what a Nielsen that Love has," Santalucia marveled. "He's gotten to virtually everyone in the airport except the kids. But what for?"

"Who knows? That cab *did* almost hit you, but it seems like a pretty inefficient way to get rid of us. Maybe they just want to keep us bottled up here. If we can't get anyone to sell us a ticket..."

"Hell, if nobody can see us to sell us a ticket, then nobody can see us if we don't have one. We'll just get on the plane and sit on somebody's lap."

But at the boarding gate they were stopped by a steward. "I'm sorry," he said. "You'll need boarding passes. You'll have to go back to the ticket counter and—"

"Shit," Santalucia said, "there's always some intellectual that doesn't watch television to spoil it for everyone."

"Please, sir, you're blocking the gate."

They made their way back through the passenger lounge under the steward's watchful eye.

"Actually, he probably just doesn't know where to put the Loveband," Santalucia said. "Keeps trying to sit on it."

"This flight originated in LA," Circe said. "He probably hasn't seen any Denver TV. Shall we try another airline?"

"Too complicated. Let's go back to the rental agency and pick up our invisible keys. We'll just drive till we're out of the Denver viewing area and then find the nearest airport."

"What about Colorado Springs?" Circe asked.

"Still too close to the Denver stations."

"Then we'll have to choose between Albuquerque or Salt Lake City or Casper, Wyoming," Circe said. "Wichita's out—I don't want to try driving Kansas after all these dust storms."

"Not to mention whatever they're planning out there for the Saucer Cult. We ought to check a map, but I vote for Albuquerque. I'm not interested in trying the Rockies when we're not sure anybody can see us. If we got stuck, we'd never get a ride."

On their way across the terminal, Santalucia paused to tweak a woman's nose, make faces at a honeymoon couple, and reverse a businessman's hat.

"You poor, sad man," said a nun.

"Another abstainer," Santalucia smiled.

Circe wasn't sure what it was about the man behind them that first attracted her attention, but there was something familiar about the large, floppy hat. Santalucia was just in the middle of laughing at what a stupid, typically bureaucratic, roundabout way Faith Limited had chosen to contain them when Circe grabbed his arm.

"That's not it," she said in a tense voice. "If nobody can see us, there won't be any witnesses to what happens to us."

Santalucia was still trying to sort out his expression and grasp what she'd said when Circe saw the man in the hat slip what looked like a two-foot chrome tube from his coat. She gave Santalucia a violent shove.

"RUN!" she shouted. "THAT WAY!"

There was a vicious *crack* behind them. A spot of flame opened like a malevolent red eye on the pebbled vinyl covering of the pillar next to them. And they were running.

"Help!" Santalucia called. "Help!"

Not a head turned. Most heard nothing; the remaining few had

201

already seen enough of his antics. A metropolitan policeman hiked his foot on the arm of a chair and bent over to tie his shoe as they pounded past.

"And they talk about being alone in a crowd," Santalucia puffed.

Crack. Someone just ahead of them screamed and fell. Another miss, fatal this time. The policeman hopped on one foot, still tying his shoe, toward the ring of onlookers closing around the victim.

"Help!" Santalucia called again. "Somebody?"

But there was no waiting for an answer. The pillared lobby opened out as the gift-laden Christmas travelers shuffled to see what had happened. Santalucia and Circe ran flat-out across the empty expanse of floor, scrambled over a ticket counter, jumped the conveyor belt for United's baggage, found a service door behind an oblivious clerk, and raced through the cavernous baggage room. A moment later they were outside on the tarmac in the frosty air. Santalucia pulled Circe back just as an electric hauler swung past with a train of baggage wagons.

"Where to now?" Santalucia panted.

"All we can do is try to lose him," Circe said.

"That way." Santalucia pointed with a quick jerk of his elbow. "Toward the little independent airlines. Then we can double back to the car rental place. We'll cut through that hangar."

They heard the baggage door slam open behind them and footsteps start out across the apron.

Circe led the way, darting amongst the fuel trucks and baggage-haulers and emergency stairs and work platforms, avoiding the floodlights. From somewhere far away came the flat, lifeless chorus of a Christmas carol from a loudspeaker.

> *Now rest you merry per-er-sons,*
> *Let nothing you dismay,*
> *Sink back into the peaceful flow*
> *Of Personal Enrichment Day. . . .*

A few moments later they reached the yawning black opening of the hangar. Too late they realized that the doors at the far end were closed. A cul-de-sac.

"There's got to be some kind of service door," Circe said, slowing to avoid the jumble of drums and parts.

"If it's not locked," Santalucia said. "At least the darkness is on our side. He can't see any better than we can."

The pursuing footsteps slowed to a walk, moving deliberately toward the hangar.

"Come on out, n-nigger!" shouted a voice. "The lady too! I want you to t-tell me all about the fucking f-fourth dimension again. About how I'm living in a f-fairyland."

Where had Santalucia heard that voice before?

21

Descensus ad Infernos

"I'm glad you've been so worried about the Saucer Cult," Santalucia hissed to Circe. "That's one of them out there that's trying to kill us. I met him in the park the first day we were here."

"What's he talking about fairylands for?"

"Me and my big mouth," Santalucia said.

"Come on, nigger!" called the voice again.

Circe swallowed and tensed. There was no escape. The laser could burn through anything, and she had no idea what its range was.

There wasn't time for mesc, and she hadn't tried since that night in New York, but she had to risk it again. She closed her eyes, contracting into herself, shutting out the sounds of the approaching footsteps, of Santalucia's breathing next to her.

Suddenly she felt herself moving forward, past the drums and the shambles of aluminum engine blocks and fittings like bones and joints in a slaughterhouse. She was there and yet strangely isolated, as though she moved in an envelope of nothingness, sealed away from the touch of air or the smell of oil or the cold she should have felt.

She saw something lurking in the shadows by the door, and she groped until it took shape, dwindled slightly, resolved itself into a human figure. A young man, ragged, bearded, the Cultist. But something was wrong. The eyes, that was it. Head cocked, mouth open in the hideous, idiotic grin of someone losing the sense of what he looked like. Blind.

The man she'd sat next to in the Dying Tiger the day she'd

met Love's double. The same man that had fired from the fire escape into her apartment.

But not blind. He had aimed the laser, followed them.

Something hidden under the floppy hat. Plastic, metal, geometric tracings of circuits. She could sense its meaning without probing deeply. He could see. Not subtleties like expressions, but shapes, forms, movements. The red TV image of her apartment and of herself she'd seen that night in New York had been what he saw through the device he wore. A laser scan that worked the same in daylight or darkness.

There was no time to wonder where he'd gotten such exotic equipment. Already he was raising the chrome tube of his laser at Santalucia and her own empty form behind her.

Without thinking she pressed in on him, feeling suddenly the resistance of his mind, a thick wall of self-satisfaction at the certainty of finishing his quarry off this time. Then doubt, surprise. He felt her probing. His consciousness drew back, the wall constricted around the central core of his being. He would not let her in again.

She surrounded him, hammered at the shrinking sphere of his will. *Brother Moonbeam, prophecies, death of Monad, where's Moonrose, necessity another Dink leader die, Beings sure to come, voices, always voices, uncontrollable urges, actions.* But the laser eyes? *Friends, voices.* The wall closing in on itself, growing harder and more resistant as it compacted into an indestructible kernel of will.

She focused entirely on it, pressed in relentlessly, pried at it like a walnut, felt the shell cracking, then pulling away. She snatched at streamers of his fright as he stumbled backwards to escape her.

Suddenly she sensed light flooding everything around her. The landing lights of an old crop-duster biplane returning from the hopeless task of spraying for spring crops somewhere, the burr of its motor shrouded from her in the absolute silence of her envelope.

He saw it an instant too late. The solid, gleaming disc of the whirling propeller sheared through the hat, headband, skull, hacking out a mist of blood that sparkled in the landing lights. But he fell locked silently within himself, determined to keep the last freehold of his will inviolate even if he had to withhold the animal scream of terror and pain.

Circe pulled back into the hangar darkness lest she see or feel the dreadful slicing. She found herself beside Santalucia's tensed body.

"Did you see that?" he breathed. "Why didn't the pilot see him?"

Circe was almost too exhausted to speak. "They made him invisible too."

"Of course. That way he'd be free to do whatever he wanted, and there wouldn't be more than a handful of people that saw him. Nobody'd take them seriously, especially without our *corpora delicti*."

"Pull his body in here," she managed.

"What for?"

"Just *do* it."

The conviction of her voice overwhelmed Santalucia's reluctance. He scurried out, the crop-duster's drone still moving off into the darkness, and grabbed the mutilated body by its feet to drag it in. Once back inside the safety of the hangar, he squatted over it, panting from the exertion, and studied what was left of it.

On the man's back were the shreds of a thin backpack and a confetti of plastic and metal ribbons that had apparently been resistors, capacitors, integrated circuits, and printed circuit boards. His right hand still clutched a small box with a handle on the bottom and what remained of a chrome tube at one end.

"Probably something like a carbon dioxide laser," he said. "Very powerful. Uses infrared light—that makes it invisible even when there's fog or vapor that would make most laser beams visible. I guess that was to make it hard to tell where he was shooting from—except that he wasn't subtle enough for that approach. Not much left at that end, anyway."

"He had a laser eye rig," she said, removing the packet of mesc spansules from her pocket and swallowing one.

"I've read about those," Santalucia said. "The laser focuses the image directly on the retinas. But that's entirely experimental surgery. They've only tried it on pigs."

"The government's used humans a few times," she said, not sure how she knew. From around her neck she took the little bell on its ribbon, and then from a pocket she removed what looked like a kerchief and unrolled it on the floor. It was the green of life, bordered by two concentric circles into which had been worked the symbols of the seven planetary spirits: Aratron of Saturn,

Bethor of Jupiter, Phaleg of Mars, Och of the Sun, Hagith of Venus, Ophiel of Mercury, and Phuel of the Moon.

"That leaves us with two problems. He could have stolen the laser from some government arsenal, I suppose. But where did he find the medical talent and hardware to get himself outfitted with a seeing-eye laser? And why would some Saucer Cultist be all this interested in us? If he were from Love, I could understand it. Do you think it's a disguise?"

"No," she said, crawling wearily toward the body and kneeling next to it. "That's why I have to follow him down. Would you roll him over for me? I'm too tired."

Santalucia looked puzzled, but he put his hand on one bloody shoulder and rolled the corpse onto its side, as Circe spread the kerchief carefully on the floor where he had lain so that, when he was rolled back, the circles would be directly under his heart. She nodded for Santalucia to put the body back. Then she placed the bell on the sodden shirt over the motionless chest.

It was the necromantic Bell of Girardius. Circe had had it specially cast of lead, tin, iron, gold, copper, fixed mercury, and silver in a little occults art shop on the twenty-first anniversary of the day and hour of her birth. She had been halfway through her year at the Institute. On the top of the bell was engraved Iesu, and on the band at midpoint around the bell, Adonai. Beneath that were the astrological signs of the planets, and along the bell's bottom rim was the word Tetragrammaton.

Circe sat back, concentrating on Moonbeam's lifeless form, focusing on the womanly convexities of the bell. She was more frightened than ever; except in historical accounts, she had heard of only one believable claim to have done such a thing successfully.

"Circe," Santalucia was saying, "are you all right? We've got to get out of here, damn it. What if he wasn't the only assassin? Circe? Circe, what the fuck are you doing? Are you on mesc again?"

Her vision swam and her head began to loll and roll and at last tumble, helplessly dwindling toward the expanding bell, whose curved metal face gave way like mist before her, closing behind as she passed through. For a moment she looked up into the blue twilight of the vast metal dome above her, and then down far below to the faint outlines of the folds and wrinkles of the shirt fabric, splotches of blood huge as ponds and meadows seen from the air.

And then she took a deep breath and plunged down, down, the giant chest spreading and then melting before her into an absolute, empty darkness, without up or down, directionless as chaos itself, so that only the unchanged momentum told her she still spiraled downward, fighting the buoyancy of her own terror.

And then, floating before her in cloudy wisps, the first of the souls. Hungrily they reached out to her, their transparent fingers brushing like pale feathers across her face and arms and breasts as she swam through them, deeper and deeper.

Great Mother, she thought. Horned God. Hunter, Goat, Moon, Snake, Virgin, Mother, Mourner, Wife.

Where was he? He should still have been among the newest of them. How did he get so far away?

A skull scaled with shreds of dry flesh grinned horribly at her, but without reflecting she knew it for Tasar, the Superior of Ashtoreth who had died only a few weeks after Circe had first joined the firm.

You've come, thought the face. *I knew when I first met you that your Gift was great.*

Where is he, Mistress? Circe asked.

Dropped through us and down, thought the face. *Like a stone to the bottom of a pool.*

She dove on through the smoky dark. As she sank she caught a glimpse of a dark-eyed, hawk-faced man, but the spirit turned and fled as though frightened. So familiar. Had it been the Doctor Love double she'd seen die in the Inner Circle car? But no, she didn't remember that; she was reconstructing it from what Santalucia had told her.

She wanted to follow him and find out, but she was after another.

She found her quarry cowering in the twilight mists, eyes closed. She reached out and took his cold hand, held it for an instant in pity.

Can't flash on where they are, the thought mourned. *Cut off. No map. Miss the Beaming.*

I'm sorry, she comforted. *It's over.*

I'm lost, stuck. Left behind. The eyes were still screwed shut. *Won't somebody help me?*

You don't understand, she said.

No, he thought, closing in on himself. *Something's happened to the headpack. There's a Lear jet over there on the other side of the*

208

terminal. Leaving in an hour. Password's "trigger." You tell them that, okay? They'll come lead me to the plane. Tell them "trigger." Don't worry, it's a Love plane. They're lowcal. Friends.

Open your eyes, she said.

No.

She took his hand again in a kind of benediction, drawing the rest from him, understanding. Then she backed away.

Snuff.

The thought came from behind her, but she knew if she turned around the source would flit away.

I don't understand, she said.

Children dying. Blood clotting plains dust. Death rises on fire from stone, darts at them like insects.

Where? she asked.

At the center.

When?

At the center, came the answer.

How can I stop it?

Heart of Love.

Thank you, she thought, wanting to reach out.

It's all right, child. The cold here warms, the dark illuminates. It pleases all of us after a time. But there is one more thing.

Yes?

Nothing is more than its essence. There is no power in paste-board and metal.

"This was a hell of a time to take a hit of mesc," Santalucia was saying.

Circe opened her eyes and found herself lying full length beside the dead man. Her head was cradled in Santalucia's lap. "Descensus," she managed through dry lips.

"Whatever," Santalucia said. "I was going to leave you alone and then you started to fall over. But I did go out to see what I could find of that eye rig. We'd have to take the pieces to Fred, but my guess is that whatever it was included a modified Loveband."

"I know," Circe said. "I . . . communicated with him. They were Love people posing as friends. They helped him and the others blow up the first double; they tricked him into the surgical implantation by telling him it would let him get the real Love. They used the second double as a decoy to send him after me. It was grotesque."

She was almost crying. "They turned him into a . . . a clearing house, pumping him for everything they could about the Cult while they were programming him to kill us . . . and, for a while, the rest of them.''

"Yeah," Santalucia said. "I guess that's the conclusion I was groping for. You use the mesc to clear your head, is that it?"

"Something like that."

"So they were planning to send him in as a kind of time bomb or something? That's why they were herding them into the Dustbowl?''

"Maybe at one time that was their plan," she said. "Even in his unconscious he didn't have enough information for me to be sure. But I do know the plan's different now."

The center, she thought. What could it mean? Blood clotting plains dust. The plains, the Dustbowl—center of the country. All right, she already knew that. But she'd asked him (*had* it been the murdered double?) when, and he'd said the center, too. Time. The center of time? Of course, New Year's Eve, the central moment between the old and new year, old and new century, old and new millennium.

And suddenly, from somewhere outside herself, she had a vision of jet fighters swooping and darting like insects above the helpless crowd of children.

"They're going to use the Air Force somehow," Circe said. "They're going to bomb the Saucer Kids out in the middle of the Dustbowl.''

Santalucia sighed resignedly. "And—?"

She had asked how to stop them, and the answer had been "Heart of Love." She thought for a moment. "We go after Doctor Love and his computer."

"In the basement of Love Central?" Santalucia said.

"Faith Limited has a Lear jet over at the other side of the terminal. I know the password."

"Not on your life," Santalucia said. "We'll go get that rent-a-car and do it ourselves. I'll take you back to New York, because it'll be easier with two of us to drive. But after that, you're on your own."

"*Drive* to New York? We've only got seven days before Project Snuff."

"Better to make it with a few days to spare than get on a Faith Limited Lear jet," he said. "It's one thing to walk into a dragon's mouth. It's something else to dress up in two slices of bread and go lie on his plate."

210

22

The Laughter of Vipers

Out in the middle of the playground's freezing cold, Sister Catherine suddenly remembered that she hadn't put any clothes on before she'd gotten into her overcoat. And she should never have worn bedroom slippers outside. Warm boots, that's what was wanted. That's what she would have told any children that wore slippers to school.

Well, it was hard to imagine how cold it was going to be outside because they were having some kind of heat wave in Indiana, some disturbance of the prevailing winds that was bringing hot air out of Mexico. It had kept up all fall and farmers, knowing how desperate the world was for wheat and corn, had risked a winter planting, and so far it had held. In fact, she'd read, even the birds had been confused, and flies and moths and crickets and grasshoppers had been hatching.

A world gone mad. New-born flies in December.

Something else had been distracting her, too. It was a painting she'd seen once in a museum. Or maybe she'd seen a reproduction of it in a book or on tape. She couldn't always be certain of little details like that anymore.

Anyway, it had been by Salvador Dali, and it had been called something like "King of the World." It had shown Christ on His cross, the whole thing tipped back so His feet were toward the viewer and He lay reclining almost horizontal above the silent ball of the sinful earth.

It was hardly traditional. It showed none of the suffering of the figure hanging in agony. And she thought she remembered that Dali had used his own feet as the model for Christ's, and somehow that seemed vaguely blasphemous.

211

But she couldn't get the painting out of her head.

"Can't we go *in?*" one of the children pleaded.

"I'm thinking," she said, waving her away.

Volunteering to run a free Saturday daycare had seemed like a good idea when she'd suggested it. It implied the proper suppression of self in her own case, provided a useful service to parents working or wanting to shop. And she rarely had anything to do on Saturdays. But now it seemed like such a chore.

And the wind was blowing right up her coat. Her thighs and stomach were already numb. She could hear the coat brush against them but she could feel nothing, as though they belonged to someone else entirely.

Lord of the Flies, that was the meaning of Beelzebub. Could it be that the Devil was at work in Indiana?

"*Please,*" whined the child. "It's so cold."

"Of course it's cold. I'm cold too. That's why we're playing outside today. Otherwise it would be hot."

Someone was laughing somewhere. She went to the playground gate, opened it, peered up and down the street. She couldn't *see* anyone laughing, but someone could laugh one minute and the next you could look at his face *and the laughter wouldn't leave a trace*.

Laughing wasn't like urinating on a wall.

She thought she ought to go at least to the end of the block to see if anyone had slipped around the corner. Because if there was someone calling her Froggie and laughing and urinating on walls, she wanted to know about it. Not to punish them. No, no. To talk to them, make them understand how much she cared for them. You didn't get anywhere with threats or punishment. You did it with love.

The way God loved her, for instance.

If He didn't love her, then she wouldn't know, would she?

In fact, the best way to show how God cared for her was to announce the miracle right away. And then whoever was laughing would naturally stop. Nobody laughed at miracles.

Just around the corner was a Salvation Army band left over from Christmas, still pumping out carols in their drive to restore Christmas to its original form.

"It came upon a midnight clear," she sang to the music, smiling and waving to the players.

"Bless you, Sister," said the trombone player, lowering his

trombone to reveal the creased red circle the mouthpiece had left on his lips. "Merry Christmas."

"Repent," she replied gaily. "For the Kingdom of Heaven is at hand."

"Beg pardon?" he called over the still active trumpet and accordion.

"I eat locusts and honey," she said. "To touch their ha-arps of gold," she sang, moving down the sidewalk.

"I am the voice of one crying in the wilderness," she called to a woman carrying a string bag of bulky packages. "Prepare the way of the Lord and make his paths straight."

The woman hurried on.

They weren't listening the way they ought to. There just wasn't any way to say this kind of thing pleasantly and have people believe you. You had to be forceful. She grabbed the sleeve of the next man she saw.

"Every tree which does not bear good fruit must be cut down!" she said firmly. "Do you see that?"

He yanked his arm away, frowning but obviously somehow upset, and crossed to the opposite side of the street.

There was nothing wrong with what she was doing. She could not be bound in conscience not to do it. She could not even be bound in virtue of Holy Obedience. Because she was the last of her Order, and there were no Mothers Superior to bind her to anything. Novice, sister, Mother Superior all in one.

And John the Baptist.

"Do you see?" she said, holding open her coat. There was a flight of stairs nearby, and she climbed slowly up it, turning to face the passersby. "Transformed, woman into man. I am come to tell you that the baptism of the Holy Ghost with fire is coming. I am John the Baptist, do you hear me?"

She looked amongst the upturned faces for even a glimmer of comprehension.

A boy carrying a bag stared hungrily at her crotch and hurried on.

"Can you look and not see? For the wheat will be gathered up and the chaff sent to the fire."

Someone was laughing again. She knew he'd come this way.

"Sister Catherine," a voice was saying. "Cover yourself."

"Look! Look! Look!" she shouted. "Generation of vipers! You can't escape the wrath to come. And it *is* coming, for I've been sent to warn you as I was the last time. To prepare the way for Him."

An arm had come around her, forcing her to bring her coat flaps in against herself. The lining was cold, terribly cold against her skin.

"Father Camillieri," she said.

"It's going to be all right, Sister."

"I'm so glad it's you, Father, because He wants you to know that He's coming. Sliding down off Calvary, flying toward us, rolling toward us. Faster and faster. King of the World. Just when we needed Him most, He's consented to come."

He was helping her up the steps, an arm around her shoulders, his other hand firmly holding both her hands against her chest. She looked down so she wouldn't fall.

"My feet are very wet, Father," she sniffled. "I should have worn my rubbers."

23

Indiana Home

Soames stood in the sweltering heat beside the tiny square of artificial grass laid over the freshly turned earth. She'd asked to be cremated, and he'd followed her wishes. But it wasn't legal to scatter the ashes, and he had no home now where the urn could be brought. There was nowhere for her but here.

If they'd stayed in Connecticut, he could have gone to Blessed Interval or one of the other cryogenic palaces in the hope that someday paychecks and medical cures could catch up with medical technology. But she'd suffered too much to want ever to wake up again. So now there was nothing—no body, no bones, only ashes that would be deaf to the trumpets of the Last Judgment.

He looked out across the flat plains of baking dirt toward the town. The hospital gleamed like a white sugar cube at the far end.

They'd taken her at last, not to excise the diseased gall bladder but to administer drugs in the Terminal Wing. They were especially proud of their specially trained death squad, brimming with the kind of compassionate candor that Soames had been searching for all these months. Unfortunately, they specialized in terminal illness. Illness their colleagues had made terminal.

He heard someone circumspectly clearing his throat behind him. "Mr. Soames?"

"Eh?" Soames said dreamily, turning from the artificial grass to find the round, flaccid face of the Mortuary Artist. Jowly, eyes nearly hidden beneath deep folds of flesh, a child's face that had unaccountably become lined and begun to sag, like an immortal cherub's too long on the job.

215

"I hate to mention this at a time like this," he began. "But I believe you neglected to give us your Omnicard number. Of course, there'll be insurance coming and all the rest of it, but these are difficult times, if you understand me, and we've had to establish some unfortunately stringent rules about extending services to, ah, transient cases."

"What? Oh, of course." Soames caught the glint of the hooded eyes, cold and hard for so soft a face. "How much?"

"Well, let's see, there was the Restorative Cosmetologist, the Permanence Artist, the Slumber Director. Then there was Studio rental and supplies for Revivification, the use of the Reunification Chapel, as well as the Eternal Sleep Crematory. Oh yes, and fuel fees, grounds fees, transportation, Repose Vessel rental, plot purchase, the actual urn—"

"Just the total," said Soames. "It doesn't matter anymore."

"Altogether, roughly one hundred ten thous—"

Soames handed him his Omnicard. "This will cover that much," he said.

"I can see it's a gold," the Mortuary Artist smiled. "We'll just take it back to the Center."

"Fine," Soames said. "I'd like to stay here a little longer. Then I'll just swing past and pick it up."

"Very good," the man said. "I'll leave it for you at the desk."

He was gone.

Soames would have to leave almost right away, before the jimmy slipped that card in the slot and their computer lit up like a Christmas tree. But it was hard to leave. After all those months, it was hard to turn his back on her forever, even when all the pain and suffering had been burned away and only elemental ash remained.

He could see clearly the state highway leading west out of the town. Along it skimmed a little van. More of the Saucer Kids? He'd thought a lot about them as he'd listened to the reports of the caravan's progress. They were so sure, so certain. They believed the end of the world was coming and that Beings would somehow whisk them away to some kind of other-dimensional heaven.

It would be nice to have that kind of belief. Kids were always so idealistic, so unshakable in their convictions. He wished he was young enough to be that way, too. He could head west, follow the setting sun into Kansas with the rest of them. More and more cars would appear, herd him toward whatever their destination was. They'd take care of him there, from what he'd heard: food, shelter, blankets. It would be nice to let somebody take care of him, even tell him what to do. He wouldn't have to think or worry.

Except that New Year's would come and nothing would happen. Another disappointment, another hurt. He didn't have the strength for it.

He made his way out of the cemetery, pausing at the gates, on which were engraved two praying hands, to nod a last goodbye. Then he trudged down the hill toward town.

He'd come in the usual Mortuary Artist's limousine, having carefully parked his car out of sight so none of them would know its license number or make or notice how it was stuffed with the few odds and ends that his wife had loved, all that was left of their household. He wasn't quite sure which side street he'd parked on, because he had had trouble remembering practical details like that during the last few days, but he figured he could find it before too long. Before the Mortuary Artist called the state troopers with a deadbeat alert, at least.

The funny thing, though, the funny thing was that at least he'd expected to feel relieved of some tremendous burden when at last it was over. But there was no relief. His shoulders still sagged as though beneath an immense weight, he still felt the same sense of dread he'd had returning to the car when she had lain in it, moaning. God damn it, it wasn't fair. All things, good and bad, had to have natural limits, fixed ends. It couldn't go on like this forever.

A grasshopper bounded from nowhere, poised on his shoulder, flicked away.

He paused before a D-store window on the dusty main street. Self-consciously he looked both ways, but there was only a frail girl in faded jeans engrossed in watching something on one of the display TV sets. He stole a glance at himself in the plate glass.

No wonder the Mortuary Artist had been worried about the bill. His denim suit was actually frayed. His hair was shaggy, his beard untrimmed. He looked like a scarecrow someone had stuck out in a cornfield somewhere.

He sensed the girl glance over at him, and he hurriedly pretended to be looking at something in the window instead of his own reflection.

Satisfied at having obscured any suggestion of narcissism, he turned to head on toward wherever his car was.

The girl was staring at him.

He gave her a fatherly wink. "Good day," he said in a husky voice.

The girl looked startled. "You say something?"

"How do you do?"

"Pretty lowcal," she said.

He balanced stiffly, sensing that she wanted to say something more.

"Are you . . . are you a Seeker by any chance?"

"A Seeker?" he asked.

"Never mind," she said, turning back to the TV with a kind of longing. "I was just hoping I could hitch a ride, that's all."

"What are you watching?"

"The Mothership," she said.

He peered through the window at the TV screen. It seemed to be a picture of a huge disc somewhere out in the prairie. On every side of it milled the ant-like specks of people.

"That's not a ship," he said. "That's just a sculpture some guy did out in Kansas. It's been getting a lot of coverage lately because all the Saucer Kids seem to think . . ." He eyed her thoughtfully. "I see," he said. "You're one of them."

She nodded. "I've been trying to get there for days, but one place I got arrested for hitching and then I kept getting all these one-town rides. It's taken forever to get this far."

"But you realize that thing there hasn't got anything to do with those Beings of yours," he said.

"I *know* that. But They must have communicated with him somehow, inspired him, maybe without him even knowing what he was doing. It's a sign. It's the sign telling us where They're going to beam us up."

"You don't have any doubts?" he asked.

"Of course not," she said. "I was in Tennessee the first time after . . . well, never mind, with a guy I'd met. And I flashed on it right after he went off, if you know what I mean. And I hadn't even seen anything on TV. It's this kind of spirit radar. You just relax, let your thoughts kind of mish around, then exhale to get rid of the bad ones, and sometimes things will just come to you."

"You really believe that?"

"Of course I do," she said. "I doubted before, but I do now."

He sighed with a kind of admiration. "All right," he said. "I'll take you."

She smiled at him. "I thought you might. I could see it in your face. You have a nice face."

"What's your name?" he asked, gesturing with his hand in the general direction of his car.

"Starbud," she said.

They moved along the highway between the bright green rows of miracle winter corn beneath the blinding noontime sun, but the sky beyond them was dark with a duster somewhere far away. Starbud studied the gloom wearily. It seemed to grow denser toward the horizon, as though there were something tangible there, clouds so thick you could reach out and tear out hunks of them. She rubbed her eyes.

Almost like the clouds were swirling. After what had happened with the boy, she'd been surprised that she'd had the spirit radar to read Soames correctly. Obviously anything was possible, and now maybe she'd somehow evolved the ability to see molecules actually moving through the air.

The car whined onward, and the ground-cloud grew bigger. But she'd been through dust blizzards a hundred times bigger and more frightening than anything she could see ahead.

A sharp *thok* and a splot of viscous yellow-green liquid appeared suddenly on the windshield.

"What was that?" she asked, startled.

"Bug," Soames said.

Thok-thok.

Two more in rapid succession.

Then all at once the air around them was alive with great black shapes like blurred ping-pong balls.

Thok-thok-thok-thok.

Soames reached down to the dash and flicked on the windshield wipers. Two nozzles squirted streamers of cleaning fluid that rilled up the windshield in the wind, and the two wipers swept across, smearing the yellow stuff back and forth, finally beginning to cut through it. Soames slowed slightly until he could see the road better.

But the *thoks* came more and more rapidly. Soames hunched forward, trying to see through his windshield, now opaque with a greenish yellow-white slime in the dimming light, against which the heads-up display shimmered lividly.

The girl felt her heart beating faster and faster, a rising panic squeezing her chest. Her breathing grew more rapid and shallow, her legs and arms numb. She crossed her arms over her chest protectively. The very air outside was closing in. It was a sign. The Beings would not let her join the others. They were going to crush and suffocate her here.

"What is it?" she asked in a strangled voice. Some of the things were hitting the side windows now, splattering, bouncing off like hail. In the dusky fields beyond, the tall corn itself seemed to be moving.

But Soames was too preoccupied to answer. All at once there was the faintest flickering through the smeared glass, a pair of headlights emerging from the gloom directly toward them. Their car swerved, skidded as though the pavement were greased, slewed in slow motion sideways across the crown of the roadway and down toward the wall of corn beyond as the other car squealed in the opposite direction. There was the whip-crack of snapping fence wires, and suddenly they were spinning into the corn like a rotary scythe, the new ears beating a tattoo along the car body and windows. They slithered to a stop.

Terrified, gasping for breath, Starbud wrenched up on the doorhandle and pulled it open. The air was black with a powerful whirring and humming.

Something sharp struck her face.

She opened her mouth to cry out, but another fluttered against her lips and teeth, and as she closed them to keep it out, a third buzzed against her left eye. She forced herself to hold just long enough to focus. Through the hail of flying shapes she saw what they were. Grasshoppers. Flying, leaping, swarming over the stalks of corn.

She felt the urge to scream burning deep within her, but she turned steadily, pulled open the car door with both hands, crushing two more of the things, and flung herself inside. Soames leaned over and swept a handful of them off her and onto the car floor. She stared down at them, stunned, as they writhed and tumbled over one another, whirring into brief flights and dropping back again. She kept thinking of the crowd in New York, the insect closeness of the jail.

"Locusts," Soames said. "They're eating up our one shot at having enough food next year. I'd heard forecasts here and there, but I guess I hadn't been paying attention to them...." He stared dazedly at the instrument display still burning against the windshield. "HED's shot," he said at last. He twisted the key as though to demonstrate. "Dead."

Outside, the insect rain continued against the metal and glass of the car. Suddenly there was a pounding at the window. It took both of them a moment to realize it was not the locusts. Soames reached back and opened the rear door, and two dark figures clambered in through a cloud of wings.

"We almost hit head-on back there," the first one said, slapping the things off his chest. He was black. "You okay?"

"We're okay, yeah," Soames said. "But our battery's cracked or something."

"Our car's still okay," the woman said. "We can give you a lift to the next town, at least."

"Thanks," Soames said.

"Is that east or west?" Starbud asked.

"East," the black man said.

Starbud shook her head. "No. We can't go even a kilometer backwards. Already we're running out of time. We've got to keep moving forward."

The man and woman in the back seat exchanged glances.

"I'm sorry," the woman said. "We were already held up with car trouble. We can't risk any delays—it's life and death. But we can't just leave you here."

Soames gave Starbud an imploring look, but she was adamant.

"Why do you have to keep moving west?" the black man demanded. "You're not going with everybody else to Kansas, are you?"

"The Beaming's in two days," the girl said. "We've got to be there New Year's Eve."

"What's the matter with you?" the black man said to Soames. "You're actually taking your own kid to get killed with the rest of those nuts?"

"She's not my kid," Soames said. "I just promised to help her, that's all."

"Look," the black man said to Starbud, "I'm a father, and I know how your father would feel if he knew where you were headed. You get in our car and we'll take you back to New York. You'll be safe there, at least."

"Never," the girl said.

"But you don't understand," the black man shouted. "You could get killed if you go out there."

221

"My parents are there," the girl said quietly. She could feel the woman staring at her.

"We'd better forget it," the woman said. "I can read her and she's not going to change her mind. Do you understand me, though?" she asked Starbud. "We're not lying. If you go on, you have to believe us that there's terrible danger."

Suddenly Starbud's mind was flooded with images. She saw the sabotage of the Denver satellite, saw Moonbeam backing away into a whirling propeller. She looked fearfully at the woman's face and realized that the flashes had come from her.

"It's all right," the woman soothed. "I just wanted you to understand the danger."

Starbud saw jet fighters swooping down toward the empty plains. "It doesn't matter," she said.

The black man sighed. "You'll take care of her the best you can?" he asked Soames.

"I'll try," Soames said.

"Then that's the most we can do," he said to the woman.

Soames and Starbud were silent for several minutes after the man and woman had gone.

"Well, what now?" Soames asked. "Do we sit and wait it out?"

"No," Starbud said slowly. "The Beings wouldn't want us to just sit. If we start walking now, we'll be that much farther along when we find our next ride."

Soames rubbed his eyes, rummaged among the junk in the back for blankets. "We'll take these," he said. "It's hot enough here, but I hear Kansas hasn't gotten any of this weather. It'll be cold there."

In pulling the blankets out he dislodged a framed photograph, a polished quartz paperweight, odds and ends of a lifetime. He stared down at them for a moment.

"We'll leave the rest, I guess," he said. "Nobody needs any of it any more. Shall we get out on my side, my dear?"

They opened the door a second time to the overwhelming buzzing. The girl batted them away from her face, felt them strike her hair, entangle themselves, flutter wildly. Each one was an electric shock, metallic thwacks up and down her arms and legs. It was like the steady pounding of feathers, no one blow painful or even forceful, but cumulatively paralyzing.

The ground was brown and alive with them, and as she stumbled forward beside Soames she could hear their shells crackle beneath her feet. Just as they reached the road she lost her footing in their ooze, and fell forward. She staggered up crawling with them, but she tugged at Soames's sleeve, always pulling him on, even when she had to close her eyelids and go by her sense of direction, feeling them jump to her neck and cling, tickling, then crawl into her shirt, while other pricklings moved up her pantslegs and sleeves.

Sometimes, slipping and sliding in the mush of exoskeletons and insect guts, she felt she couldn't breathe. At least in a dust blizzard she could always put her back to the wind and gulp down gritty air; but here the air was alive with ravenous, alien, flying things whose need to spawn and eat she could not begin to fathom because it was so far below the threshold of thought.

But perhaps the Beings could understand them.

It was only gradually that she became aware of a lessening of their impacts.

"We're through the worst of it," Soames said.

Gradually the sky began to brighten. On either side of them what had been rows of new corn was now a wasteland of shredded vegetation, flattened and lifeless except for the occasional grasshopper that rummaged innocently and industriously amongst the inedibles, somehow left behind by the swarm, and those that had succumbed to injury or age and lay squirming on the roads and fields, moving their legs in slow, useless, jerky arcs.

Starbud looked back only once to see the black cloud now low on the eastern horizon. They kept to the highway, criss-crossed by tire-track smears of insects crushed by cars and trucks trying to make their way through the storm, in places the asphalt gilded almost entirely by a layer of sickly yellow slime.

It was perhaps an hour later that they found the ride Starbud had known lay somewhere ahead. A young man in a silver jumpsuit was just finishing tightening the bolts on their car's wheel hub as his blond and shaggy companion hefted the flat tire they'd removed into their trunk.

She knew without asking that they were Seekers. She waved to them. The two looked up, and the shaggy one roared a greeting as the other waved them on. Starbud and Soames hurried forward, trying to keep their footing on the slippery surface of the yellowed road.

24

The Gathering Dark

3:45 PM Central Time, Friday, December 31

Sinbad Schwartz was ecstatic. Not even in his wildest dreams had he envisioned so vast an audience for his work. And not just the limp-wrist critics from the Art Establishment. Kids, adults, oldsters—real, average people. It was a vindication of the universality of art. It was a vindication of the universality of Sinbad Schwartz.

He'd spent every waking hour these last days at *Ode to the Forty-Five RPM,* moving among his admirers and having himself interviewed over and over by the various national and international news teams covering the event. Thirty years ago it would have been called a *happening.* Maybe he would single-handedly revive the term, he told reporters. And how would he feel if in fact his work did somehow lure a flying saucer full of aliens out of the sky to destroy the earth, as the Cultists firmly believed? So much the better. It would prove once and for all the power of his vision and the efficacy of art.

He'd gotten back to the McCallums' agristation, where he'd been staying off and on these last months, so exhausted and famished he barely had the strength to punch in a couple of lunches on their homeputer. The McCallums were out, as usual, so he slumped into a chair and hit the remote control for the TV, flicking through the channels to find something to lull him while he gathered the strength to return to his work and watch people admire it.

Considering the time he'd spent in the McCallums' living module, considering how much of the final conceptualizing had gone on within these very walls, it was altogether likely that the place would be declared a national historical landmark. Guided tours to his bedroom, his bathroom (*And this is where he used to put his HED toothbrush. The replica you see here is as close to the one he used as our research—*), the table where he ate. When his toothbrush and knife burned out, he'd have to remember to store them in a trunk with identifying notes for the art historians and biographers.

He hit the remote and backed up a couple of channels. Just what he thought he'd seen! The local ETV station was rerunning the November edition of *Art Now* that had, as far as he could gather, started the whole thing.

He stared lovingly at the footage they'd shot of his construction when he'd first finished it, back in late October. It was weird to see it again without all the people crawling around it. He'd forgotten what *Ode to the 45* looked like alone. Very good, that's what it looked like.

Mr. Sinbad Schwartz, generally acknowledged leader of the Crapart movement, the voice-over droned as the screen flickered with shots of *Ode* from every possible angle, *is already the creator of a large corpus of objects both huge and problematic which, like his cenotaph for drunken drivers, have been mainly unrealized. This time, however, Schwartz had managed to secure financing from an as yet unidentified patron for the realization of this, his latest, grandest, and most ambitious design.*

Schwartz nodded approvingly. The patron would stay unidentified, too, because Schwartz himself hadn't the vaguest idea who had sent the anonymous cashier's check. But it didn't worry him, because obviously he had admirers at every level of the economy.

One approaches the work by a series of markers which ingeniously superimpose the road to art on Route Seventy-Three.

The screen showed a long shot of the Dustbowl highway and one of Schwartz's hand-lettered signs, then cut to a full shot of *Ode*.

Before one is a soaring column bisected near the top by a great silver disc, a mixture of monumental geometric and organic volumes which, as one draws nearer, literally fills the sky. In some senses it is an emerging earth form—a mushroom, a toadstool—and yet at the same time the viewer feels the imprint of man's shaping spirit in the uncompromising geometrical perfection of the shaft.

There is none of the temporary, vulnerable, quixotic quality found in his earlier exterior plasterboard and masking-tape constructions. This, one feels with enormous satisfaction, is a statement for the ages—without wishing, necessarily, to impose the kind of "meaning" one is apt to associate with the word "statement" on what is in a variety of senses purely formal and abstract.

Schwartz's forehead wrinkled briefly. All those years he spent making things that weren't supposed to be anything and they'd always said they looked like this or that. Now he'd made something that was supposed to look like a chromed antique forty-five on a spindle and they were calling it a formalist construction. Well, he could live with that as easily as he lived with the fact that most of those people out there now thought it looked like a flying saucer. That was the secret of great art. It looked like anything you wanted it to. Albers's squares, Pollack's blizzards of paint droplets, Michelangelo's *Pietà*. The whole thing was up to the viewer.

In several portions, the announcer was saying, *the tinfoil has been torn, hinting at the interior plywood frame which exactly and miraculously fills the exterior tinfoil skin, a summation of the perfection of volume absolutely filled.*

The work demands diachronic linear contemplation—one thinks about it as one walks toward it in a kind of participatory fluidity which is masterfully encouraged by Schwartz's consciously non-painterly sculptural vocabulary of everyday builder's supplies.

Schwartz heard the high-voltage crackle that meant someone was in the dustlock. McCallum or his wife back from whatever it was they did. Growing rubber, he thought.

The construction is the positive, the space is the negative, joining to create a single unity of positive-negative yin-yang which revitalizes traditional tri-dimensional spatial notions, transcending visual intuition to draw upon our tribal and primordial sense of interlocking shapes and motifs—the column, the disc, and the void.

He'd done all that, he smiled, without half thinking about it. He ought to be taking notes so he could add a little spice to the interviews he'd be granting as soon as he'd caught a nap and had the strength to get back to the *Ode*.

Preconceptions are cast aside in the face of being/disappearing/becoming, defining the cosmos through a series of plural manifestations. Only when the viewer's nose actually strikes the column does any stasis become possible, with a consequent

226

*compression of the primarily metaphoric sense of sculptural
space, thus casting aside illusionistic symbolism for the primary
physical reality of tinfoil, through which all ambiguities are
resolved, allowing his reshaped reality to be perceived through
our altered cognitions.*

"You watching yourself again, Schwartz?" It was McCallum's
voice, as usual sharpened to an unpleasant edge. "You've turned
narcissism into a fine art."

"Actually," Sinbad said, rising to get his lunches from the
homeputer microwave, "narcissism is the essence of art. It says
that later in this show. What's your nose so out of joint for?"

"Nose out of joint? Have you been out to any of the polytents
lately? Every one's been torn apart to make tents for these creeps
while they wait for the Saucer tonight. They've trampled the
guayule, destroyed the heating lamps. In a few days they've
undone years of work. But that's all right with them—they don't
think there's going to *be* any tomorrow. They can do more
damage than the locusts in Indiana and it won't matter. Except it
will matter. There *is* going to be a tomorrow, and they're going
to have to live in it. And they've already guaranteed it's going to
be a poorer place to live."

"Then I don't see what you're so pissed about," Schwartz
said. "My whole life is creating art that raises the level of
consciousness and improves humanity's—"

"Raises the level of consciousness?" McCallum snorted. "If
you want to improve the world, why don't you get in the dustcat
with me and see what we can do about the guayule? Do you have
any idea what your piece of sculpture has done? It's focused
their worst fantasies, reduced them to pure barbarism. They're
nothing but savages out there. They think that plywood thing of
yours is going to *lure* the Beings' saucer from space. That
remind you of anything?"

Schwartz pushed the first plate away and pulled the second
toward him. "Great art is whatever you want—"

"It's like a goddamned South Seas cargo cult building bamboo airplanes and control towers to trick the silver gift-bird down
out of the sky. For over fifty years those natives have been
waiting for their bamboo decoys to bring the World War Two
cargo planes back. And I can just see this bunch doing exactly
the same thing."

"Calm down, Andrew." Carol had come unobserved up into

the room from the lab tunnel, and was standing by the house terminal. "Andrew's upset because I told him I'm going down there to look for Jessica. I know she's with them."

"She'd never be that stupid," McCallum said.

Carol shot him a sharp look. "Why is it, Andrew, that you always seem to want to think she's dropped off the face of the earth? It's like you're afraid she *will* come back."

McCallum stalked away angrily.

"Anyway," Carol said, "the baby's asleep, Mr. Schwartz. All you need to do when he wakes up—"

"Actually," Schwartz said, "I was planning to head back to *Ode* and see how—"

"Mr. Schwartz, for months I've been taking care of the baby."

Schwartz opened his mouth to protest.

"Oh, I know I wanted it that way," Carol hastened on. "I don't blame you. I was trying to replace someone I'd lost. But it's not just enough to be anyone's mother. I'm *her* mother, and if I'm going to be that then I'll have to go down there and search from one end of that crowd to the other. And that's for the best, because I think it's time for you to start being a father."

"But my work—"

"If you don't want the child," Carol said, "then let him go back to his mother."

Schwartz said nothing, poking at his tepid oat-loaf. He should have punched in a delay on this one to keep it hot.

"And now it's time to go," Carol said. "Before the light's gone. Do you want to come, Andrew?"

McCallum shrugged.

"All right," he said. "All right, I'll go."

5 PM, Eastern Standard Time

James Augustus Pilcher sat in his white Shady Pines johnnycoat, open at the back, his hands in leather manacles, tying two sticks together in a cross with a piece of yarn. Beside him the forlorn bottle brush of an artificial tree strung with more dusty yarn stood as a mute reminder of the gray Christmas just past. Or Personal Enrichment Day. Shady Pines was aggressively nonsectarian.

Sister Catherine glared at him from across the room, pulling

228

her own johnnycoat tighter about her. Miserable imposter, she thought. Liar.

"Good afternoon, Sister Catherine," said a voice kindly.

She looked up. It was Father Camillieri.

"I see you still have your Christmas decorations up," he said. "I told you you'd like it here. It's lucky we were able to work out the arrangements."

She said nothing. She was still waiting, and she'd know Him when He came. It wasn't Father Camillieri and it certainly wasn't James Pilcher.

"It was a lovely day," Father Camillieri went on. "I guess there's another storm on its way tonight, but it was still a lovely day. Maybe it means things will get better, don't you think, Sister?"

She did not answer.

"The nurse tells me they're planning a lovely party for all of you tonight," Father Camillieri said. "For New Year's. And I thought you'd want to know that I've made sure there's a party at Mill Street School. I knew it was something you'd always arranged for the children on your own all these years, so I thought you'd rest easier knowing it had been taken care of."

Silence again.

"Do you think your friend here is coming to the party?" he asked, smiling at Pilcher.

No answer.

"Do you know his name? Have you tried to meet him?"

Sister Catherine looked up tiredly. "He's an imposter named James Pilcher, and he's nutty as a fruitcake."

"I'm not anyone named Pilcher," said the boy fiercely, looking up from his yarn. "You know who I am."

"Now you see, Sister Catherine?" Father Camillieri prodded. "You haven't really tried to meet him. What *is* your name, son?"

"Jesus Christ, Son of Man," Pilcher said.

"Liar!" Sister Catherine shrieked, tearing at her johnnycoat. "I'll show you who *I* am! I know exactly how He's going to appear—"

Father Camillieri held her down in the chair and kept her from ripping off her johnnycoat until the attendants arrived with thorazine and leather straps to tie her in.

When the priest had finally gone, she glared her hatred across the room.

229

But Pilcher was ready. With a cunning smile he raised his diamond shape of sticks and yarn, now completed. A god's-eye. He stuck out his tongue.

Trembling, she shrank back before the power of the hex. She tried to form the image of Dali's "King of the World" in her mind, but she couldn't get past the huge feet that were, in fact, Dali's.

"I'll show you," Pilcher muttered. "Just as soon as I get my rollerskates back."

4:30 PM, Central Time

Starbud sat in a stupor of exhaustion and wonderment inside the little shelter of clear plastic that the others had found. She recognized it as the remnant of one of her father's polytents.

A circle of cars, vans, and trucks had been made to mark out a large clear space around the two-hundred-foot shaft and disc of silver, but Starbud had insisted they stay well back at the fringes of the crowd. So many of them, more than she had seen in New York or New Bethel or Denver. They crawled, thick as locusts, around the central circle, which they left inviolate for the true Saucer which would be drawn to the plywood imitation.

She felt more comfortable here. How well she remembered the dust drifts across old fences and farm buildings, but never before could she have imagined all the little children she saw scampering over them and wading through them. There had been an unexpected light dusting of snow, and the rising wind seemed to play with it, whipping it in fine wisps between the trampled clumps of dirt. It seemed to be growing colder.

Brother Jack, silver jumpsuit wrinkled from the long drive, stood leaning stiffly on the ax he'd used to split some old fenceposts into firewood, while Brother Bert bent his shaggy head over the pile of kindling to try to blow it into a fire. Soames, whom Brother Bert insisted on calling Brother Ray, sat slumped like a bundle of rags, knees tucked under his chin, waiting for the first warmth of the fire.

"I asked around about those names you mentioned," Brother Jack was saying. "A bunch of people knew Moonrose, but nobody's seen her."

"And Levitt?"

"He led the main group here a week ago or more," Brother Jack said, "but nobody's seen him for the last few days. One brother I met told me some people think he was a Dink agent. Except I can't figure why a Dink would actually lead us to the Beaming, can you?"

Starbud shrugged, staring off to the west where the gathering storm clouds had covered the sunset. Duster coming. Already it was growing dark. She didn't really need to ask about Moonbeam after the confusion of images the woman in the car had fed her during the storm, but she felt obliged for the sake of Moonrose's memory.

Jack shook his head. "Nothing," he said. "I found somebody that thought she remembered him, but that was about it."

The wind blew ever stronger and colder, and an anticipatory hush spread outward from the center of the milling crowd. Even Starbud could sense the growing excitement through her weariness.

From the dark center of the crowd a voice was shouting, shredded into unintelligibility by the wind. But Starbud could recite the half-heard words by heart.

And the voice which I heard from heaven spake unto me again, and said, Go and take the little book....

She rose and walked forward with the others to join the crowd, Soames rising awkwardly and following after them. Already the center of the crowd had begun to blossom with the twinkling elfin lights of candles, more and more moving ever outward into the darkness.

...and as soon as I had eaten it, my belly was bitter. And he said unto me, Thou must prophesy....

Starbud's face glowed in the dancing light of the candle she held cupped against the gritty wind. Perhaps the woman had been right, but she would wait until the bitter end in memory of Moonrose and her own dead hope.

And they heard a great voice from heaven saying unto them, Come up hither. And they ascended up to heaven in a cloud....

Starbud glanced back at Brother Jack and Brother Bert and Soames, their faces disembodied in the darkness, hanging like moons in the illumination of the candles they sheltered at their chests.

And then, whether by prearrangement or common consent, the cars and trucks that formed the protective circle about the plywood *Ode* turned their headlights on as one, and out of the night the great disc flashed suddenly into being, more real, more imminent than anything else imaginable, shimmering, floating on what seemed to be a beam of solid silver.

7 PM, Central Time

The megahype was over. Dreamily, T-Boy Tucker removed the Loveband and rubbed his eyes. Then movement caught his eye. He looked over at his son's miniature Honda hovercar maneuvering around the beanbag chair.

"Did you erase?"

"What?" His son wasn't listening. As usual.

"When you hit the table leg and then backed up and went around it—that whole sequence is imprinted on the chip now. You've got to erase it and start over or it'll repeat the whole thing next time."

"You play with it," his son said, rising and stomping out of the room.

Little prick, T-Boy thought. He picked up the ultrasonic transmitter for manual control to see how he'd do with a second car against the misprogrammed chip car.

"You playing with Todd's cars again?" his wife asked, standing in the kitchen door.

"I got to go in a little while," he said, preoccupied with directing the second hovercar. "Maneuvers."

"You never mentioned it before," she said. Her voice carried a certain irritation, but at the same time it seemed she was neither angry nor surprised. "I thought we were going to the VFW Hall for New Year's. I know we paid for reservations months ago. They've got a wall screen to show the Love special...."

"Must of forgot."

"Training again?" she asked. "It's the fifth week in a row."

"We practice till Old Fartbreath thinks we've got it right. It's tough stuff, you know. Low-level strafing runs, target practice with Lawndoctor missiles."

"But what are they training you for?"

"Jesus, you ask a lot of questions, woman," he said. "How do I know? Maybe the Texas Air National Guard is being activated and sent to Pakistan."

"What time do you leave?" she asked.

232

His hovercar plowed into the beanbag chair and dropped like a stone; his son's programmed unit brushed the table leg, backed up, and continued around it toward the fireplace. He watched it drift into the flames and drop suddenly, curling and drooping in the heat.

"I don't know," he said slowly. "In three minutes."

The charred hulk of the hovercar rolled off the flaming log where it had fallen and tumbled into the embers below.

Within the hour he was hurrying along the flight line, the nylon thighs of his flight suit swishing.

"Hell of a thing, calling out the Guard on New Year's Eve," the pilot next to him was saying. His voice was cool and level, as though he were grumbling more because it was traditional than because he minded any of it or found it in the least unexpected.

"You keep your lip zipped," the flight leader called back. "You leave planning to the general staff."

"Yes, sir."

T-Boy swung around the front wheel of his Dragoon all-weather interceptor and bounded up the ladder to the cockpit. He was busy plugging himself into the plane's life support systems and computer as the ground crew closed the canopy over his head and wheeled the ladder away. Beneath the belly of his plane, the last of the Lawndoctor antipersonnel missiles had been hoisted into place.

"We have green sequence," T-Boy heard over his headphones. "Repeat, jocks, we have green sequence. Arming procedure initiated."

Missiles armed? But somehow T-Boy did not seem at all surprised, instead adjusting his faceplate and concentrating on his instruments as a series of roars and whistles spattered down the line as one engine after another caught.

T-Boy watched the flight leader's Dragoon rise on its VTO engines and hang suspended for a moment over the tarmac. Then it turned and drifted down the runway, gradually picking up forward speed as its cruising engine wing pods tilted slowly back from the vertical. A moment later they were in flight position, and the fighter shot down the runway and arced up, followed by a second and then a third.

T-Boy repeated the maneuver, chasing after the others into the night sky. At just the right instant he slanted his ship's movable nose down, hawklike, into supersonic configuration. And he did not have to be told to keep his altitude low and to angle up to the northwest and cut across Colorado and Nebraska before circling back southward for the strike. Something about not confusing the radar net on a holiday night.

Not that the megahype ever needed to explain its orders to T-Boy Tucker.

25

The Heart of Love

They stood in the cold outside the nightmare vastness of the Temple of Love. Occasional flakes of Dust bowl-yellowed snow drifted down through the coronas of the floodlights as the crowd of middle-aged adults, prosperous and impoverished alike, pressed forward from every direction to see first-hand the miracle of the lighted ball that would descend fourteen minutes from now from the top of the highest spire on the Temple.

They had already made their way through more than a mile of people, and they had paused to catch their breath and get their bearings, clinging to the pole of an unlighted streetlamp like exhausted swimmers hanging from a buoy.

"You're still going in with me?" Circe asked.

Santalucia nodded.

Circe studied his face for the hundredth time. "It was that girl back in the locust swarm, wasn't it? Did she remind you of your daughter?"

"Of course not," Santalucia said, too suddenly. "She's over twice Erin's age."

He wasn't lying entirely, Circe thought. There was another reason for his coming with her, but it still eluded her. She stepped up on the base of the lamppost to get a better view of the Temple swarming with people.

"I feel like the Cowardly Lion outside the Wicked Witch's castle," Santalucia was saying. "Except the Witch is out here with me. The Wicked Witch of the Middle West."

Circe smiled vaguely, already filling her mind with the image of the Temple, probing the lines of its shape, its buttressing and

235

stresses, its mass to extract the pattern of the mazes within. The heart of Love.

"It's not below ground," she said.

"What's not?"

"Doctor Love's office. It's somewhere up above, over one of the vaults. Do you remember seeing any elevators that went up?"

"In Doctor Love's Temple, everything moves down. It's a philosophical necessity. But why start with Love's office? What do you expect to find there?"

Circe took one last look over the heads of the crowd at the Temple and stepped back down to the sidewalk. "I don't know," she said. "It's a feeling."

"Great, a feeling."

"I know you don't put much stock in intuitions and the occult," Circe said. "But have I been wrong yet?"

"Circe, I'd follow you through the gates of hell," Santalucia smiled.

They began to move forward again, elbowing their way through the press of bodies. Huge wall screens had been erected over the windows on every side of the Temple to broadcast the Love special, already in progress, and everywhere spectators stared glassy-eyed at the screen, their ears muffed in Lovebands. The closer Santalucia and Circe got, the more enraptured the viewers they found.

"Makes them a lot easier to push out of the way," Santalucia whispered in Circe's ear. "I just hope nobody knows we're in New York. Otherwise the carrier channel could be saying terrible things about us, and the whole bunch of them could turn on us any minute like bacchantes, and string parts of us from here to Fourteenth Street as window streamers."

But no one moved to stop them or even seemed to notice as they threaded their way through the faithful up the staircase toward the entrance to the Temple.

There had been no effort to limit the audience. It had obviously been Doctor Love's intention to counter the Saucer Cult's gathering in Kansas by uncharacteristically dragging as many of his followers away from their TV sets as possible and bringing them together in one place as an inspiring show of strength. Those who had come first had gotten the seats inside the Temple; the rest had simply filled in the aisles, the back, the lobbies in a thick fluid mass that spilled down the steps on every side and extended outward into the darkness.

In the lobby Circe and Santalucia were able to catch a glimpse of the great auditorium, fountains flashing in a golden mist, audience heads bobbing and nodding across the rows of seats like waving grain. Almost all wearing Lovebands here. Another wall screen had been hung behind the empty podium to show the special; it was flashing with black and white photographs of Love's career: as a young urologist in Cleveland shaking hands with Bob Hope at 105th Street and Euclid during a publicity tour, meeting privately with Reverend Sun Myung Moon after a rally, standing shoulder to shoulder with Ted Kennedy; as a man in distinguished middle age conferring with Senator Fonda and President Korzeniowski, accepting a toast from King Charles III, gesturing atop the shattered fiberglass peak of Disneyland's Matterhorn ride to direct Faith Ltd.'s private mission to bring food and comfort to the victims of LA's earthquake, Sleeping Beauty's deturreted castle rising starkly in the distance behind him. A mixture of the nostalgic, the popular, the religious, and the political.

What struck Circe as odd, however, was that there was not a single flesh-and-blood human being actually at the podium. Santalucia, in arguing against coming to the Temple, had reminded her that RR&D's plan, all along, had been to pretape the special. Still, she couldn't imagine Love would call out so many of his followers without at least offering them a glimpse of him in person. Perhaps he was planning to come out at the stroke of midnight for his personal appearance.

Yet even as she thought, cheers erupted from the crowd outside and trumpets blared in the auditorium. The ball was dropping. Midnight. The end of the twentieth century and the second millennium—Eastern Standard Time. She still had one hour before disaster struck in Kansas with the century's end in the Middle West.

They had made their way past the bank of below-ground elevators and had at last reached a back corridor by slipping behind a temporary barricade. The sudden emptiness was eerie, a sensation heightened by the presence of a monitor even here flickering with Doctor Love's hypnotic visage.

—*through the swirling vortex downward to unmoving Essence,* the Doctor was saying, *where amidst the healing flow of*

237

primal elements, matters of government may be handled with the same ease as we now handle matters of the spirit—

"Everything he says sounds like a description of a toilet flushing," Santalucia said.

"Shh," Circe cautioned, leading him around a corner to a single flight of stairs. "It's up here."

They started up, the scraping of the soles of their shoes on the stairway a sharp counterpoint to the deep and reassuring resonances of the voice that floated up the stairs after them from the monitor.

—with the coming of this new century and new millennium, this new age, has come the time to remove all stress from government by turning to those changeless, eternal verities of the quiet spirit—

At the top of the stairway, the same voice spoke to them muffled through a huge oak door banded with iron straps and studs, apparently brought from some old Spanish monastery and installed in the Temple.

Circe pushed against it and it swung open.

The room was carpeted in green, the walls papered a paler green. At one end of the room before a set of closed drapes was an Empire desk with ornate gilt legs. Along one wall was a mural-sized photograph of Doctor Love speaking in the Houston Astrodome, and beneath it ran a set of low bookshelves containing, among other things, several Bibles, bound religious pamphlets, from Jehovah's Witnesses back to Billy Graham and Billy Sunday, a *Gray's Anatomy,* and several worn texts on disorders of the urinary tract. Along the other was a bank of monitors; most of them showed the Love New Year's special, but a few were running the other networks' competing shows.

—a leader who can turn back the childish taunts, demands, and whining complaints of other nations with a fatherly sternness and make sure that no other people gets a bigger share of the world's valuable resources than we do. A leader whose years of study of spiritual writings will allow him to take care of everything without disturbing the rest which each and every one of you yearns for and deserves—

"I've got to hand it to you, Circe," Santalucia said, riffling the pages of one of the urology texts. "This is definitely Love's office. But as I said, he's out. Probably at home packing for the New Hampshire primary."

"Something's not quite right," Circe said. "The aura's missing." She ran her fingers along the immaculate, shimmering top of Doctor Love's desk. At one corner was a framed picture of a woman and child. Doctor Love's wife and daughter? Then a triptych of pictures of Love himself in youth and middle age, all of which had been on the TV during the special. She paused to study the one of him in a coat and tie, then went to the pair of baskets at the other end. The out basket was empty, but the in contained several internal memoranda that had yet to be attended to. Circe shuffled through them. All were campaign strategy proposals for various states.

"Sure doesn't look like the monster we've made him out to be," Santalucia said. "No sign of weird religious rites or blueprints for mass murder. Not even a simple rack or thumbscrew. Maybe we were just hallucinating."

"No, we weren't," Circe said. "But I'm not getting the kind of vibrations I got downstairs or back at Solarsystems International. There's a kind of calm here, almost an absence of everything. A vacuum. It's unnatural. There's something terribly wrong here."

"I guess you could say that," Santalucia observed, looking over Circe's shoulder toward the door.

In the doorway stood the first of half a dozen brown-uniformed security officers. "I'm afraid you'll have to come with us," the first guard said. "This is a restricted area. We'll have to take you to the security room until the police come."

"Police?" Santalucia asked.

"Of course. You're trespassing here."

Santalucia sighed with relief. "By all means, let's wait for the police."

They were taken into a private elevator hidden behind the curtain, and then down, down until an *F* lighted on the panel over the door, a level Santalucia had never been to before. All the way down, Doctor Love's voice soothed them from a speaker mounted in the ceiling of the car.

The corridors, however, were exactly the same as C level's. The guards led them to a small room bare but for several straight chairs and the inevitable TV monitor from which Doctor Love murmured. They were left alone.

"It doesn't look like they're planning to kill us," Santalucia said, trying the door and finding it locked. "At least not yet."

"It's not *our* lives I'm worried about," Circe said. "What time is it?"

"Twelve-fifteen," Santalucia said. "But I don't see what else you expected, coming here without a ghost of a plan—"

Circe waved for him to be quiet. Ghost of a plan, she thought, sitting down and closing her eyes. She tried to remember her terrifying descent into the misty wastes that night in Denver, to recall every detail of the dark-eyed man who had fled before her and then returned to whisper to her back. Then in turn she called to mind each of the photographs she had seen in Love's office.

"But honestly, Circe, thinking that you were going to be struck by some kind of inspiration after we got here is like Caesar attacking Gaul without a roadmap. When they tell Love that we're—"

"They won't," Circe said.

"Of course they will."

"Did you look at the pictures on his desk carefully?" Circe asked. "Especially the most recent one? The one where he was wearing a tie?"

"Yeah, I noticed that. I gather he's not very fashionable in real life. Nobody's worn ties for ten years."

"That's how old the picture is."

"I get it," Santalucia said. "The reason they use computer simulations and doubles is the real Doctor Love's too old for today's Pepsi generation. Lucky for him presidential candidates can do all their campaigning by television. Between makeup and electronics, no one will be the wiser."

"No, the reason they use computer simulacrums is that there's *no* real Doctor Love."

"Impossible," Santalucia said.

"Doctor Love has been dead ten years," Circe said. "He's the one I saw in the spirit world, the one who told me to come here."

"Circe, I never know whether to take you seriously or not," Santalucia said. "I suppose he wanted to trap us?"

"He wanted to help us. He's disgusted with what's happened to his movement."

Santalucia smiled indulgently and shook his head. Circe was just about to add something when they heard the door lock click open. A small, fiftyish man in an expensively tailored jogging suit entered. He was rubbing his hands nervously.

240

"I hope you can appreciate how distasteful I find this, personally," the man said, avoiding eye contact by looking at their knees. "You've done some very fine work for us in the past, Ms. McPhee, and while I've never been a great admirer of your books, Mr. Santalucia, their popularity indicates they, ah, fill a very real need in the public, which is something that I and the rest of us at Faith Limited *do* appreciate, I assure you."

"But now you're going to have us killed," Santalucia said.

"Killed?" The man looked directly at him for the first time, eyes wide with surprise. "Goodness, no. What do you take us for? While the Inner Circle has asked me to convey our regrets for the protective measures we're forced to take—"

"Do you mean to tell me," Santalucia said, "that you can burn up half of Denver and plot the mass murder of a bunch of kids in the middle of the Dustbowl and you balk at killing two people? What's the problem—you don't like seeing your victims face to face?"

"Mr. Santalucia," the man said, rubbing his hands even more vigorously, "no one could be sorrier about Project Snuff than we are. You have to understand it took us months of backtracking from the first rumors until we finally found out what Project Snuff really was."

"You're trying to tell me you didn't have anything to do with it?" Santalucia asked.

"Faith Limited is a very big organization, Mr. Santalucia. We have an elaborate system of flow charts for the chain of command, but like any organization, we have hot spots—ambitious men and women who, however mistakenly, short-circuit the command flow, start sending approvals and directives back down the chain before the requests have been cleared at the top. Naturally, they meant it only for the best, and naturally the lower echelons assumed their orders had the approval of the Inner Circle or the appropriate departments. . . ."

"You're telling me you're like Henry the Second going around asking why no one would rid him of this meddlesome priest, and then pretending to be shocked when his drinking buddies went down to Canterbury and dispatched Becket?" Santalucia laughed.

"Never mind," Circe said. "It's still not too late. You can call the Pentagon, stop whatever planes are being sent—"

"We think it's the Texas Air National Guard," the man said. "But there's no way to stop them. We can't just *call* someone in

241

the Pentagon—we have no official connections there, and they probably wouldn't believe us, anyway. And we'd be implicating ourselves in something that . . ."

"You're just going to sit back and let it *happen?*" Circe said.

"We don't want it to happen, but we've got no choice. This way, the incident will be explained away as some kind of military blunder or pilots drunk on New Year's Eve—whatever tack the Pentagon decides to take to cover itself. If the generals thought they could use us as a scapegoat, the scandal would do incalculable damage, not just to the campaign but to the Church itself."

"Somehow that doesn't seem very important," Circe said.

"Oh, but it is. Think of the good Faith Limited has done. America was suffering for years from a crisis of faith. The old belief in a remote god and an afterlife of punishments and rewards just wasn't immediate enough to satisfy the needs or alleviate the anxieties of modern people. We've given them rituals that speak to their need for reassurance through familiar things, and beliefs that don't attack their self-esteem."

"So you've gone Marx one better—you've used electronics to really make religion the opiate of the masses," Santalucia said.

The man ran his fingers through his graying hair. "Mr. Santalucia, if you could only share with me the *mountains* of testimonials to the good that our Lovebands have accomplished. Alcoholics and addicts weaned from their self-destructive dependencies, seriously disturbed people finding inner fulfillment. And that's nothing to what we *can* accomplish. We can not only orchestrate and facilitate the changes in lifestyles and attitudes that the solution to our energy and food problems will require, we can remove all pain and resentment connected with the sacrifices people will have to make."

"Once you've made Faith Limited president," Circe said. "What gave you the idea? Was it when the computer made the actor doubles obsolete, so you knew you didn't have to worry about electing a living front man to office who might turn out to be more independent than you wanted?"

"You're a very shrewd young woman," the man said.

"Wait a minute," Santalucia said. "You mean Circe was right? There's no Doctor Love? A *corporation* is running for

think of a more promising solution to America's ⸻n you?" the man said. "Time and again it's been

242

American business know-how that's saved this country when everything else failed."

"But a corporation isn't a human being," Santalucia said.

"But it's an entity—a person, if you wish. What single man or woman is capable of coping adequately with all today's problems? Not that poor old dyke in the White House now, I assure you. A corporation's more efficient, better equipped to gather and process information, identify and assess goals, reorder priorities, make sound decisions, because it has the benefit of all the viewpoints, talents, and skills of its members. It's really a conglomerate of highly trained individuals that go together to make a, well, a super-being without the drawbacks of the emotions and biases of the average fallible human."

"Like a conscience," Circe said.

"Oh, come now," the man said. "We're not monsters, we're people like you."

"Your chain of command means that no one individual has to take responsibility for what the corporation does—he can always point to the people above or below, the way you just did about Denver and the Dustbowl," Circe said. "But the fact is, without individual responsibility, there's no conscience. No single human was ever capable of the cruelty of the mob. Even Hitler didn't think up the concentration camps all by himself—it took the cooperation and talents of people up and down the chain of command."

"I'm really not interested in hearing this," the man said. "I've conveyed our regrets, and the security people will be here in a moment with the Lovebands."

"Ah, the long-awaited memory-wash," Santalucia said. "But one last thing—what did you do to Doctor Love? Was he killed?"

The man had been in the process of opening the door. He closed it hurriedly. "Of course he wasn't," he said in a voice too low to be overheard by the guards outside. "We bought him out."

"Bought him out?" Santalucia said. "You mean Doctor Love was some kind of Colonel Sanders that sold out his southern-fried religion business and hired on as your front man?"

"That's a rather crass way of putting it, Mr. Santalucia," said the man. "But he did serve as a kind of corporate image until his health started failing—of *natural* causes. After that we used

243

doubles, until very recently, when the computer simulations were fully perfected—at no small expense, I might add."

"So American business has finally turned religion into a combination TV commercial and fast-food chain," Santalucia said. "Anything for a buck."

"I don't think that a black man who wrote *Niggers in Orbit* has much to complain about when it comes to commercialism," the man sneered. "In point of fact we all considered Doctor Love a true visionary who simply lacked the means to get his story out to the people. I've seen some of the four-color promotional pieces he had done in the early days—not at all bad for their time, but they can hardly compare with today's advanced television technology when you have a message you want to send to the whole country. Fortunately, he was able to secure backing from a number of like-minded investors, and when his own interest waned, they were ready and willing to carry on. It was a lot of blood and belief and sweat that allowed Faith Limited to grow into what it is today."

"So the Inner Circle is just another term for the board of directors," Santalucia said. "I don't suppose you're going to tell us who they are."

The man shook his head. "Some very important people, and some of the finest business minds in the U.S.A."

"And you've all been amply rewarded at a thousand dollars on the dollar for your original investment?"

"I'm sure some have made an honest profit," the man said, wiping his sweaty palms on the seat of his jogging suit. "But I'm only a minority stockholder. In fact, I'm in the Inner Circle only because I happen to be custodian of a large bloc of shares kept in trust for the heirs of a distinguished civic leader until they reach their majority." He opened the door and leaned out. "You'd better come in right away. They're seriously disturbed in here, and need treatment. They're raving."

Instantly several burly guards tumbled into the room with handcuffs and two Lovebands. They cuffed Circe and Santalucia to two chairs facing the television monitor.

"Jesus," Santalucia muttered. "TV'd to death by an ersatz Doctor Love."

"There won't be any pain," the man said, backing out the door. "This is a special carrier channel directly from a unique program in the computer. After you've relaxed, perhaps I can come back and share some thoughts with you on the impact of tonight's Neilsens on the New Hampshire primary. Oh, Ms. McPhee, I do regret any damage done inadvertently to your career," he added, "every bit as much as I regret what's about to happen out there." He nodded in what might have been the general direction of Kansas. "But we'll make it up to you, I promise. Whatever you may think, we're really not very bad men, my dear. Only very bad administrators—sometimes." He closed the door behind himself.

—but seriously now, Doctor Love was saying, *I'd like you to meet a couple of my special celebrity guests for tonight who helped to make this such a profound success. So let's have a big hand for Tommy Youngtooth, that woody Indian with a forked tongue of gold—*

"We're lucky," Circe whispered as the guards stepped forward with the Lovebands. "This'll give me a direct line for a projection into the computer."

"Would you be serious?" Santalucia said as he felt the earphones and electrodes snapped over his own head. He stared glumly at Doctor Love trading quips with the young Indian comedian. And to think if he'd been smart he would have authored those gags himself and made a bundle.

Santalucia slumped down in his chair, already oppressed by the drone of Love's voice. He'd come all this way to find there was no villain to vent his frustration on by pummeling him with his fists or out-fencing him with a rapier. There was no incarnate evil. There was not even a pathetic little drummer to confess to humbuggery. Only a corporation. At the heart of Love there was nothing at all. A vacuum, a void.

Still, he thought dreamily, maybe it wasn't such a bad thing. What they'd done was to create the very first man-made god that was truly immortal. Statues of Alexander the Great and Caesar Augustus might crumble, but Doctor Love had transcended human frailties to become a computer program—ageless, immutable, untarnished by human lust or greed. An eternal being. Oh hear us when we cry to Thee, Thou IBM in majesty. . . .

Shit, he thought, trying to make sense out of the banter between Tommy Youngtooth and Doctor Love, what a hell of a way to lose your mind.

26

Caliban and Circe

12:38 AM Eastern Standard Time, Saturday, January 1, 2000

Circe watched Santalucia slipping off. Throughout most of the conversation with the little man from the Inner Circle, Circe had been withdrawn, desperately trying to think of some way to stop the inevitable. There were only minutes left.

More and more the computer had seemed the only answer: not only did it control the Doctor Love simulacrum, but its data transmission lines provided thousands of potential highways to the world outside the Temple of Love.

The alpha waves did not make her drowsy; they freed her faster than mesc could have.

This time she did not simply force herself outward. Carefully she channeled, funneled herself through the gleaming metal disc of the electrode, great cymbal, monstrous dome, tracing back the flow of electrons to their source. On and on she moved through circuits like hedge mazes and formal gardens, through arterial clusters of wires, always back like an explorer working up the meandering streams of the Delta to the body of the Nile and thence to its headwaters.

Suddenly she felt cold, terribly cold. Close to absolute zero. Liquid helium, that was it; she had penetrated to the interior of the computer itself.

Square after square of rock candy-like chips lay before her, patterned like Navaho rugs or, as she approached them more closely, like vast, futuristic cities with avenues of aluminum and silicon. She severed herself into hundreds, thousands, millions of pieces, raced along the avenues and underground chambers, leaping from gate to gate, across positive and negative zones, probing the logic circuits and then pulling back to see how the yesses and noes added up at a holistic level, then down and in again.

At last she found the nodes and clusters that created the voice and image of Doctor Love, coursed through the positive and negative pulsings until she understood how it was built, how it might be altered, had brushed the mingled bits of the dead Love and his actor doubles from films and tapes. Then she swept on, calling back and forth among the myriad fragments of her consciousness as she moved through the other IC's that were creating the background, the other guests, the music.

Part of herself she left there, the rest moving now through the encoding circuits for the carrier channel. Reverse here, activate, deactivate, a bit of her now traveling at right angles, around and back. Yes, the special channel to the TV. The briefest glimpse out the screen at Santalucia and her own inert body tied to chairs, an instantaneous return, calling parts of herself together to work up enough electrical potential to click one gate and then another until the alpha waves and the audio had been cut off there.

And then on to the exits, even as the part she left behind was still flowing through the gates and circuits, building a new Doctor Love one line at a time, moving too fast ever to know consciously what she was making her homununculus do or say.

At the output interfaces she was subdividing again. A line to the New York Public Library. From there to M.I.T. She called for the rest of her to follow. M.I.T. to Cal Tech. Cal Tech to Stanford. Nothing. Back to Cal Tech, out again, Los Alamos. At last! Los Alamos to the Pentagon.

PLEASE IDENTIFY AND CODE IN.

She summoned her separated selves, concentrated. What was the code word? Shakespeare, that was it. Prospero, Miranda . . .

Caliban.

GREETINGS. HOW MAY I SERVE YOU?

Through she went and in, searching now for the core and center through which all commands had to pass. ZICON, that was what it was called, she realized. Zone of . . . Zone of Internal Consumers. The National Security Agency clearing house with direct links to and from the Continental Air Command, North American Air Command, Central Intelligence Agency, National

Security System, Air Force Security System, Army Security Agency, Marine Corps, Canadian GHQ, the Joint Chiefs, the President.

But she couldn't find it. Elusive references, bits and pieces, a will-o'-the-wisp. She coursed through the bank of data terminal interfaces.

ZICON. Fort Meade. Direct line.

CLASSIFIED ACCESS. PLEASE IDENTIFY AND CODE IN.

Probing, waiting for the word to form. Caliban? No, couldn't be Caliban again. Child, mother . . .

Circe.

Caliban and Circe—so obvious she'd almost rejected it.

GREETINGS. HOW MAY I SERVE YOU?

On she raced through the IC's of the ZICON computer complex.

12:45 AM Eastern Standard Time, Saturday, January 1, 2000

Several stories under Fort Meade, Maryland, deep in a bunker of reinforced concrete, Staff Sergeant Wilma Seligmann, USMC, sat with the other officers and noncoms from the Army, Navy, and Air Force in the ZICON Comcenter. They were bored and irritable; they worked on five-day duty shifts and were required to sleep in a dormitory one floor above—no liquor, no drugs, and no Lovebands. And today was a holiday on top of everything else.

In anger, somebody had penciled on the outer wall today's five-digit combination for the push-button lock on the door that led from the elevator into the Comcenter. It went largely unnoticed among the fingerprints and smudges, and it would be changed at 6 AM anyway, and nobody without the necessary clearances could get as far as the elevator. But even breaking security in a vacuum afforded a little relief.

Like a great spider's web, ZICON's links to every radar and sensing installation in the American defense network was diagramed on a four-by-eight sheet of plywood against one wall, where green, white, and red LED's tracked any active phone or videphone circuits to and from CONAD, NORAD, DIA, CIA, NSS, and all the rest. At a raised podium overlooking the board and all the cubicled operatives, Colonel George Dorsey, USAF, kept watch, because Colonel Dorsey was the current Deputy

Director of the National Security Agency—Big Daddy or DIRNSA to his staff. On his desk sat direct telephones to the President, the Joint Chiefs at the Pentagon, and the War Room, one gold, one white, and one red, though at the moment he was on a conventional black audio phone on the Frankfurt-B line, patched through to a young woman named Grete, whom he'd met there on his last tour and who shared his passionate interest in handcuffs and rubber overcoats.

Wilma Seligmann had just processed two CANUKUS-EYES ONLY and routed them on to the appropriate Canadian, American, and British agencies. Then came a UKUS—EYES ONLY and she dutifully relayed it to the British and American receivers. A slight pause, then something from GHCQ, Government Headquarters Canada Quebec, on to low-level Pentagon. Another lull.

Her eyes wandered to the fist-sized red alert button beside her LC display. It would be nice to give it a good punch and then go home. Except that it sealed all the doors to ZICON. How she wished she were down at the Starting Gate having a good stiff drink after shift. Or home watching the Love special. She missed her Loveband. Now *there* was somebody who would make a first-rate president. She could never explain her reasons when she got into an argument about it, but she just knew that he was the man with the answers everybody was looking for.

A string of letters flashed across the LC screen.

MISSILES APPROACHING DEW LINE.

She waited for the inevitable THIS IS A TEST, but there was nothing. "Say again," she whispered.

MISSILES APPROACHING DEW LINE.

And she hit the great red button with the palm of her hand.

"What the fuck is going on?" crackled Big Daddy DIRNSA's voice over her earplug.

She relayed the information. "Do I call an EXLAX?" she quavered. She could imagine the missiles leaping from the silos and bomb bays toward their preset Russian and Chinese goals. There was no way the US would risk a preemptive first strike from the East, not after the India-Pakistan Five-Minute War.

"Jesus no," Big Daddy DIRNSA said. "Not till we know what they are and where they're from."

She glanced over. Already the phones on Big Daddy's desk were lighting up.

In the great cavern of the SAC Command Control room, Colonel Baskin and the senior control officers were mulling over the news from one of the flight followers that there was an unidentified squadron of twenty Dragoon all-weather interceptors at 101 degrees east longitude and 38 degrees north latitude, bearing 212 degrees southwest. Nearest town Apple, Kansas, a hundred miles from the Oklahoma border. Point of origin unknown, possibly Texas Air Guard returning to Amarillo.

If this was some kind of Guard maneuver, then Colonel Baskin ought to have been told about it. It was bad enough spending New Year's Eve hundreds of feet underground with a bunch of sweaty technicians and no TV. She didn't need a bunch of amateurs screwing around on unauthorized joyrides.

A light glowed inside the gold phone mounted on the panel before her. She picked it up. At the other end was Big Daddy DIRNSA.

"I don't care if you're not getting any readings on your radar," Big Daddy answered. "My information is we've got blips coming in from the north. We're on red alert."

"Is this a test?"

"Not a test. Full red alert."

"Is this EXLAX?"

"Not yet. But if you've got anything already in the air that's not part of the alert procedure, send them north for possible defensive action."

Baskin glanced at the data display for the four clocks. It was 9:54 in the morning in Moscow, 5:54 Greenwich Mean Time, 12:54 in Washington. The rest of the world was already into the twenty-first century while she hung suspended between the years. Hell of a time for the Apocalypse.

But it was just a malfunction in the ZICON system. It was almost certain she wouldn't have to take the keys out of the double-padlocked red safe. Still, she was going to have to go through the motions. She gave the standard orders, then called for a flight follower to redirect that maverick flight of reservists out in Kansas. Fat lot of good they'd do if they really had a flock of ICBM's coming in.

"We're in touch with a Captain T-Boy Tucker, Colonel," said one of the flight followers. "But we're having a lot of trouble getting through to him. Sounds like he's drugged or drunk or something. Insists his flight leader wants them to practice strafing runs outside this place Apple, Kansas."

Colonel Baskin snorted. She *knew* it had sounded familiar—it was the place all the Saucer kids had gathered for the end of the world. Actually, in some ways it was too bad the reservists weren't carrying armed Lawndoctors. But this was no time for idle wishing. "You tell him to get that squadron turned around and headed north. This takes priority. Jesus Christ, doesn't he know what a red alert is?"

"I'll do my best, sir, but he barely makes sense," the flight follower said. "It's like he hears me but he's not listening."

"*Make* him listen. Find out what the Texas Air Guard code equivalent for EXLAX is—if the jimmy hasn't been conditioned to respond to *that*, I'll have their commandant's ass in a sling."

12:55 AM Eastern Standard Time, Saturday, January 1, 2000

The call from ZICON had come in only a minute before, but already word was spreading through the White House as the president and her advisers interrupted their small staff New Year's celebration to follow events at the DEW Line. So far, DIRNSA had reported the ZICON readings had not been confirmed, but it was too early to dismiss it as a malfunction when there were blips on even one screen. The president kept calling them UFO's.

"I'd say there are two things to consider here," she said, her face purple in the light of her field-hockey screen. "First, whether there's anything subversive about this gathering out in Kansas that might tie in with some Soviet airlift of funds or something."

"We've had the FBI looking into that right along," someone said. "No known connection."

"That's the first thing," the president continued. "And the second is whether or not those nuts out in the Dustbowl are in on something your president ought to know about."

"Pardon, Madam President?"

"What if they're right?" the president said. "I mean, how would it look if a bunch of nobodies really *did* get to heaven in a space ship? A lot of important people in Washington would be left standing around with their pants down."

"It would look bad," somebody agreed.

"It would be the political pits," said the president, waiting for the computer to finish its free shot. "Tell them to gas up Air Force One and stand by."

11:59 PM Central Time, Friday, December 31, 1999

Overhead the sky was clear, an infinity of stars bright and terrible. Below, streamers of dust torn from the frozen earth rode the screaming wind through the blackness. The great disc and shaft, illuminated through the swirls of dust by the circle of car headlights, shuddered and groaned, leprous tatters of tinfoil flapping from its gleaming skin.

Starbud squinted against the dusty wind, wondering how long the imitation saucer could stand the battering. There was a sudden gust, a loud cracking, and a piece of plywood tore loose from the top of the disc and sailed away over the heads of the crowd.

"They're coming!" a voice shouted.

Soames, standing beside Starbud, looked up. At the blurred edge where the dust storm's top faded into the clear sky, a line of lights had appeared toward the north. He watched them for a moment.

"No," he said. "It looks like airplanes."

"It's the Mothership!" someone else was yelling. "Look how *huge* it is!"

The lights moved slowly toward them. Now they could hear the distant whistle of engines. An instant later the lights streaked high above them, banking several miles to the south and coming back low over the disc and shaft glowing in the headlights. As one, the Seekers hunched their shoulders against whatever was to come next, the liberating wrench of the Beam's golden ions or the hail of bullets.

Unmistakable now, the planes thundered overhead and diminished again to a flock of pinpoints of light headed north.

"They were just scouting," someone said.

"No, I bet they saw it. The Air Force sent them out to stop the UFO 'cause they had it on their screens. But when those jimmies got a look at how big it was, they just turned and beat it."

"The Mothership's coming. It's got to be just over there to the south where they got scared off. You see any lights?"

"Any minute now! As soon as it's midnight!"

252

Starbud looked up at Soames.

He smiled sadly. "It's past midnight," he said.

Suddenly there was a rending and cracking. The disc and shaft tilted in the wind, angled precariously in the blaze of lights as scraps of plywood showered from it and shredded flecks of tinfoil whirled and glinted away into the darkness. And then with a groan of protesting, riven wood, it fell to the side. Roils of dust billowed outward after the fleeing Seekers as it struck the ground.

1:01 AM Eastern Standard Time, Saturday, January 1, 2000

"Nothing?" Big Daddy DIRNSA was shouting. "No missiles over the DEW Line?"

"We've been through everything," Staff Sergeant Wilma Seligmann answered. "It's like whatever signals activated the system just evaporated. If there was a glitch somewhere, it took care of itself."

"Then *fix* it, goddamn it!"

And a few moments later, Colonel Baskin, hanging up her direct line to DIRNSA, spun angrily in her chair to look out over the backs of her phalanx of flight followers.

"The flight of reservists finally responded," a senior controller reported. "They're still northbound."

"Get them down at the nearest airbase," Baskin fumed, relieved to have something to vent her frustrations on, "and have the MP's out on the apron to slap those jimmies in the stockade. And if they don't respond right away, you get a goddamned wing of regulars up there and shoot Captain T-Boy Tucker and his pals out of the fucking sky. What do they think this is, Amateur Night?" But after all, she reminded herself, they were no more than errant children.

1:05 AM Eastern Standard Time, Saturday, January 1, 2000

Just when Santalucia had expected to slip under, something had revived him. Since then he had divided his attention between Doctor Love's celebrity guests and Circe, whose head had lolled over onto one shoulder and whose breathing was very deep and regular indeed. Astral projection, his foot. She'd gotten zonked on the alpha waves in nothing flat, and here he was still fighting them off successfully.

Doctor Love had just come forward to fill the screen, for some reason massaging his left arm with his right hand, his jaw set and mouth straight.

—but the secret to achieving the kind of entropic transcendence has always been the great Letting Go—

Santalucia watched his right hand move from his left arm to his chest. The words seemed labored.

—learning not to grasp but to open our arms—

Doctor Love clutched his chest, looked into the camera with a puzzled expression, and dropped from sight. The screen cut to a full stage shot, Doctor Love lying crumpled before his deep blue curtains as people rushed toward him from both sides, forming a knot around him that filled and tightened until he was hidden from view.

A moment later a figure hastened toward the camera. There was something at once odd and familiar about it. Odd because . . . well, it seemed a little out of focus, and . . . Jesus Christ, it was in black and white. Right there in the middle of a color telecast—or simulacast, Santalucia reminded himself—there was somebody in black and white.

Gosh, folks, said the face, *one minute you're dead—I don't mean in show biz, I mean really dead—and the next they're dragging you back to do a benefit.*

Something tugged at Santalucia's childhood memories. What was it about the set of the mouth, that kind of half smile on one side. And the nose.

But don't get me wrong, now, I just love being in New York. Where else do the bums come up and ask you for a hundred dollars for a glass of water?

He looked to the side. A kind of a ski-slope nose. And there was music in the background. Terribly familiar.

No, but I love New York. Even the squirrels in Central Park carry sidearms. And what about those pigeons . . .

The song was . . . holy shit—"Thanks for the Memories." It was Bob Hope. It was an animated version of the nostalgia photo they'd shown at the beginning of the show. Had the computer blown a logic circuit somewhere?

But all gags aside, folks, I gotta tell you I've just gotten some very bad news, and it's confirmed. Doc Love has just bought the big boat ride. Doc Love is dead.

Dead? The computer had killed off Doctor Love and was announcing it? He glanced over at Circe's slumbering form. Was it possible she'd actually used some weird power to get inside the computer and assassinate the Doctor's simulacrum? Except in her haste the memory module she'd activated to make the announcement was the Bob Hope unit.

I know you all share my grief at knowing my good pal the Doc is no longer with us handing out the kind of solid advice we all knew and loved him for.

The question was, Santalucia thought, whether a black and white image had credibility anymore.

Oh, and by the way, I just got word that a couple of friends of mine got locked up by accident in a security room down on Level. F. Could we have a couple of our boys in blue go down and spring them?

27

The New Age

6 AM Eastern Standard Time, Saturday, January 1, 2000

Father Camillieri looked out across the nearly-empty pews streaked with the glorious reds, yellows, and blues of the dawning sun through the stained glass windows. An old Italian woman, head covered by a black veil, sat bowed and still. A middle-aged couple toward the back, another old woman, a young man in sunglasses, perhaps the son of some parishioner now returned to the Church like the prodigal to his father.

"At that time," he read from Matthew, "the disciples came to Jesus privately, saying, 'Tell us, when are these things to happen, and what will be the sign of Thy coming and of the end of the world?' And in answer Jesus said to them, 'Take care that no one leads you astray. For many will come in My Name, saying 'I am the Christ,' and they will lead men astray. For you shall hear of wars and rumors of wars.'"

At least, he thought, they'd left the epistle and gospel in English. In a vain effort to feed a jaded world's growing appetite for mystic cults and chaos, the Church had returned to the mystery of the Latin mass, but at least they'd had the sense to leave the important things accessible to those of the faithful that still listened to the words instead of rocking mindlessly to the rhythm and music of a voice they didn't understand.

" 'Take care that you do not be alarmed, for these things must come to pass, *but the end is not yet*. For nation will rise against nation, and kingdom against kingdom; and there will be pestilences and famines and earthquakes in various places. But all these things are the beginnings of sorrows.' "

"Praise be to Thee, O Christ," chanted the little girl who had been the only one available to be this morning's servitor.

256

"Dominus vobiscum," said Father Camillieri.

"Et cum spiritu tuo," she answered.

"Thou wilt save the humble people, O Lord, and wilt bring down the eyes of the proud; for who is God but Thee, O Lord? Suspice, sancte Pater, omnipotens aeterne Deus, hanc immaculatam hostiam, quam ego indignus famulus tuus offero tibi, Deo meo vivo et vero, pro innumerabilibus peccatis, et offensionibus, et negligentiis meis, et pro omnibus circumstantibus, sed pro omnibus fidelibus Christianis vivis atque defunctis; ut mihi, et illis proficiat ad salutem in vitam aeternam. Amen."

Father Camillieri raised his eyes again to the empty pews.

He thought of the madness of poor Sister Catherine and the helpless boy who had sat across from her. But it was a madness that had swept the world. The German Heresiarch now preaching to his candle-bearing Lazarites that he was himself the risen god-king. The Monad's deluded children shivering in the center of the Dustbowl. The dull-eyed faithful vegetating before the image of that electronic Antichrist, Doctor Love.

At least the prophecies had proven false. God's creation had not ended last night as the Monad had promised. But perhaps, if they were lucky, something else had ended: the reign of the false prophets. Oh, not right away, of course. Though he hadn't seen it, he'd heard that Doctor Love had died on the air last night. And without Doctor Love's hypnotic presence, his organization couldn't survive long. It would end eventually. These things always did.

Just as the Rabbi had said. The children would return to their parents, the faithful would return to Mother Church.

And he would visit Sister Catherine in the afternoon.

5:23 AM, Central Time

Stray wisps of dust swirled through the paling headlight beams that shone steadily on the fallen jumble of plywood and tinfoil, mixing with random crystals of the night's light snow, settling gradually in the depressions in the frozen ground worn by the thousands of feet into irregular patterns that echoed the corn furrows plowed and abandoned long ago.

The True Seekers had kept their vigil throughout the night, faithful as the cargo cultists beside their DC-3s of bamboo. Now, however, a restlessness stirred through the crowd as their crystallized breaths streamed away from their mouths and noses, bright and white in the first gray light of dawn.

And then, wordlessly, they began to move away. One of the trucks that was parked facing *Ode* shook as its motor caught and its headlights blinked out. Then it backed up, turned, and threaded its way slowly through the retreating crowd. Another engine started, and another. One by one the vehicles and people began to melt away across the pathless wastes.

"Shall we try to find a ride?" Soames asked.

"Where to?" Starbud said.

"I don't know," Soames said. "I guess there's no place left, is there?"

"Jessica?" a woman's voice called. "Jessica? We've been searching all night."

She turned and saw her mother running toward her against the flow of Seekers. Behind her came her father, awkwardly, reluctantly, and behind him a short squat man carrying a baby wrapped in an old blanket.

"All those *people*," the short man was saying. "It's just *amazing*. And when the wind brought it *down*—I couldn't have *planned* a more brilliant finale. It makes Rinaldo Fawcett's 'Blood Rain' *chopped liver!*"

Starbud tried to stare at them as strangers, but wordlessly her mother drew her to her and held her. "Come home with us, Jessica," she said. "Please come home."

Starbud's eyes glittered with tears.

Andrew McCallum stepped forward. "Please, baby," he managed.

She said nothing, eyes burning as she stared at the empty western horizon, and he took her cold, gloveless hand to lead her home.

Soames watched them go, even the man with the child. Alone, he turned to the sun's red ball rising in the east.

6:35 AM, Eastern Standard Time

The sun was already flooding the canyons of Manhattan when Circe and Santalucia reached his apartment. It was still strewn with the debris of the visit by the men from Faith Limited so many months ago, though Santalucia was too groggy with lack of sleep to count up exactly how many months it had been.

It was going to be a clear and sunny day—that was certainly cause for some kind of celebration. But he still had no idea where Martha had hidden the bourbon, and the refrigerator smelled like the mummy's tomb.

Circe opened a window to flush out the months of stuffiness while Santalucia poured them each a glass of rusty water.

"Well," he said, "I guess you were really Glinda the Good after all." He toasted her. "But we haven't accomplished anything. Faith Limited is still a corporation with a hatful of subsidiaries."

"But nothing to sell. It'll take time to reprogram their computers—and they'll lose a lot of converts in the lull. And there's no way they can revive their central symbol."

Santalucia shrugged. "They'll create a new one."

"I don't think they can," Circe said, finishing her water and stretching. "Remember, Doctor Love was an extrapolation of a real human being, no matter how woody his ideas were. He was a single living mind, an individual. A computer can augment, *re*create—but it can't *create* a real personality. At least not one with the kind of magnetism that can sway people the way the original Doctor Love did."

"Maybe computers don't have charisma yet," Santalucia said. "But the technology gets more sophisticated all the time. Someday they'll crack the code of what makes people follow one man, and with all those Love adapters built into sets across the country—"

"The last suggestion I sent on the carrier channel was for everyone to throw out their Lovebands," Circe said. "No, it wasn't the war to end wars. It won't keep us safe forever. Nothing ever will."

"But you really did get into that computer?" Santalucia marveled. "I still don't believe it. The idea of a telepath . . ."

"It took me a long time to understand, too," Circe said. "It wasn't until Love told me that the Tarot and the bell and all the rest of the things Ashtoreth and the League used were just as much crutches as the mesc. The power was always in me, the Gift. I just had to learn how to call on it when I needed it."

"I still don't swallow the spirit world stuff," Santalucia said.

"Here, then," Circe laughed, slipping the bell over her head and putting it around his neck. "Maybe this will help when you're ready. Everyone has the potential to some degree, you

259

know, not just people at Ashtoreth. Maybe now we'll all learn to control it—maybe this *is* the beginning of a new age.''

''And the lion's going to lie down with the lamb?'' Santalucia said. ''Let me know the minute it happens.''

''Well, *I'm* going to bed,'' Circe said, unbuttoning her blouse.

Santalucia looked longingly at her. ''Okay, but until the new age is officially declared, this lamb will just stay here and brood while the sun comes up.'' He shook the bell at his neck and it tinkled softly.

''No,'' she said, leaning forward and grabbing hold of the bell to mute it. ''Come to bed. I'm lonelier than ever. I want you with me.''

''To be perfectly candid,'' he said miserably, ''I'm more awed by you now than I ever was in Denver, and look what happened to me there.''

She was naked now. She bent down and kissed him lightly on the lips. Then again.

Santalucia felt a nostalgic, long-dormant tingling sensation. ''Well, maybe it *is* a new age,'' he said reflectively. Sproi-yoi-yoing, he thought.

''What's the smile for?'' Circe asked, leading him toward the bedroom. ''I saw how it was going to work out. And after all we've been through together, it shouldn't surprise you to know there's a very high probability we're going to be spending a lot of time with each other. Could even wind up parents.''

Santalucia drew away from her and sat on the edge of the bed. ''I don't know about that,'' he said. ''I really screwed that up the last time around.''

''There's plenty of time to patch things up with little Erin,'' Circe said. ''Remember, the world didn't end last night.''

Santalucia lay back. ''Do you mind if we don't pull the shades?'' he asked. ''I worked so hard on this, I don't want to miss any of it.''

''You mean the sun rising?''

''That too,'' Santalucia said.

''No, I don't mind,'' she murmured at the joining of their light and dusky bodies. ''Not this morning or any other.''

EXPLICIT.

ABOUT THE AUTHOR

RUSSELL M. GRIFFIN is a teacher who resides in Milford, Connecticut with his wife and baby daughter, Anne.

MATHEW SWAIN

He's a tough-guy detective living in a seedy 21st century America. He smokes hard and drinks hard and is certainly no soft touch when it comes to the ladies. More often than not, he's smack in the middle of danger —but he thinks on his feet and has a great nose for snooping. Catch Mathew Swain in his first three futuristic adventures:

HOT TIME IN OLD TOWN

When someone ices one of Swain's friends, Swain sets out to nail the killer. His relentless thirst for justice takes him to Old Town, a radiation-soaked mutant enclave where Swain uncovers a secret so deadly it's been paid for with a thousand lives. (#14811-7 · $2.25)

WHEN TROUBLE BECKONS (*on sale October 15, 1981*)

When Swain's rich friend Ginny Teal asks Swain to visit her on the moon, he's awfully reluctant. But Ginny sounds desperate and Swain gives in. But when he gets to the Moon, Swain finds Ginny out cold on the floor next to a dead body. (#20041-0 · $2.25)

THE DEADLIEST SHOW IN TOWN (*on sale February 15, 1981*)

Swain is hired for more money than he's worth to find a missing #1 newswoman and plunges deep into the dazzling world of a big video network, a ratings war and the misty borderline between reality and illusion that makes up the video of tomorrow. (#20186-7 · $2.25)

Read all three of these exciting Mathew Swain novels, available wherever Bantam paperbacks are sold.

FANTASY AND SCIENCE FICTION FAVORITES

Bantam brings you the recognized classics as well as the current favorites in fantasy and science fiction. Here you will find the beloved Conan books along with recent titles by the most respected authors in the genre.

☐	14428	LORD VALENTINE'S CASTLE	$2.95
		Robert Silverberg	
☐	01166	URSHURAK	$8.95
		Bros. Hildebrandt & Nichols	
☐	14844	NOVA Samuel R. Delany	$2.50
☐	13534	TRITON Samuel R. Dalany	$2.50
☐	14861	DHALGREN Samuel R. Delany	$3.95
☐	13134	JEM Frederick Pohl	$2.50
☐	13837	CONAN & THE SPIDER GOD #5	$2.25
		de Camp & Pratt	
☐	13831	CONAN THE REBEL #6	$2.25
		Paul Anderson	
☐	14532	HIGH COUCH OF SILISTRA	$2.50
		Janet Morris	
☐	13670	FUNDAMENTAL DISCH Disch	$2.50
☐	13189	DRAGONDRUMS Anne McCaffrey	$2.25
☐	14127	DRAGONSINGER Anne McCaffrey	$2.50
☐	14204	DRAGONSONG Anne McCaffrey	$2.50
☐	14031	MAN PLUS Frederik Pohl	$2.25
☐	11736	FATA MORGANA William Kotzwinkle	$2.95
☐	14846	THE GOLDEN SWORD Janet Morris	$2.50
☐	20592-7	TIME STORM Gordon R. Dickson	$2.95
☐	13996	THE PLANET OF TEARS Trish Reinius	$1.95

Buy them at your local bookstore or use this handy coupon for ordering:

Bantam Books, Inc., Dept. SF2, 414 East Golf Road, Des Plaines, Ill. 60016

Please send me the books I have checked above. I am enclosing $_____ (please add $1.00 to cover postage and handling). Send check or money order —no cash or C.O.D.'s please.

Mr/Mrs/Miss_____

Address_____

City_____ State/Zip_____

SF2—9/81

Please allow four to six weeks for delivery. This offer expires 3/82.

<u>SAVE $2.00</u> ON YOUR NEXT BOOK ORDER!

BANTAM BOOKS 🐓
Shop-at-Home
Catalog

Now you can have a complete, up-to-date catalog of Bantam's
inventory of over 1,600 titles—including hard-to-find books.

And, you can <u>save $2.00</u> on your next order by taking advantage of
the money-saving coupon you'll find in this illustrated catalog.
Choose from fiction and non-fiction titles, including mysteries,
historical novels, westerns, cookbooks, romances, biographies,
family living, health, and more. You'll find a description of most
titles. Arranged by categories, the catalog makes it easy to find
your favorite books and authors and to discover new ones.

So don't delay—send for this shop-at-home catalog and save money
on your next book order.

Just send us your name and address and 50¢ to defray postage and
handling costs.

BANTAM BOOKS, INC.
Dept. FC, 414 East Golf Road, Des Plaines, Ill. 60016

Mr./Mrs./Miss_____
(please print)
Address_____

City_____State_____Zip_____

Do you know someone who enjoys books? Just give us their names and
addresses and we'll send them a catalog too at no extra cost!

Mr./Mrs./Miss_____

Address_____

City_____State_____Zip_____

Mr./Mrs./Miss_____

Address_____

City_____State_____Zip_____

FC—9/81